TikTok Readers Love *Say You Swear!*

'I've fallen in love with Noah Riley and he doesn't
exist. I'm dead. RIP me'

'This book broke me and put me back together! One of
the best books I've ever read'

'This book was PERFECTION'

'I don't even know how I'm supposed to read any
other books after this one'

'The hangover I have from this book is not ok. I can't
go on with life after this'

'I have read almost 300 books this year and this one is
still my top'

'Whoever recommended this book to me . . .
I love you'

'I've never cried so hard reading a book in my
entire life'

'Noah Riley has my heart'

'Omg this book!!! Nothing will ever match it'

'Read this book in less than a day. I was that addicted'

I wish I could read it for the first time again'

'I will never recover'

'Noah is my favourite book boyfriend of all time'

USA Today and *Wall Street Journal* bestselling author Meagan Brandy writes New Adult romance novels with a twist. She is a candy-crazed, jukebox junkie who tends to speak in lyrics. Born and raised in California, she is a married mother of three crazy boys who keep her bouncing from one sports field to another, depending on the season, and she wouldn't have it any other way. Starbucks is her best friend and words are her sanity.

SAY YOU SWEAR

MEAGAN BRANDY

ORION

This edition first published in Great Britain in 2023 by Orion Fiction,
an imprint of The Orion Publishing Group Ltd.,
Carmelite House, 50 Victoria Embankment
London EC4Y 0DZ

An Hachette UK Company

5 7 9 10 8 6

A CIP catalogue record for this book
is available from the British Library.

ISBN (Paperback) 978 1 3987 1948 4
ISBN (eBook) 978 1 3987 1949 1

The Orion Publishing Group Ltd
Carmelite House
50 Victoria Embankment
London, EC4Y 0DZ

An Hachette UK company

Typeset by Born Group
Printed and bound in Great Britain by Clays Ltd, Elcograf S.p.A.

www.orionbooks.co.uk

For the one who feared the fall
but dared to jump anyway.

This one is for you.

Chapter 1
Arianna

The drive to Oceanside is usually a peaceful one, but my brother, Mason, and his two best friends, Chase and Brady, came to an unspoken agreement last night that "one more" meant one more twelve-pack. So out they stayed, saying drunken goodbyes to our classmates at the very last summer party to be had in our hometown.

My girl Cameron and I knew better than to party hard the night before a drive, so we headed home early to finish packing for our final trip to the beach before college life begins.

A trip that *should have* taken no more than three and a half hours, yet we've already been in this damn SUV for five. We learned years ago that long drives with pouty, hungover man-boys are not fun, but here we are again, willing yet slightly annoyed participants in the 'how many times does one man have to stop to piss' experiment.

The answer is seven. We stopped seven times already, thanks to Brady's baby bladder.

At least they seem to have sobered up in the last fifteen minutes, finally allowing us to turn the music up loud enough to where we can actually hear it.

Honestly, I shouldn't complain.

Group car rides are pretty much the only time I get to feign innocence when I lean a little farther into the star player of my fantasies, more commonly known as my brother's best friend.

'Play but don't push' is the game I'm forced to settle for

and I'm good at it. Probably because I've had the better part of six years to perfect it.

See, the day Chase and his family moved in across the street, I saw *him* first. It was as if an invisible stamp came down and pressed across his forehead, a big fat red label that screamed *mine*.

Sure, I was only in junior high, but I'd seen *The Boy Next Door*. I understood the power of obsession, and mine started the minute I laid eyes on him. Granted, mine wasn't the murderous sort and watching that movie gave me hardcore, unachievable body goals, but all that's beside the point.

Chase Harper had arrived in the neighborhood, and I was determined to be the one to show him around it, so I pressed the brakes on my bike at the edge of his lawn, gaining his attention.

The minute his brace face smiled at me from across the yard, my twin appeared out of nowhere, something he's inconveniently good at.

Mason rushed him, tackled him to the ground, and when he stood, he fed Chase a line I sometimes wish he'd choke on.

He growled, *"Stay away from my 'little sister!'"*

In horror, I watched as Chase hopped to his feet, literally, like some sort of spider monkey shit. I held my breath, readying for the fight I suspected to follow—yeah, my brother was known to knock a kid out when it came to me—but then Chase laughed, and we all fell silent.

The brown-haired, green-eyed boy turned to my brother with grass in his mouth, a grin curving it, and asked Mase what football team he played for. He was looking for one to join.

I huffed and rode off because I knew with that single question asked, Mason and Brady had a new best friend, and I was, once again, colored in red, an invisible circle-backslash symbol painted across me.

In the span of five minutes, my brother's duo grew into a trio, and our house became their hangout spot of choice. I never understood the whole forbidden fruit thing until then, how not having something only made you want it more.

It's a bunch of bull, if you ask me.

Unfortunately for me, no one did, so I sat back, forced to watch as the jocks of junior high became the hotties of high school.

Every girl wanted a bite, but who could blame them?

They were model students, star athletes, and undercover bad boys. No matter a girl's type, one of the three was sure to fit the bill.

I like to joke that they're every shade of Dwayne Johnson since he seems to be different yet extremely fit regardless of the role. Brady would definitely be the WWE version.

No, but really, all three were gifted with good genes. Mason, my overprotective twin, is tall and trim and could literally stunt double for a slightly younger Theo James. Brady's a bulked-out Ken doll, and Chase is, well, the epitome of perfection.

Unfortunately for me, *every* girl agrees.

He has the same height and build as Mase, but his brown hair is a few shades lighter. His eyes, vivid and upbeat, are a mix of grass and seaweed. He's kind, strong, and confident. Almost as bossy as Mason and Brady, but out of the three, he's the only one who cuts us girls some slack from time to time.

I've convinced myself it's his way of differentiating himself from protective older brother to a man with eyes and hidden desires, but I'm known to be a wishful thinker.

Nine out of ten times, I'm thinking about the man beside me. It's the oldest cliché in the books to want who you can't have. Unrequited love for your brother's best friend, a brother who is insanely protective and, yeah, admittedly slightly psychotic when it comes to those he cares about. He can't help it though. As soon as we were old enough to learn how my dad lost his baby sister, Mason made it his mission to shadow my every step. Combine that with the death of our friend Payton's boyfriend a couple weeks ago, and he's a pile of paranoia.

The fact that Chase was passed out for most of the drive today likely saved me from a solid dozen glares through the rearview mirror. Pretty sure that's why Mase insists I sit in the middle every time we ride together, so he can keep eyes on me at all times.

It's sweet how my twin takes his 'big brother' role so seriously.

It's also really annoying.

Had we stayed on track this morning, we would have rolled into town around eleven, but here we are, turning into the long driveway of the beach house at a quarter to one.

Mason barely has time to put his Tahoe in park before Cameron is throwing her door open and hopping out. She runs halfway up the steps and spins on her bare feet, throwing her arms out with a smile. "Come on, you guys! Time's already ticking!"

"We have the rest of the month!" Mason shouts out his open window.

"And we're already down half a day!" Cam fires back.

I smile, patting my brother's shoulder. "Come on, Mase, we're a half day down," I tease, and my brother grumbles as I slip out the door, following Cameron along the wraparound deck.

She beams, hopping up to sit on the edge of the banister, so I join her, and Brady's stepping up in the next second.

"This is fuckin' insane!" Cam shakes her head, eyeing the area.

"Fuck yeah, it is." Brady faces the ocean with a grin.

Heavy footsteps behind us let us know the other two have walked up, and together, we spin.

The five of us stand there a moment, silently breathing in the fresh seaside air as we stare into the floor-to-ceiling window of the beach house.

Of *our* beach house, as of a month ago.

Mine, Cameron, and Brady's mom have been best friends since college, and before they even married our dads, they bought a beach house together. As the years went by, marriage and us kids followed. They kept that place as a spot to always come. Then, when we were young, I guess there was a crash in the housing market, and all our parents were lucky enough to snag vacation homes along the beach, and ever since then,

4

this is where our families spent every school holiday. We never understood why, but they never did sell the original home they purchased, and that's the house we're about to enter, but it looks nothing like the place we saw as kids.

They had it gutted, parts torn down, and not only rebuilt but also added onto. It's completely renovated.

Coastal blue in color, the place is huge. It has a massive wraparound patio, leading to a massive back deck, the one we're currently standing on, and a private pathway leading to a beautiful dock surrounded by California poppies. There's even a full sound system with speakers embedded into the corners of the walls, patio, and wood paneling every few dozen feet—there isn't a single spot in or around the place the music can't reach. Being on the opposite side of the condo strip, it's more secluded, so the sound doesn't bother others who are trying to have a more relaxing vacation.

It's the perfect escape, a palace on the water.

And it was just given to us.

To *all* five of us.

Our parents surprised us at our graduation party, handing us a deed to the place, all our names listed as equal owners. They said they decided to do this for us years ago as a way to try and keep our crew close, no matter where life may take us after college, as the place did for them afterward.

Splitting it equally among us meant no one can decide to sell without the others, and should life take us away at some time, we'd always have this place to come back to at any point.

To say we were excited is an understatement, but for me, it also brought a hint of dread. It was sort of a depressing conversation, to be honest. I'm not so naive to assume that our lives would stay the same, that it would be us five for always, but it is kind of terrifying to consider the alternative.

New people will come into our lives. I know this.

Some might be for the better, others for the worse.

But what happens if one of our worlds is flipped upside down?

What if we drown from the capsize?

5

If we lose each other along the way, who will be there to pull us from the water?

Maybe that's a little dramatic, but it's a real possibility. A shitty one.

Less than a month from today, the future begins.

My brother and the boys will head to Avix University for the official start of their college football careers, and Cam and I will drive home to pack, getting ready to meet them on campus a few days before orientation.

Leaving home is as real as it gets.

It'll be the first time my brother won't be a door away. While it's slightly terrifying, it's also a beautiful thing how the football house is on the complete opposite side of Cam's and my dorm. Meaning, Mason won't be able to "check in" on us as often. That alone is going to be worth celebrating on move-in day.

I love my brother but damn. Sometimes he needs to back off. He's lucky I didn't pick a college across the country.

He also knows there is no way I would have.

I don't do well without family being nearby. Some might call that being codependent.

I simply call it a twin thing.

"So, we're still good with how we picked rooms a couple weeks ago, right?" Mason breaks the silence. "Girls upstairs with the joining bathroom, leave the spare room, a spare, and us downstairs?"

"Mom decorated our rooms when she came to check on Payton and stocked the fridge last week, so—"

"No take-backs!" Cam cuts me off with a smile.

The boys laugh, and then Mason takes a deep breath, pulling the key from his pocket.

"No take-backs." He grins. "We ready for a do-over? No parents, no rules."

"No one left under eighteen this time around." Brady playfully shoves Mason and me since Brady, Mason, and I became legal three days ago.

I look to Chase, who happens to glance my way at the same exact time. He smiles, and I match his with one of my own.

"Oh shit," my best friend teases. "Things are about to get real up in here!"

I wish I knew how true Cameron's statement would become then, but I didn't have the slightest clue.

Chapter 2
Arianna

"Fridge is open, alcohol's in hand, so get your asses in here and let's get this party started!" Cameron repetitively knocks a bottle against the countertop and doesn't stop until we're rounding the corner into the kitchen to join her.

"Easy on the granite, Cami baby. Take it out on me instead," Brady teases, leaning on his forearms.

"Next time, Brady, next time." She grins.

As she starts pouring the shots into the glasses Chase helped her pull down, I let my eyes roam.

The kitchen is everything you'd expect in a beach home, light in color and wide open. The dining table is a large U-shape bench-style seat with white and light-blue pillows in the corners. It sits in front of the large bay window, allowing you to peer out over the beach and watch the sun set or rise without stepping foot outside. There's a large marble island in the center, the stovetop, and double ovens circling behind it, which is where Cam's now perched, five shot glasses filled to the brim at her side.

She waits for us to claim a shot, seizing the last as her own. "Let's toast to all the stupid shit we are going to do while we're here and to the blast that we are going to have while doing it."

We laugh, and her blue eyes narrow with playfulness. "I'm serious, assholes. This little vacay is now officially going to be our last memory before our new lives begin. This is huge!"

"She's right." Chase steps beside Cam with a grin. "Let's make the most of it."

"When do we not go balls out and have a kick-ass time?" Brady reaches over, squeezing her knee. "We're about to run this beach, girl."

Cameron grips his cheeks, pinching his lips like a fish. "That's the spirit, big boy." She pecks his lips, downing her shot in the next.

The rest of us follow suit, knocking our shots back.

My eyes pinch from the burn of the liquor, and I laugh when Cameron shakes her head, her tongue sticking out.

"Okay, that shit's nasty." She laughs, happily passing the bottle off to Brady when he reaches for it.

"I'll meet you bastards at the beach. Mase, call your cousin, tell him to get his ass down here, and one of you pansies bring the football!" With that, Brady disappears out the back sliding door.

Cam turns to me, mischief written all over her. "Come on, girl, let's get changed. There's a gang of beach boys out there calling our names."

I wiggle my eyebrows up and down. "Maybe those Brazilians will pay off after all."

"Oh, fuck me, I'm out," Mason grumbles, rushing toward the patio door. He stops as he steps through, turning back to pin Chase with an expectant glare. "You comin'?"

At first, Chase doesn't move, but then he shakes his head, and Cameron covers her laugh with a cough, knowing we've painted a mental picture in his head.

"Yeah." He clears his throat and snags the football from the bucket by the door. "Right behind you."

As soon as the door is closed, Cam and I bend over, laughing.

"That was gold." She high-fives me, and we quickly rush up the stairs, dragging our suitcases away from the wall where the boys placed them before disappearing into our rooms.

"I call hot pink today!" Cam shouts.

"I figured so! I think I'm going with my black one!" I flip open my suitcase, planning to unpack later and pull out my bathing suits.

I'm just getting the bows looped on the bottoms when she barges through our joining bathroom.

"Tie this for me." She gives me her back. "Also, I'm vetoing the black suit in favor of the red one."

I roll my eyes and fix her top as she looks over her body in the full-length mirror mounted to the wall in front of us.

"Thank you, Victoria, for your super summer sale," she mutters.

"She must be doing something wrong because I don't see any secrets in this thing," I tease, and she blows me a kiss.

My best friend has an amazing body, toned and tight in all the right places and nearly opposite of me in every way.

Cam is an easy five-ten where I'm pushing five-five. She's tall, fit, and model-like with crazy, crystal-blue eyes. While there's no denying it, she hates to be called thin.

Growing up, people would tease her for being *too tall* and *too skinny*. I mean, they'd then get beaten up by Mason or Brady, but still. It was bad for a while. The boys always tried to make her height seem insignificant, even when, for a minute there, she was taller than they were, but they couldn't take away the hurt the words of others caused her.

She's tried everything from all-carb diets to pharmaceutical drugs, even adding Ensure to her meals every single day for months and nothing. Her metabolism simply doesn't work that way. Now that we've gotten older, she's learned to own it, has filled out more in other areas, and is constantly going with the boys to the gym to keep the bit of muscle she's added to give her more weight. Regardless, she's always had a confident attitude, the 'never let them see you sweat' type.

Cameron throws her long blonde hair into a high ponytail and turns to me.

"Now." She tosses me my new red suit. "I'm dying to see how those babies look in this." She gestures to my chest.

"Seriously?"

"Oh, yeah, go hard or go home."

"Mason might just drag my ass home if I start with this." I

scoff, picking it up, and look over the deep cut of the front. "This thing is like 'fifth date, trying to get lucky' worthy."

"You're talking like you didn't already undo your top to swap it."

"Touché." I strip out of the black suit, slipping into the tiny red one.

Cam sprawls out on my bed, quickly checking her notifications, but then faces me when I spin, giving her my best Marilyn Monroe pose.

"Whatcha think?"

"I think you better thank the big man upstairs on the daily for those Dolly Ds he blessed you with." She looks me up and down. "These new-gen *Baywatch* babes got nothing on you."

"Why, thank you, friend. Now let's go."

I head toward the door.

"Wait," she rushes, crawling to the edge of the bed. "Let's talk for a sec."

It's clear she's nervous about something, so I drop onto the mattress next to her, waiting for her to speak.

"Our last trip ended in a sad shitstorm with your cousin and Deaton's car wreck. That was heavy, but this is our chance to end the summer on a good note."

"That's why we went home with our parents for a couple weeks, to press the reset button."

"No, I know, it's just now we're closer to the start of school, and once we get to Avix, our schedules are going to be all over the place. For the first time, we won't have a ton of free time together," she begins, a bit overly serious for her.

"Cam, we're roommates." I laugh. "We'll see each other plenty, and we'll always have the weekends."

"Yeah, but," she huffs. "I guess I just want to live it up, you know? This is the last time we'll have virtually no responsibility outside of not getting shit-faced and murdered."

I laugh, but she doesn't even pause.

"So, I vote we do like we did on our secret little trip and have some fun flipping invisible middle fingers at the boys along the way."

"We're gonna sunbathe topless, the boys be damned?"

An amused groan leaves her, and she sits up, shaking my shoulders. "I didn't say try to get them to murder us," she teases with a grin. "But yeah, same vibe."

The two of us laugh.

"So real eighteen-year-old fun, swim, layout, barbecue, drink, dance, flirt . . ." I lift a brow.

"Make out with a couple of beach boys we'll never see again," she adds with a shimmy and ends in a shrug. "The boys are going to, so if we want to do the same, we should. And the best part is no one here will be afraid of 'big brother and his boys.'" She grins.

Chuckling, I pull myself up, walking backward toward the door. "No overanalyzing, no second-guessing, just go with the flow kind of fun that we may or may not have to sneak around the boys."

"But if we can't . . ."

"Invisible middle fingers, and we do it anyway."

"That's *exactly* what I'm talking about. Screw these boys and their obsessive need to know! Let's have as much fun as possible and whatever happens, happens."

"Whatever happens, happens," I agree.

Cam squeals, hops up and tosses her watch onto my bed. "Now, let's go make some poor fools drool. We didn't spend the last four months in Booty Boot Camp for nothing."

She pushes her forehead into mine, and we smile at each other.

"It's game on, bitches."

We search the beach as we step off of the back deck, spotting the boys about thirty feet down the sand line, so we make our way toward them.

"Looks like Brady's already found the hottest girl on the beach to keep him occupied," Cam jokes, nodding her chin in his direction.

I squint, skimming over the small group, stopping on the gorgeous, tan-skinned, dark-haired girl perched on a rock, and a smile takes over my face.

12

Kalani Embers is her name, and she's definitely the most beautiful girl around, but she's not free for the taking. She's my cousin Nate's soon-to-be wifey, who we had a chance to meet and hang with when we came down to set up the house at the start of summer. She's also the only girl to ever beat Brady at sports trivia. He literally bought every game in the book to 'study' the answers, so the next time he saw her, he could take back his know-it-all title, but Kalani, or Lolli as we call her, was born into the game, her entire family having been a part of the NFL world, and stats are her jam. Poor guy doesn't stand a chance.

She's not only the youngest but the first female franchise owner in NFL history.

"Aw shit, here comes trouble!" Brady whistles, gaining the others' attention.

Mason groans, shaking his head, shouting across the sand. "You guys tryin' to see me knock a fucker out?"

"What's the matter, Mase, afraid someone might take the bait?" Brady throws back with a grin.

It's no secret Cameron has a thing for Mason, but none of us really knows how he feels about her. He does things like running off guys who try and talk to her and will hold her when she cries, but it's hard because that's who Mason is. Protective by nature. He looks out for her as he does me, is there for her when she might need him, as are the other boys. As I am. It's what we do. We're family, the five of us, and where we come from, that little fact trumps all else. It's also what makes it so tricky to understand. It's like I said, Mase treats her as he does me, so there's a chance there's nothing romantic about it. He doesn't know how to care a little; it's always with all of who he is.

It's a blessing and a curse sometimes because he stresses and overanalyzes more than necessary, but he can't help himself.

My brother is the toughest person I know. He's everything a father would hope for in a son and more than I could ask for in a brother. He's the most important person in my life, and if there's one person in this world I want to make proud, it's him. My twin is the other half of who I am, but that doesn't mean I understand his every move, even if I wish I did.

Either way, Cameron refuses to think on it to keep herself from getting her hopes up. She's not lovesick, by any means, and she doesn't sit around and hope like I might be pathetically known to do, but as it stands, she'd take his hand if he offered it in a heartbeat.

What makes it a bit more difficult is the fact that Mason is the biggest flirt known to man, possibly neck to neck with Brady, but he means no harm and would never intentionally lead her on, so I guess only time will tell.

I look to Mason as he flips Brady off, but Brady only laughs.

Lolli smiles, pushing off the rock she was sunbathing on. "Well, well, looking fresh as always."

I grin, reminding myself not to go in for a hug. Lolli isn't the touchy type. "Had to try and keep up with you."

"Girl, please. You should have seen the suit she tried to wear today. I had to sex her up myself."

"So Chase has you to thank, huh?" Lolli smirks.

I squash my lips to the side, and she laughs.

Lolli guessed my feelings for Chase the day we met, and she loves to pop off with off-color jokes to make the boys uncomfortable while still attempting to be stealthy, but only for my sake. She'd outright tell him to strip me in the sand if it were up to her. She's down like that.

"Have you heard from Kenra yet?" I ask about my cousin, Nate's older sister, as the events of a few weeks ago flash through my mind.

Kenra just got out of an abusive relationship, one that took a turn for the worse when her now ex-fiancé crashed with her and his younger brother in the car. He and Kenra made it out okay, but his younger brother, the father of Payton's unborn baby, wasn't so lucky. He was only seventeen.

Talk about a cruel mess.

"How's Payton doing?"

Lolli lifts a shoulder, glancing behind her, where I spot Payton walking down the beach. "I try not to ask. I'm better at entertainment, so I keep her busy when I can."

"I bet that helps more than you know." Cam smiles at her.

Lolli looks off, uncomfortable with the deep stuff, so I change the subject.

"So, what's the plan for today, or do we have one?" I ask, looking around at everyone.

Brady shrugs, tossing the football in the air. "I figure we'd start it off right, go out to eat, dance, get fucked up, then bum it and bonfire tomorrow?"

Cam and I nod. "Sounds good to us. Lolli, you guys in?"

"My man reports for practice in two days, so that would be a no." She smirks. "We'll be locked in our room all night, but we'll see you guys tomorrow, I'm sure."

"On that note . . ." Nate steps up, hugs us hello, and waves goodbye in the next second, quickly carting his fiancée toward their house.

"Well, okay then." Cameron laughs. "A night of dirty dancing it is, but first!" She takes off, charging right into the open waters, Brady on her heels.

"Hold up, I'm snaggin' Pretty Little." He jerks his head in the direction of Payton. "She could use a little distraction." With that, Mason jogs a few feet down the beach toward the young blonde sitting alone on a rock, searching for answers she won't find in the California waves.

Slowly, Chase and I make our way closer to the water's edge.

He bumps his shoulder into mine. "You happy to be back at the beach?"

"Always, you know that." I grin his way, but a heavy breath leaves me as I face forward. "Let's hope this time is less traumatic."

"Yeah." He nods. "I can't imagine what she's going through."

We glance Payton's way in time to witness her eyes widen, having spotted Mason coming at her at the last second. He bends, swooping her up with no effort, and she squeals into the air, making us laugh.

I smile after my brother, a calm only the ocean seems to bring me settling over my shoulders. "I think this trip will be different."

He glances over. "Yeah?"

"Yeah." I nod. "When we came at the end of June, it still felt like we were fresh out of school, you know? Like we had the whole summer ahead of us, but we don't anymore. Summer is almost over, and we're moving out on our own the minute we leave here. It's just . . . different. Like we're grown, and this is life now." I scrunch my nose and turn to look at him. "Don't you think?"

That one-sided smile of his I love appears. "Yeah. I guess it is different." He's quiet for a second before he adds, "Maybe a lot of things will be different now."

It's as if he's speaking more to himself than me, so I don't respond.

A moment later, he stops walking and faces me. He frowns at my swimsuit, and I can't help but laugh.

"Is there a problem?"

"Yeah." He nods, his eyes lifting to mine. His frown doubles, but not even a second later, a grin pulls at his lips, one I recognize.

"Chase," I warn, but before I can make a break for it, he's already tossed me over his shoulder and is running for the ocean.

The others laugh as I'm tossed on my ass and swim over to join us.

I wish I could freeze this moment, our entire crew enjoying the last bit of the summer sun because who knows what the summer's moon will bring.

I look to Chase, who smirks at me from across the water.

I, for one, can't wait to find out.

Chapter 3
Arianna

"Hurry up, brats! The cab should be here any minute!" Mason yells from the bottom of the stairs.

"Ugh, that man, I swear, he's wound so tight." Cam smirks into the mirror. "Think he'll let me help him out with that?"

"Cameron." I laugh. "Ew!"

"Oh, chill, Virgin Mary." She hip checks me and leans across the sink to finish her mascara. "And what do you think you're doing?" She glances at my dress. "Take that horrid thing off. You look like you're about to hunt Easter eggs, not have a wicked time on the dance floor."

"It's not that bad, and I can't wear that scrap of fabric you call a dress."

"Yes, you can."

"Do you *want* to have fun? I have to pick and choose my sexy, and night one is not the night."

She pushes her pointed finger in the air, raising one perfectly shaped blonde brow. "*Au contraire,* my flowery friend . . ." She spins. "Tonight is the perfect night for sexy. It's time to get tipsy and if that means Mason is forced to face the fact that you do, indeed, have a vagina, then so be it."

I squeeze my eyes shut, not going anywhere near that comment.

"Come on!" Cameron laughs. "We agreed to have fun!"

"We will, but I can't go balls to the wall the first day."

"Honey, I speak for your cha-cha when I say that dress has got to go. As in, into the trash."

I try and keep from laughing, but it's no use.

Cam and I are still cracking up when Brady begins pounding on my door.

"Yo! You guys sound like you're having way too much fun. If there're pillows and panties involved, I want in!" he shouts.

"Fuck off, Brady!" Mason's yell follows from . . . who the hell knows where. He's never too far away.

Brady's chuckle reaches us. "For real, though, 'bout ready? Uber's pulling up!"

"Shit. Yeah, we're coming!" Cam yells, turning her evil eye on me.

"Ugh! I hate you," I grumble, tugging my dress over my head and holding my hand out to her. "Give me the damn thing."

Triumphant smirk in place, Cameron slaps the slinky black number in my palm.

I slip it on, quickly stepping into the black pumps with a gold heel she sets in front of me next.

"Happy?" I cock my hip.

"Ecstatic." She smirks. "Now, let's go before your brother barges in."

My dress is simple but sexy. It's a halter top that cuts low in the front, snug and slinky down my waist, and loosens at the hips to allow for flirty dancing. My dark-brown hair is pulled back in a tight, high ponytail, and the smoky eye is in full effect.

I don't go 'full makeup' on a daily basis, but it's one of my favorite parts about going out.

Snagging a pair of black stud earrings from my bag, I rush into the hall behind Cam, smirking at the view as I take her in.

She's wearing a deep purple tube top dress that's tight from her chest down to her ass. She paired it with nude pumps and left her lids bare of shadow, only going with a thick coat of mascara. Her long blonde hair is left down, with big beachy waves. My bestie's fine.

"Okay, bitch!" She links her arm through mine as we hit the last step of the stairs. "Showtime!"

I clasp my earring and hold my head high.

Brady, as usual, is the first to spot us, and his infamous whistle follows.

"Hot damn!" Brady stalks over to us, planting a kiss on our cheeks as he grabs us both by the hands. "Do a little spin for me. Show me whatcha got."

We laugh but twirl as he asked.

"What do you think, Brady? Do we pass?"

"With flyin' fuckin' colors." He grins. "Come on, shots in the kitchen before we head out."

"I thought our Uber was here?"

"Had to get your fine asses down here somehow," he admits as he smacks both our butts.

Mason spins as we enter, instantly frowning.

"What the hell?" he snaps. "I swear you want me to go to jail."

"Chill." I laugh, shaking my head. "There will be no handcuffs tonight."

"I mean," Cam begins, batting her lashes overdramatically. "Unless you want there to be—"

"Okay." He throws his hands up. "Whatever. Wear a dress that would fit our first-grade neighbor all you want, but I'm gonna need a double for this shit."

"I got you, my man." Brady's grin grows. He sneaks a glance in my direction, mischief written all over him.

He reaches over, running his hand up and down my arm slowly, stopping to rest it on my hip. He uses his other hand to pour my shot, then brings it up to my lips.

"Open up, Ari baby," he says in a low, gravelly tone.

I lock eyes with him, playing his little game, and do as I'm told.

His eyes never leave mine, a laugh on the tip of his tongue as he pours the hot liquid down my throat. Once I've swallowed, he reaches up to swipe his thumb across my bottom lip to get the single drop that didn't make it into my mouth.

"You're a dick." Mason groans playfully, and we can't hold it in, both of us laughing.

19

"Okay, fucker, enough with the show." Chase frowns, nodding toward the bottle. "Now pour us a shot so we can get out of here."

Cam slyly slips a hand behind her back, and I meet her with mine for a secret high five, both of us facing forward, grins pulling at our lips.

Brady claps his hands together. "All right, y'all, to our first night out as legal drinking adults!" He grabs his shot and lifts it in the air. "Well, according to the badass fake IDs I got us anyway!"

"Woo!" Cam shouts.

We click our glasses together in cheers and down our liquor.

"Let's roll, bitches!" Cam throws over her shoulder on her way to the door.

The four of us follow.

Brady spends the entire ten-minute drive going over the dos and don'ts of what to say and how to act when we pull out our fake IDs, but it turns out his worry is a waste.

The bouncer at the door lets us pass after Cameron smiles at him. She may have also asked him to check the zipper on the back of her dress, but hey, he's happy to help.

The guys, however, did have to show their IDs, but the Tom Hardy look-alike didn't blink twice at them, so they must seem legit. That, or he really doesn't care.

The moment we're past the threshold, Cam squeals, gripping my arm. "This place is awesome!" she shouts, already moving her body to the music.

The club is a giant circle with an open floor plan. Circular booths with white tables and chairs line the right and left sides, with the bar stretching across the back wall. The lighting is dark with a blue tint, but not in a black light kind of way. More of an enchanted, frosty feel. The floor shines a metallic silver, adding to the illusion.

Cameron leads us to a booth near the bar, and we sit to have a few drinks.

An hour and three Midori Sours later, my body's humming, and I'm ready to hit the dance floor. To be fair, us girls were ready as soon as we walked in, but the boys wanted to 'scope out the scene' first—overprotective brutes.

Contemplating my next move, I look around me. I'm blocked in the booth, Chase on my left, the others on my right, so there's only one logical direction to go. Logical, but potentially problematic. The liquor in me doesn't seem to care, though, as my ass is lifting off the seat.

I move quickly before I can be stopped and before I chicken out, sliding my body across Chase's, his every muscle locking up on contact. There isn't much space between the tables and the seat tops, so the only way to get through the gap is to press my ass into his lap a little, so I do.

Instantly, his hands fly to my hips, and he swiftly pushes me by, carefully setting me on my feet beside the table, his eyes flying to Mason just before he speaks.

"Could have asked him to move, Ari." My brother's glare burns into my cheek.

I ignore it. "As you can see, dear brother, there was no need. I'm standing, and now . . . I'm going to dance."

Cam shrieks, quickly placing herself beside me. "Not without me, bitch!"

"Goddamn," Brady draws out, causing all our heads to turn in the direction he's drooling.

With a giant grin on his face, he nudges Mason's shoulder. "Move it, brotha man." Hooking his thumb over his shoulder, Brady points to the brunette leaning over the bar. "I gotta get over there."

"You can't even see her face from here." Cam scrunches her nose.

"Dat ass, though," he says, looking at me expectantly.

I smile wide, picking up what he's putting down. "All that ass . . ."

"In them jeans," Brady finishes on a laugh, raising his hand for a well-earned high five. "I knew you wouldn't disappoint."

"Okay, Waka Flockas, let's go." Cameron rolls her eyes, pulling me toward the dance floor.

21

We wedge ourselves between a few groups of people, finding a nice, crowded spot near the center, and let loose.

"Girl, I'm feeling good right now!" Cam shouts over the music.

"Same!" I laugh. "That last drink snuck up on me."

Ne-Yo's "She Knows" begins to play through the speakers, and we lock eyes.

"Aw shit," we scream in drunken laughter, and then we go to work.

Swinging our hips, rotating our bodies to the beat, we soak up our very first night in a club.

I close my eyes and let the music take over my body like it always does. When I'm happy or sad or mad, anything, music is what I seek. I relate life to lyrics, tone to mood.

The beat can wake me or break me down. The words can lift me or leave me a soppy mess. A lot of people avoid songs that make them remember pain when they're drowning in it, but I say let that sucker take you under. When people feel good, they tend to blast some bubbly music that makes them dance around, so if you'll dance when you feel like dancing, why not have a good cry when you need one?

I need music like my twin needs football; it's in our souls, and right now, my soul is feeling sultry.

It's not long before a blond guy makes his way through the crowd and begins to slink his way closer. I smile, giving him the okay, so he slides right in, and we begin to dance. In my peripheral, I notice Chase and Mason dancing with some girls only a few feet away. I have no doubt it's purposeful, their way of keeping an eye on us girls, but to give them credit, they don't interrupt.

Probably because we keep our partners a shuffle away. A few songs later, Chris Brown's "Loyal" comes on, and Cam squeals beside me.

I throw my hands in the air again, ditching my partner for my best friend, and we sing along like a couple of drunk girls at a karaoke bar, loud and out of tune.

Cam jerks her chin in the direction of our boys, and I know exactly what she's thinking.

We make our way to the boys, just in time to sing along with the chorus, sending each other into another fit of laughter.

"Cute, girls." Mason laughs, stepping away from the scowling redhead. "Real cute."

Cameron grins, fanning herself. "I need a water and another drink!"

Mason glances around, assumingly in search of Brady, and then throws his arm over Cameron's shoulder. "I'll take her!" he shouts, pulling her toward the bar, but not before he points at me, his eyes on Chase. "Stay with her."

They walk away, and I face Chase, dramatically shimmying my shoulders around, and he chuckles, shaking his head, but he doesn't accept the invitation, so I dance without him.

My eyes close, and I fall into the music, and about a half song later, the heat of Chase's nearness washes over me. It takes a serious amount of effort, but I don't open my eyes, not yet. I wait, continuing to sway to the music, and finally, he moves a little closer. My senses are flooded with his clean, sandalwood scent, and my eyes fly open, locking onto his bloodshot gaze.

His movements are a little loose from the liquor, but he keeps up, and when I brace my hands on his shoulders, bringing myself in a little more, he allows it.

"Well, look at that," I tease. "We're almost dancing."

A grin pulls at the corner of his mouth, and I suck in a deep breath when his free hand falls to my hip. "You're brave for wearing this thing." He tugs at the stretchy fabric.

"Do you like it?"

He frowns, and a low laugh leaves me, but I don't say anything else, the heat of his hand frying my brain. It's all I can think about.

His hands on me.

With each passing second, my fantasies pull me deeper, my heartbeat growing erratic.

Moving with his body brushing mine serves as an accelerator, pumping my blood at a quickened rate, sending the alcohol coursing through me straight to my brain, and with it, washing away my sense of reason, or at least that's the only thing I can come up with as to why I suddenly dare to drag my hands a little lower.

Hips still rolling, I slowly run my palms over the curve of his shoulders, gliding them over the cuts of his pecs.

Chase's eyes fly to mine, and my hands decide to climb up, higher and higher, until my fingers are spanning along his corded neck. Chase swallows, a small frown building along his brow.

The bass of the music pounds wildly beneath our feet, the lights change colors, dimming the space around us, and the crowd seems to shuffle in. We're barricaded now, Chase and me.

We've danced before. At birthdays and our parents' anniversary parties, a couple school formals, but not like this. Not close and never after a few drinks.

This is new. Foreign.

My fingers find their way into his hair, and I scratch at the base of his skull in a gentle, massage-like motion. I shift the slightest bit, on accident, and he hisses as my thigh brushes the proof of his arousal.

He's hard.

Holy shit, he's hard because of me.

I start a new rhythm, my body applying the smallest bit of pressure to his package with every move, and his hands come up, clutching on to my wrist, his lips finding my ear.

"Ari, what are you doing?"

Tequila is heavy on his breath and sends a zing of anticipation down my spine as I remember mine and Cameron's conversation, a newfound confidence floating through me.

"What am I doing?" I repeat his question, and I pull back to meet his drawn-in gaze. "I'm doing whatever I want." *Boys be damned*.

His features pull, tightening at every inch.

I crush my lips to his.

24

Chase tenses, his hands twitching against me one second, flying to grab hold of my biceps in the next, and then he's pushing us apart, his long arms stretching to their max. Wide, bloodshot eyes find mine, and his face pales.

Chase shakes his head, and his features begin to crumble. "Arianna . . . no."

My mouth opens, but nothing comes out, and his hands come up to rub along his face.

Tears prick the backs of my eyes as I take in the mortified expression on his face. My skin flushes, and I look away.

Mason and Cam break through the crowd then, and Chase's hands fly from my body, sweeping into his hair, as he plasters on the biggest, fakest, tightest smile I've ever seen.

My insides crack as reality sets in.

I wanted to kiss him, and he didn't want to kiss me back, but nothing stings more than the look of horror in his eyes when he realized what I'd done.

Without his permission, I forced him across the line he kept ten feet in front of him. That little line is now covered in a layer of wet sand, and everyone who's ever set foot in the ocean knows it's not so easily wiped away. It grows thicker with wind and waves, and we're in Southern California, so we've got those in abundance.

Not that it matters, because if his panic-stricken expression said anything, it's that he'll shovel that shit to the ends of the ocean if he must.

Thankfully, alcohol not only sloshes through the two of us but also the two who have now rejoined us, so they don't notice a thing, and when my brother passes me a water bottle, kissing my forehead before turning to his best friend with a sloppy smile, I accept it with a tight grin. I finish off half of it and spin to Cameron. She hands me one of the shots in her hands, and before we throw them back, Brady appears out of nowhere, ready with a drink of his own.

All five of us form a small circle, downing our drinks in one go, and it doesn't stop there, the need to get wasted higher than ever, so, anytime someone suggests another, I'm there to eagerly egg us on.

I feel like a fool, but the low lights and loads of liquor fogging my vision hide the tears that slip without permission. Thank hell for that, and thank heaven for generous bartenders who serve us past last call.

It's not until well after two that we're stumbling out of the Uber and trekking our way up the driveway to our front door.

Cameron tugs her shoes from her feet and begins bouncing on her toes. "Hurry up, Mase! I have to pee soooo bad. You don't even know!"

He chuckles, struggling with the doorknob. "I'm trying, but this key's broken or something," he slurs.

"Oh my god!" I gasp, looking around. "We forgot Brady!" I kick Mase.

"Shit, Ari!" He starts hopping around but loses his balance and falls into the wall beside us.

A laugh spurts from me, and I stumble on my heels, quickly catching myself on the porch post to my right.

"Brady left with that girl," Cameron whines, still dancing around, waiting to be let inside.

"The big butt girl?"

"No, the big boobed girl."

Oh, yeah. I remember her.

Mason fumbles with the lock again, and just as he manages to align the key with the hole, it slips from his fingertips, crashing to the deck floor. "Fuck." He laughs, wrapping his hand around the knob and shaking it.

Chase chuckles behind me, and I turn to find him slouched over the railing, holding on for dear life. A loud crash sounds, and I jerk around in time to witness Mason toppling over as he attempts to grab the lanyard.

"Shit!" Cam yelps, dropping to her knees in front of him.

Half a second later, Chase's "oh fuck" rings out.

I whip around as he stumbles backward, landing on his ass

at the bottom of the porch, his legs stretched out on the steps in front of him.

I'm stuck staring, my head bobbling from one side to the other, making me nauseous.

Cam begins laughing uncontrollably, drops onto her butt, and leans her upper body against Mason, who has stopped trying to get up, his eyes already closing.

"We could totally take advantage of them right now." She grins.

I can't help but laugh, and then I kick my shoes off, fall onto one of the porch lounge chairs and let out a deep breath.

Alcohol for the win.

Chapter 4
Arianna

The sun is warm and inviting today, the complete opposite of yesterday when the four of us woke up to Brady's loud ass laugh around five in the morning.

We never did make it into the house, passing out on and around the patio set, which is exactly how Brady found us. After getting some sleep, we tried to head down to the water to hang with our cousins and friends, but we didn't make it past the deck, our hangovers taking a victory lap. So, we turned right back around and threw ourselves onto the couches. It was a movie marathon kind of day.

Today, though, we woke up juiced and ready for some fun. We went for breakfast at Oceans Café, a place Lolli swears by, and then we hit the store to test out Brady's fake ID there. It worked, and we're double stocked, just in case.

Since we've got all we need for the bonfire tonight, we unpack the party favors and hit the sand.

Cam, Mason, and Brady run off, going straight into the cool water, but I lay my beach mat out and waste no time dropping onto it. I close my eyes and smile as the sun soaks into my skin, but the slight shuffle beside me has me looking up.

Chase stands there, staring after our friends with a twisted expression, so I suck it up and pull on his trunks to get his attention.

He looks down, and I push up on my elbows, using my palm to shield the glare from my eyes. I motion with my head for him to join me.

He hesitates a second, then, without looking at me, drops down, mimicking my position.

A hint of anxiousness washes over me as I know we can't escape what happened at the club any longer. This is the first moment we've had alone since that night, and I know I'm not the only one who realizes it.

I admit, I woke up a little embarrassed the next day, but not enough to regret it. Had he shown any sign of anger or ignored me after, I likely would, but he hasn't. He hasn't exactly met my eye, but he hasn't avoided it either. He is right now, though, the tension in his shoulders doubling with each passing second as he tries to focus on the others goofing off in the ocean before us, but I know he's not even seeing what's in front of him. His mind is muddled by me. Or more, *because* of me.

His chin meets his chest, and here it comes.

"Are we okay?" he asks, his focus pointed at the sand beneath him.

"Why wouldn't we be?"

"Come on, Ari. Don't do that." He shakes his head, looking off.

A wave of apprehension washes over me, and I take a deep breath. "Chase, look at me, please."

He does, revealing sadness and confusion.

"Talk to me. What's going on in there?" I ask, tapping my temple with my free hand.

Sighing, he lies down next to me, turning his head to stare directly into my eyes.

How the heck I am supposed to concentrate with him so close, I don't know, but I give him a small smile, encouraging him to speak.

He's staring at me so intently that I want to look away, but I won't.

"What was that at the club?" he eases into the topic.

A knot forms in my throat, but I swallow past it.

"I was letting loose."

"Having drinks with friends is letting loose."

His eyes narrow, and I sigh, pushing up into a sitting position. "If you're looking for an apology, I can't give you one."

"I'm just trying to understand."

A wounded, humorless laugh leaves me, and I look to the sky. "Don't pretend you don't know," I whisper. "And don't pretend you weren't as curious as I was, even if you didn't want it. I know you thought about it."

"What does that mean?"

My head jerks his way, and I frown. "You might have pulled away, but not before you held me tighter."

"I was shocked!" he whisper-yells. "That was the last thing I expected you to do."

"Yeah?" I pop a brow. "Was it the *shock* that made you hard?"

"Whoa!" His hands fly up, and again, he cuts his gaze around us. "That was the liquor and the mood and——"

"And me." I shake my head. "Maybe you didn't want anything to happen, but you can't deny that. I know we were drunk, trust me, I don't need the reminder. I probably would have been too chicken to do it sober, but I'm not sorry I did. I'd do it again."

"Don't," rushes from his lips with his next breath so quickly that he himself didn't realize it was coming out until it did.

We both tense.

Chase drops his eyes to the sand once more, slowly bringing them up to me. "Don't," he whispers, so low it's almost missed. "That can't happen again. I love you, Ari, you know that, but this isn't . . . we can't."

"Can't as in, shouldn't?" I swallow, forcing my gaze not to drop from his when I want to cower away. "Or can't, as in you don't want to?"

Chase exhales harshly, a tragic smile pulling at the edge of his lips. "Both, Ari."

I scoot over, putting more space between us, and he reaches for me, but I tug back.

"I'm sorry." His shoulders fall in defeat.

I inhale, returning my eyes to his.

I want to be angry. To yell and scream, but I won't allow my disappointment to cloud the truth because I know better.

Chase isn't saying this to be cruel. He isn't malicious or manipulative.

He's just . . . my brother's best friend.

We stare at each other a moment, and then his lips twitch. "What?"

"I'm just a little surprised you had it in you." He grins.

An embarrassed chuckle slips from my lips, and I bury my face in my palms, but he reaches out, pulling them away.

I laugh again, but Chase, he doesn't, and slowly, the humor on his face begins to fade.

I swallow. "Chase—"

"Heads up!"

Before I can react, I'm hit in the head by something, the impact of the foreign object knocking me over slightly.

"Shit!" Chase's arms lift, freezing midair. "Ari! Are you okay?"

I rub at my head, spotting a football lying near my feet.

"Yeah, I'm fine. It didn't hurt, it—" My words lodge in my throat as my skin prickles, the weight of a warm hand falling onto my bare back just below my bikini strap.

I peek over my shoulder, and my breath hitches as I lock eyes with a stranger.

A blue-eyed stranger.

A blue so deep, like a tropical stormy ocean's night.

No, that's not right.

They're more like midnight. Like when the moon is at its brightest in the sky, casting a shadow over the dark sea.

Or is it metallic blue, like a rainbow fish?

I can't say for sure.

I look to his hair, a deep, dark shade of brown; it's as if he just stepped out of the water, and maybe he did. I don't know. It does have that slightly styled, messy thing going on. I wonder if it's soft.

31

It looks soft.

And those lips. I—

Wait.

What the hell am I doing?

I don't even know the guy.

But seriously, though, who has such perfectly shaped lips like this? And the way they move when he speaks is like the perfect sync of a symphony—

Hold up. His lips are moving.

He's talking to me. And now he's . . . grinning?

It's a really good grin, too, kind of crooked and cute.

Oh my god, he's totally laughing at me. My eyes fly up, finding humor and inquisition swimming in his gaze.

"I—" I swallow. "What?"

Heat spreads along my chest, and I know there's nothing I can do to hide the flush taking over.

Mystery man lets out a low chuckle that causes something to burn in the pit of my stomach.

And it's official. I'm *officially* losing my mind.

A throat clears behind us.

It's Chase.

Oh my god, Chase!

I quickly jump to my feet, giving myself some distance, leaving Chase sitting on the ground with mystery man bent at the knees beside him.

"You okay?" mystery man asks, hiding his grin.

Did I say hiding? I meant attempting to hide his grin and failing. Miserably.

"Yo, nineteen!" a familiar voice calls from somewhere in the distance.

The man turns his head, refusing to take his eyes off mine until the very last second when he glances over his shoulder.

I follow his line of sight to find Brady walking up.

Brady nods his chin, the universal *I'm about to bullet this ball, and you better be there to catch it* motion all guys seem to understand, and then he does just that.

The guy catches it effortlessly. Seriously. No effort. He pretty much pushed to his feet, lifted his hand, and boom. Ball meet open palm.

There's that laugh again.

Brady jogs over, Mason and Cameron on his tail.

Mystery man looks back at me and smiles, briefly flicking his gaze over my body, but not in a pervy way, maybe not even on purpose. More like, 'you're a woman in a tiny bikini, and I'm a man with eyes.'

Chase must notice, too, because he snaps out of whatever fog he was in, hops to his feet, and positions himself directly behind me. I'm talking flesh to flesh. So close my head jerks around in shock, spotting the scowl building across his face

Brady reaches us, instantly taking note of mine and Chase's nearness. He frowns, quirking a blond brow in question. Just like that, Chase shuffles away from me.

My chest heats for an entirely different reason now.

"Wud up, man?" Brady smiles, going in for the infamous bromance handshake, slap thing. "Didn't know you'd be back in town."

"Wait." I look between the stranger and Brady. "You two know each other?"

Mystery guy looks at me with a sly grin. "Ah . . . she speaks."

Brady's gaze narrows expectantly.

So I explain, "I was a casualty of a rogue football."

Another earned chuckle, but when my eyes pop toward him, I don't get to see his expression because Brady steps into my space, kissing my hair.

"You okay, Ari baby?" he asks sincerely, petting my hair like a dog.

"Fine." I try to push him off, but he shifts, now throwing his arm around me.

He nods, facing his apparent friend. "I take it you haven't met my girl yet?"

Mystery man grows curious, cutting a quick glance toward Chase.

33

Oh, awesome, he thinks I'm a groupie now.

Before I can defend myself, Mason arrives and does it for me.

"She's not your girl, asshole." My brother's annoyance is evident in his tone.

Brady laughs, and I slip from his grasp, looking toward my brother.

Mason slides up with a full-blown smile, the kind you wear as a kid when stepping into the stadium at your first pro football game. "Bro, what up? How you doin'?"

Mystery man is staring at me but addresses Mason. "Good, just relaxing while I can." He cuts a glance toward Mase but quickly makes me his focus once more. "Are you sure you're okay?"

"I'm fine, no big deal."

As quickly as I respond, Mason is before me, frown in full effect.

These boys, I swear. "I said I'm fine, Mason. Chill. I got knocked by the ball. I'm alive and breathing. Like I said, no big deal."

"It was my bad," the stranger speaks, a hint of hidden humor in his melodic tone. "I misread the pass."

Mase nods, backing off as a grin splits his lips. "A missed pass. That doesn't sound like the guy I know."

"I'm sure I can teach you a thing or two about following through," Chase spits with unmistakable arrogance.

My spine goes straight, but I force myself not to look his way.

"Harper." The guy jerks his chin. "How's the shoulder?"

"Perfect."

"Uh," Cam draws. "Are we about to drop trou, maybe pull out a ruler?"

I can't keep my gaze from flying to Cameron, who grins at the newcomer.

"Nah, we're good. I think he's worried about his girl," mystery man says, his eyes never leaving mine.

I bite back a smirk, and somehow, he knows it, his tongue slipping out to hide his own.

Now that's one hell of a way to fish, cast your line out right in the middle of chaos. It's a guaranteed bite, and he knows it, just like I know Cam will jump on this one.

She doesn't disappoint.

"Oh, she is sooo not his girl, ain't that right, Chaser?" Cam pins Chase with a sharp brow in challenge.

Get him, girl.

Instead of allowing Chase to answer, not that he would, Mason takes the lead, as usual.

"Not sure where you got that idea, but you're way off, bro." Mase motions toward me. "Ari, this is Noah Riley. He's our team captain. Noah, this is my twin sister Ari and our friend Cameron." He points to her. "They're headed to Avix with us."

'Noah,' as Mason introduced him, smiles a hello.

"Wow," Cameron speaks the second Mason stops, looking Noah up and down. "If you're any indication of what's to come, we're gonna get into some serious trouble this year." Eyes on Noah, she cocks her head to the side. "Ain't that right, Ari?"

"Don't answer that." Mason pins me with a hard glare, quickly serving Cameron with it just the same.

"Okay," I interject before either of them decides to open their mouths again and turn toward Noah. "It's nice to meet you, Noah, and since I get the feeling you're going to ask again, yes, I swear I'm fine. These three have hit me in the head with a football more times than I can count. It's nothing but normal at this point."

He stares at me, a flicker of some unknown purpose painted in his eyes. "Right, quarterback for a brother."

Noah smiles, and I will mine not to follow.

God, this guy is too gorgeous. It's unnerving.

"So, what's up, man?" Mason asks him. "You stickin' around for a few days?"

Reluctantly, Noah shifts his attention.

"I wish. I have a couple meetings, so I have to get back to campus. There're always a few overeager freshmen who show early. If I'm not there to show 'em the ropes, Coach will have my ass." He grins, glancing my way. "I'm actually out of here first thing tomorrow."

Chase pipes up then. "Too bad, guess we'll see you back at school."

Noah nods, eyeing Chase a moment.

"Well, tomorrow's tomorrow, so you have to come to our place for a bonfire tonight." Cameron swipes her wet hair from her face.

"Yeah, man, come," Brady adds.

Noah glances behind him, a little unsure. "I came with a few other guys from the team, so I'd hate to crash your party."

Cam gapes. "There's more of you?!"

"Jesus fuck," Mason grumbles.

"There are." Noah nods, fighting the smile threatening to take over his full lips. "Four of us, to be exact, and my buddy's sister is here with a few friends." Noah meets my gaze.

"Well, the sister we could do without."

"Cameron!" I hiss.

"I just said what we were both thinking."

My asshole best friend clearly interprets my wordless *What the hell* expression and feeds me with her own that screams, *you know you agree* while waving her hand dismissively.

This bitch winks at me.

I'm going to kill her.

"Don't mind her," Brady says, then points at Mase. "I think she's got some pink puff goin' on."

Noah's brows pull in. "Pink puff?"

Oh god, no. Please don't—

"Yeah." Brady shrugs as if his nonsense should make total sense. "You know, we get sucked in, tight as fuck, achy ass blue balls, and they get swollen, sensitive as hell, pink puffs."

I bury my face in my hands.

I love my little group to death, but holy what the hell?!

Mason chuckles, and I don't have to look at Cameron to know she's nodding in agreement.

"Who's all here?" Chase wonders, his tone cordial for the first time since Noah showed up.

"Nick and Jarrod and my buddy who wasn't at camp, Trey Donovan."

My head snaps up, eyes locking with Cam.

"He's on the team, defensive lineman."

"Didn't think camp was optional," Brady jokes, making Noah smile.

"Trust me, it's not, but he's a senior this year, missed the draft last year, so he's got a little wiggle room. He was invited to Pro Day in—"

"Tampa," Cam and I blurt out at the same time, causing everyone's head to jerk in our direction.

"Yeah, actually . . ." he draws out.

"Holy shit . . ." Cam whispers, slowly looking to me. Her smile finally grows, and then she's squeezing my arms. "Holy shit!" She beams. "So much for never seeing him again!"

"How do you two—" Noah cuts off midthought, and a slow grin tips those lips of his. He stares at me for a beat before his eyes fall to his feet. "Butterflies?" He glances up.

"Aw," Cam gushes. "He told you about us?"

"What the hell is going on?" Chase asks.

"That's exactly what I wanna know," Mason snaps.

"I knew it!" Brady yells.

Cam and I freeze, our wide eyes locked on each other in a moment of panic.

Oops.

"Knew what, damn it?" Mason growls, his eyes flying around the group.

"You two," Brady accuses, pointing at Cam and me. "Took off the minute we left for camp." He crosses his arms over his chest, frowning.

"What?!" both Mason and Chase shout, each taking half a step forward.

I gape at Brady. "How do you always do that?"

Noah lifts his hands. "Hey, I didn't mean to—"

"No, Noah, this isn't your fault." Cameron glares. "These assholes try to keep us on a tight leash, without the benefits, if you know what I mean. So, yeah, shitheads, we did. We went on vacation without you. My bestie and I flew free for three whole weeks in St. Petersburg." She puts her hands on her hips, refusing to feel bad about it. "We met some amazing people, including Trey Donavan, who's apparently your new teammate, and we had a fan-fucking-tastic time."

"Son of a bitch!" Mason shouts, lifting his arms just to slap them back down against his sides. "And Mom went for this? *Dad*?"

I lift a shoulder. "Paul was there for work," I tell him about Cameron's dad. "We checked in with him, stayed in a room next to his."

Mason's glare doesn't budge, but his body loses a hint of tension.

It gives him comfort to know we weren't out there alone, or, well, without him, but not enough to keep him from being pissed off. He'll call our parents later and feed them every reason in the book why they should never allow that again, but it will fall on deaf ears. Finally. We're eighteen now. They'll advise, but my parents aren't the controlling type. Where Mason gets it from, I don't know. My dad says he was the same when he was young and that Mase will grow out of it, but I'm not so sure about that.

"All right, let's put a pause on this, huh?" Brady pats Noah's shoulder, holding on to Mason's and taking him with him as he walks away, Chase right behind them. "Noah, we're the dock property at the end. See you at seven. All of you."

Cameron sighs, offering Noah a small wave before she too heads to the house.

I stare after them until they reach our back deck and then turn to face Noah.

"Sorry about that. It's nothing personal against Trey. It's just, well . . ." I let out a defeated sigh, glancing toward the house again. "God, it's a lot of things, I guess."

Noah meets my gaze, nodding as if he understands.

Weird thing. I get the sense he does.

"Cam can be complicated on the calmest of days." I laugh lightly, rubbing my arms with my hands to rid myself of the chill making its way across my skin. "She's into my brother, but he's, I don't even know."

I peek up at Noah, expecting a bored expression or for him to be searching for a way to get back to his friends, but instead, I find Noah's ocean eyes staring intently, his head tilted as if he's interested in what I have to say, even though it has nothing to do with him.

"Sorry, I was rambling."

The corner of his mouth lifts. "Don't be. I kind of like the sound of your voice," he teases.

"Sure you do." I laugh lightly, motioning toward the beach house. "I better go help them get ready for the bonfire."

He nods. "Yeah, that's probably a good idea."

"Well, maybe we'll see you tonight." I smile and walk away, making the conscious effort not to look back.

My steps are slow as I replay the last half hour.

Chase finally acknowledged our kiss, but not in the way I had hoped he would.

Whether he wants to admit it or not, he was feeling me for at least a moment. He was hard, pressed against my body.

He wanted me.

Or maybe he was just turned on by the mood and the vibe like he'd said.

Maybe it wasn't about me at all.

So, what was with the long, slow, wretched expression today?

What was he thinking?

What was he about to say?

He was about to say something, right?

A harsh breath pushes past my lips, and I pause at the foot of the deck stairs.

If only we weren't interrupted by Noah.

I bite the inside of my cheek.

Noah. A random guy on the beach.

Or not random, but the guys' new team captain.

My hand meets the railing, and before I know what I'm doing, my eyes are gliding over my shoulder, drawn to the exact spot in which I left Noah Riley.

The spot where the blue-eyed stranger's still standing, his attention pointed this way.

I don't know why, but I lift my hand and wave, and the moment I do, my cheeks turn pink because, somehow, I know the action has him chuckling, even if I can't hear him from here.

I had a feeling this trip would be full of surprises, and it seems there's more to come.

Chapter 5
Arianna

"Hey." I nod at Mason as he sets the last ice chest down, officially completing our setup for tonight's bonfire. "Anything else I should do before I go get cleaned up?"

"I think that's it. Brady ran down to Nate's to grab the cups, and then we're good." He glances over his shoulder. "Chase is starting the fire now."

"Awesome. I'll get Cam, and we'll head back out in a few." I turn for the house.

"Ari, hold up."

I shift, and he puts himself in front of me.

He's already shaking his head. "You really took off without us? To Florida? Somewhere we've always talked about going."

"You got to go stay on campus for training camp. We just wanted some fun too."

"So why not come here, hang with Lolli and Nate? They were settled by then."

"You mean why didn't we come here, where Nate could keep an eye on us?"

"No." He crosses his arms. "I mean, where someone who cares could protect you and keep assholes away from you."

"So, this is about Trey."

His eyes narrow. "That is not fair."

"But is it?"

Mason shakes his head, blowing out a long breath. "Tell me about the guy."

Staring at my brother a moment, I decide to push. "Why, Mase?"

"Ari," he grumbles.

"Don't *Ari* me on this. Tell me why you want to know, and I will."

"This guy is going to be my teammate. Dudes talk in the locker room, Ari. *A lot*. If there's something to be heard, I need a heads-up, so I don't rip someone's head off and ruin everything before it even starts." He huffs, dropping his hands to his hips.

Is he serious?

"Are you serious?" I stare, slack-jawed. Before he has a chance to respond, I put my hands out to stop him. "That's what you're worried about, truly? Or maybe you don't know what's bothering you because you're too stubborn to consider it might be something else."

"What do you want me to say, Ari, huh?" he shouts. "That I care about Cameron? Of course I do, you know that, but that's not what this is about! I need to know if some asshole has something to say about my sister that I don't want other people hearing, and you know what, yeah, I need to know if something went down with Cameron too."

"For rumor purposes, right?"

"If it were something else, do you really think I'd be standing here right now and not locked inside that room with the girl to make damn sure when she came out, it was to come to me and only me?" His tone is strong, his eyes clear and locked with mine. "You know me better than this." His gaze seems to soften, almost as if he's apologizing in advance for what he says next. "If I wanted her, Arianna . . . she'd know it already."

A small sting shoots through my chest at the thought of my friend. My brother might be aggressive and possessive and everything else that comes along with those two things, but he's not a liar.

I nod, doing my best to keep the sorrow I feel from showing.

"Trey likes her, a lot from what I could tell. They had a little fling, but she told him she was emotionally unavailable for more, and when we left, that was it. They didn't exchange numbers or share where the fall would take them. He wanted to, but she said no. We left, and she never thought she'd see him again, but now that he's here . . ." I shrug. "Who knows."

He gives a curt nod. "And you?"

I pull my lips in, shaking my head. "There're no stories to be shared."

"If this guy talks down on her, I will fuck him up," my brother swears.

"I know."

He won't hesitate to stand up for the people he cares about, team be damned, but I don't think he has to worry when it comes to Trey.

I'm going to let him figure that out on his own, though.

So, with that, I link my arm through his and drag him back to the house with me.

Bonfire, here we come.

The party is in full effect. Drinks are flowing, the fire is blazing, and everyone seems to be having a good time.

Linking my arm with Cam's, she and I plop onto an open log the boys rolled over for seating. The second our asses are planted, Brady flies in behind us, holding two new beers over our shoulders.

"Aww, thank you, Brady." Cam takes hers, but I shake my head.

"Not ready for one yet, Ari baby?" he slurs.

"Not quite, big guy." I laugh, looking up at Mason and Chase as they approach.

"You girls good?" Mase finishes off his cup, taking the one Brady had offered me.

"Aside from your sister making me drink alone, yes." Cameron grins. "Thankfully, Brady is keeping me well hydrated," she jokes, pulling back to kiss Bray's cheek.

"Where's mine, butterfly?" a rich voice calls from behind.

Cam whips her head over her shoulder, and a big, beautiful smile lights up her face.

With a loud squeal, she runs and jumps on Trey, her arms and legs instantly weaving their way around him. He laughs, holding her tight as he whirls her in circles.

I peek at the boys, each staring right at him, unsure of how to take this.

Setting her down, Trey lets out a deep breath.

"Damn, girl." He steps back, but not so far he can't keep his hand on hers, and takes her in from head to toe. "You're a real-life Malibu Barbie." He smiles. "Never thought I'd see those eyes again."

Cam blushes, glancing my way, and Trey follows.

"There she is!" He pulls me in for a tight hug. "How you doin', girl?"

"I'm good, you?"

"Better now." He looks to Cam and then to the boys on my right. All three have slipped a little closer. He nods, sticking his free hand out, the other still holding on to Cameron. "Trey."

My brother's chin lifts, and he slaps his hand into Trey's. It takes him a moment, but his grin comes. "Mason Johnson."

"Ah, okay." He nods, cutting a quick look at Cameron before settling on me. "Brother, right?"

"Twin." I smile.

"And the man looking to fill the QB spot next year, right?" Trey nods. "I've seen some of your film, bro. Excited to hit the field with you."

Mason's shoulders go lax, and he smirks. "Yes, sir. These are my boys, Brady Lancaster and Chase Harper."

"Watched both y'all's film, too." Trey laughs, shaking their hands. "We're gonna make shark bait out of these teams this year."

"Hell yeah." Mason brings his drink to his lips, secretly throwing me a look that can only be taken as 'so far so good.' "I could use a refill. Trey, you want a drink?"

"Hell yeah." Trey drops his hand from Cameron's, who gently pushes him to follow the boys.

And off they go.

Cam and I sit back nervously, eavesdropping as Trey tells the boys a little bit about his trip to Tampa and how he met the two of us. The last thing either of us ever expected was for these boys to be in the same place.

Cam, the poor thing, will have no nails left by the end of tonight, the way she's biting at them now.

She was immediately attracted to Trey when we met him in Tampa, understandably so. He's tall, almost as tall as Brady, with short, dark-brown hair and hazel eyes. Not to mention we met him on the beach, where his muscular body was on full display all day long for her to continue to drool over. His skin glows like roasted caramel, and he has a large tattoo that covers half his back and upper arms. He's definitely pretty to look at, but that's not his only appeal. From what we saw, he's also a great guy who loves his family and is loyal to his friends, things we value just the same. Most importantly, though, he treats Cameron the way she deserves.

I can't believe he's here.

I turn to Cam, and she smiles, knocking her shoulder into mine. Together, we look toward the beach house, smiling at the hanging lights my dad added last time we were here.

"I love this place."

"I can't believe it's ours." Cam laughs. "We can legit come here whenever we want now."

I chuckle. "Right? Good luck getting us home for school holidays now."

"Yeah, they didn't think that one through."

"Butterfly!" Trey shouts as the music switches, his grin wide. "Mind coming over here?"

Cam giggles, looking to me.

"Go." I shove her away, and I lean back on my hands.

I let out a long, wistful sigh, smiling at my friends.

Straight ahead, Chase and Brady are playing a game of flip cup with a group of girls, while Parker and Nate start tossing the football around. Mason stands near the heat of the fire, chatting with Lolli and Payton.

He grins, reaching up to tug on Payton's ponytail, and I shake my head, laughing at the way she entertains his playfulness.

A gust of wind rolls through, so I wrap my arms around myself to keep warm, and not a moment later, a familiar voice meets my ears.

"Cold?"

I look over my shoulder, smiling at the lone walker making his way over.

"You made it."

He tips his head teasingly. "You were waiting for me, huh?"

I turn toward the fire when it crackles as an excuse to avert my gaze, jumping a little when the bend of his knuckle brushes against my hand, effectively regaining my attention.

"I was only playing." His voice is soft, but then his mouth curves to one side. "No way am I that lucky."

"Sit down, Romeo." I tug my lips to one side, unable to hold back a smile because he totally knows what he's doing.

A sinful chuckle escapes him, and he drops beside me.

"Romeo, huh? I like it."

I don't have to look at him to know his mouth is curved; it's clear in his flirty tone.

"Really, though, sorry I'm late. It took me longer to pack than I would have liked."

"Well, as you can see"—I gesture to the small crowd around us—"the party survived without you."

He grins. Leaning forward, he rests his forearms on his thighs. "So, what are we looking at?"

I mirror his position, tipping my head toward Cam and Trey.

Noah smiles instantly. "You should have seen his face when I told him you guys were here today."

"I can imagine." Warmth fills my chest for my friend, but unease is still present.

"She looks happy to see him."

My eyes move his way, studying his profile, taking in the sharp edges of his jaw, the firmness of his shoulders. After a moment, he meets my gaze.

"How much did he tell you?"

He tries his best to shrug it off as if he knows nothing, but I've got a feeling . . .

"Oh my god, he told you everything?" I gape, lifting one knee onto the log as I turn toward him.

Noah lifts his hands in front of him, playing innocent, but I snatch them out of the air.

"Oooh, no you don't. Spill it, Mr. Riley." I laugh.

His chuckle is low, his eyes falling to where my hands are still locked onto his. I quickly pull back, but he's faster, grabbing and flipping my wrist, so my knuckles are pointed at the sand.

"All right, I'll tell you." Noah begins drawing shapes into my palm, his featherlike touch bringing goose bumps to the surface.

He feels them because he suppresses a grin and doesn't bother to look up as he speaks. "Trey told me he met two fun, free-spirited girls who were out experiencing life on their own for the first time. He told me no matter how hard he tried not to, he fell for one of them overnight, even though he knew she was in love with someone else." He lifts his gaze to mine. "He told me about her best friend. How amazing and kind and beautiful she was."

"He did not say beautiful."

"You're right, he said sexy, but I was trying to be a gentleman," he admits, and we both laugh. Noah flicks his gaze to our hands, swiftly bringing it right back. "He told me he knew I would adore this best friend, and he's not in the habit of being wrong." He winks at me, his eyes roaming my face as it goes up in flames, but then Noah faces forward. "He missed an important piece, though."

"And what's that?" I didn't intend to whisper.

Dropping his chin the smallest bit, he motions for me to follow his line of sight.

Hesitantly, I break my eyes away, peering out over the flames in search of his intended target.

I find it instantly.

Or should I say I find *him*?

Chase stands on the other side of the fire, staring this way, but he looks off the second he realizes I've caught him. A hint of embarrassment washes over me, and I turn to Noah, who is far too perceptive for a stranger.

"Is it that obvious?" I mumble meekly.

"Is it supposed to be a secret?"

A heavy exhale escapes me, and I shake my head. "No, not really, but sometimes it feels like he really has no idea." It's not some girlish crush. It's got roots grown deep beneath the surface. It's real.

"Trust me," Noah assures quietly. "He knows."

"How can you be so sure?"

"Because he's been staring this way since the second I sat down."

While my muscles lock up, I shake my head, denying what he's trying to say. "It's not what it might seem. They're always watching, especially when the male species is within twenty yards."

"It's only him, Ari, and you're the only person he's looking at." Noah lifts my hand, kissing the inside of my wrist, and when he pulls back the slightest bit, his eyes hold mine. His mouth opens, blowing a warm breath over the damp spot, and a tickle makes its way up my arm.

"Trust me, it's not about me. It's about you."

"Exactly." His eyes flick to mine, and with cautious movements, as if I might withdraw, he reaches up, pushing my hair behind my ear. "Nothing, and I mean *nothing*, forces a man to face his feelings for a woman . . . than the interest of another man."

"Interest, you say?"

Noah's chuckle is instant, and I bite at the inside of my lip to keep from smiling. "You're a handful, aren't you?"

I pop a shoulder. "I try."

Noah's arm falls to his lap, and I tug my sleeves over my hands. "I bet you do."

He stares a moment, his chest expanding with a full breath, and when his head jerks to the side once more, my brows pull in confusion, but I peek the way he's pointed.

Sure enough, Chase is watching. Only this time, when I make it known I've seen him, he doesn't look away, but I do.

I face Noah, searching for something to say, but words seem to evade me.

A moment passes, a low exhale slipping past his lips as he slowly pushes to his feet, and I find myself rising with him.

"I should go." He nods.

"You don't have to go," flies from me before I can stop it, and I scramble to make sense of what I'm truly saying. "I mean, you haven't even said hi to your friends yet."

"Yeah. I really do. Besides, I saw the person I came to see." He winks.

"Uh-huh, sure," I mock myself, my lips curving to one side.

Noah remains perfectly still, staring at me for a long moment, and his hand lifts as if he wants to reach out and touch me, but he doesn't.

My skin prickles regardless.

"It was really nice to meet you, Arianna Johnson," he whispers, and then he turns and walks away.

I stand there, my gaze glued to his back, and just before his silhouette disappears into the night, I jerk forward, calling out his name.

Noah spins, eyeing me curiously.

"I'm . . . glad you suck at catching."

A loud laugh leaves him, the sound sending a strange vibration through my body. "Me too." He beams, pausing in place as a small, covert smile pulls at his lips. "Bye, Juliet."

"Juliet?" I question.

His grin grows impossibly bright. "If I'm Romeo, then you've got to be Juliet!"

"You know that was a tragic love story, right?" I shout, smiling all the same.

"Epic." He turns, walking backward. "It was an epic love story!" He waves, and after a second's hesitation, turns around. Noah Riley disappears into the darkness, and I stand there watching him go.

Chase

Pushing the sleeves of my hoodie up, I move toward the keg, my body and head facing forward, but my eyes on her.

Or maybe they're on him.

Why does he keep trying to touch her? I swear, every time I look over, he's got his hands an inch away from her.

Where the fuck is Mason?

Why isn't he jumping on this fucker like he always does?

Like he would me.

The dick runs his fingers along the length of her hair, and my skin heats.

Liquid splashes over me, and I jolt, looking down to find my cup crushed in my palm, the contents overflowing onto my damn shoes.

"Fuck." I jump back, flinging my hand to rid it of the cheap beer.

Brady scoffs somewhere nearby, and I whip my head around to find him sitting on a boulder not three feet away, his eyes on me. He pulls his cup to his lips, glancing toward Arianna and back. Leisurely, he climbs to his feet, fills a cup, and holds it out with a firm frown. "Her hands are empty."

The inquisition in his tone has my pulse jumping, and my eyes dart away with guilt.

But why?

What do I have to feel guilty for?

I'm just keeping an eye on her, and that's because I care.

I've always cared. Shit, I care as much as him, as much as Mason.

Mason.

My muscles clench, and I look back to the brown-haired girl at the edge of the party.

With my mind spinning like this, I shouldn't make my way to her, *I really fucking shouldn't,* but I do, and before she's even spotted me, I'm speaking.

"You two seemed comfortable."

Her eyes flash to mine, confusion bringing creases to their corners.

Confusion I feel just the same because that's not why I came over here.

That's not what I meant to say.

"We just met," she hesitantly defends.

"Didn't seem like it."

She blanches, and all I can think is, what the fuck is wrong with me?

Slowly, Arianna tips her head. "Okay . . ." She drags out. "I'm not really sure what to say to that, so . . . if there's something *you* want to say . . . you can."

Her tone is gentle and curious, and I find myself swallowing.

"No, no, uh . . ." I clear my throat, backtracking, torn by the irritation burning through me and refusing to think on the reason for it. "I'm sorry, it's just I hear you were out of town, hanging with this Trey dude, and then Noah shows up, gets one look at you, and—" I cut myself off, my mouth clamping shut as I look to her.

She slips closer. "And . . . what?"

My chest lifts and falls with a full breath, and I frown. "Don't tell me you didn't notice."

Her eyes fall, and I tip my head, catching the small curve of her lips she tries to veil.

Why's that make her smile?

Is it him?

Is it me?

Why the fuck does it matter?

"He might as well have asked you out right there in front of us all."

"He didn't."

"That's not the point."

"Then what is?"

"The fact that he wanted to." I frown. "You know that, right? That he wanted to?"

Arianna steps forward, grabbing the drink I brought over from my hand. As she goes to step past, her gaze lifts to mine, and with a hidden smile, she whispers, "*I know* . . . that he's gone."

"Do you wish he weren't?"

Her lips part, and I tense, rushing to speak before she can. "Don't answer that."

"What if I want to?" she rasps, peeking up beneath her full lashes.

"Arianna."

"Chase."

I glare, and she grins.

A low giggle follows, and she steps past me. "I'm going to check on Cam."

She smiles at the sand, and I'm about ready to bury myself beneath it.

I don't know what in the fuck is wrong with me right now, but it better be right by tomorrow.

If not, who the hell knows what'll happen?

I sure as fuck don't.

Chapter 6
Arianna

The five of us are up early the following morning, but only for long enough to finish cleaning up from the night before. After that, Cam and I tuck ourselves beneath the covers, eating chips and dip for breakfast. We're on episode three of *Emily in Paris* when she presses pause with a sigh.

I already know what she's going to say, and to be honest, it took a little longer than I expected.

"Mason shook his hand," she rasps, and our eyes meet. "He shook his hand . . ."

My smile is sad because we both know what it means.

Mason didn't feel threatened by Trey, no jealousy or anger.

He didn't pull a Mason and make a scene, knock Trey on his ass and dare him to rise to his feet.

My brother shook Trey's hand.

It was the first time my brother's feelings had been truly clear.

He loves Cameron, but not the way she wants him to.

"You know what's weird," she whispers, tears brimming her eyes as they meet mine. "It doesn't hurt the way I thought it would. It stings, but I kind of thought I'd feel like I was dying." She chuckles through her sniffles. "Does that even make sense?"

"Of course it does." I curl onto my side, tucking my hands beneath my head.

"I'm sad, but I don't know. I'm also kind of happy Trey's here."

"As you should be. We said we're having fun, boys be damned, remember? So damn them. You've now got a fine-ass man willing to turn your nights from a five into a ten. That's more than I can say."

"True." Her laugh is laced with a sob, but she shakes her head. "I can't believe Trey's actually here."

"Maybe it's a sign."

"A sign I need to get laid."

I grin, and Cameron's famous smirk comes back.

"Attagirl."

With that, she presses play, and we binge the rest of the season, eating the same thing we did for breakfast, for dinner. We don't leave the room once.

By seven, Cam retired to her room, and we both passed out. It was a fantastic day, but too early to go to bed, especially when we basically took mini naps all day.

Now I'm wide awake, and my room is dark, despite the curtains being drawn, and when I look to the clock, I find it's only one in the morning, still a crap ton of hours left in the night.

I try finding another show, but after thirty minutes of watching trailers, I give up and tiptoe down the stairs for something to drink, careful not to wake the others.

Snagging a water bottle from the fridge, I step up to the floor-to-ceiling windows, admiring the ocean beyond them.

The glow of the moon against the dark waters is unreal and one of my favorite sights. It's peaceful, scary as shit after a horror movie marathon, but peaceful any other time.

"Hey."

I scream, but a large hand quickly wraps around my mouth, and I spin, coming face-to-face with Chase.

"Shit." My shoulders settle, a huffed laugh leaving me. "You almost caught a water bottle to the face."

He grins, slowly letting me go as he looks around the room. "Walking around in the dark?"

I rub my lips together, tipping my head at him. "That's where all the fun happens."

A scowl forms along his face, and I bite back a laugh.

He says nothing for several seconds, so I nod. "I'm going back to bed." But before I can slip away, Chase gently grips my wrist, so I look over my shoulder into his green eyes.

"I got a smoothie earlier. It sucked," he tells me randomly.

I suppress a grin. "That's too bad."

"It was Brady's fault."

I chuckle, and his smile slips free.

"I'm craving a sundae." His eyes search mine. "You know you want one, too."

"It's the middle of the night."

"So." He shrugs.

"So . . ." I glance around the room, having no idea why I'm trying to escape. "I'll get the spoons?"

"That's my girl." He turns to the freezer, and I pretend he meant that in a far more literal way. He moves over to the cupboard for toppings, quickly setting them on the counter to his left.

With his eyes on the floor beneath his feet, he heads my way. Assuming he's coming for the spoons, I slip to the side, but Chase shocks the shit out of me when his left arm darts out, caging me in.

My eyes slice up to meet his, and his palms find my hips. He lifts me, slowly lowering me onto the kitchen island.

The unexpected chill of the granite has me squealing, my body lurching forward, right against Chase's chest.

He chuckles as my hands latch on to his shoulder, and I ease my ass down.

As I look up, my breath hitches. His mouth is no more than an inch from mine, and I'm not the only one who noticed.

All I would have to do, all either of us would have to do, is tilt our heads the smallest bit, and our lips would be touching, but I tried that once, and we both know how that turned out.

I won't try again, even if, since that night, something's shifted. I can see it in his eyes, in his words.

I can sense it in his touch.

It's almost as if, for the first time, he's testing the feel of my skin. His hands have grabbed hold of me thousands of times, but not with a firm grip, and never did they linger. Not like now.

Chase is frozen, standing completely still as he stares at my mouth, and I can't help but wonder if he's replayed our kiss, as fleeting as it might have been, in his head as many times as I have.

Heat spreads through my abdomen, so in an effort not to embarrass myself more than I already have this week, I avert my gaze. The second I look down, I jerk with realization.

I climbed straight out of bed and only came down for a quick drink, maybe a snack . . . in nothing but a T-shirt cut around the collar, and a thong—the countertop freezing my ass cheeks should have reminded me of this.

Chase follows my line of sight to where my tangled shirt rides high over my hips, to the bright-yellow V of my underwear, currently getting cozy with his abs.

He jumps, swings around, and gets right back to his original task.

"You want caramel syrup?" he rasps, promptly clearing his throat.

"Chocolate." I curse myself for sounding all breathy, but son of biznatch!

Who is this man, and can I keep him?

I scoff internally because, yeah, right. He's just high on summer. Or something like that.

Whatever, I'm not about a wasted opportunity, so I sit back and watch the way his muscles move as he works.

Did I mention he's shirtless? 'Cause it's glorious.

His brown hair is perfectly messy, his skin tan from spending as much time as possible beneath the sun, and so smooth. He's been talking about getting a tattoo for years, but as of right now, he's still all natural.

I lick my lips.

So fine.

"I can feel you checking me out." He doesn't bother turning to confirm.

"Yeah, well." I grip the countertop and lean forward a little. "When the man above blessed us with wine, we indulged. It's only fair his other masterpieces get the same treatment."

Chase sets the ice cream scooper down and spins with a smirk. He leans his ass against the granite, one leg crossed in front of the other, and holds his arms out wide. "Then, by all means." He surprises me for the third time in three days, encouraging me to openly gawk.

He's being playful, and I'm so here for it.

So I take his unexpected invitation before he comes to his senses.

For the first time, I have no time limit, no need to peek beneath my lashes or hide behind shades. I look my fill, unabashedly taking him in from the tips of his brown hair to the bottoms of his bare feet.

At first, it's a quick run of his body, and then I start over. I trace the firmness of his jaw down his neck, noting the way it thickens, widening into his broad shoulders, courtesy of years of football. I move to his arms and the deep cuts that disappear behind him, roaming over every ridge of his abs, daring myself to travel farther south.

My knees meet each other as I trace the sharp lines of his hips, his pajama pants sitting loose and perfectly low. I suck my cheek between my teeth, fearing I might make an incredibly embarrassing sound as I do my best to conjure up the shape of the bulge pressing against the thick, striped cotton.

My eyes dart up, and the look in his . . .

It's new.

Dark.

Desperate?

Chase's throat bobs with a heavy swallow, and my core throbs. I drop my left shoulder, aware my T-shirt will slide with it, and it does. The gaping neck allows it to continue

down my skin, and it only pauses when the m
hollow of my chest, outlining the swell of m

Just a tease . . . just enough.

His gaze slices to mine, narrowing. "Wh

"That seems to be your question of chc

His frown is small. "Maybe I should wou

My stomach hollows. "Maybe you should."

Feeling brave, I allow my hands to slide farther back, willing him closer, trying to make it as clear as possible, just in case he's not getting it.

I want you.

Instantly, his gaze drops to my mouth, so with nerves running through me, I glide my tongue across my lips.

That does it.

Chase pushes off the counter, and like an animal after his next meal, he makes his way to me.

Three more steps.

His fists flex at his sides.

One more . . .

He reaches me.

I push up.

My brother appears.

Shit!

I jerk upright, and Mason's sharp eyes fly between us.

"What the fuck is this?" Mason shouts, the patio door slamming him in the ass as he's frozen halfway through it.

I damn near jump and run, but my body went from flight to frozen in two-point-five seconds.

I'm once again teen me who got pulled onstage at a One Direction concert and threw up all over Zayn Malik's shoes while he was still wearing them.

Thank God Chase isn't wide eyed and tongue tied like me.

"Nothing, man, just getting some ice cream. You want?" Chase asks him as he casually reaches behind me, finding something to grab from the cupboard, and moves back to the forgotten ice cream cartons.

go to bed."

t snaps me out of it.

'm having ice cream." I don't bother trying to hide my
noyance.

"Have it in your room," he demands, his nostrils flaring.

"Maybe I don't want . . . wait." I look him over, finding
he's still in jeans and a hoodie, and he just came through the
back door. "Where were you?"

"Go. Now."

Dramatically rolling my eyes, purely to annoy him, I snag
my water bottle and hop off the counter, my brother's glare
burning into my back as I curve around the countertop.

I bump Mason's shoulder as I walk past him, and he's quick
to grab my arm. His hold is gentle, but his eyes are hard and
pointed at his best friend. "You have pajamas for a reason,
Arianna. Wear them," he grits out.

"Tell you what, when you start wearing a shirt in the gym,
I'll consider it."

He frowns, and I slip past him.

Mase can have his little tantrum all he wants. Meanwhile,
I'm over here trying to muster up all the control I can find to
keep from skipping my way up to my room, but the minute
I'm inside it, I do a little happy dance.

Holy. Shit.

He couldn't look away.

He couldn't *stay* away.

I don't even know that he realized it.

Maybe it was best Mason slipped in when he did. Had it
been fifteen seconds later, he might have walked in on something else entirely.

Because Chase can't pretend tonight was all me. It wasn't.

He asked me to stay.

He stalked toward me.

He—

My door is pushed open, and I jump, spinning around.

"Chase," I breathe.

60

"Forgot your ice cream." His brows are drawn tight, and he blindly sets the treat down on the desk near my door.

I glance at the bowl, layered in caramel. "That's yours."

"Right."

He spins, stepping out into the hall.

Frowning, I push it closed, but before it clicks, he's there again, and then his hand is sinking into my hair. I'm spun and pressed into the frame.

He glares, his hand shaking, and then he says, "Fuck it."

His mouth crashes down on mine, and I gasp around him.

He presses closer, holds tighter, and when my mouth opens, allowing his tongue inside, he groans.

And then he pulls away, his retreat is as quick as his kiss, and I'm left frozen, my hand in the air.

"Bitch!" is hissed, and my head jerks right.

Cameron peeks from the shadows, stepping out of the joining bathroom, her jaw dropped in awe.

I face her, and we both quietly squeal, jumping onto my bed top.

My smile couldn't be wider because I *finally* got a sign I'd hoped to find.

One that can't be denied.

Chase Harper isn't as immune to me as he would like me to believe . . . or had *liked* me to believe.

This was all him.

Where this man came from, I don't know, and I don't care.

His eyes are open, and that's more than I could have expected.

I smirk, burying myself under the covers.

Cam sighs. "Maybe we'll both have a hottie to hump this summer."

We look to each other and laugh.

May-freaking-be.

Today is one of those summer days in Southern California where the warm sun decides to pop out after lunch and disappears before you've even gotten the chance to eat. So Cam and I put our towels away and met Lolli and Payton downtown for tacos while the boys stayed behind watching football highlights on YouTube.

As soon as we got home, Cameron went upstairs to paint her nails, and I dropped onto the couch.

I'm just ending my phone call when Mason steps into the living room.

"Mom?" Mason wonders.

"Yeah. She talked to Aunt Sarah about Kenra and tried to check on Payton, but she didn't answer. I told her she's probably taking a nap."

He scoffs a laugh. "Mexican food will do that to you."

"And growing a human might add to that." His lips twitch. "Dad said they're about ready for their trip."

"Good, they need to take a vacation now that we'll be out of the house. Scoot over." He taps my knee so he can fit into the spot beside me and throws his arm over the back of the couch.

"Did you just get out of the shower?" I take in his wet hair.

He nods, snatching the remote from my hand with a smirk. "Yeah. We got that new weight set Brady's dad sent him all put together. It's legit. Once we have a chance to haul his bench press out here, we'll have everything we need and won't have to pay to use the gym downtown anymore."

"I'll have to check it out."

We look at each other and laugh.

"Hey, you would have been proud of me at the boot camp me and Cam went to. I only took like . . . five unapproved breaks." I smile.

He chuckles. "Just stick to the treadmill, sister, and you'll be fine."

I grin, snuggling up again and pulling the fleece blanket up to my chin.

After a few quiet minutes of relaxing in front of the TV, the smile on my face begins to fall.

It's the small stuff like this I'll miss most, and it's a little too heartbreaking to think these times might fade away.

"Hey, Mase?" I ask quietly, my eyes on the TV. "You think we'll still come here every summer after this?"

He nods absentmindedly, scrolling down to *SportsCenter*. "Yeah, for sure."

"Do you really? Like seriously, really?"

He chuckles, his eyes flicking my way. "Like, seriously, really. Why?"

"A lot can change in college." I shrug against the cushion. "We might be on the same campus, but that's nothing like all of us living in the same court at home."

Small creases now frame his eyes. "I'm sure we'll get busy with life at some point, yeah, but we'll always make time for each other and this place. I mean, that's why they gave it to us, right? Keep us linked?"

I nod. "Yeah, but will it really be that simple?"

"I don't know, Ari. Shit." He runs his hand over the back of his head, his eyes moving to the TV. He scowls. "It should be."

I stare at Mason a moment.

The possibility—or likelihood—of change is a topic my brother hates. Plain and simple, it scares him, and when Mason is afraid or sad or anything, the like, anger, and frustration are what you get. Period. He's been that way all his life.

I don't know if all twins feel the same, but me and Mase? We're a bit codependent. The thought of being alone doesn't sit well with either of us. It could be because we've never really been alone. It could be because we have a large, loving family, one that Cam and Brady have been a part of since birth, and Chase joined when he was twelve.

Mason looks at me, accusation in his eyes. "You think I don't see, or know, but you're wrong." He doesn't have to say the words. We both know what, or more who, he's referring to. "I am the way I am for reasons you don't understand yet. I'm just trying to save you from—"

"From what?"

He sighs. "From a letdown. All our lives, you've been by our sides, doing what we do, and you never complain, but what about outside of us, Ari?"

"I tried that in Florida and got shit for it."

"That's not what I mean." He shakes his head. "Maybe I overreacted a little, and that's because I was caught off guard, but I'm talking about friendships . . . experiences you haven't had yet." My cheeks grow a little pink, but I don't look away. "There's more out there outside of us."

"Maybe I don't need more."

His smile is small. "How do you know?"

I pull my knees up, wrapping my arms around them with a shrug. I guess I don't, but they've always been enough. I don't see that changing.

I understand what he's saying, and he's not wrong. The five of us, we literally do everything together.

Vacations, holidays, and all the small things in between.

We've shopped together, thrown birthdays together, and rode to school together every single day since forever. First, we all sat in the same rows on the school bus, and then we piled into Brady's mom's van when he got his permit. Mase was the first to pass his driver's test, so from that day forward, we rode with him. Every. Single. Day.

The five of us. We were inseparable. A unit.

And we loved it. Still do. It's why we're all headed to the same school for yet another four years.

Does he want that to change?

"Getting away at Avix, it's going to be good for you." He speaks gently. "And I'll still be right there when you need me. And when you don't."

Unease settles over me. "You're talking like it's going to be the end of this. Of the five of us."

"We're family, and family doesn't end." He shakes his head, easing into his next words. "But that's exactly why it's important for all of us to stay friends, so things don't get weird." Mason faces forward, kicking his leg out. "So things don't get ruined."

"Right."

He points his frown at the TV, and mine falls to the lint on my socks.

See, the day before junior high, Mason asked Chase and Brady to help look out for us girls, which meant we were friend-zoned all around in order to avoid the extra drama our teenage years were sure to bring. And they did, here and there, but that line was clear, and we all knew it.

Me more than anyone, but we're not in junior high anymore.

And that line?

I'd say it's as good as gone.

There's just one problem.

And he's sitting right beside me.

Chapter 7
Arianna

As we pull out of the restaurant parking lot—Payton in the back seat beside me—her hands fall to her stomach, and I shift in my seat to face her a little better.

"Have you felt the baby kick yet?"

"I think, but it's hard to tell," she shares. "It sort of feels like I'm a bowl of water, and every time I move, it splashes around."

Mason and I chuckle and look to her tiny belly, just beginning to show through her clothes.

"You want to feel, don't you?" She lifts a perfectly manicured blonde brow.

My smile is instant, and I laugh. "I don't want it to be weird, but yeah."

She shakes her head. "You guys are too much," she muses with a grin, and my eyes narrow, but then she grabs my hand, placing it on the highest point of her stomach.

Warmth spreads through me instantly, my skin pricking as I gently cup her belly over her shirt. I glide my palm forward and backward and then down the bubbled slope a tiny bit.

"It's so hard," I whisper. "Perfectly round and tiny." I lift my gaze to hers.

She nods, moisture building in her eyes as she tries to smile, but I imagine she's all over the place. Happy she has a piece of the man who won't be here to see their child come into the world, and sad for the very same reason.

I can't imagine.

"My mom and Aunt Sarah," I mention Nate's mom. "Are going to have a heyday. Seriously, he—"

"Or she," Mason pipes up.

"Is going to be so spoiled. You'll basically have a babysitter anytime you could possibly want one."

That makes Payton chuckle, and her head falls to the headrest. "Yeah, your mom literally calls or texts every day to see how I'm feeling and all that."

"She's been talking about grandbabies for like four years now. As soon as Nate got engaged, I swear she flew out to see Aunt Sarah just so they could go celebrate the fact that a baby was in the near future."

"Have they met Lolli?" she teases. "'Cause that girl won't even share Nate's hoodies. His baby? Forget about it."

We chuckle, and then Mason pulls up in front of the driveway of Payton's place.

Her brother meets us in the driveway, opening Payton's door before she has a chance.

She climbs out, and Parker pokes his head inside.

"Lolli said you're headed down to the beach bash?" He looks to Mason, then glances behind him to make sure Payton isn't in earshot. "What happened? She changed her mind?"

"She only agreed to brunch beforehand, and she kept yawning and shit, so we didn't push," my brother tells him.

Parker nods. "She says she's sleeping fine, but she's been up as early as Lolli all week. She keeps reaching out to Deaton's mom and people back home about where he was buried since there was never a funeral announcement, but no one knows a thing, and that shitty woman won't respond."

"Can Kenra ask around now that she's back?"

"She's asked a couple people but got the same answers." He shakes his head, knocking on the roof. "All right, well, have fun. I'm staying home with her, but Nate and Lolli headed that way about ten minutes ago."

"Let us know if we're needed," Mason tells him, a frown pulling at his brows.

"Yup."

My brother nods and puts the car in gear. "We gotta pick up our shit at the house. See you later."

With that, we head home.

Cam, Brady, and Chase pull up at the same time, having stopped for gas on the way home from the restaurant.

We've got the paddleboards and ice chest loaded into the folding wagons in minutes, and then we're on our way.

Cam wraps her arm around my shoulder. "Beer, barbecue, and beach boys, here we come."

An hour later, we're dancing in the sand to a live hipster band, our paddleboards laid out and ready to hit the waters. The boys decide to have a drink before joining us, so me and Cam head out on our boards to play around.

A little while later, Lolli joins us, so we make our way to the small cove where a large group has formed.

"Okay, Ari," Lolli begins, dropping back on her board to sunbathe. She cups her hand over her eyes to shade them from the sun and looks to me with a smirk. "Share the dirty deets. There's a reason that Abercrombie model of yours keeps glancing this way, and it's not the same reason Mason and Nate are."

I grin, glancing over my shoulder, and sure enough, he's staring, but they all are at this point, each pushing their boards into the water, so who knows. "He has been a little more—"

"Frisky? Touchy? Noticeably horny?" she fires off, making the three of us laugh.

"Something like that." I chuckle. "I don't really know what to think of it. On the one hand, he's just Chase being Chase, and on the other, he's . . ." I lift my shoulders, unsure of how to explain it.

I try not to read too much into things, but it's getting harder and harder not to wonder what if.

Lolli nods, facing the sun with her eyes closed. "I say you grab his junk underwater and see what happens. Bet he pokes you with it."

Cam and I laugh, mimicking Lolli's position on the board, but it's not long before the others join, and we're all playing around in the ocean.

Brady and I race from the flatland to the cove. Mason, of course, paddled out to the middle point ahead of us and hovers there *just in case I get a cramp*.

Got to love him.

The boys play a game of paddleboard dodgeball with a group of guys, and we sit back to cheer them on.

Brady is last man standing, so when Chase knocks Mason's leg with his hand, and the two slowly begin to climb to their feet, Cam quickly pulls her phone up from around her neck—waterproof sleeves are a must when you live ocean life.

Brady faces the crowd, gloating in the way only Brady can, and the boys throw their bodies at him, tackling him into the water.

"You sons of bitches!" He laughs as he goes down and then takes turns catching each in a headlock, swiftly dunking them under.

Prepared for what *always* comes next, we ready for them, quickly covering our faces as we're flipped into the water and tossed from one to the next like hot potatoes.

Lolli shrieks when Nate does the same to her, and then she's shoving us. "Thanks for the warning, assholes!" She laughs. "Handsome, you're so not getting any tonight!"

"Baby, I'm sorry!" Nate grins, grabs her face, and lays one on her, effectively changing her mind.

"All right, we ready to hit the sand, eat and toss a couple back?" Brady grips his board, pulling himself up into a sitting position.

"Yeah, I'm starved." I move toward my board but lay across it longways to use my feet rather than paddle to get me back.

Everyone agrees, and it's back toward the shore we go.

Brady pulls out a few beers, pouring them into Solo cups, so the beach patrol has no reason to come over and question us. They know what's up, but it's a 'no harm, no foul' kind of thing.

Once our hands are dry enough to wipe the sand away, we head over to the barbeque station set up and grab some tri-tip sandwiches.

The sun falls behind a wall fog, not long later, and the firepits are put to use, so while the others dance around to the music, refilling their cups for the third time, I move toward the flames.

It's not exactly cold, but there's a slight chill in the air, and my hair is still wet, so I wrap it in my palms and hold it away from my skin, spinning, so the heat warms my back.

"S'more?"

I glance to the side to find a blond guy, his hair tied back in a tight man bun and a grin on his lips.

"Yeah, actually." I turn, letting my hair fall, and step up beside him.

He hands me a stick, and I poke it into the bag of marsh-mallows. "Thanks."

His smile deepens. "No problem. I'd offer you a hot dog to roast, but I ate the last one already."

I chuckle. "You roasted a hot dog right here?"

He holds his finger to his lips. "Don't tell, technically, this fire belongs to the food truck, and I don't think they'd be cool with me grilling my own and not buying theirs."

Glancing around, I nod and hold my marshmallow over the flame. "I think they're doing just fine without your sale."

"It is a pretty good turnout, huh?"

I blow the fire out over my stick, and he squeezes it between two graham crackers, right over a slab of chocolate, and hands it to me.

"You here on vacation?" he wonders, perching himself on the edge of the rock.

"More like a quick trip. We come here all the time, so it's become a second, way better home than a vacation spot."

He chuckles, looking out over the party. "I hear you. I'm here during the summer mostly, but I try to make it this way a couple times a year other than that." He bends, digging into the small ice chest near his feet, and pulls out a beer. "Want one?"

"She's got one," comes from behind me, and the guy's head snaps toward the voice.

Chase slips between us with a glare, completely blocking me from the surfer boy to my right, and holds out a freshly filled cup.

I lean forward to meet the man's eyes and smile, lifting my cup. "Thank you, but I've got one, and thanks for the s'more."

The guy nods, an easygoing grin on his lips. "For sure, you guys have a nice night, huh?" He waves, grabs his bag, and moves over to a group of people a few feet away.

I face Chase, bringing my drink to my lips.

"What?" He frowns.

"That was rude."

"You don't even know the guy. Why would you take anything from him?"

"He was just being nice."

Chase scoffs, facing away.

Now I'm the one who's asking, "What?"

"Nothing." He shrugs. "Didn't think Cam was being serious about the whole beach boys thing, that's all."

My mouth opens, but nothing comes out, so I busy myself with my beer.

Is that jealousy?

It can't be, can it?

It's simply him being an ass, mimicking Mason as he's known to do.

Before I can think on it anymore, Cam walks up.

"'Bout ready to head back? It's getting dark, and I've got sand in places eyes have never seen." Cam laughs.

"Yup." Chase kicks off, and Cameron raises a brow but wipes it away before anyone can see.

The walk home from the party feels like it takes twice as long as the walk there.

We're beat from the sun and surf, and the bit of day drinking added to it.

71

Nate and Lolli wave us off as they keep forward toward their place, and we drag ourselves down our driveway.

Cam and Brady beat us out in rock, paper, scissors, so they got dibs on first showers, assigning us as the cleaner-uppers.

Together, we haul the ice chest up onto the deck and move back down to secure our equipment.

Mason and Chase drop the paddleboards into their slots, and I come behind them, looping the lock through the fin boxes. I get them all laced together, but the lock itself has sand in it and won't clamp.

"Piece of crap." I sigh, trying to jam the stupid thing in place.

Chase wipes his hands on his shorts and comes up behind me, his arms coming around, caging me in. His hands cover mine, and he gently takes the lock from my hands. "Here, let me."

I'm not sure if he whispers, but it feels like it, his warm breath rolling over my wet skin with slow accuracy. I look up over my shoulder, and his eyes meet mine, a covert smirk trying to break free.

He brings the metal item to his mouth, blowing into it, and my eyes fall to his lips.

I want to feel them again. I want them to glide along my neck as his breath is.

The lock clicks and Chase chuckles when I jump from the sound.

And then I jump again when the paddles are tossed at our feet, Mason's body pushing itself in front of us, so he can begin sliding them into their posts.

Chase backs away and does the same, so I slip away, heading up the dock.

As I reach the platform, my eyes glide their way once more, and, what do you know, Chase's are on me.

I pinch my lips to the side and continue into the house, where my smile breaks free.

As I cut an apple and scoop some peanut butter into a small bowl, I can't help but remember the words spoken in the dark only a few nights ago.

Nothing forces a man to face his feelings for a woman more than the interest of another man.

I'm not sure if that's what's happening here but bless you, Noah Riley, for your man knowledge.

You might be the very reason I get everything I've ever wanted.

Chapter 8
Arianna

We came down to Lolli's today for breakfast, and after eating, moved out to the patio for a couple games of Cornhole, but us girls didn't last long, so everyone decided to take a walk down the beach to the coffee shop.

Mason, Chase, and Brady all hover over Payton as she climbs up the small set of stairs to sit beside us on an abandoned lifeguard's post, the only place on the beach that offers any shade if you don't pop up a canopy.

So protective, our crew. We may have only met Payton earlier this summer, but she's Parker's sister, and Parker is like family to Lolli, making her important to all of us. At least that's how it started, but that was just the start. It didn't take long for each of us to eagerly welcome her into the fold. She comes from a shitty situation. Her mom, while richer than dirt, was cruel and controlling. Outside of Deaton, Payton didn't really have any true friends, so sometimes I catch her sitting back, watching the rest of us, kind of like I'm doing now with the boys.

It's an unnecessary reminder of Mason's massive inability to find his chill.

I imagine Chase being the leader on the board of *stay the fuck away from my sister,* but he hasn't been so good at upholding his title.

Sure, he pulls back and cuts me off at the ankles with his 'no, hell no' speech, but he's slowly coming around. We hadn't drunk a drop when he kissed me in my room. That was all him. At this point, I just want to feel his lips on me again.

Anywhere.

Everywhere.

"Girl, stop," Cameron's chuckled whisper pulls my eyes to hers, and her grin deepens. "Your face is straight-up flushed right now."

"Shut up!" I whisper back. "For real?"

"Oh, yeah." She nods, and I recognize the mischievous glint in her eye and my own narrows.

"Cam, don't—"

"Hey Chase, toss Ari that drink, will you?" She bites back a laugh, nodding at Mason's half-empty bottle. "Our girl's *thirsty*."

Chase looks from her to me, a knowing smirk pulling at his lips as he grabs it, Mason's glare moving among the three of us before pointing back to the other blonde not twenty feet away.

But Chase doesn't toss it.

He does me one better and saunters over, but instead of placing it in my outstretched hand, he leans closer and sets it beside me, his bare chest brushing along my shoulder. His eyes meet mine as he moves away, but he doesn't say a word, moving back to where he stood with my brother.

Only once he's out of earshot do the three of us let our chuckles free.

Lolli makes a gagging sound, and we look over to find her pretending to suck a dick, her brows wagging, so I toss the chair pillow at her head, moving my eyes to Chase once more.

I let out a tortured sigh, but sensing my brother's attention on me, I look his way. I'm met with a frown, but what's new? He's never been one to hold back his displeasure when it comes to one-on-one attention from anyone with a dick, especially one of his best friends.

Jerk.

Trudging up the back deck, Cameron groans. "Why did I agree to walking to the coffee shop? My body aches."

"Same." I yawn, using the railing to help me make it up the last few steps. "How can I be so tired when we were lying in bed by six last night?"

"That's exactly why you're tired." Chase grins.

"That . . . or the two hours you spent paddling *against* the tide." Mason shakes his head. "If you learned how to take instruction in the gym, you wouldn't feel the need to work your muscles out there so much."

"You mean she wouldn't feel like she was dying for days after?" Cameron teases.

"I don't feel like I'm dying days after, one for sure, but not more." I laugh. "Besides, I like how water exercise doesn't feel like exercise. That's why I do it. And not taking instructions would mean I don't do as you say, but I do. The problem is, I am physically incapable of the shit you give me."

"I only ask you to try."

"To try and bench an obscene amount of weight."

"If you focused, you could do it, but you laugh the second your muscles strain." Mason glares.

I laugh then, and he quickly follows.

Mase drapes his arm around my shoulder and jerks me to him, kissing my head. "You're a brat, that's all."

"Yeah, but my 'big' brother turned me into one."

"I'll own it." He nods, unlocking the door and letting us inside.

"I'm taking a nap. Wake me before you put the pizzas in the oven." Mason takes off down the hall, the rest of us plopping around the living room.

"I don't know about you guys, but I'm feeling him on this nap time shit." Brady kicks out of the recliner and switches on the TV. "Any movie requests?"

I snag the blanket off the back of the barrel chair and curl up beside Cam. "Your call, big guy."

Of course, he picks something he's seen a hundred times and knocks out in the first five minutes. Not ten minutes after that, Cam starts fidgeting.

"Go away if you're going to keep twisting and turning." I give her a teasing nudge.

"My body is in pain," she whines and then gasps. "Chase!" she practically shouts, looking to him. "You took that massage class on a dare last year."

Chase tips his head back, grinning. "I did."

"Don't make me beg, Chaser, 'cause I will."

He laughs, sitting up and onto his knees from his spot on the floor. "Come on, then."

"Yes!" she squeals, dropping onto the floor in front of him.

After a minute or two, Cam lets out a soft, sedated moan, followed by another, and Brady, of course, hears it in his sleep. He tosses a pillow at the back of Chase's head.

"Dick." He laughs.

Cam turns so she can see me and winks, and I roll my eyes playfully, letting my eyes close.

On the cusp of falling asleep, Cam's hand falls on my arm, and she gives me a little shake.

"Your turn, bestie," she whispers with a smirk. "I'm going to bed."

I glance to Chase, who sits back waiting for me with a small grin, and then peek at Brady, his face now buried in the crease of the cushions.

I take Cam's place.

"Hang on," Chase whispers, careful not to wake the others, I'm sure, and stretches to the right, snagging a blanket from the wicker basket by the fireplace.

He motions for me to lie down, so I follow Cameron's lead and pull my T-shirt up over my head, then lower onto the carpet.

I'm keenly aware of Chase's every move, holding my breath as he climbs over me, positioning his hips right against the curve of my ass. I try, unsuccessfully, to suppress a chuckle.

"Something funny?" He moves my hair to one side, his open palms falling to my shoulders.

Well, since he asked . . .

"It's just when I imagined us being in this position, it went quite a bit different." I smile into the crook of my arm.

He freezes, but after a moment, his throat clears, and he begins applying pressure to my muscles.

Chase starts high and works his hands down, rubbing and kneading with his knuckles. I'm not even sure how much time passes as I lie there completely relaxed, but right when I feel myself start to drift off to sleep, the change in Chase's touch has my eyelids flying open.

It's slower, almost forced, as if he has to remind himself of what to do . . . or, dare I say, what *not* to do.

Chase's next move has me leaning toward the latter.

Slowly, and with a slightly shaky touch, the pads of his fingers meet my skin as he takes the strings of my bikini top in his hand.

He waits a beat as if I might protest, and then he tugs.

His hissed breath fans along my bare skin, and I squeeze my fists tightly to keep myself from squirming beneath his touch.

I've gotten a massage before, from Brady and a few others, all in good, relaxation-seeking fun, but I never wanted any of them to strip me down. So yeah, totally different.

Shit, I don't even want to breathe in fear he pulls a Chase and backpedals.

There's no denying he's grown more brazen. Untying my top is proof of that, as is the way he pushes it to the side in the next breath.

He runs his open palms along my back with no barrier to break the contact of his skin from mine.

I pretty much play dead, dying for his next move, while telling myself his only purpose is to make it easier: a smooth surface to work on.

His hand leaves me, and he stretches, a blanket draping over us in the next second. *All* the way over us. My eyes fly open so fast it takes a moment before I can see.

My hands are folded under my head, and Chase's fingers curl over to meet my collarbone, gently sliding back down until his fingertips meet the highest point of my ribs. His palms flatten there, his touch light, and he glides them in a—not at all—massage-like motion.

It's a touch of curiosity.

It's him exploring the feeling of my skin against his.

It's as thrilling as it is shocking.

His body lowers, the heat of him hovering over me, and I swallow.

I attempt shifting, a desperate need to face him washing over me, but he doesn't allow it. His forehead meets my back in the space between my shoulder blades, and he gently shakes his head back and forth.

His hair tickles at the base of my neck, and I shiver beneath him. My lungs expand, starved, and I drag a choppy breath through my nostrils, one that's forced right back out when warm, wet lips meet my spine.

My eyes flutter closed, and then another kiss falls.

"Chase," I pretty much moan, gasping when his lips find my ear.

"Shh . . ." he croons, his nose gliding along my jaw. "Tell me to stop. I don't know what I'm doing . . ."

"You're doing great."

His body shakes with a low chuckle, and then his hands are on my side, slowly gliding up until the edges of his fingers meet the edges of my breasts.

He twitches, and then his hands fly back off of me completely.

I use that to my advantage, quickly flipping under him, my bare chest now hidden beneath his loose shirt.

He wasn't expecting it, and his eyes snap wide.

Chase begins shaking his head, a flash of panic falling over him, so I offer a small smile.

Please don't run . . .

His brows cave in as he contemplates how we got here, so I give him a gentle push disguised as a yield.

I drop my head back, this time straight to the carpet, leaving the pillow beside me, and stretch my chin the slightest bit to expose my neck, leaving it up to him to decide what to do with it, if anything.

His Adam's apple bobs with a hard swallow, and after a moment's hesitation, he drops his face into the crook of my neck.

For a moment, he doesn't move, the heat of his breath working on its own and creating an ache between my legs, but then he pulls in a long breath.

I twitch when his tongue meets my skin, tasting as his lips press against my collarbone.

Quickly, before he has time to object, I push my palms under his shirt, and my insides twist as my hands meet his abs.

I've stared at his muscles hundreds of times, imagined exploring them thousands, but I'm not sure I believed I'd ever get the chance to freely learn their cuts with my own touch.

Chase pulls back, just enough to meet my eyes, and wears the same tense expression as before.

Still, I smirk as if to say *I dare you to follow my lead* as it's clear he's battling himself on the inside, trying to decide what's okay and what's not. What's right or wrong. What he bases his decisions on, I have no idea, but I help him out by taking one of his hands in mine and placing it at the curve of my left ribs, just below my breast. I leave it up to him to decide what he wants from there while pleading with my eyes for him to touch me.

He drops his mouth to my ear, whispering, "You can't look at me like that. I'm trying to—"

"Stop trying. Whatever it is, just . . . stop."

He chuckles, but his frown comes back quickly, and at the speed of a snail, he glides his hand up the tiniest bit. My breathing speeds up, and I run my hands from his abs to his back, pulling him into me.

His thumb meets the swell of my breast, and my lips part with a low whimper.

Unfortunately, the second the sound leaves me, Chase's eyes grow wide, his hands fly from my body, and he quickly falls to the space beside me.

Unable to meet my gaze, he hands me my shirt, slowly removing himself from under the cover, but I get angry and sit up, letting the thing fall around my waist.

Brady's still facing the cushions, so I pretend I don't give a shit if anyone comes in and slowly pull my shirt over my head.

I jump to my feet, my bare feet slapping against the hardwood on my way to the kitchen.

I yank water from the fridge, and when I close it, Chase's right there, frown in place.

"You're mad."

Does anyone, since the existence of humanity, *enjoy* whiplash?

I push past him, but he grips my arm, spinning me back around.

"Don't be upset."

"What if Brady woke up?" he speaks low. "What if Mason walked in?"

"What if you figure out what you want without worrying about other people?"

His mouth opens, but nothing comes out, and his eyes fall to the floor.

"Right." I turn and head up the stairs, locking myself in my bedroom.

My head falls against the door, and I close my eyes, willing tears not to follow.

My hopes are officially up, and it's my own fault.

Chase is being playful, pushing the boundaries a little, and I might as well be a damn bulldozer. I need to let him call the plays, and even if I'm frustrated in this moment, something tells me he will.

All I know is I'm ready when he's ready.

No matter when. No matter what.

Chapter 9
Arianna

"Hole in one, baby!" Cam lifts her hands over her head in victory.

"That's three in a row!" Brady shouts, crossing his arms in a pout. "You're cheatin'."

The rest of us laugh, and Mason slaps the big guy's shoulders.

"It's the same shit every time, my man. Why do you think mini golf is always her idea?" He grins, bowing when Cameron lifts her chin with a smile.

"It's okay, Brady baby," she teases. "We all know you're the best athlete out of all of us."

I chuckle, and warm breath meets my ear.

"Does that laugh mean you agree?"

I shift to look at Chase, but he's already slipping away, his lips curved around his water bottle, and my nerves fire off.

He knows I'm still staring his way and—

"Payton," Parker speaks slow, as slow as his body lifts off the bench beside me as if he's approaching a wounded animal and fears for them to run. "What's wrong?"

All our heads jerk in her direction, the clubs falling from our boys' hands as they quickly follow behind Parker.

She makes not a sound, but as her head lifts from the screen of her phone, tears fall like a waterfall, rapid and nonstop.

She doesn't blink, and while she's looking at her brother, I'm not so sure she sees him.

"Payton." Lolli tries this time, stepping beside her, and

gently curves Payton's wrist, so she can see the screen. Her eyes scan over it a moment, and she glares, her head snapping toward Parker, anger bringing heat to her skin.

"He's gone," Payton says, voice scarily void of emotion.

"Who's gone?" Mason says gently as he slowly approaches.

Payton brings her eyes to his, tension framing her features. She shakes her head, hands him her phone, and takes off toward the exit.

"Fuck me." Lolli tosses Nate her drink and chases after her, while Mason reaches down to pick up the phone.

He leans his body toward Parker, the two reading over the screen at the same time.

Mason shoves it into Parker's hand, turning to stare in the direction Payton disappeared. "Lolli said it right." He shakes his head. "Fuck me."

"Talk, man." Nate glares at Parker.

Parker's shoulders fall in defeat, and he glances at the phone once more. "The funeral. They held it. They couldn't be decent for one minute and allow the girl carrying his baby to be there."

Oh my god.

"How do you know for sure?" Cameron chews on her fingernails.

"Mase . . ."

"His bitch of a mother sent her a picture from a funeral." Mason turns to face us. "Casket is in the background and all."

I gasp, my hand flying up to cover my mouth.

"Holy shit," Cameron whispers, turning to me and wrapping her arms through mine.

"What do we do?" I ask Parker.

He shakes his head. "I don't know. I don't know what we can do. Lolli hired someone to look into it, but he was a minor, and his family must have paid a fuck lot to keep it all under wraps."

"Yeah, I fuckin' bet." Nate frowns. "I'd want to keep as much of that shit under wraps too if my oldest son was the reason for my youngest son's death. How she continues to blame Payton and not him, I can't understand it." He tosses Lolli's soda in the garbage and pulls the keys to his Hummer from his pocket. "Come on. Let's get her home."

Nodding, we follow after them, quietly slipping into Mason's Tahoe, and not ten minutes later, we're pulling up in front of Lolli's place.

Payton's face is stoic as she steps out.

She looks at no one, her hands stiff at her sides as she follows her brother into the house, going straight for her room.

The bedroom door is closed with cautious movements, but the second the door clicks, every one of us freezes as Payton's piercing screams echo from the hallway, bouncing off the walls around us.

We stand there, helplessly staring at one another, and not much changes over the next hour. Lolli makes a fresh pot of coffee, and we pace the house, jolting every time her sudden outbursts reach our ears.

"This isn't good for her." Chase shakes his head, worry etched along his face.

I reach over, squeezing his hand, and Mason scrubs his hands down his chin.

Lolli excuses herself, stepping out onto the deck—she doesn't do well with emotion, but she's learning, and the man who taught her how to love follows after her.

Chewing on my inner lip, my leg bounces in place.

If it were me, I'd be begging for my mom, but Payton doesn't have one who cares, but I imagine she could use the soft touch of one right now, and my mom is the best woman I know. So, I don't hesitate to call her, but I don't get past the first sentence before I learn my brother beat me to it.

I look to him, and as if he knew what I was going to say, he rasps, "They're already on their way."

I nod, and he sighs, coming up and wrapping his arms around me.

"Is she going to be okay?"

"Yeah." He nods, sounding as unsure of his answer as I am.

"What mother would hide something like this?"

"She's not a mother." My brother glares. "She's a heartless bitch. Payton is carrying a piece of that woman's son. She should be worshiping the girl, begging for forgiveness for treating her like shit their entire relationship. She's not a mother," he repeats.

Those are the last words spoken for several hours, and finally, my mom and dad are knocking on the door.

Nate welcomes them in, and they give their round of hugs.

Parker answers the questions he can and shows my mom to Payton's room, where she stays for the rest of the evening, my dad in the kitchen whipping up something warm.

Hours go by, and we fall asleep all to wake up every so many minutes, a restlessness in all of us.

Around four in the morning, my dad shakes my shoulders, and my eyes pop open. "Come on, sweetheart. I'm driving you guys back."

I begin to shake my head, but he gives a stern nod, so I climb to my feet, finding the others all around doing the same thing.

My dad drives us all back to the house, parking at the curb. He turns, squeezing my hand. "Get some sleep, honey. We'll cook brunch down at Nate's around noon or so. We'll call you, okay?"

"If she wants us to come back—"

"I'll let you know. I think she just wants to be alone a minute."

"Mason is camped outside her door."

"Well, Mase is Mase. We just gotta let him do what he thinks he needs to do."

"You traumatized him when you told us about Aunt Ella's death."

He nods. "You might be right, but you guys had just started taking off on your bikes and roaming through the neighborhoods, so you need to know how dangerous that was."

"Was it hard after she died?"

His smile is sad. "Yeah, honey, it was. I didn't ride a bike for years after that, and when it was time for me to get my license, I was too afraid to drive, thinking I might hit someone like someone hit her."

"Your parents shouldn't have blamed you," Brady mumbles from the back seat. "That wasn't your fault, Uncle E."

My dad sighs, nodding slightly. "I know, son, but death is hard for people, and you don't really know how you'll handle it until it happens." His shoulders seem to fall, but he jerks his chin. "Go on. We'll see you guys tomorrow."

With that, the four of us go inside.

Everyone drops onto the couches, but I silently slip out the back door, making my way down the dock. The sun is still hidden behind the horizon, but it will be rising soon.

I walk to where the water meets the wooden posts, strip my shoes off, and submerge my feet in the cold water.

It's always been a peaceful place for me, the ocean, so full of possibilities and hope.

I've always loved how, while nothing changes here, it's also never the same. The waves vary minute by minute. The lines in the sand crease then curve. It's a true wonder, the ocean. Strong and dominant, yet soft and fragile, like the shattered shells pushed to the surface, just to be swept away with the tide. The imperfections are there but hidden, buried. Only those willing to dig down deep will discover the flaws of the sea.

With a soft sigh, I close my eyes, listening to the roar of the waves before me, and inhale as much as my lungs will allow. The salty wisps in the air hit my throat, and the suffocating sensation plaguing me begins to wash away.

Today was horribly tragic and serves as yet another reminder that no matter the choices we make, anything can come in and stir up our lives at any moment. Chances are, we'd never see it coming, and that's terrifying.

I think about my family and friends, of my own personal dreams, and the life I want for myself down the road. And then I think about it being stolen from under me, just like it was from Payton. Like the waves are stealing the sand from beneath my feet this very moment with their fight for dominance, leaving the ground beneath me unsteady, as unsteady as the world around me suddenly feels.

Maybe it's dramatic or silly, but moisture fills my eyes as they open to stare at the moon's gleam bouncing along the water's surface, fading more and more the closer it gets to shore.

The waves splash higher then, the cold burning my skin, but I don't move away, and in the next moment, someone steps beside me.

I don't have to look to know who it is. Chase's chilled fingers brush mine, and the tears in my eyes fall.

"How could that woman do this to her?" I shake my head. "She loved him, and from what we've heard, he hated his mother. How could she deny the one person who meant the world to him her chance to say goodbye?" My voice breaks. "She's having his baby. Her grandson."

"I don't know. I can't imagine," he barely whispers.

"I hope she got the chance to say all the things she wanted to say. How devastating if not." I swallow. "My dad didn't. His sister was only ten. God, life's just . . ."

"Unpredictable . . ." his pensive tone drawing my eyes his way.

A soft frown creases his forehead. Ever so slowly, his green eyes lift to mine, and his hand follows, gently finding its way to my cheek.

The airways in my lungs constrict as his palm glides higher, the tips of his fingers now lost in my hair.

We must shift because the next thing I know, we're facing each other, the shine of the moon creating a soft glow over the right side of his handsome face.

"Ari . . ." he breathes, his throat bobbing with a hard swallow, his fingers twitching against my chilled skin. A low curse leaves him next, but he doesn't pull back.

Chase doesn't let me go.

In fact, his other hand comes up to meet my left cheek and his lips part.

It's obvious he's struggling to come to terms with whatever's going through his mind, and that's understandable. It's like I said, it's been a long, hard day.

I should stand here and wait him out, give him all the time he needs, be here when he's ready to speak the words sitting at the tip of his tongue, his tongue that slides along the insides of his lip, as if fighting to slip out, but forced to remain hidden.

But I can't . . . not with him so close and not when his eyes are darkening by the second, drawing me in and drowning me without a single word spoken.

So, I make a decision that benefits me.

I rise to my toes and press my lips to his.

Chase sighs into my mouth, and I begin to pull away, but as my body slides backward, Chase's hands drive deeper into my hair. He closes the space between us.

He kisses me, and this time, he doesn't stop.

His tongue dives into my mouth, exploring deeper, and I'm putty in his palms.

Somehow, at some point, we moved toward our dock because the next thing I know, my arms are coming down, our tops are long gone, and our hands are roaming each other in foreign ways. My back meets the cool sand, nothing but my bra and underwear left on. A chill runs through me, but then he settles between my legs, his warm body heating mine from above.

His skin is soft, his body hard, as is the bulge beneath his jeans, jeans that my fingers gingerly glide lower to meet.

I flick open the button, and Chase doesn't protest.

He doesn't lift his lips from mine once as I wiggle his body free, pulling my feet up to help them off of him.

My panties are next to go.

Without a wasted moment, I push my hips up into his, grinding myself against him, and he groans, tearing free of my lips and pressing them against my cheek and jaw, settling at the curve of my shoulder.

I roll my core, and he hisses, a low curse leaving him. A sudden urge to feel him washes over me, so I reach between our bodies. I grip him, willing my hand to stop shaking.

Every muscle in his body freezes, his lips included.

His pinched gaze slowly lifts to mine.

His green eyes are begging me to stop while pleading for me to let this happen, to keep going.

Does he not know I've thought about this for years, dreamed about it even?

"I want this," I whisper. Soothing the worry lines on his forehead with one hand, gripping him harder with the other. I don't take my eyes off his. "I want you."

I'm not sure if it's the sureness or desperation in my voice that propels him, but he sits back on his knees, locating his discarded jeans.

He grabs a condom out, locking eyes with me when he tears it open, watching me watch him as he sheathes himself.

Nerves flip through me, my muscles tensing, but I pull in a deep breath, and the anxiousness eases as he settles over me again, his hands sinking into my hair at the back of my head.

His fearful, hesitant eyes ask for permission a second time, and I answer by lifting my hips, forcing the tip of him inside me. He groans, and I slide my hands up his body until I'm holding his cheeks in my palms. I run my thumb along his lower lip.

"Please," I rasp.

Chase caves.

He moans, and I hold my breath as he slowly works his cock inside me.

I clamp my teeth together, swallowing the painful hiss that threatens to work its way up, and thankfully, he drops his head into the crook of my shoulder. My eyes squeeze closed, my grip on him tightening as he pushes all the way in.

I gasp, my hips locking, and he kisses my skin.

It burns more than it aches, the unfamiliar pressure something to get used to.

Chase begins to rock, nice and slow, pulling out and pushing back in a little more each time. He moves as if following the sound of the waves crashing below us. I mirror his movements, and a low moan escapes.

I block out the slight sting and focus on the swell of him inside me.

I close my eyes and lose myself in the brown-haired, green-eyed man above me.

Chase kisses along my jaw, his palm coming up and slipping beneath the bra we never got around to taking off.

He squeezes, his thumb grazing along my nipple, and I begin to shake beneath him.

His breathing picks up, short hisses slipping past his lips, creating goose bumps where it blows along my skin. He moans.

My core clenches, and I know I'm going to come.

Chase's thrusts grow quicker then, his groans deeper, and when he moans my name, right against the hollow of my ear, I explode.

My body fires off, my pussy locking around him as he pulses inside me.

"Ari . . ." he whispers into the night once more, and my lips curve into a smile.

I run my hands through his hair, and when my body goes limp in the sand, the weight of the man I'm in love with settles over me.

I close my eyes, etching every second of this into my memory to the tune of the late-night ocean's swell.

Sighing in exhausted satisfaction, I know I'll never forget this night.

I had no idea just how much I'd come to wish I could . . .

Chase

Ari pulls the blanket up over her shoulders, her head shifting on the wicker seat, so she can look up at me.

I grin, kicking my legs up onto the edge of the stone firepit. "The fire's getting low. Should I add another couple logs?"

She shakes her head, not taking her eyes from me.

"I could get us some—"

"What the *fuck*?"

I fly up so fast my feet get tangled in the blanket, and I trip, my hand quickly darting out to catch myself on the back of the chair.

My eyes snap toward Mason.

His jaw is set firm, and he jerks forward, snagging the blanket and rolling it in his hands. "Ari," he forces past clenched teeth. "Get up."

"Mase, come on," she argues.

"Don't," he hisses.

"We're just sitting here, bro. It's nothing." I shake my head, and only after the words leave me do I realize they were the wrong ones.

Out of the corner of my eye, I see Ari's head jerk in my direction.

Unease settles over me as she slowly climbs to her feet, takes the blanket from Mason's hands, and steps through the back door.

I raise my eyes to Mason as she slips closer to me.

He opens his mouth, but then he closes it, shakes his head, and storms past.

I fall back into the seat, burying my face in my hands.
Fuck!

Chapter 10

Arianna

When my grandma died, it felt unexpected. Even though we knew she was sick, knew the treatments weren't working, and the poison was taking over her body, *I* didn't expect it. Not when the day before, she was awake and alive, smiling, seemingly feeling better or okay . . . unlike every other day the six months prior.

I guess that was the giveaway—the white flag of surrender. That perfect day of laughs and smiles and memories she gave us. That *she* herself was given. That was her last strong, happy, full day before she joined my grandpa.

. . . Maybe that should have been my first clue, the uninhibited happiness and relief I felt not two hours ago when Chase was mine for those few minutes in the sand.

It was perfect, and it meant something, and Chase wasn't that guy. He'd never sleep with me, then disregard me after. Sure, he screws around as much as Mason, and not nearly as much as Brady, but he'd never do that to *me*, to our friendship. Not when he knew how I felt. I may have never spelled it out in big, bold letters, but he knew. He had to.

Last night, or early this morning, depending on how you look at it, we dressed, making our way to the house. Chase brought out a blanket, lit the firepit, and we sat there under the stars, enjoying each other's company, watching as the moon disappeared with the rise of the sun.

About twenty minutes after dawn was when Mason came home. I didn't move, but Chase, he jumped ten feet.

We were only sitting close, our bodies touching but not wrapped in each other. I think the fire and the sunrise made it look as intimate as it felt, and maybe that was a bit much for the first time he saw Chase and me together. Then again, I lie with Brady all the time, and while Mason will make a remark, he doesn't lose it the way he does when it comes to Chase.

Does he not trust him?

Does he not trust him with me?

Everything was as perfect as it could have been prior to that. I finally had what I'd wanted for so long—that perfect moment with the perfect person. Everything was perfect.

Yet, here we are, the morning after, staring at each other from across an entirely different fire.

We're sitting on the deck, and Chase is gauging me, a torn expression written along his features as he begs me to understand him when he's yet to say a word.

Not that he could right now, and for that, I'm grateful because he doesn't have to for me to know exactly what will leave his mouth should he try.

As promised, we made our way to Nate's, where our parents cooked us a giant feast. It's meant to lift our spirits, but the tone is solemn, so I can hide a little behind the hurt we all feel for the young woman who has yet to leave her room this morning.

My brother joins the rest of us on the back deck then, scrubbing his hands down his face as he plops beside me.

"How is she?" I manage to whisper, forcing myself to stay focused on my brother.

Mason sighs. "She said she's fine, but who knows. Parker said she's the 'suffer in silence' type, so I'm guessing she's full of shit. She's safe and where she belongs, though, so I guess she's taken care of. She let Lolli stay in there, so that's got to be a good sign."

I nod, and he drops his head onto my shoulder, closing his eyes a moment. Mine flick across the flame.

Chase's brows draw in so tight they're practically touching, and his gaze falls to his lap.

I jolt from the literal pain that shoots through my chest, and Mason's head snaps my way.

He frowns instantly, and I know my eyes are glossed over, but I offer a tight smile, one he convinces himself is for the pain our family is going through.

My mom comes out then, hands full, but refusing help as she lays out a buffet on the picnic table my uncle Ian made as a gift for Lolli and Nate.

My mom stacks all our plates full, something I know she'll miss, and my dad delivers them to where we sit.

The meal is more or less eaten in silence, or if there is conversation, I miss it, too lost in the whispers in my own mind to hear anything around me.

A little while later, everyone's shuffling again, and my mom slips up. She hugs me, quietly sharing something with me, but I miss it too.

The next time I look up, it's just us again, Chase and me, his plate sitting untouched before him.

He hasn't moved.

I wish he would.

I wish he'd leave, but I know better than that.

Especially since his eyes, they're locked on me, again or still . . . I don't know, but I want him to look away because I can't, and it's slowly killing me inside.

The troubled and tormented expression staring back at me right now, imploring me to understand, shouldn't be there.

I should be looking into the eyes of a determined, resolute man ready to hurdle mountains, tumble, and fall as we climb to our feet again until we find the steady base at the top. Together. That's what love looks like, right?

A mess of emotions?

A bumpy ride?

A thrilling experience?

But who the hell am I to say what love is?

All I know of it is what I've seen from my parents, and this is nothing like that.

This is agonizing.

Gazing at him now, at the flick of the flame as it bounces off those green eyes of his, both dim and dejected, I wonder if I'm being unfair.

Chase and I, we hadn't really gotten to a starting point, then this morning happened.

Our emotions were out of sorts. We were hurting and confused, focused on loss and lost in what-ifs. The moment got the best of us.

We went from spunky attraction to sex on the beach under the bright moon.

From nothing to one hundred—*real quick*.

I want to grin at my inability to lock lyrics out of my head, but I can't find it in me to acknowledge that piece of me right now.

The certainty of the situation is clear. Only a fool would deny what's more than obvious, and that is what meant more than I'll admit to myself, must have meant so much less to him.

I know Chase felt something, just like I know this is painful for him, too. A different kind of painful, but painful nonetheless.

I've always wondered if we were a long shot best not taken, but now I know it's true.

Reality is sad.

I'm sad, but I'll have to get over it, because like my brother has been trying to tell me, keeping our friendships tight is more important than anything.

We didn't make promises; I didn't ask him for more before I gave him everything, and that's on me. I'll bear the burden if it means I get to keep him in some way.

With that thought in mind, I inhale, offering a soft smile to the man across from me.

It's as if he was holding his breath, as a gush of air whooshes from his lips, and he jolts to his feet, finding his way over to the empty space beside me.

His gaze flies to mine. "Arianna . . ."

"I know." I nod, swallowing the lump in my throat, unable to keep my eyes dry. "You don't have to say it."

His features pull. "I feel like a jackass. I knew what I was doing, and . . . I wanted it." He looks into my eyes, and I see his truth. "I wanted *you*, Ari. I just, I don't know. I didn't think. I just jumped." His head jerks away in frustration. "I feel like I'm screwing you over, like I'm treating you like you're not important to me when you are."

"Chase." I fight hard to keep my voice from cracking. "Look at me."

He looks over, but only with his eyes, as if the thought of facing me head-on is too much.

"I know better than that." The left side of my mouth lifts sadly, a tear making its way down my cheek. "You were good to me." I place my shaky hand on his knee, afraid to touch him but needing him to hear me. "I don't regret it."

He studies me, searching for sincerity, but his nod is unsure.

"You're not some random girl, Ari. You're more. You mean . . . so much more." My heart punches me behind my ribs, and I wish he would stand and walk away, stop talking or something, but he continues.

"I don't even know what happened," he whispers earnestly. Regretfully. "We were standing there in the dark, your hair was blowing around, and you . . . you looked so beautiful, Ari. And sad." I clench my teeth to keep a sob from breaking free. "Everything with Payton, I don't know. I had to kiss you. Once I did, I couldn't stop." He swallows, and I use every bit of strength I can muster not to look away.

Chase drops his attention to the ground, and I brace myself, adding a couple of nails into the organ beating behind my chest to keep it at bay because I know what's coming. I know what he's about to say, and it's going to sting like no other.

Soft green eyes lift to mine, and I dig my nails into my thighs, focusing on the physical pain rather than the emotional torture he's about to inflict.

And he does.

Chase's voice is low and regretful as he whispers words I will never forget. "It was a mistake."

I gasp on the inside.

"I don't know, Ari. Maybe if things were different, I . . . we . . ."

That's all I can handle because things could be different. Things *would* be different . . . if he wanted them to be.

But at the end of the day, the facts are clear.

I mean a lot to Chase, but his friendship with my brother means more.

And that's okay.

I've known it for years. I'll know it for years to come.

Hopefully the ache doesn't last as long as the hope did.

Pushing to my feet, I can hardly force a smile.

"I'm going to go home with my parents tonight."

He's on his feet in the next second. "No—"

"I need to leave, Chase," I cut him off. "I'm fine. I just—" *I can't be around you.* "I need to leave." *I need to figure out how I'm going to be able to face you after this.*

"Yeah, okay," he says quietly, dropping his chin to his chest. "What will you say to Mason when he asks why you're leaving?"

A flicker of anger burns in my chest, but I push it away. "I don't know, but after last night, I'm sure he'll be happy to see me go."

I start down the steps, both of us knowing my words are not true. My brother will be upset, angry even, but I can't possibly be in that house with Chase just down the hall a day longer.

At the edge of the dock, Chase's heartfelt words reach me, but they don't soothe as he intended.

"I don't want to lose you. It might not feel like it right now, but you mean a lot to me, Ari . . ."

"Yeah," I breathe, while in the back of my mind, it whispers, *just not enough.*

Later that night, as I cross the road to climb into my dad's truck, headlights catch my attention from a block down, blinding me. I lift my hand to shield my eyes, to try and see better, but then the light flicks off, and there's nothing but darkness once again.

I climb into the back seat, close my eyes, and hope like hell when we get to Avix, it will be like nothing ever happened.

Chapter 11
Arianna

"Where you at, girl!"

Holding back a sigh, I let my pen fall from my fingers and use the moment's interruption to stretch. I don't bother answering Cam's obnoxious ass, knowing she'll pop her head in my room any second, which she does.

"Hey!" She face-plants onto my bed, quickly rolling onto her stomach to face me, her grin far too telling.

Unease wraps around my shoulders, but I've gotten decent at hiding it, so much so she doesn't seem to notice anymore.

Cam wiggles her brows. "We're going out."

I force a chuckle, picking up my pen once more. "I can't tonight. I have to study."

She grabs my pillow, growling into it dramatically.

"Ari, come *on*. We're three weeks into the semester, and you still haven't come out with me. I get you want to stay on top of your classes, but, shit, we were supposed to be living it up together, and you keep ditching me, making me look like the hooch caboose."

I raise a brow.

"You know?" She speaks with exasperation. "The ass at the end of the train. It's three guys and me everywhere we go. That shit sucks! I need another vagina with me to even it out a bit."

A small grin pulls at my lips, and I shake my head. "You're an idiot."

"You love me."

"I'm not going."

"Please."

"Cameron, I can't. I have a lot of homework." Not exactly a lie, but she knows it's more than that.

She's quiet for a minute, sighing as she pushes herself up. She walks to my dresser, running her fingers along the photos lining the top of the cheap carbon fiberboard, and picks up the one of the boys holding the two of us. Still in their uniforms and fresh off their big win in the championship game, we're lying across their hands, our faces smiling into the camera.

I've almost stuffed that one in the drawer so many times, but I can't bring myself to do it.

"First regular-season game's this weekend, you know."

"Yeah." I swallow past the burn in my throat, avoiding her gaze. Of course, I know.

I wrote it on my wall calendar months ago, knowing it was coming with me, even circled it with blue and gold sharpies.

Cam blindly sets the photo down, gently reminding me of what I already know. "You'll break Mason's heart if you don't go."

The day I left the beach house, Cam left with me, and while I knew she suspected something had happened, I waited until the drive to campus a full week later to lay it all out for her. I told her everything, and like I knew she would, she got angry, and a little while later, she cried.

I didn't want to keep it from her, but I also didn't want my own inner issues driving a second wedge in our little group. It took a half gallon of mint chip ice cream and a six-pack of beer to get her to drop the Chase-aimed pitchfork and understand the situation for what it was: a night of overflowing emotion that drove us past the point of no return.

No one was at fault, and no one did anything wrong. It simply was what it was, and then it was over.

We got to Avix two weeks before school began, and during that time, she was attached to my hip in all her best friend glory. We slowly unpacked and decorated what would be our home for the next year, went on walks, and got to know the area.

We went to the movies and hung out with some girls from the first floor of our dorm. Had lunch dates and coffee breaks. She kept me busy with any and everything she could think of, and for the most part, it worked, but as soon as I was alone in my room again, the ache would creep back in. She knew that, which is why we didn't spend a single day indoors from move-in day to the night before classes officially began.

That was also the first night the boys were allowed even a minute of free time.

They asked us to come over, see their place and meet their friends.

Cam was so excited, but I was the exact opposite. Dread fell over me, and I felt trapped.

My best friend tried to backtrack, but I didn't allow it. I encouraged her to go. After all, it had been seventeen days since we hung out with them . . . since that last day at the beach.

Mase would call at night, and Brady would push his way into the frame, but Chase never did more than linger in the background, and for that, I was grateful.

Cam went to see them that night, and though I didn't ask her to, I know she lied to my brother when she showed up without me. She had to have, or he would have been on my doorstep within the hour.

But that was the middle of the month, and now August is almost over.

Her patience is running thin, and it's understandable. I came here to live it up with my best friend, and she was left to do it all without me while trying to pull me out of my cyclical state of drowning in my sorrows.

It's not that I don't want to go because I do, and I've talked myself up to it more times than I can count, but I can never pull the trigger. It's frustrating, but I physically can't stomach the thought of seeing him, and it would be naive to assume he wouldn't be nearby. He definitely would be, probably with a gang of girls flocked around him, as they always have been.

My heart can't take it.

I can't take it. Not yet.

Cam said I needed to get out, to get my mind off things, but how can I do that when he's *always* around?

It was torturous enough forcing myself to keep our tradition of studying on the bleachers while they practiced, but I had to show some sort of normalcy, or my brother would flip out and demand answers. He has no idea how to approach things on a normal level; he goes all in in an instant, and that's the last thing I need, so a couple days a week, Cam and I park our asses in the stadium seats to do homework while the boys work in the heat below us. It's something that started as a way for us to stay 'safe' under their watchful eyes, and it turned into something they looked forward to. Every good run or new play, they'd look up with grins, knowing they'd get one in return from one of us.

We never did get much homework done there.

A small smile graces my lips, but a twist low in my stomach steals it away, and I grow angry with myself because of it.

I'm so sick of being sad.

The good thing about carrying the tradition on here, if there is one, is the boys have to go into the locker rooms afterward too. In high school, they brought their bags home at the end of the day, so it was from the field to the car. Here though, I can slip out before I'm forced to face them, cutting out the possibility of Chase's awkward glances that would lead me to do something embarrassing.

Other than those days at fifty yards away, I've seen Chase once since we arrived. It was during our mandated Sunday dinners together—a precondition from our parents when they agreed to house us in the higher-end, studio-style dorms.

They started the first week of school, and while I sucked up the pain his distant eyes caused, I couldn't make it past the first ten minutes, so I lied. I said I had a stomachache and locked myself in my room the rest of the night. I thought Brady would bust my door down because, not a minute after they all walked in, he began giving me what we like to call *The Brady Eye*, the one that says *I know something, but I won't call you on it just yet*. Bless his heart.

The week that followed, I said my study group wouldn't budge on the time, and I couldn't miss it. I wasn't even in a study group, but I've been searching for one ever since.

The only reason I didn't get shit for it is likely because I've been smart about my absence, finding times I know the others are in class to meet with my brother for lunch or homework sessions then. Same with Brady. Some days I'll meet one at the coffee shop, or we'll meet each other outside of our classrooms and chat during the small breaks before the next one.

But never more than one at a time, because that would lead to them realizing one corner of their triangle is missing. I can't have that. Not yet.

It's hard when you realize you simply aren't enough for someone, and it's even harder when everyone you're connected to is connected to that person as well.

While it's not every day anymore, I still sometimes quietly cry myself to sleep at night. I know it's irrational, some might say dramatic, to cry over someone who was never really yours to begin with, but as cliché as it sounds, my heart aches like he was.

Or maybe it's the fact that reality forced my hand that night as those waves rolled up over my feet, stealing more than just the sand from under me. Everything I thought I might one day have washed out to sea.

My second home took my maybe, my hope, and my virginity.

When I thought of the future, the possibility of my brother's best friend and me was always present. I spent so many years with the same images in my head that I don't even know how to imagine anything else. It's as painful as it is annoying.

But miss our boys' first game as college athletes?

I could never.

I meet Cameron's gaze. "I'll be there."

She nods, inspecting her cuticles, her voice barely a whisper. "I hear you some nights, you know." Her eyes lift to mine. "You're not as quiet as you think you are."

I pull in a long, steady breath. "I'm okay, Cam. I swear."

"I can't help you let go if you don't let me try."

"I know." I look away. "But this is on me, and I have to work through it on my own. It's the only way."

"Promise you'll try harder?" she whispers.

My lips curve, and I lift my hand, my best friend coming in for a quick hug.

"I will."

"K." She squeezes me before pulling away and heading for my door. "I'm going to get ready. I leave in twenty if you change your mind."

I nod, appreciating Cameron even more. She knows my staying in has nothing to do with homework, and she's allowing it because she knows it's what I need.

I meant what I said about trying harder. I'm so over myself and ready to get rid of this hollowness consuming me, but despite our conversation, I still pass on her every invitation the days that follow, and when game night finally rolls around that next weekend, my nerves are going haywire.

I'm rigid all over, the ache in my shoulders bone deep from drawing them in so tight without realizing it. I'm just ready to get there, and sadly, for it to be over.

"Hurry up, hooker!" I shout, pacing the entryway to our dorm room.

I take a deep breath, wringing my hands in the air, quickly dropping them to my sides when Cam's door is thrown open.

"Chill, ho-bag, I'm ready."

She walks down the hall, and I can't help but smile.

"Aww, you look so cute!"

She has Chase and Brady's numbers written on her cheeks in eyeliner and Mason's painted on her white T-shirt in big, bold, blue glitter paint. She's got her famous Cam daisy dukes on and strappy gold gladiator sandals. Her blonde hair is up with big curls in it. She's adorable.

"Wait, wait!" She spins, and the number four is written along the back. She peeks at me over her shoulder. "Had to rep Trey, too."

We laugh, and she turns to the long mirror hanging on the back of the door, rolling her eyes when I tug it open.

"Good thinking. Now let's go." I nudge her into the hall, and we make our way to the elevator.

Inside, Cam looks me over. "You could have worn Mason's practice jersey or something."

I scowl at her reflection in the standard silver doors. "I'm wearing an Avix football shirt."

"Yeah, with joggers and your old dog-walking Uggs."

"Don't start."

She tightens her ponytail. "I take it you're not going to party with us after?"

"No."

She growls. Literally, and whips around to face me. "I swear to Jesus, Arianna Johnson—"

The door pops open, and I shush her, but she flips me off.

"Don't shush me, get a grip and come out!" she hisses, but her pout slips as does the slouch of her shoulders. "Chase will be there, so what?! Big freakin' deal!"

Panicked, I look around, taking in the curious glances we're getting as we walk through the common area. "Cameron, stop."

Her eyes flash. "Fuck these gossipy bitches. Like I care."

I jump forward, planting my feet in front of her. "*I* care, all right? I don't need people to know my business!"

"What business would that be, 'cause the way I see it, you have none!"

"Would you stop and process this for a minute? Do you really think I want to go watch girls throw themselves at Chase—a football player, in a football house, after the first home football game of the year?" My brows rise.

Her eyes fall.

"I want to go watch my brother and my friends play, that's it. Find someone else to sit with or get over it."

"Whatever." She purses her lips, studies me for a moment, then stomps past me. "But for the record, I'm not going to stop asking you to come out, so *you* can get over *that*."

A grin slips over my face, and I step through the door she holds open for me, a big, fake smile on her rosy lips.

Only once we're through the gate and taking our seats in the stadium do I turn to Cameron.

"For the record, I don't want you to stop asking."

She glares, but a glaze falls over her eyes, and she nods, reaching out to squeeze my hand. "You're just . . . I'm worried, you know?"

I swallow past the knot in my throat. "I know."

She sniffles and straightens her spine. "Okay, do you think we can convince those guys over there to buy us beer?"

We laugh and face forward.

Twenty minutes later, the crowd is roaring, the stadium packed full of blue and gold.

It looks like half of the student body made it out tonight to catch the opening game of the season.

It's a little bittersweet to look around, knowing none of our families are here, something the boys have never experienced before. There wasn't a single game as kids where at least one parent wasn't in attendance, and ninety-five percent of the time, both were. We were lucky like that.

They were always there for us, so the moment we got to campus, they took off to travel through Europe, something they've been planning and saving for the last four years. As soon as Brady's dad was given the okay to take the leave, they put everything in motion. Once my parents knew Kenra was okay, they left, but I have no doubt they're huddled around a TV or computer right now, wherever they are, watching.

The very first play of the game is a wicked fifty-yard pass, the kind that gives you chills as you trail the perfect spiral, and your entire body lights up when it falls effortlessly into the waiting hands of an Avix U receiver. It only gets more exciting from there.

The air is electric, the crowd passionate, and the team feeds off the hype.

It's exactly what I needed, a bit of normal. Game nights have always been a favorite of mine.

Time flies as we stand, shouting and cheering under an entirely new set of Saturday night lights.

Being the beast he is, Brady's lucky enough to be in for the majority of the game, while Chase and Mason had most of their playing time in the third and fourth quarter. Chase didn't get to touch the ball, but he laid some good blocks, and while Mason didn't get to show off his arm, his handoff in the backfield was on point, his footwork even better.

My brother has always been slick on his feet, and from the few minutes he was on the turf today, it's obvious he's only gotten better.

But the time clock is almost out, and the starters are back on the field now, nearly the entire stadium on their feet as we watch, waiting to see what the play call will be.

It's a quarterback keeper, and the man wearing the number nineteen steps and jukes past a corner, who threatens to take him down, spins off the shoulder pads of the second defender, and the crowd erupts, chills breaking out over my arms as I push onto my toes in time to watch as he leaps over a swarm of determined Sharks, who drive the defending team into the backfield.

The buzzer sounds right as the quarterback jumps to his feet in celebration, and it's touchdown number four. Avix University takes the win with a one-point lead in the last five seconds of the game.

Cam and I jump up and down with the rest of the crowd, hugging and cheering.

Tears fill my eyes, and I pull my lips in. This is a day Mason, Brady, and Chase will never forget. Hell, I'll never forget it. They worked so hard to get here, and I'm so proud of all three. I can't wait for them to earn more time on the field.

Cam squeals, pulling me alongside her through the crowded tunnel. "That was so cool, Ari!" She high-fives a random group of guys that run by chanting in playful drunkenness. Laughing, she turns back to me, her tan cheeks flushed with excitement. "You have to wait with me and congratulate them!"

"I am." I smile, but even I realize my nod is a little overeager.

She squeezes my arm. "You got this, sister."

"Yeah." I inhale deeply.

Maybe.

It's a good forty minutes before the team begins to file out from the stadium tunnels and the tailgaters erupt in cheers once more. Our boys' smiles can't get any wider as they glance around at the madness they didn't get to see on their way in. Still, through the roar of the crowd and beyond the half-naked girls, they spot us perched against the light post and make a beeline right for us.

My smile's uncontainable. I push off the cement pole and throw my arms around Brady's neck when he comes at me full speed. He picks me up and whirls me around, laughing into my neck.

"How'd you like that, Ari baby?!" he shouts, laying one on my cheek and then trades me out for Cameron.

My brother steps up, wrapping me in his arms with a laugh. He shakes me. "I can't even tell you what that felt like."

I pull back and look at Mason's smiling face. We've talked about this day since we were seven, and he started youth football. This is the beginning of something big for my twin, and I can't help but tear up over it.

"Stop it." He laughs, shoving me lightly. "God, you're just like Mom, crybaby," he teases.

I laugh through my sob. "Yeah, well. I'm proud of you guys."

Mason's face softens, and I know what he doesn't have to say. Having me here with him at Avix means the world to him. He might be bossy and moody, but like me, my brother needs family and people he cares about nearby. He does about as well as I do alone, which is probably why it's taking me longer than it should to wake up from my self-pity stage because I've been pushing my family and friends away instead of taking comfort in the fact that they're here for me. If only I'd allow them to be.

And they would be, but like I said, I won't drive a wedge between my family. I'll deal with it alone so that they don't have to feel the void that comes with it.

A hand hesitantly brushes along my lower back to gain my attention, and I glance over my shoulder, my breath lodging in my throat as my eyes meet moss-green ones.

Chase.

His smile is small, cautious, and it's heartbreaking.

My shoulders fall, and I step from my brother's embrace, turning to him.

He breathes a sigh of relief when I force myself to hug him as I did the others.

His heavy inhale has my ribs constricting, and I swallow the emotions threatening to give me away. "You did awesome tonight, Chase," I whisper. "I'm so happy for you."

I squeeze my eyes shut, hoping he lets go soon, unsure if I'll be able to.

His arms fall from my body with ease.

Why wouldn't they?

Chase clears his throat as he steps back, smiling with uncertainty. An apology lurks behind his lashes, and I hate it. I don't want his apology or guilt or anything else relatively related to regret, so I do my best to pretend I don't realize he's silently begging for forgiveness and understanding.

"How did it feel?" I ask, my insides churning, trying to block out the pathetic girl conversations I made up in my head for this exact moment.

God, how different those went.

We were lying on the couch while he ran his hands through my hair, whispering, replaying the images of his first college game, a night that will forever be stamped into his memory.

A memory I won't be a part of because it's not my pillows he'll be lying on tonight.

Why am I such a girl?

"It's kind of surreal." Chase's eyes light up, creating a strain behind my own. "It was crazy out there. Those guys were massive."

"You're telling me. They looked like a team full of Bradys!" Cam laughs, hopping onto Brady's back.

Mason grins, glancing around. "I guess everyone's getting ready to head out." He turns to me, his smile flipping to a frown when he looks at my pants. "You're not coming again." His tone is accusatory.

I shrug, looking anywhere but him. "Not tonight."

My brother waits for me to peek up and then pointedly flicks his eyes to Chase, who is chatting with Cam now, all to bring them right back to me.

I hold his gaze but give him nothing.

After a moment, he blows out a frustrated breath. "I'll walk you back."

"Our dorm has a group walk, they're at the left gate, but I have to get over there because they leave in ten minutes."

His eyes narrow. "Fine, but text me when you get home. Forget, and I'll be bangin' on your door."

"I won't forget." My lips twitch, and I look to the others once more. "Good job tonight, guys. I'll see you—"

"Tomorrow." Brady pins me with a pointed look. "Dinner."

"Right." I nod. "Bye."

I rush away, joining the buddy walk back as promised.

Along the way, I battle my brain.

I curse myself, wishing to wake up tomorrow morning and everything be back to normal, while simultaneously begging for a stroke of genius that leads to an excuse my brother will buy when I tell him I won't be joining them for dinner tomorrow. Again.

But when I drop onto my bed, alone in my dorm while my friends are out celebrating this milestone that'll never repeat itself, I remember the promise I made to Cam.

I remember the reason our families gave us a beach house

and the purpose of us all working hard to make sure we could end up at the same college.

My feelings don't get to take all that away.

So I'm going to suck it up, get up and go out.

Starting *after* tomorrow's dinner.

Chapter 12
Arianna

The following week goes by in a blur, and before I know it, the weekend has arrived once again, but this time, I'm prepreprared for Cam and her grilling.

The slamming of the front door has me scurrying from the bathroom so fast that I slip, but I dart a hand out just in time to keep myself from hitting the floor. Once I'm back to standing upright, it takes all I've got to keep from laughing.

Quickly tightening my robe around my waist, I ease my way into the living room and lower onto the couch while Cam hastily shoves shit into the fridge.

"Hey!" Cam shouts, hearing me enter. "I ran into the little store on campus, paid a million dollars, but got stuff for breakfast, figured we'd camp out on the couch all day tomorrow, brunch it up."

She doesn't wait for a response as she dashes past me without a glance, rushing into her bedroom. Her closet door hits the frame, and the click of hangers has my knee bouncing. Not a minute later, she's moving toward the bathroom in her bra and underwear, a coral dress half over her head, muffling her words behind the stretchy material as she tries to tug it on.

I knew she was coming home before she headed out for the night; she had told me so after tonight's game. I had decided not to hang around to congratulate the guys this time, opting for a text in our group thread instead, and came home with the dorm crew again while she found a few friends from her classes to wait with.

Cam slips out of her room a few seconds later and falls onto the couch beside me, shoving her feet into a pair of gold wedges. "So, I'm meeting Trey tonight for drinks at Screwed Over Rocks. It should be fun . . ." She throws me a hint but doesn't look up.

"I'm sure it will be. You always seem to have a good time with him."

"Yeah." She pulls on the left wedge. "I guess the team's having a little party at the house, but he's not feeling it so . . ."

I bite back a grin. "Yeah, Mason texted me a few minutes ago, letting me know."

"Oh." Cam pushes to her feet, her annoyance clear as she stomps toward the door.

I almost get nervous, but my friend doesn't fail me. She never has. Never will.

She pauses the moment her hand wraps around the knob, her shoulders falling. "You could come, Ari. Chase won't be there."

Finally, Cameron looks over at me, her downcast eyes meeting mine. It only takes half a second, and then she's whipping around with a frown. "What the fuck?"

I bust up laughing and literally hop up on the cushions as I tear my robe wide open.

Her hands shoot up.

"Hold up, are you . . . what are you doing?" She takes in my made-up face, commercial-worthy curls, and slinky, midthigh plum dress, the one she picked out for me the last time we went shopping.

"What am I doing?" I jump over the side of the couch, slipping my feet into the heels I put at the edge of it, and smile. "I'm going to get drunk with my best friend."

"Yeah?" she whispers, her eyes growing glossy.

I could punch myself for it, but instead, I bite back my own emotions and nod. "Yeah."

Cameron squeals, tackles me, and then we're both falling back onto the couch.

Once we're standing again, she sighs and then smacks me with her wristlet.

"Never again, Arianna Johnson. I will fuck you up if you even try." She glares, but her eyes are full of unshed tears, and her voice drops ten octaves. "You were scaring me."

"I know. I know. I'm sorry. I still need to get my head straight, but right now, I need to have some fun more."

"That's what I've been saying. Get out of your head."

I link my arm through hers. "Think you can help me with that, bestie?"

"Oh, hells yeah!" She smiles, tugging me forward.

With that, we're out . . . but not before pausing at the counter for a quick pre-party shot.

Screwed Over Rocks is a student bar a few blocks up from campus, and from what they told us at orientation, they're sticklers about the drinking age, but looking around, I'm pretty sure it's a 'don't ask, don't tell' operation when it comes to fake IDs. Meaning, show an ID that says you're legally allowed to drink, and in you go.

This is my first time here, but I already know I'll want to come back.

The place is wide open and relaxing, with a dance floor that spreads across the entirety of the square room. There are tables lining both the left and right walls, allowing for some to sit back and relax. Or perv.

There're typical barstools that line the curved bar top, stretching along the back corner, and the lights hanging above let off a soft red glow, an alluring contrast against the gold glitter-infused, black-tiled floor.

The DJ is isolated in the farthest corner of the bar, and the sound system allows for the melody to be heard in various volumes throughout it: thunderous in the center of the dance floor, soft and airy near the tables, and clear and raw at the sides of the bar.

Cam stretches her neck and advances forward, my hand in hers. "Come on! He's over there!"

When we reach him, Trey smiles brightly, tells us how nice we look, and immediately places a shot in our hands.

"What is it?" I ask him, eyeing the dark liquor.

"It's your fun juice, girl. Heard you needed it." He holds out two limes.

I pin a glare on Cameron, and she shrugs, not waiting for me before downing her own shot. She bites into the lime and then wipes her mouth with the back of her hand, smirking at me.

"You gonna deny it, sweet cheeks?" She grins, her head tilted.

Popping a brow, I throw mine back, loudly knocking my glass on the bar top with a grin. "Nope." I toss my lime at her, and she laughs, her eyes lighting up with excitement from just having me with her.

I love my best friend

"I'm going to dance!"

"Attagirl! Meet you out there!" Cam shouts while Trey calls for another round.

The minute my feet hit the center of the dance floor, where the music's blaring the loudest, the rush takes over, and instantly I feel better than I have in weeks.

My lungs open, and even though I'm in the middle of a growing crowd, I can breathe.

Two songs come and go, and then Cam and Trey join me, fists full of liquor.

We knock back two more shots.

An hour or so in, I'm feeling good. My smile grows a little lazy, my body the perfect amount of loose, my mind on nothing but the beat blaring around me.

I look over to find Cam watching me, her back pressed against Trey's front.

I reach out, squeezing her wrist, and she jumps at me, making me laugh as she wraps her hands around my neck.

She gets my message.

Thank you, friend.

"I love you, biatch!" she shouts, louder than necessary in my ear, and we laugh, separating from one another.

Trey puts his arm around her middle, and my eyes flit from his arm to hers.

She shrugs, biting back a smile.

Trey catches it but lets his smirk fly free. "Another?" he asks.

"Might as well do it right." I shrug. "And a water?"

"You got it."

"I'll go with, back in a minute." She blows me a kiss, and they slink away.

"I'll be right here."

I keep dancing, swaying my hips to the music, enjoying every minute of freedom the music offers me.

When the song closes out, and the DJ changes tracks, I give myself a mental *fuck yes*, and let my body lead me into more seductive movements as Ariana Grande's "Dangerous Women" plays in the background.

Two verses in, and someone joins me from behind, his shadow wide, enveloping me completely. While the heat of my new dance partner's body is ridiculously present, he doesn't slip closer, hovering the smallest bit away instead, and it's as if a switch is flicked.

My heart rate spikes, my body warming. I grin into the dim room and keep moving to the music, my hands gliding along my ribs as I softly sing the song to myself.

Strong hands come up to cover mine then; he's not actually touching my body, but he uses the position of my own hand to press just below my belly button, bringing me closer to him.

I allow it, feeling the provocative rhythm of the song as it courses through me, and when his fingers span out on top of mine, I lace them together.

I test my dance partner, swaying my hips one way while rolling my shoulders another, making an *S*-like shape with my back. My head sways slightly with my movements, and my god, he keeps up, matching every twist and turn of my body with his own. Not once does he have to pause, pull back or readjust. We're in perfect sync.

It's intoxicating. Cathartic.

It's exactly what I needed, a fresh, healthy way to release all my pent-up emotions without breaking down and bawling my eyes out.

116

Simultaneously, my chin lifts as his dips, but only the slightest bit, his warm breath now feathering across the sweat-slicked skin at the nape of my neck. It's as if fire meets ice and has me gasping. I'd swear his chest swells at the sound.

He pulls our joined hands away from my body, lifting them above my head, his fingers never once leaving my skin. He trails them oh so slowly down my form until he reaches my hips. Abandoned in the air, somehow my hands know what to do, know what he *wants* them to do.

They dance down in time with the beat, my fingertips meeting the tips of his short, soft hair. While my right hand glides across his neck, latching on there, my left lowers, now clasped over his strong knuckles this time.

His grip on my hips twitches in response, and my body decides to push into his in return, my head falling back, the sudden weight unbearable.

As if sensing my next move, his right hand flies up, gently stopping me from looking his way.

He can't see my face but somehow senses my pout, his chuckle giving him away, and my eyes close, soaking up the deep, raspy sound.

His smile is evident in the way he breathes, his amusement in the way he's dancing. It's as if his exhilaration runs through my own veins, and when he unlinks his hand from mine, sprawling his fingers across my ribs, his curiosity is written in the way his heart beats, peaking my own.

I want to see you.

He knows I do, so when the song rolls into another, it's no surprise we both stop moving.

My toes curl in my heels as I begin to pull from his grasp, but I'm rooted in place in the next second when his lips press gently to the edge of my ear.

"You can turn around now, beautiful." He speaks in a deep whisper, and an airy sensation whirls through me.

I suck in a breath, biting my lower lip as I turn, but I don't short myself of the fun by darting straight for his face;

instead, I drop my gaze slightly, coming eye level with a strong, corded neck, tan skin and the collar of a simple gray T-shirt. I don't tip my chin but allow my gaze to travel down as much as the position allows, finding a hint of ink settled under his right sleeve.

His hand lifts from his side then, and I admire the way his muscles grow more pronounced. He chuckles again, and I close my eyes, readying for the touch I sense is coming, and it does.

Strong, rough-to-the-touch fingers press on the underside of my chin. He gives a small nudge, wordlessly asking for my attention, and my lids fly open.

His jaw is firm and flawlessly curved, his lips drawn into a side smirk, but not the kind that says he's full of himself. It's soft. Charming.

Familiar?

His chest rises with a full breath, then his free hand twitches beside me, and finally, my eyes rise.

When I meet an open metallic-blue gaze, I stop breathing.

He doesn't say a word, just stares unblinking, and when his mouth hooks higher, I snap out of it, my wide smile breaking free.

He laughs, allowing his hand to fall to his side. "Hi, Juliet."

"Noah."

Chapter 13
Arianna

"Wait a minute!" Cam chokes through her laughter. "She convinces you to take her home, then what?" Her brows shoot up. "Says hang on a sec, let me pull the plug to my red river, but hurry, so I don't make a mess?"

Noah laughs into his fist while my palm slaps over my mouth to hold back a giggle, so I don't spit water all over, as tears of laughter leak from my eyes.

Trey grins. "No. She waited until I got sheathed, reached between her legs, pulled the shit out, and tossed it to the floor like it was fuckin' normal."

My mouth drops open, and Cam laughs so hard she *does* spit water . . . all over Trey's lap, but he only smiles, nudging her shoulder with his.

"Okay." Noah frowns in amusement. "No more of your frat stories tonight." He smiles, not a hint of judgment present.

"Let's hear some of yours?"

Noah's gaze darts to mine, eyes bright. "Me?"

I nod, taking another small drink of water.

His chuckle is low, and he licks his lips, but it's Trey who speaks.

"Unless you want a detailed description of the practice field, gym, grocery store, and maybe a local gas station or two, you probably want to stick to me for entertainment." He laughs, whipping his head to the side to avoid the peanut Noah throws his way.

Noah grins good-naturedly, throwing his arm out along the back of the booth as he settles more into it.

"A homebody then?" I wonder.

Noah brings those eyes back to mine, a hidden grin threatening to slip. "Depends."

"On?"

His gaze narrows the slightest bit, but a smile is written in the creases framing his face. "On the day, the situation, and the reason I'd have for going."

"I didn't mean he's a grandpa." Trey laughs. "He's a focused-ass fucker, is all. Surprised I got him out tonight." He looks to his friend, and then Trey's smirk widens. "Actually, I'm not."

They share a secret laugh, and I smile, glancing around the table as the conversations flow, truly enjoying the easiness of the evening.

After my dance-partner surprise, Noah and I tracked down Cam and Trey by the bar, quickly grabbing an empty table to hang for a while longer. We've been sitting here for about an hour now, listening to Trey's hilariously horrific tales from his first year in college when he pledged a fraternity at UCB, where he completed his first year. He transferred to Avix his sophomore year, and he learned quick football and fraternities don't always mix when you want to be on top of your game, ergo the football house Mase and the boys live in.

Chase.

My stomach turns at the thought of him, and I fill my glass with the remainder of the pitcher. When I set the heaving cup back down, my eyes rise, finding Noah studying me, his head tilted slightly.

His tongue peeks out, wetting his lips, and his dark brows slightly pinch, strangely making his face all the more handsome. Thankfully, Cameron begins to speak, so I have an excuse to look away.

"I'm wiped." She turns to me with a drunken smile. "You must be dying if I'm tired."

I grin but drop my gaze to my glass. I hate how a simple, unintentional thought that was linked to Chase leaves me sulky, even through the buzz.

Honestly, I'm not tired yet, and the last thing I want to do is go home and lie in bed for hours, thinking about things I have no control over and a man I need to *get* over. Still, I am ready to agree, turning back to her, but Noah speaks before I can.

"How 'bout Trey walks you, and I make sure Ari gets home safely after she finishes that glass she's just poured?" He flicks my cup, smiling at my friend.

Cam scowls, whipping her head my way. "Ari?"

I bite back a grin, but she knows.

"Go on, bitch." She smirks, sitting back. "Let's hear it."

Trey grins, and Noah's brows draw in farther.

"What'd I miss?" He looks between the three of us.

Trey reaches over, smacking Noah's arm. "Dude, didn't I tell you this girl comes equipped with a jukebox?"

Noah's gaze flies to mine with growing intensity. "No."

Heat makes its way up my cheeks, so I lower my chin slightly.

"Everything everywhere reminds her of music. She's physically *incapable* of not thinking of a song, no matter the situation. It's weird, but you get used to it." Cameron laughs.

My mouth drops open. "It is not weird, asshole."

Noah looks between Cam and me with confusion.

Cam rolls her eyes, and I grow more self-conscious. "I said I was leaving. You offered to walk her home and, in her head, miss thang sang . . .?" She looks to me with an expectant eyebrow raised.

I laugh lightly, trying to calm my nerves before singing out of tune. "If you get there before I do, don't wait up on me . . ."

"See." Cam smiles at Noah. "That. The song has nothing to do with what we're doing. In fact, it's sad as shit, and she changes the words when needed, but the me going home thing was the trigger." She shrugs. "Weird, but all Ari."

Noah laughs and crosses his arms on the table, his biceps flexing as he leans forward, capturing my brown eyes with his crazy blues. "Earlier, you grinned at yourself and looked away when Trey set the pitcher down . . ."

My smile is wide, surprised he caught that. "Ever seen *Grease*?"

He nods, eyes full of wonder.

"At the dance, Doody, Sonny, and Putzie drop their pants to the camera."

He shakes his head slightly, not quite picking up what I'm putting down, but my lifelong movie partner beside me begins cracking up.

I look to her, and together we sing in a low baritone, "Blue moooon."

Noah throws his head back, laughing, his blue eyes brightening by the second.

I grin, picking up my full glass of fresh off the tap *Blue Moon* and take a large drink.

Noah nods, resting his back into the seat, his eyes never leaving mine, never losing their intensity. "Go ahead, guys. I've got her."

Seeming unsure, Cameron turns to me.

Tonight's the first night I've ventured out, so I know she's uneasy about me not coming back with her, but one look, and she knows I need to stay.

She nods, moving to her feet. "For the record, if Mason blows up my phone looking for you, I'm totally ratting you out."

I laugh, nodding. "Fair enough, but I'm betting he's pretty wasted by now."

"As if there's a level of drunkenness Mason Johnson could reach that would erase his need to know where his precious twin is and what she's doing."

"Considering he has no idea I'm out with you right now, I'd say we're good."

"If you say so, still throwing you under the bus if it comes to that!" She blows me a kiss, then off they go.

Laughing, I watch them disappear before facing forward again to find that Noah, while still leaning forward, has scooted to the center of his side of the booth and is watching me intently.

I let him, not shifting or shying away from his thoughtful gaze.

Finally, he sighs and sits back, a sad smile tipping his lips. "You slept with him." His tone is low, gentle, and sure.

My mouth opens, denial on the tip of my tongue, but the words never come, the truth somehow marked in his gaze. It's as if he'd know if I even tried to lie.

So I don't.

I nod.

Something indecipherable passes over him, and his slow nod follows my own, as does his recognition. "He hurt you."

I dip my chin, pull in, and release a deep breath, then look up. Something in Noah's candid expression has me spilling all the things I've held on to for the last few months, things I didn't want to tell Cameron because I didn't want her to inadvertently take sides. It was hard enough for her to witness the change the summer had on me.

So when Noah asks me to start from the beginning, and I sense his sincere desire to understand, that's exactly what I do.

I tell him about us as kids and our interactions. I replay how, at my and Mason's fifteenth birthday party, Chase beat up the guy who gave me my first kiss, saying he was an asshole who didn't deserve it and then wouldn't talk to me for two weeks. I share how on the night of our junior prom, Chase got drunk and pulled me into his arms on the dance floor, singing along to David Cook's rendition of "Always Be My Baby" . . . all to pass me off when Mason came back.

I tell him how over the years, my feelings grew stronger than I meant for them to, and I sat back like the naive girl I clearly was, waiting for Chase to realize while explaining Mason's take on everything. I don't leave out any details from our time at the beach house, apart from our sexual experience, neither Mason's reaction nor Chase's response.

I lay it all out, and not once am I hit with a feeling of judgment or pity by the man in front of me. It's a strange sense of comfort.

"I mean, the night before was heavy. We were mentally messed up and exhausted, so I guess I should have known better, but I wasn't thinking about what would happen later. Even if I had, it wouldn't have changed anything at that moment." No way would I have backed out. Not with the way Chase looked at me that night; he actually saw me, and even though it didn't last past that, I'll always have that one desperate look from him, his visible need for me. I'll never forget the desire in his eyes that night.

"Looking back, I didn't really handle the situation well." My nose scrunches in thought. "Or at all, really. I was unfair. I've *been* unfair. I just . . . left, and now . . ." I blow out a heavy breath. "Now, I guess you could say I hide." I peek at Noah.

As my downcast eyes lock with his, his bounce along my face, concern pulling at his own as mine gloss over.

"I never thought getting something you always wanted could be more painful than wanting but never having it. There really is no in-between."

I'm not sure if it's in my expression or laced in my tone, but Noah detects my self-reproach and refuses to allow it.

"Juliet . . ." He speaks with a tender firmness, waiting for me to look up once more, and when I do, a single word slips past his lips, his expression leaving no room for argument. "No."

At his pained, sorrow-filled whisper, the dam breaks.

"Ugh." I look up at the ceiling, willing the tears away.

Noah curses, shifting from his seat, but I only look to him when he takes my hand and pulls me to my feet, gently wiping tears from my cheeks with the pad of his thumb, and leads me toward the door.

My feet are a little unsteady from the alcohol, but Noah keeps me grounded with his body.

We walk back to campus in silence, and despite my leaving the place in tears, there's no awkwardness to speak of between us.

Twenty feet in front of the brownstone building my dorm room is located in, Noah reaches out to grab my hand, halting my footsteps, and when my eyes find his, he nods his head toward the fountain.

With a light laugh, I follow his lead, lowering onto the cement edge beside him.

He angles himself so he's facing me, and after a moment of holding my bloodshot eyes with his own, he nods. "You didn't tell him, did you?" he speaks softly.

"Tell him what?"

"That it was your first time," he guesses.

A sharp pain knocks against my ribs, my attention dropping to the ground beneath my feet.

I shake my head, somehow not at all surprised by his perceptiveness.

"Shit," he mumbles, then shifts closer to me. He lifts my gaze to his, leaving his hand to rest on my cheek. His forehead is pinched, torn between a few emotions I can't quite name.

"Was he gentle?" He works hard not to frown; I can see it in the strain between his brows.

"Noah—"

"Tell me," he quietly cuts me off. "Tell me, Juliet."

His voice's barely above a whisper now, and something in my chest warms.

This man, who I've met a total of three times, feels like the furthest thing from a stranger.

My lips curve up slightly, and I reach out, placing one hand on his chest.

"He was gentle. Maybe even too gentle." I scoff a laugh. "He had no idea, but he treated me better than I could have asked him to. We have a complicated relationship, more so now, but he'd never hurt me." I smile sadly. "Never intentionally anyway."

Noah nods and brings his right hand up to cover mine on his chest.

"You know this has nothing to do with you, right?" he stresses. "This is all him and his uncertainties."

When all I offer is a twitch of my lips, his eyes narrow slightly.

He squares his shoulders. "Trust me, I'd bet he's just scared and doesn't know what to do."

"He doesn't see me, Noah. Not like I wanted him to."

"He sees you." Noah's steady gaze floats across my face. "How could he not?"

His sweet words have me pushing down an airy feeling in my stomach, but he's wrong. Thinking that way is what got me into this mess.

"He loves and respects me the way I do Brady, the way Cameron does him, but that's all." I shrug. "I get it, but it still sucks, and it's taking longer than I wish it would to come to terms with that fact." I reach down, running my hand through the fountain water beside us. "I'll get over it, and hopefully, our friendship will make it once I do. It has to, for my brother and the others. For us too, I guess."

Noah's quiet for a few moments before he speaks. "This is why I haven't seen you at the house."

Not a question.

I grin at the water, admiring the way the moonlight beams through. "Been looking for me, huh?" I tease, tossing his words from the bonfire back at him.

"Yeah."

His instant response has my gaze flying to his.

We sit there, staring at one another for a moment, and then suddenly, Noah jumps to his feet.

"Come on, Juliet." He holds his sturdy hand out. "Let's get you home. You mixed whiskey and beer tonight. Your head'll be killing you come morning."

I groan and allow him to pull me to my feet. Noah insists on walking me all the way to my door, so I ignore the nosy rosies in the halls as we pass.

Love how it's totally normal to be up at three in the morning in college.

"You'll be all right tonight?" He leans against the frame as I unlock the door.

I grin, slipping in and using the door as leverage. "I'll be fine."

A small frown slips over his face, but he nods.

"I really needed tonight. Thank you for . . . you know, all of it." I glance away, heat sneaking up my cheeks. I can't believe I unloaded all my problems, but Noah erases the unease swimming in my stomach.

"You have nothing to be embarrassed about." He stares at me a moment, his low exhale following not long after, and he takes a step back. "Do me a favor and drink some water before bed tonight."

My head falls to the frame. "How is that doing you a favor?"

He cocks his head the slightest bit, making me smile.

"I will, swear."

Satisfied, he backs away. "Night, Juliet."

I lift my hand, and once I close the door behind me, I only have a single thought.

I wasn't ready for him to go just yet.

Chapter 14
Arianna

It's ten to ten when there's a knock at the door. Several seconds of groaning into my blankets pass, but Cameron's feet never stomp along the linoleum floor, and then I remember she poked her head in earlier to tell me she was leaving.

A second knock sounds, and I flop onto my back, huffing at the ceiling, slowly pulling myself to my feet.

"Com—" I try to speak, but my voice is a croaky mess, so I clear my throat and try again. "Coming," I yawn midword, using all the muscles that are working right now to unlock and open the door.

My eyes widen, my body freezing, and autopilot has me slamming the thing closed as soon as I've opened it.

A deep chuckle echoes through from the other side, and I lightly bang my forehead against the cheap wood.

"You have got to be kidding me," I whisper.

"Come on, Juliet. Open up." Humor is clear in his tone. "I've already seen you now."

I groan, shifting slightly to look in the mirror beside the door. I lick my fingers and rub beneath my eyes, attempting to rid myself of some of the black eyeliner that made its way down my face and smooth the Alfalfa-esque hair down that's sticking up all over the place.

Taking a deep breath, I shake the sleeves of the hoodie I stole from Mason until it's swallowed my hands and bring it up to my mouth.

I pull the door open, and I'm met with a big, bright morning smile, the kind that demands one in return, despite the horror and embarrassment of my appearance.

"Morning, sunshine."

My eyes narrow playfully, and I take a step back, welcoming him inside. "Good morning, Noah." I close the door and lean against it, crossing my arms over my braless chest.

I watch wordlessly as he takes the few steps toward the kitchen, setting a drink holder of what I assume are coffees and a café bag on the bar-like countertop. Noah pulls a water bottle from the pocket of his hoodie, twists off the cap, and sets it down beside the other items. His hand slips into the front pocket of his jeans next, sliding right back out with a small bottle of Excedrin, and finally, my tired, hungover mind catches on.

Noah didn't only come here to check on me; he came to take care of me.

It's clear he's been up for a while. He's bright eyed and fresh in a pair of jeans, a lightweight gray hoodie similar to the one I'm wearing, and his dark hair is swiped to the right like he ran a quick hand through it and called it a day.

He turns to me, his face all business

"Here." He lifts his closed fist, holding my gaze with his.

I suppress a grin as I push off the door and meet him where he stands, opening my hand as requested.

He pushes my sweatshirt back with the inner part of his middle finger, and my eyes drop to the contact, confused when the exposed skin of my wrist prickles. Noah sets the pills in my palm, quickly passing me the water bottle.

Water in one hand, pills in the other, my eyes lift to his.

A soft smile forms along his lips as if in answer to the question I didn't have to ask.

"I wanted to make sure you were all right. Cam showed up at the house about an hour ago and said you were still in bed," he tells me.

My face transforms into a frown before I can stop it, let alone process the reason why, and Noah laughs.

"I didn't decide to come after I heard." He grins. "I was already planning on coming here before I spotted her."

I squish my lips to the right, fighting the blush threatening to spread.

Noah sees it, the heat rising along my neck, but he's a gentleman about it and turns away, leaving me to my awkwardness.

Why would it matter if he only came because Cam likely made it sound like I died and came back a zombie? I wasn't *that* drunk, and it's not like I expected him to show at all. Why would he?

I squeeze my eyes shut and give myself a mental shake before dropping the pills in my mouth and finishing off half the water bottle.

"So," Noah speaks with his back to me. "I got plain coffees to play it safe—figuring if you were a coffee girl, you'd have creamer already—and a couple breakfast sandwiches."

I walk around him and pull out both Cam's caramel creamer and my thin mint one, placing them on the counter in front of him.

He looks at the bottles, his eyes narrowing in thought. "I think caramel's too basic for you."

"I don't know . . . I am kind of basic," I tease.

"I disagree." He smirks, removing the lids and adding one creamer to each until the paper cups are full, and then places them both in front of me. "Prove me wrong."

I lift a brow, grabbing the caramel one as he eyes me, and then I set it in front of him, our laughter following.

A satisfied grin pulls at his lips as he pulls the sandwiches from the bag. "Ham or sausage?"

I scrunch my nose, and his face falls.

"You don't like either?" he nearly pouts, and my smile is instant.

"I like both, and I'm dying to drink this coffee, but . . . mind if I shower? Maybe, I don't know . . . put some pants on?"

He frowns, his attention immediately dropping to my bare legs, and then his dark brows jump. "Shit. I'm sorry." He

130

spins on his heels, running a hand over the hair at the base of his skull.

I laugh. "I'll be quick if you want to find something to watch. Unless you can't stay, of course, then thank you for—"

He glances over his shoulder. "I can stay."

"Okay, then." I grin, grab my coffee and lift it. "Thank you, Noah. Seriously."

He nods as I make my way into my room to grab my things. It's times like this I appreciate the private bathroom Cam and I were blessed enough to get.

In the shower, I think about Noah being here, as well as how Mason would murder the man if he knew. Actually, maybe it's me who he'd murder for allowing Noah in like nothing, but I don't know. He lives in the same house as my brother, plays on the same team, and so far, no one has had a bad word to say about the guy. Mase would have never left me on the beach with Noah that day if he didn't trust him in some manner, let alone invite him to the bonfire that day, so it doesn't feel like a bad move.

Plus, I had a lot of fun last night. Having someone to talk to outside of my normal group was refreshing in a way I've never experienced.

I love talking to Cam, and I'd trust her with all things in my world, but I had a fresh mind with a fresh outlook, and I think it was exactly what I needed. While it seemed to bother him that I was upset, he wasn't wounded by the situation like me, Chase, and Cameron were, or as Brady or Mason would be if they knew. It's different, and I love that.

We didn't sit around the entire time working to wash away or prevent awkwardness. It was fun and stress-free. It was easy.

Noah being here now, though, I one thousand percent did not expect. It was easy to see he was being genuine last night. That he honestly wanted to hear what I had to say, but I didn't exactly think past that conversation.

Now I can't help but wonder if Noah could use a new friend as much as I need one.

Hurrying out of the shower, I throw on my favorite Death Before Decaf T-shirt and a pair of leggings. I run a comb through my long dark hair, brush my teeth, then grab my coffee and step out of the bathroom, wet haired and fresh faced.

Noah's on the couch, as I expected, so I fall into the space beside him. He grins my way, passing me the ham breakfast sandwich and remote as he takes a bite of his own breakfast.

I look up at the TV as the commercial ends to find he's about twenty minutes into the movie *Grown Ups*, so I toss the controller to the side and settle in to watch with him.

Once I'm done eating, I cradle my coffee in my palms, folding my legs up on the couch.

"Thank you, Noah," I tell him again, peering at him over the rim of my cup when he looks my way. "For last night and today. For right now. I've locked myself away a lot lately, so it's really nice to have you here."

"You don't need to thank me."

"I do."

"You don't." Noah twists to face me. "I came because I wanted to."

I let my head drop onto the cushion, smiling up at him. "Well, thank you anyway."

A small shadow falls over his eyes, but he nods.

"I was too busy being a baby last night, I didn't get to tell you, but you play like a boss."

That brings a wide smile back to his face, but he turns away, shielding it from me.

"I'm serious. Your very first throw the first game and that quarterback keeper? So smooth." I chuckle when he shakes his head, still not looking at me. "And last night, that flea-flicker was genius. I feel like a jerk because I totally spaced on you being the main man until I saw you last night and remembered. You're a badass, number nineteen."

Noah's mouth is still upturned, but he stays facing forward, only moving his eyes my way as he attempts to downplay his skill set. "Last night's game was a tough one, but we did it. As a team."

I pull my lips in to bite back my grin.

He's so different from my brother and the boys. Mason would have said something along the lines of 'hell yeah, I'm a badass' or added to the plays I listed, but I guess that's not Noah's style. He's humble, and that's rare, considering his position. For any athlete playing at this level, really.

He almost has this tortured soul vibe going on, but not the kind that makes you bitter or cruel. The kind that stems from loss and letdowns, where you're almost afraid to want because the universe might decide the jokes on you, and down another tor you tumble.

"Mason's been killing it at practice," he shares then, shifting the attention from himself. "He's going to do really well if he keeps it up."

I study his features, finding not a hint of insincerity. He truly believes what he's saying, and he speaks with no malice or jealousy, no threat or fear that he'll lose his spot to the rookie superstar. And my brother *is* a superstar.

"You want him to do well." I meant it as a statement, but the awe of the situation seeps into my tone, and it sounds like a question.

Noah's head tugs back a little, taken off guard, and I almost worry I've offended him, but his chuckle soon follows, my muscles easing as a result.

"Hell yeah, I do." He nods. "Mason's got it. He's good. Great even. We needed him tonight, and he delivered better than expected if I'm being honest. When I took that last hit, I had to step out. Their defense had my timing and footwork clocked by the fourth quarter. When that happens, and we've got a solid second, it's a no-brainer to make the swap. Mason went out there and shook 'em up with ease." He laughs, and, for some reason, the boyish sound makes me grin. "No one expected the rookie QB to come in there and raise hell, but he did. Showed 'em up too." He smiles, finally turning toward me.

I like his smile. It's a pinch higher on the left, revealing a sliver of his white teeth. The hint of stubble along his jaw wasn't there last night and allows for a nice little shadow, helping his smile burn brighter, also making his eyes appear more aqua than midnight ocean waves.

"He'd be happy to hear that, but if you tell him, he'll get an even bigger head," I joke, and while Noah's lips twitch, his features smooth.

After a moment, he nods, opening his mouth to speak, but then he faces forward and clears his throat.

"I have to get going." He pushes to his feet, looking over at me. "Sundays are a little busy for me."

I nod.

What's on Sundays?

Noah stands there a second longer and then gathers our garbage, heading toward the kitchen, but I stay where I am, watching.

It's so strange he's here in my space.

Not as strange as how it feels as natural as it does with the boys.

Noah reaches the door, pulls it open, and pins me with a smirk over his shoulder. "I put my number on a napkin and stuck it on the fridge. If you text me your number, maybe next time, I'll call ahead." With that, he winks and walks out.

Smiling, I push to my feet and grab said napkin. I make my way back to the couch, phone in hand, and I type out a text while hoping he doesn't think my musical crackhead syndrome is too much. He said maybe he'd call next time so . . .

Me: here's my number in case you want to, you know, call me . . . maybe.

I grin at my lyric of choice and wait for his reply.

Romeo: hahaha. Wanna know a secret?

Of course, I wanna know!

I respond a little more subtle.

Me: it's not a secret if you tell me.

Romeo: I knew you were going to send me something about a song.

My brows pull in.

Romeo: Don't frown.

What the . . .

I bite my lip and type out my next message.

Me: how?

Romeo: Well, Juliet, it won't be a secret if I tell you.

Damn. I grin.

He's good.

Noah leaves me in such a good mood this afternoon that I completely forget what Sundays are about for my crew, and a couple hours later, while I'm still sitting in the spot Noah left me, the door to my dorm opens.

My lungs seize as Cameron steps in, Mason and Brady right behind her. The door begins to close, and I grab the blanket, covering my lap tighter as it grows closer and closer to the frame, but the second it touches, it's shoved back open again.

Chase steps inside, his eyes instantly finding mine.

Shit.

Considering they found me lounging with a pile of blankets and a half-eaten box of pinwheels, tossing out a random excuse was a no go, which is why I'm now sandwiched between Mason and Brady, who just dropped onto my living room couch, pretending I planned to be here all along.

Mason wraps his arm around my shoulder and tugs me to him with a playful growl. "Miss you, sister. Feel like I see less and less of you. It bites."

A sharp pain knocks against my rib cage, and I look to my brother, guilt heavy in my mind but a smile on my lips. "Me too, brother." I hug him, shoving him away when he bites at my scalp.

"What the hell?" I laugh, and he smirks, snagging the remote from my lap and switching over to ESPN. *Of course.*

"How's that study group going?" Brady calls, and I look his way. His gaze is narrowed, aware I'm a big fat liar, so I do the one thing he's asking for.

I nod in admission.

Brady nods back, yanks me to him, and kisses my hair, stealing the other half of my blanket as he straightens.

Chase files over next, and I lift my hand to wave, but he does what I *don't* expect, leaning over for a hug. So I hug him back as I have a hundred times before, only it feels the furthest thing from normal.

It aches.

I don't know if it's his way of keeping up appearances, but the way his grip tightens on me and how his palms widen across my back, makes it feel like a plea, but I couldn't tell you for what if I tried.

When he pulls back, I quickly turn to glance over my shoulder at Cameron as an excuse to hide the unease in my eyes before he has a chance to look into them.

"You need help?" I offer, ready to jump from my seat.

Everyone laughs, and I frown.

"Ha freaking ha, I am not useless." I shove Mason, and he only laughs more.

"No, honey cakes, you're not," Cameron placates me teasingly. "But I cooked the last two weeks, so it's officially their turn."

And cue more guilt.

From there, thank God, the boys get straight to work, cutting produce they brought and frying burgers, and Brady delivers on his mom's famous homemade garlic fries. Cam and I pull some plates and drinks out as they're finishing up.

We settle around the small kitchen, and I finally get to hear some of the stories the boys have from their first couple months here, laughing at Brady's horrible luck in picking up batshit crazy women. We play a few games of our favorite dice game, Tizy, next, and then settle into the living room with root beer floats.

A soft sigh leaves me as I peek around the room, realizing how much I miss this, how much I miss them.

I gasp when something cold hits my thigh, and Brady's eyes widen.

"Shit!" He looks to his tipped-over drink, still spilling into my lap.

I wave my hands up and down, and the others laugh. "It's so cold!"

They scurry around for napkins, but it's Chase that lifts one, and as he passes it over, he does a double take.

My muscles lock as his frown slowly builds.

Cameron swoops in, tossing a towel at me, and I jump, making quick work of wiping it with one hand and yanking the still extended napkin from Chase's hand . . . all to have it torn away by Cameron.

She zeros in on Noah's name and number, her head snapping my way.

Please don't.

"Yes." She drags out the word with a hiss, being overdramatic as she eases it to the floor beside her. "Let's not lose this."

It takes all I've got not to glance at Chase, but when I finally do, I'm relieved to find his eyes pointed at the TV, and then I get annoyed with myself for assuming he might care.

Not five minutes after that, I'm painstakingly reminded why I've skipped Sunday dinners, and everything else for that matter, as Mason starts talking to Chase about the girls from their party last night . . . and their walk of shame this morning.

My stomach turns, and for the first time today, last night's alcohol threatens to show itself. Heat builds in my chest, spreading up my neck, and I'm about to start sweating.

I want to cover my ears. I want to get up and run out before anything else is said, but I can't. The others will look at me like I'm mad, and then they'll get mad and demand a reason for my freak-out, but I can't sit here. I don't want to sit here. I—

My phone beeps then, and I hastily pick it up, finding a text from Noah.

Romeo: I've been thinking and there's something I should tell you.

Oh no.
I pull my knees up, a small scowl building along my brow.

Me: go for it.

His response is instant.

Romeo: I hate caramel flavored coffee.

A laugh spurts from me, and in my peripheral, all eyes snap my way, but I don't look up, not even when a certain pair of green ones burn into the side of my face.

I settle in my seat with a smile and text my new friend back.
Bless you and your perfect timing, Noah Riley.

Chapter 15
Arianna

My phone beeps, the timer for my mile going off, so I slow my strides.

As soon as I pull my earbuds from my ear, my phone vibrates, so I free it from my armband.

I smile at my screen and open Noah's text.

Romeo: I had eggs for breakfast.

My feet come to a complete stop, and I grin as I message him back.

Me: Billy Ray Cyrus "Achy Breaky Heart."

Romeo: Really?! How do you even know who he is?

He's totally smiling right now.

Before I can respond, another text comes through.

Romeo: It's from Hannah Montana, isn't it? You were one of those crazy girls who cried when little Miley grew up to be . . . my kinda Miley.

He sends a little winky face, and I bust up laughing, partly because he's right, mostly because this conversation is ridiculous, but that's exactly why it's so much fun.

Me: Liar. Miley's too wild for you and you know it. I feel like you're more of an Emma Watson kind of guy.

Romeo: You sure?

I suck my stomach in, a small cackle slipping from me.

Me: No, I guess I'm not . . . but I still win. Again.

Romeo: I'll stump you, Juliet. Just wait.

I grin, locking my phone back in place, and finish off the rest of my lap since I couldn't manage to trim anytime off my mile like Mason challenged me to.

Monday morning, when I woke up, Noah had texted me, saying the coach gave Mase a shout-out after the team's film session that morning. I texted him back Sage the Gemini—"Good Thing."

His response was a bright smile. I know it.

That night, I got another message, claiming he saw something odd at the grocery store—peanut butter flavored Oreos. I sent back the link to KC and JoJo's "Tell Me It's Real."

Ever since then, it's been a game between the two of us. He hits me with something random, and I prove Trey's words right. I am, in fact, equipped with a jukebox. Like I said, it's fun, lighthearted and I'm pretty sure the sole purpose is to simply make each other laugh in case one of us needs it. It's not the only time we talk. Like this morning, I sent him a picture of my shoes after I mindlessly walked into a mud puddle, a broken sprinkler left behind, and he sent back a photo of the notes he was taking in class.

No big deal, just us chatting a bit like new friends will.

Wiping my brow, I step off the track and head for the girls' locker room for a quick shower before meeting Brady for my promised study session.

I'm dressed back in my jean shorts and a burgundy long-sleeve shirt and headed for the library, not fifteen minutes later, braiding my hair along the way.

I spot Brady's behemoth body the second I walk in the door and quickly tie off my hair as I rush over to save the poor student helper who has *no* idea what she's in for if I don't rescue her. Her rigid stance and the way she's clutching those books to her chest tell me she's not ready for all the Lancaster charm, but the wide sparkle in her eyes screams she wishes she were.

He sees it, which is why he's inching his way closer, towering over her small frame.

Big dummy.

I step up and slap my hand on his shoulder. He doesn't flinch in the slightest, doesn't even look back at me. "Welcome to the party, Ari baby."

The poor girl's eyes shoot even wider, and she drops her gaze to the stained carpet beneath her feet.

"Come on, big guy." I laugh. "Time to study."

"I'm tryin' to study." His body sways slightly, trying to hit every nerve with his little innuendo. I can only guess his grin has turned feral because when the girl peeks up at him, her fair cheeks turn a bright cherry red.

"I should go," the girl whispers and sidesteps out of Brady's cage before darting away, disappearing behind the closest bookshelf.

Brady stands tall, exhaling loudly. "Almost had her."

I laugh and shove him toward the open tables. "No, you didn't."

He grins but doesn't argue.

We drop into the seats, and Brady pulls out two water bottles and four ham and cheese Lunchables, setting them on the table between us.

I laugh, quick to open a pack and stack my first bite. "Always coming in clutch."

"You know I got you." He winks, digging in.

We get lost in the world of psychology, and before we know it, it's late in the evening. The library is quickly filling up with a whole new breed of humans, the obnoxious procrastinators and those forced here for after-hours tutoring.

I slump against my chair, and Brady mimics my position.

"My brain is done, Brady." I drop my head onto his shoulder, and he rests his on top of mine.

"Right back atcha." He tosses his pencil on the table. "Wanna eat?"

I laugh because, with Brady, it's either football, food, or, well, sex. I nod. "I could eat."

"Cool." He gently nudges me off and stands, shoving his books back in his backpack. "Let's meet the boys at the burger place off campus."

I must hesitate too long because he stops midpack and stands to his tallest height. His earthy green eyes narrow in on me. "Don't give me no lip. You're coming."

I huff and shift to stand. "Can't you just come to my house?"

"Don't want to."

"We could go to that pizza place down the road?"

"Fine. I'll see if they want to go there."

"Brady . . ." I drop my eyes to my bag.

He sighs and walks around my chair, enveloping me in his big one-of-a-kind bear hug. "Not gonna lie, you're pissing me off a bit here, Ari baby. But I got eyes, I know some shit went down with you and Chase, and you're trying to steer clear, but that ain't fair to the rest of us. We're your boys. You're *our* girl. Suck it the fuck up, or I'll end up laying out my best friend."

A sorrowful laugh slips from me. "I don't want to make it awkward for anyone, and it's kind of . . . hard for me."

Brady tenses slightly. "I know." He drops closer to my ear to whisper, "Good thing you've got that game face down, huh . . . need you to put it on for me right quick."

I pull back as he does and frown up at him.

He gives a subtle nod before his attention lifts over my head.

"Wud up, pussies! Come to scope the scene?" He grins. "'Cause if you did, I got dibs on the shy little redhead over there." He hooks a thumb over his shoulder.

Great.

My heart rate spikes, and I take in a shallow breath as the boys walk around the table, making themselves seen.

"Sister." Mason's smile falters the longer he looks at me, but I force one for his benefit.

"Brother."

His eyes thin the slightest bit. "We're going to get some food, thought maybe you guys were 'bout done." Mason looks to my half-packed bag. "Seems you are."

Chase looks to me, but I keep my focus on Mason.

Shit. Think, Ari!

"Oh, well, uh, I—"

"Hey."

My already accelerated heart goes into overdrive, yet I sigh in relief as my gaze flicks over my brother's shoulder.

In that second, all three turn to face the man walking up behind them.

My brother grins wide, offering his team captain a fist bump. "Noah, what up?"

Noah meets Mason's knuckles with his own, tossing a subtle wink my way when my brother says something else I don't catch.

Noah chuckles. "Nah, man. Just came to get Ari."

Oooh. Shit.

My pulse is jumping from my skin; it has to be. I'm too scared to look at my brother, so I don't, locking eyes with Noah instead. His chin lowers, probably unnoticeably where the others are concerned. "Ready?"

"Wait, what?" Brady's shadow crowds me from behind, and to my right, my brother moves closer.

Noah doesn't move an inch, keeping his blue eyes on me. "Sorry I'm late, got caught up at the student center."

"Don't worry about it," I keep up. "We barely finished."

One side of Noah's mouth lifts into a grin, and I fight my own.

"Uh . . ." Mason drags out, clearing his throat, and I finally face him. He reaches up, scratching at his head, his frown flicking between mine and my rescuer's. They settle on me. "You got plans . . . with him?"

I start packing my stuff again as a reason to look away, unsure of his reaction and what he'll do next. There's honestly no telling.

"Yeah, I do." Not exactly a lie as of now. "I didn't know you guys were coming, or I wouldn't have made plans." That was definitely a lie.

Brady's stance widens beside me, and I nearly tear off the zipper on my backpack due to nerves.

"Hold on a damn minute." Brady, while quite calm, speaks slowly, so I'm not sure how to gauge him either. He looks at me, then Noah.

Noah doesn't falter but keeps his eyes strong as steel on Brady's, respectfully so. Brady swings his puckered brow to me. "Want me to take your bag home?"

My shoulders ease. "I got it, Brady, but *thank you*."

"Mm-hm." He kisses my head and turns to grab his own things.

I think we're getting off easy, but then a sudden, yet expected question comes from the most *unexpected* source. "Where are you going?" Chase asks.

Noah stands in silent support, stepping closer to take my bag when I begin to pull it over my shoulder, and with a tense smile, I look to Chase as if the sight of him doesn't mess with my head.

"We haven't decided."

His green eyes narrow. "So why not come with us?"

Instantly, I seek out Noah, for help maybe, and while he doesn't look away, he gives nothing more than a blank expression. It's his way of allowing me to make the call and letting me know he'll be there for whatever I choose, rather than choosing for me.

"Um . . ."

Noah's eyes pierce mine.

I don't know what to do. If I say yes, I might die a little more inside, and Noah did slide over in rescue mode as if he knew I needed it. But if I say no, how will that look?

Why do I care?

"Ari?" Chase prompts, with a little less bite this time.

Noah must note the indecision in me because his blues become more vibrant with every breath he takes, and his chin

rises a fraction of an inch, encouraging me to make a choice.
A choice for myself.

Something in me settles.

"No, I don't think so." I face Chase.

"Why not?" The guy who pushed me away dares to ask.

"I don't feel like it."

His frown deepens. "That's it, huh?"

Undeserved guilt curls around my muscles, but before I can
respond, Mason—my crazy controlling, over-the-top brother,
who normally asks these kinds of questions—shuts his best
friend down.

"Dude, Chase. Back off her, man." He scowls at him, flicking
his gaze across his form. "She said she don't wanna go."

My mouth wants to gape open so hard right now, but I
force it to stay closed, watching in . . . well, I can't figure out
if it's horror or fascination, as Mason turns to Noah, gives him
yet *another* fist bump.

Um . . . *what?*

"Get her home safe, so I don't have to go and get myself
kicked off the team?" Mason's face is dead serious.

Noah simply says, "Will do."

Brady chuckles next to me, pulling me into a hug. "Funny
how these plans popped out of nowhere, ain't it, and the dude,
too?" he whispers.

"Sorry," I mumble into his sweater.

Brady hates lies. He's our voice of reason in his own crazy,
horndog way, and he pretty much just covered my ass. "Don't
worry about it. Had they asked outright, I'd have told 'em.
Lucky for you, they didn't, so all's good."

I pull back and smile. "See you in class tomorrow."

"I'll be the sexy one in the front." He grins, and I smack
his shoulder.

With a refreshing inhale and a new sense of ease, I turn
to Noah.

He smiles, forcing one from me in return.

"Ready?"

Slowly, he nods.

"Bye, guys," I say but don't look their way.

I fall in line with Noah, and together, we head for the nearest exit.

"Oh my god, Noah, it smells stupid good," I say as I step out of the restroom.

I follow the sound of his soft chuckle into the little kitchen nook, right as he pulls a chicken breast off of the small countertop grill and begins slicing it into long strips.

"Where did you learn to cook?" I ask. Peeking over his shoulder as he stirs the meat into the bowl of homemade chicken alfredo, he whipped up like nothing and in no time at all.

"My mom." He smiles. "She had me help her with dinner every night, said I'd need to learn for moments like this." He tosses me a wink.

"Smart woman." I smirk, resting my chin on my elbow against the counter.

"Yeah." He chuckles, but it's a weighted sound that makes me look from the food to him.

A small frown creases his forehead, but he doesn't say anything, so I don't ask what brought it there.

I want to but don't.

"Where are your plates and stuff?" I push up. "Least I can do is get those ready."

"There's a stack of paper plates above the microwave. Hope that works for you."

"*My* mom said she had children so she wouldn't have to wash dishes ever again. So yeah, paper plates are perfect." I laugh, and he joins in.

"Smart woman."

"Right? It was a joke, but I can see the appeal."

Noah chuckles as he turns the burner off and rinses his hands in the teeny sink next to the teeny stove. "Want to grab some drinks, and I'll clean off the coffee table so we can eat more comfortably?"

"Yep." I set the paper plates next to the stove, my eyes flicking to the small table against the wall. It's a two-seater table, not quite big enough to fit Noah's long legs under, let alone a second person's.

"This place is pretty dope," I shout. "From the outside, you'd never know it was here."

He steps from around the wall that separates the kitchen from the living room. "Yeah, my coach calls it the perks of being team captain, but sometimes the space isn't worth all the shit I have to deal with in the house. It does make it easier to try and keep the first years in semicheck, though."

"So, you're basically the designated party pooper?"

"Nah." He pours the pasta into a large bowl and nods his head, motioning for me to walk ahead of him.

Snatching the plates, I lead us into the living room, listening as he explains further.

"I let them have their fun. It's a part of the whole experience they earned by getting here. As long as they're respectful and keep it to a minimum through the week, they know Saturdays are usually their free nights to live it up."

I nod and take the seat next to him on the corduroy-looking couch, setting our drinks down.

"Now in the off-season . . ." He shakes his head with a grin. "It gets a bit wild."

"I bet." I kick off my slides, folding my legs up. "Spring back home was nuts, but definitely more fun around the house. The boys weren't so strict on themselves since football was over, which meant they weren't so hard on us." I shake my head with a grin. "Not that football was ever really 'over.' There were always camps or something or another, but no actual games meant we could party a bit."

"Yeah, light training and no coach on your ass." He laughs. "I'm just glad there's a door at the bottom of the stairs instead of the top. Keeps the wild ones away, and I don't have to worry about drunk people falling down and busting their heads open when they're lost looking for the bathroom."

"Come on." He nudges my shoulder. "Scoop your plate first, so I feel like a gentleman."

Leaning forward, I do as he asks, admitting, "And I was over here trying to be polite by waiting for your go-ahead, but fair warning, I'm known to eat like a man, so no judging."

He chuckles. "Wouldn't dare." He clicks on the TV, turning down the volume, leaving reruns of *The Office* to play quietly around us.

Food piled high on my plate, I chew on the inside of my lip. "Thank you for this, Noah."

"Juliet, look at me."

My eyes slide his way, and he smiles.

"Stop thanking me like I'm doing you a favor. I'm not. I saw you sitting there with Brady the second I stepped through the door. Went in specifically to find you, if you really want to know, and I was about to walk over to ask if you wanted to hang for a while when I saw Mason and Chase slip up behind you. All they did was beat me to the starting line." He looks back to his food, and then, as if deciding to go with his last thought, he hits me with a sly grin. "Looks like I won."

My hand comes up to cover my mouth as I laugh, and I flick my eyes to his. "So what you're saying is . . . I'm looking at a winner?"

He turns to me with a mouthful of food and winks, pleased with my lyric of choice.

Giddy, I focus on my meal.

It seems Noah gets me.

I think I like that.

Once we've eaten, Noah tosses our plates into the trash and comes back to join me on the couch.

He's quiet for a minute, and when I twist to face him, he does the same.

"You've never been here, have you?" he asks.

I sigh and drop back against the old cushions. "Nope. Now that you mention it, I feel like a jackass." I shake my head.

"They are definitely going to get their feelings hurt when they find out I came here today."

"They've been waiting for you to come?"

"Mason and Brady have invited me so many times, but I just . . . haven't."

He eyes me. "Chase hasn't been? Begging you to come over?"

Pulling in a full breath, I say, "No, he hasn't. I can't decide if he's giving me the space I've made clear I need or if he's giving it to himself, but either way, I'm kind of tired of it now." I look down, scratching at the glitter polish on my fingernails. "I want to be able to hang out, watch movies and do absolutely nothing other than be with my friends again. Dumb, right? Since I'm the one messing it all up, to begin with."

"You're not messing anything up if you're doing what feels right."

"That's the thing," I say quietly. "It doesn't feel right. Necessary, but not right. When we'd fight growing up, it was over the next day. We just don't get mad at each other, you know? None of us. Annoyed, pissy, all the time, but not angry, like *for real* angry. It sucks, and we didn't come to college together for this to happen during our very first semester."

Noah doesn't say anything at first, but once I look to him, he gets more comfortable. "How did that happen?"

My gaze drops to where his jean-covered knee now touches mine, and a small smile pulls at my lips. He doesn't notice, he's simply relaxed, and I realize I am too. My shoes are off, my legs tucked under me, and my body settled into the cushions as if I've sat in this spot a thousand times.

It sort of feels like I have.

I look up and find his insane blue eyes surveying me, and for some reason, I feel the need to look away.

"Ari?"

"Hm?"

Noah grins. "How'd your whole group end up at Avix?"

"Oh." I laugh. "Right. So our counselors in high school thought we were crazy because, literally, the first day of freshman year, we went to the office as a group, notes from our parents in hand, and told them our plan, asking for schedules that would help make it happen. We took summer school every year to get ahead and just in case we struggled later. Once we agreed we'd make it happen, we started narrowing down schools based on what everyone wanted. None of us wanted to leave California, so that tightened the list, but we still applied out of state, just in case. We pretty much knew the boys would get in anywhere, so we looked for the best team versus the best child development program for Cameron. In the end, we chose Avix."

"I didn't hear your name in there."

"You're right. You didn't." I grin. "I didn't care where we went."

"Really?" He's more curious than surprised. "Not a single stipulation?"

"Nope."

The corner of Noah's mouth hikes up. "Why do I get the feeling there's a reason behind it that you're choosing not to tell me?"

"Because there is." I laugh. "It's too embarrassing to share, but I will admit I did push for a fat house off campus, but my dad shot that down so fast. After the boys had their meeting with the athletic director, who was kind of a dick, by the way, we learned that was out regardless. Honestly, the level-three dorm we scored is perfect anyway."

Noah grins, nodding.

"What about you?"

"What about me?"

"How did Noah Riley, superstar quarterback, end up in Oceanside?"

"Ha ha," he teases as he looks away, only to turn right back.

At first, I wonder if he won't share, but then he nods.

"I'm from near here, stayed around so I could be close to my mom."

"Aww," I coo.

Noah gives a playful glare, and I can't help but laugh.

"I love that. It's pretty much why we wanted to stay, too." I lean back, wrapping my arms around my drawn-up knees. "She's the real master chef, isn't she? I know you told me she taught you how to cook, but I'd bet a dollar the recipes you use are hers."

"A whole dollar, huh?"

"What can I say? I'm a broke college kid." I shrug.

Noah chuckles, but it's solemn, and I can't help but search his eyes for more.

"You and your mom, you're close." My tone is gentle.

"Yeah," he admits. "She's all I ever had."

"Here in Oceanside?"

His eyes find mine. "Anywhere."

"Really?"

He nods.

"No siblings . . . a long-lost dad, maybe?"

"Nope, neither. No cousins, aunts, uncles, not even grand-parents. It's just us."

A small ache forms across my ribs. "That's sad."

He shrugs, looking away. "Normal for me. I never had more than her, so there was never anything to miss."

"You must miss seeing her every day. You must get lonely here."

Noah's blink is slow, but he doesn't say anything.

Now that I think about it, I never see him with anyone. It's always him on his own.

I wonder if he likes it that way?

I can't imagine life without my friends and family. It would be so hard if I didn't have open arms to fall into when life got tough.

Who does he have in his life to catch him should he fall?

"So, you and Cameron," he changes the subject. "Have you two always been best friends?"

"Since birth, yeah." I laugh.

"She comes here often."

"Yeah." I nod. "Trust me, I know. She makes sure I'm aware."

"Why don't you tag along with her next time? Make your way up here with me," he suggests.

My cheeks grow warm, and he chuckles.

We stare at each other a moment, and his grin slowly fades. His tongue slipping out to wet his lips, calling my attention to his mouth, but only for a second.

I push to my feet. "I should go."

"Yeah . . . I'll drive you."

I smile. "I can walk, Noah. I'm only across campus."

He frowns, standing tall, forcing my chin to lift in order to meet his gaze. "You really think I'd send you down those stairs, into a house of twenty or more guys, and leave you to walk out alone?"

"You realize my brother and best friends are among those, right?" I smirk, and his eyes narrow more, making me grin. "Come on. Walk me down, and if Mase *isn't* around, I'll take you up on that ride."

"How 'bout we plan for me to take you, but you can still see if Mason's around for fun?"

My cheeks grow warm, and I laugh, leading us down the stairs. "Come on, Romeo."

At the bottom, Noah reaches over my shoulder and unlatches the lock, pushing the door open before me.

A couple big guys nod at Noah as we slip out, grinning my way as if they know exactly what we were doing. Their grins are very Brady-like—a mix of proud papa with a naughty little twist. While Noah pauses to answer a question from one of them, I step through the entryway and into the common room area, allowing my eyes to travel the large space.

There's a TV on both walls, a pool table in the center, and a couple of couches pushed against opposite sides. The walls are a deep blue, a giant white Avix Sharks logo painted dead center. The mantel has trophies—hopefully they're glued down—scattered along it, with a few abandoned beer cans, adding to the reality of a houseful of college boys.

I grin, seeing the place for the first time. This is exactly what I'd imagined, maybe even a little cleaner than I'd have thought. Gliding my hand down the frame of the entryway, random beer bottle caps stuck all along the edges, I scan the area for Mason, but I don't get far before a clipped voice breaks through from behind me.

"Thought you were going *out* for dinner?"

I whip around, coming face-to-face with Chase.

My breath freezes in my throat, and I cut a quick glance toward Noah, who's still talking to his teammate. I force myself to look back to Chase, praying my voice comes out steady as I say, "Noah cooked for me instead."

Chase scoffs. "Yeah, I bet he decided to get you up in his room *last minute*."

My head tugs back. "Are you really acting like this right now?"

Chase slips closer, his voice a tense whisper for only me to hear. "What do you expect, Arianna?"

My chest tightens with anger, but beneath that is the ache, the sting. I blink, shaking my head. "Nothing." I cut a quick glance toward Noah, who has yet to spot Chase but is now moving toward me. "I don't expect a thing from you, Chase. I learned my lesson."

Chase's brows crash, but he says nothing.

Thankfully, Mason walks around the corner in the next second, his eyes narrowing as he takes in our awkward face-off.

"Ari?" My brother swings his pinched gaze to Noah as he steps up beside me. "What are you doing here? Come to check out the place?" he asks me.

I don't break it all down, instead sticking with the simplest of answers. "I was looking for you."

He steps closer, propping his elbow onto the wall to block my face from the others, worry lines building across his face, but I shake my head.

I'm okay. Swear.

Mase nods.

"Can you take me home?"

"Yeah, I'll grab my keys," he says, right as a blonde girl tucks herself under the arm he has posted up. As soon as he looks down, he grins.

"You know what, it's fine," I rush out, a sudden, desperate need to get away creeping in.

"What, no." He rolls his shoulder, essentially giving the girl the brush-off. "It's fine. Course I'm gonna take you."

"I'll take her." Chase starts walking toward the door as if his words are final, but my brother jerks forward.

"No, I'm good." Mason shakes his head, giving the girl a quick glance.

I offer her an apologetic smile, glancing at Noah as he steps closer, and that breath I'm holding quickly turns into a lump I swallow past.

Nerves tingle along my skin as I wait, knowing what's coming, and having no clue how it will unfold.

"I got her, man." Noah grins easily. "Wanted to take her anyway. Told her so before we came in here."

My stomach clenches at his direct admission, and I wait for my brother to snap back.

Mason swings his gaze my way, his frown hard and on me, but then he grins, swinging his attention to Noah. "Bet she turned bright red, huh?"

My mouth gapes and Noah chuckles, but he doesn't confirm. He keeps that knowledge for himself.

"You sure, bro?" Mason reaches out, and they clap hands in the way boys do.

"Positive." Noah turns to me, nodding toward the door.

As I prepare to pass, my eyes slide to Chase.

He stands with his jaw set firm and pointing straight ahead, but he says nothing.

Why would he?

Noah takes me home, tells me good night, and leaves.

I lie down. Another day ruined when tears I can't hold back begin to fall.

Chapter 16
Arianna

"How is it so fucking hot?" Cam whines as she peels herself from the bleachers and begins packing up her books.

"Sitting on these plastic seats doesn't exactly help. I'm a pile of sweat."

"We should make the boys put a canopy up for us."

"Because they have time to do that before practice."

She laughs, knocking my feet from the back of the chair in front of me so she can pass. "True, but can we talk about why it's still so hot, and we're officially in October? I mean, what the hell is this shit? We're in Southern California, for fuck's sake."

"It's the metal and the turf and the sun. You know this. Step into the shade, and it'll drop a solid fifteen degrees."

"Which is why I suggested the canopy." She smirks. "K, bye. My professor wants me at the child development center to meet some of the parents at pickup today."

"You'll be home tonight?"

"Yep. See you later."

I wave and lay my book on my chest, closing my eyes to bake in the sun's soft glow.

I'm not sure how much time has passed when the clacking of cleats against cement meets my ears.

I shield my eyes with my hand and squint at the approaching figure.

"You trying to get a sunburn?!" Noah shouts from a few rows down.

I still can't see his face but sit up in my seat with a smile. "No way, the sun and me, we go way back. She's good to me."

Noah chuckles, and as he climbs the next two steps, he finally comes into view.

He's red in the face, dripping with sweat, and . . . ridiculously attractive.

He smiles, swiping a hand through his slick, dark hair, and the soft, sun-made highlights show themselves.

"What are you doing up here? Come to watch me?" he teases.

"Ha! Sorry, but been doing this for years. I guess you're simply a bonus."

His shoulder pads lift, and he winks. "I figured as much, considering I spotted you up here weeks ago."

"Did you now?"

He only grins, so I tap on the book covering my chest. "Cam and I started coming out to their practices back in high school, so we carried it over once we got here."

"Nice." He nods.

"You guys done for the day? It's a little early." I peek at my phone.

"Yeah, we doubled on film this morning, weight room right after, so it was more a run day today." He grabs the towel tucked into the back of his pads and wipes it along his brows. "Worked up an appetite though."

I grin. "Is that right?"

"It is." He cocks his head. "Feel like helping me cook again tonight?"

I drop my feet, lowering my book to my lap. "And what help was I to you last time?"

"You helped me eat it." His lips curve up on one side.

A laugh slips from me, a little too loud apparently, because I catch the attention of several of his teammates as they head into the tunnel, and of course, Brady and Chase are among them. They both stop, their eyes darting up and over to where we're standing. Subconsciously, I sink into my seat.

156

Noah catches my movement and glances over his shoulder, nodding his head as he turns back to me.

I want to shrink into myself, embarrassed by my childish reaction, but as I look to Noah, not a hint of judgment slips over him, quite the opposite really.

Noah's soft smile has me releasing a breath, the understanding glint in his gaze leading me to admit, "I hate it."

Noah's lips twitch. "I know you do."

"Practice is over, Arianna!" Chase yells, still standing in the same spot, but my eyes are on Noah, who turns his head to hide it, but not before I spot the frown that's slipped over his face.

Forcing myself to look toward the tunnel, I spot Mason a few feet back. He's following behind his team, pulling his shoulder pads from his body as he walks, and when he looks up, he spots Chase standing there. Mason's eyes follow his line of sight to Noah and me. He frowns, hesitates for a split second, but then nudges Chase's shoulder from behind to get him to move.

They disappear from sight with their next steps taken.

A sign escapes me, and I push to my feet, unable to bring myself to look at Noah.

"I don't think I'll be good company tonight. Rain check?"

"Rain check," Noah speaks without a hint of displeasure. So why does a heavy sense of disappointment weigh me down?

It's not until later that night, when I'm rummaging through the freezer, that I realize the disappointment I felt earlier . . . was my own.

"God *damn*," Cam drawls slowly. "That man is flawless."

We sigh, look to each other, and bust up laughing.

"Seriously, Ari. You need to jump all over that."

I smile, watching as Noah does the same, but his is directed toward a beautiful blonde girl who is walking toward him with what looks like a plate of cookies.

Something in my stomach stirs, bringing a small frown to my face.

"Who is that?" Cam wonders.

I shrug, noting the graceful way in which she moves, like a floating prima ballerina. "The Sleeping Beauty to his handsome prince."

"Mm-mm, no. You got it all wrong."

Quirking a playful brow, I turn to her. "Do tell?"

"Sure, the man may look like a prince, and by the way, it's Cinderella's man who has dark hair, not the prudy SB chick." I laugh, and she continues, "Anyway, yes, he's all pretty and shit, but under all the gorgeous is an animal. Has to be. He's far too fine to be tame."

Cameron sits back on her elbows, smirking my way. "Bet he comes alive in the bedroom."

"Shut up." I laugh.

"I am so not playing. I bet he morphs into another man, giving that best of both worlds' vibe." She thinks on it a minute. "Yeah. He doesn't have sex; he love fucks."

I gape at her, and simultaneously, we laugh again.

"Okay, enough before he hears you."

"I'm telling you, he's a beast, and you're the closest thing to Belle I've ever seen."

"You're an idiot."

"Let's ask." She quickly jumps to her feet, and my eyes shoot wide, my hand snapping out to wrap around her wrist, but she opens her mouth before I can jerk her back.

"Yo, Noah!" she shouts, and my face turns into a tomato as he—and the ballerina—turn their smiles on us. "Quick question, but no questions, only an answer, yeah?!"

Noah shifts his eyes to me quickly, then back to Cam. "Let's hear it!"

Cameron throws a wink at me over her shoulder, turning back to Noah just as fast. "Sleeping Beauty or Beauty and the Beast?"

He looks my way, my skin igniting as his gaze burns across my face, attempting to decipher Cam's nonsense. Quickly, almost unnoticeably fast, Noah's eyes cut to the girl beside him, and then they return to me. Now I might be reading into nothing, but I also might swear he follows the length of my long brown hair until it disappears over my left shoulder.

I pull in an involuntary breath as he turns his grin to Cam.

"Come on now. Don't make me say it."

His response is very, very *Noah*.

My lips twitch.

Satisfied, Cam drops back down, whispering through her teeth, "You realize he totally caught on to that right, like, he picked up what I was putting down?"

"Quit biznatch, you don't know for sure," I whisper-hiss.

"Dude, Ari. It's cute that you're pretending otherwise. Now, be discreet, but look at him."

"No."

"Please," she begs. "Bet you a lipstick he's waiting for you to."

"Fine, but I get to pick it out."

"Deal."

I sit back, running my fingers through my hair to try and appear nonchalant as I glance his way. Unfortunately for me, I freeze, visibly so, and the man . . . who is totally looking at me catches it. Ever the gentleman, he licks his lips to hide his grin, and my skin threatens to give me away, but then I realize that's not all.

"Oh my god, you bitch, he's walking over! With the girl!"

Cameron's head falls back as she laughs. "This keeps getting better. He's about to clear shit up, watch."

"Shut up."

"You'll thank me."

"You're an ass."

"You love me."

"Hey."

Our heads dart toward the newcomers, a big fat fake, *embarrassed* smile plastered on my face, a legit entertained one on Cam's. "Hey!" we say in unison, and I fight the urge to ram her ribs with my elbow.

"Cameron." He hardly looks her way.

"Noah." She sits back, propping herself on the palms of her hands.

Noah's dark hair is mostly hidden under his hood, his blue eyes brilliant against the heather-gray color. Slowly, he pushes it off his head.

"This is my friend Paige." He nods toward the beautiful little creature beside him.

I don't have to look at my best friend to know she's smirking with satisfaction.

I lift my hand in an attempt to wave, but she steps forward, wrapping me in an unexpected, light hug, before taking her place again, right at Noah's side.

"It's so good to meet you, Ari." She folds her hands behind her back. "I've heard a lot about you."

My brows shoot up, and I search for the right words, but my brain is stuck, so I laugh to cover my nerves.

I peek at Noah, and he gives me a playful wink.

"It's nice to meet you, Paige."

Paige smiles, showing more perfection. "We should get together sometime."

Uh . . .

I smile.

She turns to Cam. "It's nice to meet you too, Cameron. I hate to leave right away, but Sundays are kind of crazy for me."

My eyes dart toward her.

So both she and Noah are 'busy' Sundays?

Noah clears his throat. "I'm going to walk her out to the parking lot."

Paige smiles, waving as they begin to walk away. "I hope to see you again, Ari."

We hold our smiles in place until they're gone and then turn to each other.

I glare.

Cam scrunches her nose. "Maybe she's gay?"

I groan and stand.

"He likes you, Ari," she tells me.

160

"Shut it, Cam." I walk away.

"Don't act like you don't care!" she shouts.

I flip her off, head over to the row of community coolers, and grab a water.

Being Sunday, it should be family dinner tonight, but since the team had a bye week this week, the football house is holding what we've been told is their annual cookout. They invite family and friends and anyone else they don't get to see regularly, and it's a giant potluck-style hangout at the edge of campus. Thankfully, the boys are all about counting this as our meal date.

After a few small sips, I make my way over to my brother, who is manning one of the many grills. "Hey, brother."

"Hey, sister." He glances at me, then back at the chicken he's flipping. "Having fun?"

"I am." I glance around.

"Good." He picks up his beer and takes a drink, eyeing me over the neck of the bottle. "You doin' okay?"

My mouth opens, but I clamp it shut, offering instead a small nod.

"You sure?" he prompts.

"I . . ." I sigh, caving a little. "I had a tough couple months, but I'm feeling better now."

"Better, or a little better?"

"Depends on the day."

His features tighten at my honesty, and his shoulders fall. His brown eyes search mine. "If something was wrong, if you needed me, you'd tell me, right? Even though I can be an ass sometimes, you'd never not come to me if you needed me?"

"If I needed you, *when* I need you, I won't hesitate, you know that," I answer him quietly and truthfully, and the corner of his mouth lifts. "But maybe it needs to be said that sometimes, there will be things you won't want to hear, and those will be the things I decide not to share."

His jaw tightens, and he looks away, but when his eyes come back to mine, they're soft. "That's fair." He nods. "I love you, you know. More than anyone."

I smile and lean in to hug him. "Yeah, Mase. I know."

The sorrow in my tone is accidental, but he hears it. My brother simply doesn't understand it, which is why he's frustrated with me.

He has no idea he dug a Hoover Dam—sized hole between Chase and me because I didn't tell him we leaped without looking. He knows something, but he doesn't have the slightest clue how deep that something runs. In his mind, everything he does related to me stems from protection, but what he's very, *very* slowly beginning to understand is we're not children anymore. Some things he can't and shouldn't shield me from.

Regardless, only a fool would push the blame on Mason.

He might have been the one to blow out the match, but Chase is the one who tossed it in the ocean.

That was a decision he had to make, to push me away or pull me closer, and he decided to push.

And that's okay.

If there was one thing I wish he and I had, it would have been the opportunity for us to figure out together we weren't meant to be. Maybe then I could have worked up to the point of understanding without all the mess.

It sucks to hurt for a man you never even had.

The pain within me makes itself known at random, and that pain stems from a love that never even *lived*. One that never had a chance to flourish.

It's that feeling of being robbed that stings more than anything at this point, but if there's a positive to take away from this experience, it's that growth can only come from heartache.

How else are you supposed to discover what you truly want?

What you refuse to let go of?

What you deserve in a partner?

I don't think you can possibly know without the hurt to force your hand.

I want someone's all.

I want someone's all and absolutely nothing less.

Chase couldn't give me that, and maybe I should be thankful he realized before things got any deeper.

Maybe that's my way of finding an excuse for a shitty move.

I sigh, stepping back.

"Ari," Mason calls, sensing my retreat. "I miss hanging out with you. Stay?"

With a squashed smile, I wrap my arms around my brother, and as I look over his shoulder, the universe decides to test me.

My eyes lock with golden-brown ones.

"I'm not going anywhere." I pull back, flicking the tray of cooked meat. "Should I take this to the tables?"

"If you could." Mason nods, turning back to the grill.

On my way toward the rows of food, I catch Chase's eyes from across the yard once more, but this time, I'm the one who looks away.

A hand slips in front of me, nudging a bowl of pasta out of the way, and I lower the mountain of chicken onto the tablecloth.

"So your brother got the cooking gene," Noah teases.

I nudge him with my arm, pinching down the edges of the tinfoil. "How hard can it be to flip chicken?"

"Who knew that's all there was to barbecuing?" he jokes. "Flip it, and you're good."

I cross my arms and face him with a playful glare.

Noah chuckles, his gaze flicking in the direction I plan to ignore. "I have to go, but I wanted to say bye first."

"You didn't have to come back just to tell me that. You could have texted me."

He nods, his blue eyes searching my face. "I don't get a whole lot of free time on the weekends, but maybe you want to do something during the week? The cooking lessons are still on the table."

"That's because you haven't seen how bad I am yet."

"I'm taking that as a yes." He smirks. "So, this week, right?"

I bite back a smile, nodding.

"Good, 'cause I was going to keep asking until you said yes," he adds, making me laugh.

Noah glances past me once more as he shuffles back. "I better go."

"I want you to stay."

He freezes for a second before a bright smile takes over his face, and he laughs, forcing mine to slip free. "Your jukebox plays all genres."

"Yes, it does."

Noah takes a step toward me, and as he comes closer, his eyes, a little darker than their usual blue, hold strong on mine, and suddenly, I'm not so sure I'm breathing.

It's confirmed I wasn't when a low gasp fills my throat as he presses his lips to the highest point of my cheekbone. They skim along my skin, maybe by mistake, as he pulls back, but either way, the heat of his lips burns all the way down my neck.

Noah gently squeezes my bicep, and then he walks away.

My eyes refuse to leave the back of his head and only do when my bestie comes up and hip checks me.

She tears open a bag of chips and throws one at me. "Sleeping Beauty, my ass."

Chapter 17
Arianna

"Okay, let's hear it."

Noah grins, glancing over as he stirs. "What do you want to know?"

"Your secrets." I pause for dramatic effect. "'Cause there's no way you whipped up this sauce in the half hour it took me to drop my stuff off and get here."

"You're right." He nods, setting the long wooden spoon down smack-dab on the counter. "I didn't," he admits as I reach past him, lift said spoon, and set it back down on a paper plate. "I made it in ten."

My head snaps his way. "I'm sorry, what?"

He smirks and begins walking backward into the living room, so just as he wants me to, I follow.

"Okay, Gordon Ramsay." I set our drinks on the tabletop, and we lower into the spots we've come accustomed to eating in the last couple Mondays. "Tell me how."

"Sorry, can't do that." He shakes his head, no longer waiting for me to serve myself but rather portions it out for me.

I reach out and scoot an extra piece of chicken onto my plate. "And why not?"

Noah's eyes glide my way, and he smirks. "Only way to learn is to do it with me."

"That sounds a lot like coercion."

He lifts a dark brow. "Did it take coercion to get you here tonight?"

I stick my food-covered tongue out, and Noah shakes his head and laughs.

After a few bites and tuning into the scene in *Superbad* where McLovin first gets his fake ID, I turn to Noah. "So, do I get to pick the menu?"

"Only if you take turns doing the cooking."

"Yeah, sure, if you want a Top Ramen night with a side of Takis."

"I happen to like ramen."

"Big fat liar."

"Nope."

"How could a guy who can cook like this possibly like Top Ramen?"

"You ever dress up your noodles? Little lime, some Tapatio and cilantro?"

I gape at him, and he chuckles, adding, "How about with a boiled egg, soy sauce, and sriracha?"

I blink dramatically, and he tosses his napkin at me.

"Okay, you win." I accept defeat. "You're on menu, but we need a noodle night in there somewhere. I want to learn all about this from poor to polished ramen stuff."

Noah nods. "I want to teach you."

"Good." I jerk my chin, and he beams. "Let's start Sunday?"

When he frowns, I quickly add, "Or, I mean, whenever you have time. You know, after the season maybe."

Stop talking, Ari.

"I don't want to wait until after the season, Juliet." Noah tries to hide his amusement as he looks my way. "I can't on Sundays, that's all."

Because you and the ballerina are both busy that day . . .

That thought has a frown threatening to creep over my face, but I manage to hold it in.

"How about we make these Mondays official and add Wednesdays?" he asks. "Those are the easiest for me since I have morning practice, and my classes are done before lunch. What about you?"

"Yes."

He looks to me, and I shake my head, clamping my eyes closed a moment. "I mean, same." *No, wait.* I twist toward him a bit. "No, not same. I don't have practice, obviously, but yes, those days are good for me too."

Noah drops his grin, and I wonder what the hell is wrong with me.

Thankfully, I manage not to ramble on the rest of the evening, and when Noah walks me home, the short trip is full of jokes and laughter.

The next morning, I wake to find a text of our 'proposed' menu. So making it official, I add our plans to my calendar and search for him on Venmo. He said he would hit the store, so I send him a small chunk of my monthly food budget.

Noah sent it right back.

It's Wednesday, we're about done with the first meal, so I sneak away to the bathroom and stuff forty bucks into the front zipper of his backpack. I'm back in the kitchen before he has a moment to get suspicious.

Noah lifts the spoon to his mouth, where my attention is stuck as he blows on the hot mixture. Once satisfied it won't burn my mouth, he brings the spoonful toward me. "Taste this."

His eyes, they're so unlike a shade of blue I've seen before. So mythical and bright, yet stormy, like what you'd expect the find on the god of the sea. A little lost and lonely maybe. A hint of wild. It's intriguing, the color. Or maybe it's the emotion I can read within them.

How can I read the emotion within them?

"Juliet?"

I blink, dropping my pinched gaze to the spoon.

"Sorry," I mumble, closing my lips around it.

The savory glaze concocted of homemade chili with cranberry hits my tastebuds, the explosiveness of the flavors pulling a satisfactory moan from me.

"So good." I leave the sauce to sit on my tongue a moment.

"You know, if the whole going pro thing doesn't work out for you, you could totally be a chef."

I hadn't realized I closed my eyes, and when I look to Noah, he tears his from my mouth.

He quickly turns to the sink, dropping the spoon inside. "You think it's good like that, or does it need more crushed red peppers?"

When I don't respond, he looks over, meeting my frown.

"The little pepper flakes . . ."

". . . like pizza peppers?"

He grins and turns to lean his tailbone against the small countertop. "Were you paying attention when we put in the spices?"

To the food? No. To the focus and peacefulness that takes you over when you cook? Yes. Yes, I was.

"No?"

He laughs, playfully hitting me with the dish towel.

I pop a shoulder. "I figured my job was to hand you stuff and give you honest opinions on taste."

"Uh-huh, and how are you supposed to make it on your own if you do that?" he teases.

"Okay, wow. If I gave you the impression that would be a possibility, I am so sorry." I grin, a laugh slipping through. "Basically, I'm going to need you and your black jacket–worthy skills to survive away from home."

I expect him to laugh or joke back, but he doesn't.

Noah's gaze floats across my face, and he gives a nearly undetectable nod. "I think that could work out."

I don't know why but heat slowly spreads up my neck.

He sees it, and rather than turning around and pretending he hasn't, he follows the warmth past my collarbone. I should look away, but I don't want to. I want to watch him watch me. When his midnight eyes land on mine, something low in my gut twists. It tangles and pulls, and I whip around to face the counter. I move the bag with the chili ingredients in it to the side, setting the one full of stuff to make potpie in its place.

My limbs are heavy, fuzzy, but I breathe through it, swallowing beyond the knot in my throat.

"I swear to God, Noah, if this potpie tastes good, there will be no freezing of anything. I'll be eating it all tonight, no joke."

Noah's laugh is low and sultry.

Or I'm losing my mind and need to get a grip. I can't be sure.

He takes the hot pot of chili to the tiny table covered in potholders, setting it down beside the tray of meatballs. "We're not making one big one. We can't freeze it like that. We have to make a few small ones."

"K, let's do that . . . but also make a big one we can eat tonight?" I smile like a psycho, showing all my teeth. "We can veg out until my leggings are too tight."

He looks at me over his shoulder. "You want to hang tonight?"

My eyes bulge. "Oh my gosh! I . . . totally invited myself to stay." I avert my gaze. "Ignore me, keep going. What do I do next? Set the oven temp, right? That's step one?"

"Juliet."

My muscles tense the slightest bit. "Yeah?" I line up the ingredients, no clue what order they should be in or if it even matters.

"You're my only plans," he shares.

I don't know why, but I'm suddenly nervous.

Noah senses it, chuckling as he comes to stand beside me, calling my gaze to his. He lifts his hand as if he was about to reach out and touch me but decides better of it, quickly lowering it to the bag beside us. His eyes, though, they stay on mine. "You wanna stay, veg until your leggings are too tight, and I've gotta loan you a pair of sweats?" His mouth hooks higher. "Watch a movie with me?"

"Yeah." My brows pull. "I do."

He nods several times before blowing out a breath and turning to the sink to rinse the chicken. Who knew that was a thing?

The potpies take the longest out of all the meals we made today if you count the baking time. Once the big one is ready to be cut into, Noah grabs plates, but I put them back, stuff two forks into my hoodie pocket, and carry the entire pie into the living room.

We eat straight out of the throwaway tinfoil tray, watching *Bad Boys For Life* in comfortable silence.

At some point during the movie, I shift closer to Noah. My shoulder is now pressed to his, my bent knees resting against his thick, football player thighs.

When I tuck my hands into my lap, he reaches behind us, grabbing a blanket. He drapes it over my legs without a word, leaving his arm to rest along the back of the couch.

I sink in a little more as he settles into the cushions.

When a low sigh escapes him, my mind begins to wander.

I watched him closely tonight. The peaceful look on his face. The ease of his movements, it's so obvious he's at home when cooking as if it's second nature for him. It reminded me of being at home, watching my parents in the kitchen.

He kind of reminds me of home.

And that . . . is kind of scary.

Chapter 18
Arianna

Putting the car in park, Noah turns off the engine and looks at me. "You mean to tell me you've never had sushi?"

"I have never had sushi," I admit, picking my bag up off the floorboard.

He drops back against the seat. "How is that possible?"

"It's always grossed me out." I shrug. "I like catfish."

"Cooked catfish, I assume?"

"You assume correctly. There's this little place my grandparents used to take us called The Catfish House; we'd go eat fried catfish, okra, and hush puppies. It was out in the country in a little town on the way to the bay. But sushi?" My nose pinches, and I shudder. "Heck no."

"I'm gonna make you some, change your mind."

"No way!" I pretend to gag. "Homemade sounds so much worse."

"Trust me, Juliet."

I sigh, playfully, a single thought running through my mind as I stare at him, and that is, *man, is he easy on the eyes*.

A small smirk tips his full lips, and he steps out, so I follow, and as usual, he walks me all the way to my dorm room.

At the door, I turn to face him. "Just to be clear, I should get my game face on, ready to try some sushi soon?"

He smiles wide, glancing down the hall.

A short piece of hair falls over his forehead as he does, and before I realize what I'm doing, my hand is brushing it back into place.

Noah doesn't tell me no. He doesn't reach out, halting my hand, warning me that I shouldn't touch him. Not even as it lowers from his thick, dark hair, but instead allowing my fingertips to test the feeling of his skin from his temple to his jaw.

My eyes lift to meet his, and then the door behind me is ripped open. Laughter flows from the room but cuts to silence in the same second.

My hand flies down, and I whip around, coming face-to-face with a glued in motion, wide-eyed Cameron. Brady's at her back with a frown in place.

"Uh, hi," I offer lamely, my face growing hot, even more so when I peek into the place, spotting Mason and Chase inside. Both slowly rise from their place on the couch, matching glares on their faces, and I quickly look back to Cam.

Cam's smirk slowly slips into place, and she crosses her arms. "Well, hell to the oh."

I snap my attention to Brady, too nervous to allow it anywhere else.

Come on, Brady. Help me out.

His features twitch the slightest bit, but he eases up, offering Noah a small grin. "Perfect timing. FunWorks is closing the bumper boats for the season this weekend, so we're going to get a round in. Looks like you guys are free to join us."

I glance at Noah over my shoulder, and his eyes snap from where they're pointed across the room to mine, and I don't have to guess to know what—or more who—he was looking at. His expression holds so many questions right then, but he says not a word, waiting to see what leaves my lips instead.

Do I want to go with my friends to ride the bumper boats? Sure. We used to do that kind of stuff all the time, but do I want to be on edge and anxious all evening? Not even a little bit.

I had such a good-ass day. I deserved a good day and won't allow anyone to ruin it this time. So maybe we pass on the outing?

I search Noah's face.

What do I do?

Noah gives a slight jerk of his chin, reminding me we're not the only ones standing here, and I need to move my ass.

Right, right.

I take a step inside, past a stunned silent Brady and Cam as they shift backward, making room for us to enter. Reaching back, I grab hold of Noah's T-shirt and drag him with me.

"Hey, guys," I absently wave toward the others, without so much as glancing in their direction.

"Hey, man," Noah says behind me, and I can only assume he's talking to my brother when he says, "Harper," in greeting next.

"Long time no see," Mason jokes, and an easy chuckle slips from Noah.

They're quiet after that, and I have no doubt the bags hanging from Noah's hands are being inspected as we slip into the kitchen.

I quickly spin, facing him.

"Do you want to go ride the bumper boats?" I whisper, the second we're as far away as the space allows.

He moves in closer, using his body to shield me from the others. "Do you *want* me to go with you?" When I frown, he continues, "Just because I was here when they asked you to go doesn't mean you have to invite me." His blue eyes hold mine.

I glare. "You already know the answer. You just want to hear it."

I swear he wants to smirk right now, his hand skimming mine as he starts pulling the containers from the bags. "Maybe, but had to be sure."

"So you'll go?"

"I'll go."

Satisfied, my shoulders ease, and I move to pull the freezer open, pushing shit around to fit the first few items inside. When Noah steps around me with more, I move away, and the moment my eyes lift, they lock onto Chase's.

He frowns, Looks to all the containers on the counter and back. He pushes to his feet as if to come closer, and my muscles clench. He doesn't miss it, and the creases along his forehead double. He stays where he stands.

My brother leans against the back of the couch, his arms folded over his chest, legs crossed. His face is blank as he takes everything in. The food, Noah, me . . . Chase.

Mason's brown eyes lift to mine, his head tilting the smallest bit.

I don't look away.

"No study group today?" he asks.

"No."

"Do some cookin'?"

"Yep."

"You cookin' for me, Ari baby?" Brady walks up, reaching toward the bags, but I dash forward, blocking him with a brow raised.

"Not happening, big guy."

Brady makes me laugh when he pokes his bottom lip out.

"Don't feel bad. Half of these I won't even be sharing with Cam this time."

"Hey!" she whines, leaning over the countertop to look at all my goodies. "But those soup bowl things were so good!"

"I know, and if you liked that, you'd devour what he made for me today. Way too good to share." I turn to her with a smile.

"Wait." She turns to Noah. "You guys *made* those?" She pushes containers around, trying to figure out what's inside, her smile wide. "I've been meaning to ask where they were coming from, but we've been missing each other at home the last couple weeks, and when we are here together, we're too busy eating 'em for me to care. I thought you signed up for one of those meal things all those Instagram models try to sell."

Noah and I look to each other with a laugh.

"You don't know how to cook," Chase interrupts, his tone flat.

My throat grows thick, but before I have a chance to respond, Noah does, and with a tone far more friendly.

"She can cook fine." Noah's words fan along my hair.

He's slipped closer.

174

We both know that's not exactly true, that I'm better as the test dummy, but that's not the point right now, and I could kiss Noah for having my back without pause.

"Yeah?" Chase keeps pushing. "Since when?"

Undeserved guilt washes over me, but it quickly shifts to annoyance.

Who the hell does he think he is? He isn't being conversational or friendly. He's being an ass, and he knows it.

I look him in the eye. "Since now. He's teaching me."

Chase's lips press into a firm line, and after a moment, he gives nothing but a curt nod, heading out the door, Brady, and Cam right behind him.

"Be downstairs in five, you guys!" she shouts, and then they're gone.

Mason wears a blank face as he looks from Noah to me and then to the door Chase just walked out of and back. "What's his problem?"

I sigh, grab money out of my purse, and shove it in my back pocket. "I don't know, Mase. Maybe you should ask him."

"I'm asking you."

"And I said I don't know, all right?" I lift my shoulders.

He glares a second longer, then lifts his hand and clasps Noah's shoulder. "Ready to get your ass soaked on some bumper boats, Riley?"

Noah glances at me, and when I nod, he turns to Mason. "Lead the way, Johnson."

Off we fucking go.

Laughing, Cam and I turn our boats, strategically making our way past the rock waterfall without getting sucked under it.

On the other side, we split.

"Okay, tuck into that corner, and I'll take this side." She backs up, so she's hidden from the opening. "And now we wait."

We wait a good three minutes and are just about to give up and go back out to the main water hole when it grows eerily quiet.

Suspicion flourishes between us, and I mouth, 'what do we do?'

Her eyes narrow instantly, and she shakes her head knowingly because she understands exactly what I'm likely to do.

This kind of thing makes me nervous and giddy, and I can't stand it. It's that feeling you get when you're walking through a haunted house, knowing full well you're about to get scared, so you start laughing or screeching, your stomach twisting.

I can't handle it; I turn my boat back on, and she rolls her eyes with a smile.

We come together, ready to creep around the side, but the second we do, we're met by a strong front of four smiling men, their water cannons pointed right at us.

We scream and squeal, and they crack up as they do their worst.

The excitement and freezing water have adrenaline taking over, and I gun it over to the water's edge, hop from the boat, and dart up the side of the waterfall.

"What the hell, Ari!" Mason yells through laughter, but I keep going, dipping around the fake palm trees that make a nice little lagoon setting. The water splashes behind me, my friends' laughter loud and growing nearer, so I know they all jumped out too.

"Hey!" the ride attendant shouts. "You guys can't be up there! And you can't take the guns off the boats!"

I yelp, cutting to the left where she can't see me.

The others are yapping away behind me, but I keep moving. I hop over the small stream running through the rocks and tuck into a shaded corner behind a shadowed boulder.

I smile wide, squeezing my eyes shut, trying to calm my breathing.

"You ditched me, bitch!" Cameron yells from somewhere, and in the next second, she's squealing. "Goddamn it, Mason!"

He laughs, both of them shouting, "Oh shit!" in the next breath.

The place echoes with a call to security.

"Look what you started."

My eyes fly open, landing on a gun-yielding Noah. I jerk right but I'm met with more rock, one too tall for me to climb. I whip around, facing him once again.

Noah's blue eyes gleam as he glances around. "Looks like you're stuck."

"Or you could be nice and give me a five-second head start?" I give a giant, cheesy smile.

His eyes crinkle at the sides as he takes a step closer, his mouth taking on a devious grin. "You mean let you go?"

Another step.

I nod, but my smile slips as I look at him. I mean *really* look at him. His hair is drenched and dripping, the dark even darker, shinier. His T-shirt is soaked, along with his athletic shorts.

As I look at his face, I find his smile has faded too, and his eyes, they're on my lower legs, dripping wet just as he is.

Step.

My breathing grows labored as I try to figure out what's happening here.

Noah's my friend. We're friends.

Friends don't look at friends this way . . .

He's directly in front of me now, all tall and gorgeous and confident, and so close we're breathing the same air.

"I'm a smart man, Juliet," he whispers, his gaze dropping to my lips. "Only a fool would let you go once they had you where they wanted you."

"Oh," I breathe.

Noah apparently appreciates my breathy response because a slow smirk takes over his face, and he steps into me. I place my hand on his chest, a little unsure and a lot curious, as he runs his tongue along his lips, his teeth sinking into his bottom one a second later.

And then our bodies are thrown into shock as a bucket of freezing water is poured over our heads. I gasp, and Noah shoots back in laughter.

"Holy shit, it's cold!"

Noah smirks, tossing his water gun into the water below us. "Gotcha."

My mouth drops open, and I look up at the dirty trickster. Brady busts up laughing.

"Thought the cold shower was for her, asshole," he jokes with Noah and grins my way. "Run, Ari baby, security's coming." He shoots to his feet, shouting, "Security's coming!"

Wide eyed, Noah and I look to each other.

"They're over there!" one shouts.

"I spot two!" another screams.

"Shit!" I look around. "What do we do?"

Noah yanks me by the hand, and we jump along the rocks, headed away from the park.

"Over here!" Cameron and Mason shout.

We follow the sound of their voices, spotting them on the other side of the fence, Chase just landing on his feet next to them. Noah and I jerk to a stop in front of it, and in the same second, his large hands are gripping my calves. I grab hold of the teal fence and help hoist myself up, throwing my legs over the side.

Chase rushes behind me, guiding me down by my hips.

Noah is over a split second after my shoes hit the ground, and I throw my head back laughing, my arms shooting up and around his neck.

He spins me, letting go of my right side on my way back down, so I'm tucked under his shoulder.

"Run, fuckers!"

All our heads snap toward Brady's voice, realizing he's already halfway to Mason's Tahoe.

"Get back here!" security yells, and we book it.

Mason peeks behind us to see how close the staff is while hurriedly digging in his pockets for his keys.

"Hurry, shithead!" Cam shouts, jumping up and down, her eyes widening as the mini golf cart grows closer. "They're fuckin' coming!"

"I'm trying, woman!" Finally, Mason tears the keys free, the lock clicks, and we're shuffling into safety.

Noah tosses me onto the seat before climbing in next to me. No one takes the time to hop to the third-row seating, so I scooch up onto Cam's lap, and Mason peels out from the parking lot.

Once we're a good five blocks away, the entire car erupts in laughter.

Brady yells, hitting the dash in excitement. "That shit was fun!"

I grin, dashing a hand out when Cameron shoves on my back.

"Bitch, get off me. You're soaked!" She chuckles.

"So are you, asshole. What difference does it make?" I smile and try to wedge myself in at her side.

"I have room—" Chase begins, but Noah's already grabbing me.

"I got her." He places me on his lap, pulling the seat belt over me awkwardly and buckling it.

I giggle. "I think I'll be good, Noah. No one else has their seat belt on."

"Leave it on for me, yeah?" He speaks low, but we're closed in a truck with no music, so I'm positive nobody misses his concern.

I nod, willing myself not to blush.

A minute or two later, I look up, catching Mason's eyes in the rearview mirror. He stares at me, looks to my seat belt, and then his attention goes back to the road ahead, his mouth curling into a small smile as he does.

Something inside me settles right then, only I'm not so sure what it is.

Chapter 19
Arianna

"I don't feel like partying tonight. I'm fucking exhausted." Brady drops onto the tailgate of Chase's truck, the game having ended a little over a half hour ago.

"Same, dude," Mason agrees, tossing his bag in the bed. He turns to us. "What about you girls? How 'bout a night in, come to the house with us? We can order pizza or some shit. Camp out in mine and Chase's room?"

A party I could talk my way out of but a chill night at their house, when the celebratory party tonight is elsewhere? Not so much, so I shrug, nodding along with Cameron.

My phone vibrates, so I pull it from my back pocket.

Romeo: You see me get laid out on my ass tonight?

I grin.

Me: I did. You got knocked down . . .

I wait a good ten seconds, letting his mind race, then send him the rest.

Me: But you got up again.

He sends back a laughing face emoji, and I chuckle.

Romeo: In case you were wondering, this will never get old.

I stare at his text, a strange warmth washing over me, and I gnaw at my bottom lip.

"Earth to Ari!"

My head snaps up, and I'm met with four sets of narrowed eyes.

"Sorry." My face heats, but it's dark, so I don't think they see it. "Are we ready or . . . ?"

"Yeah, sister." Mason rolls his eyes. "We're ready."

The boys hop in the back to make the short drive around campus, and Cam and I slide into the main cab. If my attention wasn't half somewhere else, I would have realized I was the first to climb in, forcing me into the middle seat.

I can't help but think about the last time I rode in his truck. It was during spring break, senior year.

"You didn't have to come get me. I told Mason I had a ride."

Chase scoffs, flipping a U-turn, and heads for home. "If you think I would let that asshole bring you home, you're mistaken."

"He wasn't an asshole when you invited him to your New Year's party," I remind him as he rolls to a stop at the light.

"He became an asshole when he tried to kiss you at said party." He shoots me a quick glare. "I told him to stay away from you. Looks like I'm going to have to remind him of that on Monday."

"Okay, Mason." I roll my eyes, taken aback, when his head snaps in my direction.

"I'm not your brother." His gaze narrows. "And I didn't tell him that for Mason's benefit."

I do my best to nod, attempting to breathe as air evades my lungs, the alcohol adding to the flush of my skin.

The light turns green, and Chase faces forward, so I do the same, but my eyes, they refuse to stick to the road ahead.

I stare at his profile, at the way he pinches his lips together when he's annoyed or angry. At the rapid rise and fall of his chest as he works through whatever is running through his mind.

Is it me?

Am I on his mind?

My stomach flip-flops at the possibility.

"I can feel your eyes on me, Arianna."

My giggle is low and slightly slurred. "I could have sworn I was being as stealthy as ever."

His chuckle is as quiet as his next words, "Maybe, but I always know when you're watching."

"How?" I don't mean to whisper.

Chase's hand tightens on the wheel, a small frown building along his face. "I don't know."

He's parked in front of my house moments later, and when he turns to look at me, I hold my breath.

He has something to say. I know it.

His lips part, and then Mason is there, tearing my door open with a drunken grin.

"Hi, sister."

I hold in my sigh. "Hi, brother."

I sat awake that night for hours, wondering what that moment meant. If anything at all. Hope bloomed within me then, but it was obliterated the next day when I learned his then girlfriend became his ex earlier that night, and that 'asshole' he had referred to my date as was the *asshole* behind his breakup.

He was frustrated and angry, and I read into it when I shouldn't have. It was such a rookie move to think he wanted what I had wanted for quite some time.

Wait.

Wanted?

My chest stirs, and I have to focus on keeping my breathing steady.

It seems Chase has to, as well. His body is stiff beside me, his shoulder rubbing against mine with his every calculated inhale.

He's anxious or nervous or something. Or maybe he's annoyed I ended up in the middle.

Thankfully, we're turning onto the boys' street a moment later.

"What the hell?" Cam sits forward. "I thought the party was down the street tonight?"

"It was supposed to be." Chase kills the engine. "Let's see what's up."

We roll the windows down as Brady and Mason hop over the side.

"Let me ask the doorboy what's going on." Mason taps the frame and makes his way toward the house.

Cam decides to hop out and join them on the curb, leaving Chase and me in the truck.

My pulse jumps at the silence, knowing neither of us can sit here long without speaking. What sucks is it will be nothing but wasted, random, meaningless words to erase the discomfort. Before, that would have been ok, normal even, to talk about the game or make a comment about the swag in Mason's walk. Now it's just . . . sad. And that's pitiful.

"BJ, what up, man? Why's everyone here?" Mason shouts from the grass rather than walking all the way up to the door.

"The Blevens' house is under investigation for pulling some prank on the sorority behind them. Can't party for thirty days."

"Damn."

Chase opens his door and steps out, offering me a hand.

When I don't move, a grim smile curves his lips. "It's just a hand, Ari."

A low, nervous laugh escapes, and I nod, slipping my palm into his.

When my feet hit the ground, his fingers don't release mine, and we look to each other.

It seems like he has something to say, but I know better.

He won't say a word.

With a withdrawn smile, I gingerly pull my hand from his, already turning away. "Let's go see what the others want to do."

As I glance up, my feet freeze in place.

Noah stands at the top of the porch, staring right at me.

I raise my hand in a small wave, averting my eyes as something that feels a lot like guilt knots inside my stomach, and I'm not sure why.

That might be a lie.

Mason steps up with a groan. "You guys want to go back to your house?"

I glance around, seeing girls and guys filing in from all angles of the street, settling on Cameron.

She crosses her arms, yawning into the air. "Yeah, I don't want to party."

A warm hand meets the small of my back, and I look over as Noah slides up beside me.

"Hey." I wrap my arm around his waist, hugging him, and only after the fact do I realize this might be the first time I've done so.

He's warm and solid and smells like . . . Noah.

Like fresh cotton and clean sheets. Like the winter's breeze and pine, a hint of mint mixed in.

Noah releases me, nodding his chin at the others. "Just find out about the house switch?"

"Yeah, I guess we're headed back to our place." Cam shrugs.

Noah's eyes slide my way, and after a moment, move to my brother. "You guys want to come up instead?" He pauses before adding, "All of you."

"For real?" Brady grins. "You want to bring us lowly fuckers into the captain's quarters?" He teases.

My brother laughs.

They all seem to agree, but I find myself frowning, and I don't realize it until Cameron is elbowing me in the side.

She bulges her eyes at me briefly, and I drop mine to the sidewalk.

I don't think I want to be in Noah's space with them.

It's always only the two of us, other than the occasional pop in of one of his teammates, and I like it that way. I want to keep it that way.

The others. They're involved in every aspect of my life, and while I love that about our group, I don't want to share the one thing I have outside of them.

I don't want to share my time with Noah.

With them, we'll talk shop, drink beer, and watch ESPN or Ninja Warrior. I always loved those nights, but I don't know.

With Noah, it's just . . . different.

I'm Arianna Johnson, not Mason Johnson's little sister.

I like it.

I need it.

I need—

Noah's fingers brush along the back of my arm, and I meet his gaze.

"We'll order in." He speaks with purpose.

You see it, don't you?

His thumb glides along my elbow as if in answer.

Noah knows what's going on in my head. He's telling me it'll be fine, that we won't share *our* fun. We won't cook together or chat about nothing and everything, about things that don't matter and things that do.

He wants to make sure I know I can say no, and the idea will be tossed out, just like that.

I don't have to share him; it's my choice.

Warmth spreads throughout my chest, but it doesn't stem from a blush. It's on the inside this time.

Noah's lips begin to curl before I even nod, but I do. I nod.

"Okay, Noah's it is. Now, let's go before more people get here and try to follow us or something," Cam chirps as she pulls me along as if she knows where she's going.

I lead us to the right, and we step aside so Noah can unlock the door. He lets us go first, so I head up the stairs.

Inside, I curve into the living room, pulling the string hanging from the fan to turn the light on, and Noah flicks the switch by the stove.

Noah peels his jacket off, setting it over the small chair, and I drop my sweater on top of it.

He opens the fridge to grab some beers for the others and a water for himself while I grab the menus in the drawer below the microwave. I hop up on the countertop, and he leans over, reading the options aloud to me, even though he knows I'm reading them in my head.

"We could do the family pack and get a little of everything like last time?" Noah suggests, taking a long pull from his water bottle.

"Yeah, but not the shrimp. I swear it was raw."

He grins and pops open a bottle, handing it to me. "We've been over this. You can't consider shrimp sushi."

"Of course I can." I laugh, pointing the neck of my bottle his way before bringing it to my lips.

A shuffle grabs our attention, and both our heads snap up, finding our forgotten guests standing there, frozen in the entryway, staring at us like we're mutants.

My stupid cheeks rush with heat, and I dip my head, trying to get my hair to cover it.

Noah clears his throat to hide his smile and stands tall, blocking me from my friends. "Beer?"

"Hell yeah, man." Brady darts forward then, tugging Cam along, his arm wrapped around her shoulder. He steps around Noah on purpose, raising a strong blond brow my way.

I offer a tight-lipped smile, but then Brady winks, and my shoulders ease a little.

"Cam, there's Mountain Dew, too." I hop off the counter, and Noah slides a few feet left, so I can reach inside the fridge to grab her one.

"Yes, please." She tugs her hoodie off, sneaking me a smirk as she sets it down on top of mine and Noah's.

"Sit wherever you want. I've got YouTube TV and Netflix, or there's a shitload of DVDs in the drawers." Noah pulls his phone from his pocket, readying to call in our order.

Frown in full effect, Chase disappears around the short wall into the living room, and when I look to my brother, his eyes narrow.

He's angry, but something tells me it has nothing to do with the situation and everything to do with the fact that I know his teammate's studio well. He knew we hung out here some-times—no reason to share exactly how often that 'sometimes' is—but knowing and seeing are a lot different. There's no telling what's running through his mind right now. He's taken a step or two back lately, and honestly, I've been grateful. I know it's in part because he's so busy right now, but staring at him, I'm pretty sure he's regretting it. I think he might be a little hurt, almost feeling like there's a part of me he doesn't know, and, I don't know, maybe there is.

Mason takes lazy steps toward us, blindly digging into his wallet.

"Here." He hands Noah two twenties. "Toward the food, and don't say you got it."

Noah nods, taking the cash, passing Mason a beer in trade.

Mason accepts, glancing around the room. "This place is cool." He looks back to Noah, tipping his drink. "Thanks for inviting us up." Pulling Cam along, he rounds the wall to the living room.

"You got ESPN?" Brady shouts.

Noah chuckles, looking to me.

"Go. I'll order."

He winks, joining them while I place our order. I stay in the kitchen a minute or two after hanging up, and then, with a deep breath, I pile into the small space with my oldest friends, choosing the open seat beside my newest one.

Where the boys have to wait until their coach releases game film on Mondays, Noah has early access to the website, so he pulls it up and signs into his captain's account. Just like that, the awkward tension I might be the only one feeling is gone, and I couldn't be happier.

This has the boys on the edge of their seats, watching their own game as if they didn't have the best seats in the house, and it's not long before our food is delivered.

For the next hour or more, they're completely entertained.

They hop up between bites, point out different things they saw, rewinding and rewatching several plays while Cam and I sit back, laughing at the personality they show on the field. Far too much swag for one team.

Full of food and beer, we settle in for a movie, allowing Brady to talk us into a two-hour Marvel movie.

Somewhere along the way, I must have passed out because the next thing I know, Noah's whispered, 'hey,' has my eyes peeling open.

I sit up, adjusting my head on the couch pillow. "Hi."

His lips curve to one side. "Brady went to his room a while ago, but the others knocked out with you."

I shift, looking to find Chase asleep in the recliner. Mason and Cam passed out on a pile of blankets on the floor.

"I notice she's been hanging out with Trey more and more," he says quietly.

I nod, staring at them. "Yeah. I'm glad. I got it wrong about my brother. He loves her, but not the way she hoped."

"And her, how does she feel?"

"She's . . . happier now." I nod, my smile gentle, and pointed at my best friend. "Done waiting."

When a minute goes by, and Noah doesn't speak, I look over to find his eyes on me.

My lips turn up, and I reach out, brushing his hair aside. It's so soft, so unexpectedly soothing, that I don't stop.

He stares, unblinking, and when he speaks again, his tone is lower than a whisper. "Are you?"

"Am I what?"

"Waiting." Deep lines cover his forehead, and his chest inflates with a full inhale. "Are you still waiting?"

My heartbeat jumps. Thumps. Does a fucking somersault.

But a small sting still follows when I move my eyes to the brown-haired boy in question, who isn't asleep after all, but lies there in the dark, wide awake, staring right at me.

I swallow, slowly turning back to Noah. To my hand, still caressing his hair.

To his eyes, still locked on me.

"No," I find myself murmuring, and something stirs along his face. "I'm not."

"Whenever you're ready to tell your best friend, you know, *me,* what the hell that was last night, I'm all ears."

I drop onto the sofa next to Cam, propping my feet up on the coffee table beside hers. I grin to myself, tossing a piece of stale cereal in my mouth. "What are you talking about?"

"I will cut you." She holds her eyebrow razor out, looking over quickly before focusing on the small hand mirror in her palm. "Give me the juice. Are you boning our mega-hot quarterback and not telling me?"

"Get real!" I laugh, snagging the remote from her lap. "Like I wouldn't tell you if I were."

"But you want to."

"Cameron."

"Have you kissed him? Touched? Anything?"

"Oh my god, no."

"Why not?" she gapes. "You like him."

"He's my friend." My temples thud after I say it, and I rub my lips together. "I like hanging out with him."

She scowls, gauging me. "You know he wants you, right?"

When I don't respond, she shifts toward me.

"Ari." Her eyes widen. "It's so obvious."

Pulse pounding, I shake my head.

After a moment, Cameron sighs and pushes to her feet. "You know, for a girl who spent so much time hoping for a guy to open his eyes . . . you might want to open yours this time."

With that, she heads into the shower, and I don't move from my place on the couch.

I know what she's saying, and I think she's right, but . . .

What if she isn't?

What if Noah cares for me like Chase does?

A lot, but not the same?

Not enough?

I'm not so sure I could handle another let down.

Something tells me I couldn't.

Especially from Noah.

Chapter 20
Arianna

Finally home, I strip out of my clothes and head for the shower.

The second the warm water soaks into my scalp, Cameron's voice reaches me from the hall.

"Hey!" She knocks twice and opens the door to slip inside. "How was the workout with Brady?"

"About as successful as you'd expect."

"How many times have they told you to stick to jogging?"

"Too many to count." I smile, massaging shampoo into my scalp. "How'd your test go?"

"Good until I got to the stupid essay question, but I don't think it'll hurt me too much. I basically made up a bunch of shit and worded it like a mastermind, so I'm hoping he just gets confused and gives me the points anyway."

"Sounds like a solid plan."

"I thought so," she jokes. "Hey, so, I'm going to dinner with some of the girls from the first floor. I can wait for you to get ready if you want to come?"

"No, I'm going to stand here with my eyes closed for a solid ten minutes, and then it's Spanx game strong."

"Sounds like a blast." Cameron chuckles. "I'm going to change and head out. I'll be in late; I think Trey's picking me up from the restaurant after for a movie or something."

"K. Love you."

"Love you."

Cam takes off, and I soak in the shower until the water runs cool. Slipping into a pair of spandex shorts and an old varsity

T-shirt Mason tried to toss out, I make my way to the kitchen.

My stash of meals isn't exactly low, but I'm in the mood for something fresh, so I drop onto the couch, deciding to text Noah.

Me: my freezer sucks right now.

I set my phone on my chest and begin scrolling through the new movies on Prime. A couple trailers in my phone beeps.

Romeo: Running low, are you, Juliet?

Me: I'm running on empty . . .

Romeo: Taking it back?

Me: That's the great thing about music, Romeo. It's timeless.

Romeo: Kind of like Shakespeare?

I can't help but laugh.

Me: Yeah, Noah. Just like Shakespeare.

I wonder if he knows how twisted the real story of Romeo and Juliet is?

Me: I happen to have the necessities to make college girl spaghetti. Meaning I have a can of cheap sauce, meat, and noodles. Want to come over and make sure I don't burn the place down?

I bite at my lip. He could have plans, and that's totally fine.

Maybe I should have asked what he was doing before I invited him over?

Maybe he's with a girl.

Maybe . . . he's with Paige.

I frown but shake it off when my phone beeps again. I squeeze it, but now I'm too nervous to look at the screen.

"Screw it." I hop up and make my way back to the kitchen, deciding even if he can't or doesn't want to come over, I'm cooking. It's not like I don't help Cam make stuff for the boys a lot. Usually, I'm the utensil grabber or box opener, the stirrer and stuff, but still . . . I help. Plus, Noah's taught me some basics, so yeah. I can make it by myself.

Only, I don't want to make it by myself.

Once I have everything lined up on the counter, I flatten my palms and stare at it for a while. With a heavy huff, I pick up my phone to check his message. Instantly, my smile breaks free.

He's on his way.

Less than thirty minutes later, we're settled in my kitchen as a nice little change.

"Why are you doing that?" I stand on my toes, trying to peek over Noah's shoulder, making him laugh. Turning slightly, he gently moves me aside so he has room to bend his arm.

"You put salt in the water to help season the noodles."

"That makes no sense. It's in water." I hop onto the counter next to the stove. "Won't it wash away or dissolve or something?"

"Or soak into the noodles themselves," he teases as he sets the spoon down next to me.

I roll my eyes playfully, pick up the spoon, and place it on the small saucer meant to hold it.

Noah turns to the bag he brought with him, pulling out a can of olives, fresh mushrooms, and something green.

He looks at me and grins. "You can turn a dollar can of sauce into something worth eating with just a few extra ingredients."

I watch him prepare it all and stir it into the simmering sauce. "Another tip from your mom?"

He nods, and while it takes him a minute to share more, he eventually does. "We didn't have a lot of extra money, but she always found a way to make cheap taste expensive."

"How do you know what tastes good together?"

"Google."

A laugh spurts from me, and he chuckles, continuing with his instructive cooking.

I love how he talks me through each step.

"You should always start the sauce before the noodles. The longer it simmers, the more the flavors come out, but we're doing this the quick way."

I tuck my hair behind my ear, watching him. "You know I meant what I said before about the chef thing. I really think it's something you'd be great at."

Noah glances up at me a moment before looking back to the pot. "I appreciate that."

"Did you really cook dinner with your mom all the time?"

"Every night."

"Yeah?" I grin, resting my elbow on my knee, my chin on my palm.

"Yep. I'd go home after practice or after games, and she'd be getting home from work right about the same time, so we'd make something together. Sometimes it was nothing more than grilled cheese, and other nights we'd ruin a couple batches of risotto until we got it right."

"So, on game nights, instead of going out with your friends after, you'd go home and make dinner with your mom?" I ask, my voice giving away my thoughts with my stomach full of flutters.

That's the sweetest thing.

"Don't get me wrong, I went out." He chuckles.

"But after dinner with your mom."

"Yeah, after that."

Even though he's not looking at me, I nod. "You were good, though, weren't you? You were a good kid?"

Noah's eyes are on me now.

"Yeah, you were good." I smile softly. "And you're doing all this for her, school and football. You push yourself to be the best you can, so she can see that from you. So she knows you appreciate her and all she did for you." His brows pull to the center, and he shifts toward me. "Because she gave you everything she had to give and more, and you want to do the same for her."

"I couldn't live with myself if I let her down, not when she was always there. Not when she gave me everything she could and made me who I am. I owe it to her to do my best with what I've been given."

"You haven't been given anything, Noah," I say quietly, a small smile on my face. "You earned what you have, and that's something you should be so proud of."

Noah's chest inflates, and he turns back to the sauce. He clears his throat, takes the wooden spoon, stirs, then lifts it to his lips, blowing gently.

He steps in close, holding it in front of me. He's done this before, many times. Every time, really. So why does a sudden rush of nerves swirl through me?

I open my mouth, and he slips it between my lips. My fingers gingerly wrap around the stem of the utensil, and he releases it. Stretching my torso, I set it down, and my body slips slightly.

Noah's quick to push close, keeping me from sliding off the countertop, his firm, large hand instantly locking around my upper thigh, steadying me.

My eyes fly to his, my breath catching in my throat. The distance between us has been completely erased, and he doesn't seem to want to put it back.

His nearness, his touch, it's unexpected, and I can't deny the way my pulse spurs to life. The hairs on the back of my neck rise, and I have to remind myself to breathe.

Slowly, his rough palm leaves me.

"Good?" His voice is deep and raspy, his attention locked on my mouth.

"Yeah. Noah?"

He looks up.

I want you to kiss me.

I freeze at the thought, my eyes popping wide as if I shouted my desire out loud, and my cheeks burn out of control.

He sees it, but he turns to the food before his grin breaks free.

I watch as he puts the final touches in our sauce, drains the noodles, and grates a small mountain of parmesan cheese. He then pulls the garlic bread from the oven and cuts it into small pieces.

The preciseness of his movements, the flex of his arms, the focus on his face, *him*.

I can't look away, and when he turns, catching me staring, he stops moving.

Spaghetti bowl in one hand, bread bowl in the other, he smiles, soft and easy. Thoughtful.

I should look away, but instead, I move closer, my eyes locked with his.

There's an ache growing within them, each second that passes.

Was Cameron right?

My brows pull in as I try to figure out what's happening here. Within me.

All around me.

Noah . . .

He looks my way. "You want to eat in the living room here too?"

"Yeah. Noah?"

He tips his head.

"Do you want to kiss me?" I rush out, and then I freeze.

So does he.

He doesn't move, blink, or breathe.

Noah stares at me, deep into my eyes, and swallows hard. "Since I met you."

My skin prickles, my stomach flipping like I've done a dozen cartwheels. "Really?"

"Yeah, Juliet." Blindly setting the bowl down, he slips closer. "Really."

My spine tingles, my limbs jolting as his palm meets my cheek, slowly gliding up until the pads of his fingers are in my hair, his thumbs caressing the edge of my bottom lip

A shiver runs through me, and Noah's lips twitch.

"Kiss me," I breathe. *Please.*

"Fuck." His eyes squeeze closed, his forehead falling to mine. "You're killing me."

"But what a way to go."

His chuckle is deep, and when it fans along my lips, my hand shoots up to grip his wrist.

Noah's chest rumbles, causing the muscles in my core to clench.

I want him to kiss me, to devour my mouth with his own.

I want his tongue to slip inside, discover the taste of mine, and commit it to memory as mine does the same.

I want him to move me the way he wants, however the hell he likes, and I want him to haul me closer than I'd think possible.

But Noah's lips don't move.

And when I try to open up for him, to beg without a word, he shakes his head against me.

I open my eyes, finding his still pinched tight as if he's fighting himself.

His pulse beats wild at his temples, and for a solid thirty seconds, Noah stands frozen until, finally, a heavy exhale leaves him.

He steps back, his gaze finding mine as his knuckles feather along my jaw. He stares with a tenderness I've never known eyes could hold. It's raw and painful, beautifully confusing.

My heart stops, jumps, and I can't breathe. I can hardly feel my own limbs.

What's happening to me?

A knowing smile graces his lips, but I'm not sure what he's figured out because I'm lost.

Finally, he speaks again.

"I can't kiss you yet," he rasps, his voice thick with desire, causing my toes to curl in my socks and confusion to swirl in my mind.

Embarrassment swells within me, but before I can shake my head and attempt to backpedal my way out of this, Noah shakes his, having anticipated my reaction.

"I said *yet*," he whispers gently, shifting nearer. Want whirls in his eyes, but they're drawn tight with torment. "Trust me, I want to."

"Are you sure? 'Cause I'm getting the opposite vibe right now."

Noah's chuckle is instant and adoring, and I bite the inside of my lip at the sound.

"I'm sure." He smirks, but it slowly smooths out as he pins me with a soft yet stern expression. "In case you haven't figured it out yet, there isn't a thing about you I don't like. Nothing."

". . . but."

"But a loss as big as you might be too much for me." His voice drops to a whisper. "So I can't do what you're asking me . . . not yet."

"I don't . . ." I trail off, swallowing the sting burning up my airway.

I don't understand, but the longer I stare into Noah's blue eyes, the clearer it becomes.

The calm understanding of his gaze leads me where he intended, and a sharp pain knocks against my chest.

Chase.

I'm not sure why, but shame falls over me, and as it does, I realize that's the point.

Not the shame, but the fact that I don't fully understand where it's stemming from.

It might be the fact that I realized what his concern was without his saying it aloud.

It might be because I'll always love Chase.

It could be because the thought of him still hurts, even if it's nothing like it was before.

It might even be because I can't remember the last time I thought of him at all . . .

All I know is it has nothing to do with my desire to kiss the man in front of me.

But that doesn't make it any less complicated.

I understand what Noah is asking, and it only strengthens his character more.

Noah Riley is a good-ass man.

What if he was my man?

My cheeks heat, and I tear at the inside of my cheek. "You know what I think this sauce can use?" I try to change the subject.

It's obvious.

His smile widens, stretching over his beautiful face, and I'm blushing again. "What's that?"

"A kick."

"A kick?"

I give a curt nod, spinning on my heels.

"A little something called . . . " I open the drawer on my right, lifting out two old packets from Mountain Mikes. "Crushed red peppers." I lift a brow. "Also known as crushed red peppers, in case you didn't know that," I joke.

"I had no idea." He plays along, picking up the bowl of now lukewarm spaghetti, leading us toward my couch. "You might be onto something."

We're half a bowl down when he looks over.

"What?" I ask over a mouthful of French bread.

"For the record, that about killed me, and it was a one-time thing that will *never* replay itself." His lips pull into a one-sided grin. "So next time you ask, be sure because I won't deny you again."

"Say you swear."

A laugh flies from him, and he nudges my leg with his own, shaking his head as he turns back to his food. "I swear."

I smile into my bowl, and just like that, everything is fine. As I think that, I realize it already was.

There was no awkwardness that followed, only a moment of mortification on my part that Noah quickly washed away.

It's always like this with him. Simply effortless.

Once our bowls are empty, Noah turns his body toward me, so I do the same.

After a moment, he says, "Tell me something."

I pull in a lungful of air. "What do you want to know?"

"Everything."

I freeze for a split second, my stomach muscles tightening, and a low laugh leaves me.

"Hm," I think. "I like comedies."

"I know."

"I like pasta."

He shakes his head. "Already know that too."

"Okay . . . I don't like flowers." His brows rise. "Or I do, but I think they're wasteful as gifts. Overpriced just to be tossed in the trash a couple days later."

"Noted." He chuckles, an expectant look on his face.

"More?"

His nod is slow.

I laugh again, and with a hint of bashfulness, I share something else, something he definitely doesn't know.

"My uh, my favorite color is blue."

Noah's blue eyes sharpen, and he holds mine a long moment, and when the grin that follows is far too charmingly cocky, I toss a pillow at him to erase it.

He chuckles, and we settle into the cushions.

We spend the next several hours eating popcorn, chatting about our childhoods and the things we miss.

By the time he goes home, it's after three in the morning, and before I've got the door locked behind him, I'm already looking forward to next time.

Chapter 21
Arianna

Come Wednesday, midterms are in full effect, and caffeine is the food of choice. Most of those on campus are hunkered down with study groups, essays, and a million other things that keep all of us busy and on the go. I've seen Cameron twice all week, talked to my brother once outside of a few texts, and while I haven't seen Noah either, we've both found the time to respond to each other's messages.

Except for today.

Today, I didn't hear back from him, but they traveled all day yesterday and this morning played their first early game. I'm not sure what his game-day routine is, so I figure he likes to stay busy and focused, and maybe he'd text me later, but then the game ended. Badly.

His receiver fumbled with three minutes on the clock, and the opposing team picked it up, running it back to score a touchdown. If that weren't bad enough, he was sacked twice in the next drive, and the coach pulled him out of the game when he hopped up, limping.

Mason got to go in as his backup, but it was already third down. There wasn't enough time left, and the Sharks took the loss.

Noah was okay, though, because I watched him walk off the field after interviews.

I tried to text him after the game, but he didn't answer then either, so I think he might be the sit back and reflect after a defeat type, which is why I'm sitting here staring at Cameron, unsure of what to do.

She cocks her hip. "Well? Are you coming or not?"

"You said they just got home two hours ago. Are you sure they're partying? Shouldn't they, like, sleep?"

She scoffs as she moves to my desk and snags a pair of dangly earrings. "Please, they had midterms, just like the rest of us. They're pissed, tired, and in need of a pick-me-up."

"Who called?"

"Brady. He said he left you a message too."

Frowning, I pick up my phone, and sure enough, I have a voice mail from Brady and one from Mason. "They must have called when I was taking out the trash."

I look at her, and she folds her hands in front of her in a prayer-like motion.

"What if he doesn't feel like hanging out? Or what if he's busy?"

"Honey, he will get unbusy when you show up. Trust that." She stomps like an excited child. "Come on, please! You're already looking fine, fresh face, hair did, so let's go!"

Biting my lip, I push to my feet. "Okay, hurry before I change my mind."

Cameron squeals, throwing her arm around my shoulders, and we're out the door.

Less than an hour later, we're walking up the porch to the football house.

Mason spots us the second we step inside—I'd swear he had GPS trackers on us if I didn't know any better.

He steps up, wrapping me in a hug and lifting me off the ground a moment. "My baby fucking sister came to party! Finally!" He smiles drunkenly, steering us toward the keg in the corner.

I grin up at him, patting him on the back while he fills up a few cups, passing them over.

"How you feeling?"

"Pissed off." He laughs with a shrug. "But ready to get back out there."

"Yeah, sucks to be a loser," Cameron teases, and he playfully flinches her way.

Cameron gets the familiar giggle she always does when Mason shows her attention, but she quickly swallows it.

He pulls his phone from his pocket with a frown. "Be back. My buddy's here, needs help carrying shit in. Stay away from all these fuckers 'til I get to tell 'em you're my sister."

I salute him with my middle finger, and he smirks, but Cam and I find ourselves two cups deep, and still, Mase hasn't returned.

"I'm beginning to think his friend was a girl."

"His friend was totally a girl. Oh, shit. Okay, hurry, tell me how you want to play this." Cam squeezes my arm.

"Play what?"

"Bitch—" she hisses.

"I spy Trey."

She whips around, her grin instant. "Okay, fine. I'm going, but run away or cry, and you're so dead."

"Wait, what?"

She points two fingers at me as if to say she's watching me and skips off.

With a laugh, I spin around, and as I face forward, my spine jerks straight. I did *not* pick up what she was putting down.

Shit is right.

Chase stands not ten feet away, and he's headed right for me.

A lump instantly forms in my throat, but I force myself to swallow past it.

This is his house, of course he would be here.

Why didn't I think of that?

"Hey," he steps up, but before I can respond, he's wrapping his arms around me in a hug.

My body goes stiff, but only for a moment, and I find myself hugging him back.

I can't help but inhale as my face buries into his chest, and I'm immediately hit with the warm, familiar scent seared into my memory. Suddenly, images of our night on the beach are front and center.

The gentleness of his touch as his hands slid over me. The softness of his lips when he bent to kiss me. The way he held me, the things he whispered. His soft eyes looking down at me like I was . . . more.

Like I was worth something.

Tears spring behind my eyelids, and my fingers grip onto him before I can stop them.

The sad part?

He grips me right back, pressing into my skin like he's missed our friendship as much as I have, like he needed this. To hold me, to feel me close, when he was the one who pushed me away to begin with.

"Arianna . . ." he whispers.

His voice, it's so low and gentle that I tear myself away, placing a few steps between us. It takes effort, but I bring myself to look up at him, and it's as if he's confused as to why I'd pull away.

He steps toward me again.

"Chase, I—" My eyes are pulled over his shoulder, my words dying in my throat.

That's when I see him.

Noah.

He's standing next to the gorgeous girl from the barbecue, Paige. His shoulder's perched against the wall, a water bottle in hand, while she leans her back against it, staring up at him with admiration.

He says something, and she laughs, her hand lifting to shove him lightly, and he smiles down at her.

A sudden sense of heaviness falls over me as if a weight has been dropped on my chest, forcing me to work harder for air.

Chase says something else, reaching out, but I don't feel his hand if it's touched me. I don't hear his words, though his mouth moves in my peripheral.

I see Noah and all I can hear is Paige's laugh echoing through my mind. Something stirs in my gut, low and repetitive. It doesn't stop.

Chase follows my line of sight, landing on the frame-worthy couple not twenty feet away. His head yanks my way once more. "Are you serious?" he spits.

My eyes flash toward him, and his glare flits across my face in flustered snaps.

Chase jerks right to block my view, but my arm shoots out, stopping him. His lips press into a firm line, his nostrils flaring.

I look back to Noah.

The moment I do, he glances over his shoulder. He spots me, and he doesn't turn away. He doesn't glance toward Chase or the hand that's still touching my arm. He doesn't return his attention to Paige when her palm falls to his chest, creating heat in my own.

Why is she touching him?

Noah *does*, however, hold a hand out, those eyes never leaving mine as he excuses himself and heads right for me.

I can't keep my lips from twitching or my gaze from growing soft.

The tension in my muscles eases, but then Chase is gripping my arms, forcing me to face him. He stares, glares, and then he shakes his head, tearing his hands away.

Chase's jaw clenches, and he focuses on everything or anything but me. "Find one of *us* when you're . . . done here. Don't walk around alone."

"I know," I say, but he's already gone, and Noah is stepping beside me.

"Hi."

"Hi." He looks from where Chase disappeared to me, a tenderness in his gaze that has me smiling. "You didn't come find me."

"I didn't know if you were home."

The corner of his eyes crease. "Mason said he texted you for me, telling you I lost my phone."

"I probably should have read those." I chuckle. "I stopped looking after the fifth or sixth one came through."

A small grin forms on his lips. "I was waiting around a bit in case Cameron showed. Figured it was better to ask her to call on her phone than it would be to ask Mason."

"And if she didn't show?"

"Then you'd be opening your door for me when I knocked on it."

A low laugh slips from me, and I sway slightly on my feet, giving myself a moment to take him in, as if in search of a change in him from the last time I saw him. His hair is a perfect, silken mess of dark strands with freshly trimmed sides, and he's ever flawless in a T-shirt and jeans.

No effort looks good on him, especially with the way his tattoo peeks from beneath the fabric around his bicep. It's the textbook tease—not enough to show you what's to be found, but just enough to lead you on the hunt.

I've never seen the full image, how far the dark markings travel, and I kind of want to.

I'm tempted to push his sleeve up now.

The hand on my lower back spans out, pressing into me more firmly as he nods, a tangled yet content expression blanketing his face.

"I thought for sure I'd have to head your way." He speaks in a curious, husky whisper, his eyes imploring. If the spark that flickers within his gaze tells me anything, it's that he's pleased.

My gaze slides past him then, toward the doorway he slipped from, where Paige still stands alone and staring our way.

I try to turn back quickly once I realize where my gaze has subconsciously pointed, but Noah catches me regardless.

He slides in front of me, and I tip my head back to look up at him.

"I was talking to Paige about her students. They're giving her some trouble, and since I was in youth groups as a kid, she thought I'd have some advice."

"Oh, I wasn't . . ."

Wasn't what, Ari? Jesus.

My face heats, and I attempt to avert my gaze, but Noah doesn't allow it.

His fingers come up to skim under my chin, and my lips part for a shallow breath as he guides my attention right back to him.

He says nothing, but it's as if he doesn't have to. It's all right there, written along his handsome face and in the way his thumb feathers over my jaw. It's brief, unnoticeable, but it's felt. Everywhere.

My god, I'm in trouble.

Once he's satisfied, his hand falls. "I can't let Paige leave by herself. It's not safe."

I nod and go to step back, but he doesn't allow that either.

I don't know why I'm acting like this.

Chase must have thrown me off.

"Her friend bailed on her, so I need to take her home—"

"Oh my god, I'm so sorry." I shake myself out of the weird fog I've fallen into. "Go. I didn't mean to keep you, do whatever you need to."

His eyes narrow.

"Seriously, enjoy your night. You don't have to babysit me. Cameron and the others are around here somewhere; I'll be fine. I won't roam around alone if that's what you're worried about."

Noah's stance widens a bit, and his tongue comes out, rolling along his lips. "I'm gonna lay this out for you, so pay attention because I need you to hear me." His response is instant and strong, and he steps closer, holding my eyes hostage. "I don't want you to think Paige is here with me tonight. She's not, but she is my friend, and I need to make sure she makes it home safely. I don't want you to stay here because I'm thinking you came here for me tonight, and if I'm completely honest with you right now, I don't want to share you with the person who I'm damn sure has just realized that. So, if you came for me, come with me." He pauses, but only for a second. "Because I was on my way to you just the same." Noah takes a deep

206

breath, nodding to himself. "I'm coming off a loss today. Make my night feel like a win. Come with, Juliet."

"Okay."

He scowls, his head tipping slightly as if he's surprised. "Okay?"

"Yeah . . . okay."

Noah chuckles, subconsciously rubbing at the back of his head. "That was easier than I thought."

I shrug, smiling at him. Before, I might have paused and thought about it, but I don't want to. I don't need to.

Noah is face value, and he takes me just the same. As I am.

"Let me tell Mason I'm leaving so he doesn't flip out." I stop. "Well, he may still flip out, but at least he'll know where I am."

Noah grins, taking backward steps. "I'm going to grab my keys."

We part, and I only have to spin, take a single step right, and my brother's within sight, as always, with Brady and Chase at his side.

I head for them.

Brady spots me first, and a low whistle slips from him as he turns to face me fully.

"Ari baby!" Brady holds his arms out, and I slip into his embrace.

He attempts to lift me in the air, but Mason shoves his shoulder down, making him laugh.

"What's up, sister?" Mason raises a brow, cutting a quick glance in the direction I came from. "You look like you got something to say, and I bet it's not hello."

"Hi again. Missed you for the last hour. Sorry a second time about the game." I chuckle when he gives me a playful roll of his eyes, jerking forward to kiss my temple.

I smile. "I'm just letting you know I'm riding with Noah to take his friend home. I'll be back later. I think."

He lifts his beer bottle to his lips, staring over the brim as he takes a drink. "Just you?"

"Just me."

"You can't take Cam with you?"

"She's with Trey."

"Right." He nods, eyeing me.

My brother knows I've been hanging out with Noah alone, and I'm standing here alive and well today. He didn't throw a fit when I went with Noah before, but this is different. It's night; people are drinking; *he's* drinking, which makes him more protective and paranoid, but he knows where Noah lives. Likely has a plan of kicking his ass already mapped out in his head should he feel a need to do so. I guarantee that is the only reason he doesn't press me more. "Answer your phone if I call you."

"I will—"

"Why can't you wait here?" Chase pushes off the wall. "Why do you need to go with him to take some girl home?"

Mason's head yanks toward his friend, and Brady coughs, turning to the side to hide a laugh.

I force myself to meet Chase's stare. "I want to go."

"Why?"

My pulse jumps into my throat, and I shake my head. "Why do you care?"

His eyes narrow, and he steps closer . . . and my brother follows.

Chase shakes his head, pushing past me. "Whatever. I'm going for a refill."

Mason points his frown at me. "What's his problem?"

"He's your friend. Ask him."

"He's *our* friend."

"Right." I almost forgot. "I have to go. Noah's waiting."

"Yeah, all right." Mason nods, and I spin, annoyed as I head for the door, where Noah waits, but the annoyance slips away as I find him waiting there for me, a hoodie in his hand.

"Ready?" he asks.

I nod, turning to Paige with a smile. "Hi again."

"Hey, I'm glad you made it." She beams, slipping out the door. "Noah was about to have a pity party."

I look to Noah, and he winks down at me.

208

I don't know why, but my whole body heats, so I quickly slip out the front, welcoming the cool air.

As we reach Noah's truck, Paige pulls the door open, but she steps back, nodding her head for me to go in first, so I do. We head toward the opposite side of campus, and surprisingly, it's not awkward.

Paige picks up with the conversation Noah said they were having, asking my opinion, and I do my best to offer a solution that might help. It's kind of cool being included in a discussion they could have cut short or picked up at another time.

Once at her building, she climbs out, turning back to us with a wave, and we watch as she disappears inside. Noah waits for the door to close behind her completely, and then we're pulling out of the parking lot.

He pulls into a gas station, and we both choose ICEEs, despite the chilly air. We climb back into the truck, but when I take the seat by the door, Noah looks over, jerking his chin the slightest bit, his lips curved at the corners. So, with my stomach threatening to tangle into a thousand knots, I slide over until we're thigh to thigh.

"Can I take you somewhere?" he asks.

I nod, pulling my straw between my lips, and his eyes follow the movement.

It's with a deep breath that he faces forward, and off we go.

We drive with the radio off for a little over thirty minutes before Noah pulls off the main road, parking on the shoulder.

I unbuckle my seat belt and lean forward to try and see beyond the darkness.

"This looks like a good place to bury a body."

"I don't know about burying, but definitely to lose one at sea."

My head jerks toward his, and he laughs, pushing open his door.

He grabs the hoodie he carried out of the house and waits for me to slide out his way.

Taking the half-gone Icee from my hand, he sets it on the hood, tugging the sweatshirt over my head.

I laugh, slipping my arms through the cuffs hanging well over my hands. It's soft, fresh cotton on the inside and smells like Noah.

"Thank you."

He smirks, handing me my drink. "Welcome."

"You planned this, didn't you?"

"I figured you'd be up for a little road trip."

I pull my lips to one side.

"Come on." He nods.

We walk side by side up a small hillside that leads to a wide trail, and beyond it, nothing but ocean.

My smile is instant.

"Holy shit," I whisper, stepping ahead of him toward the extended peak of a cliffside in the center.

The moon bounces off the sea the way I love, but it's even better as we're up higher than I've ever been before, so it shines like ice below us. I laugh, glancing back at Noah as he slowly steps up beside me.

"You like it?"

Nodding, I face forward again. "It's amazing."

"Come here." Noah takes my hand, leading me left a few feet, where there's a slight dip in the rock, allowing us to sit and dangle our feet, another flat stone a few feet below to catch our fall, should we scoot too far over the edge.

I can't help but laugh again, nudging him in the shoulder. "This is crazy."

"It's called Sunset Cliffs."

"Man, we have to come back to watch the sun go down. I love the moon over the water, but the sunset is definitely a sight I have to see from right here."

I look to him.

"You want to come back, I'll bring you back," he tells me.

"Say you swear."

Laughing, he faces forward. "I swear."

"When I was little, my parents would drive us to the coastline every Sunday for a picnic dinner. My dad would set up a little tent, you know, the kind that's all netting?" I smile.

"My mom would put up a table and lay out the food while Mase and I set up chairs and piled them high with blankets. We'd eat, play board games, and then when the sun would start to set, our parents would tell us stories about when they were young or when we were babies. It was always something new, something we hadn't heard yet." I loved those nights.

"Your family means a lot to you."

"My family means everything to me. I want to be everything my mom is. Strong and independent in my own way, a solid example, but human in my mistakes. I want to be proud and encouraging, accepting but firm, even when it hurts. Even when it's hard. I want to make chicken and dumplings when my daughter feels like her world's falling apart like teens think, and I want to bake cupcakes with stupid sweet frosting when my son's too hard on himself for a bad grade or dropped pass." I laugh, lowering my head. "Clearly, I have some work to do to get there, but . . . "

I look to Noah.

He runs his hand over his forearm, a look of reverence adorning his face. "You want to be a mom?"

My lips spread wide. "Of course I do."

He shakes his head, and a slight frown builds along my brow.

"No," he begins. "That's it. That's why you didn't care where you went to school. That's why you had no opinion when it came to choosing, and that's what you didn't tell me when I guessed there was more to it."

My throat grows thick, but I nod.

"You said it was embarrassing," he reminds me. "It's not."

"Telling you is."

He almost looks offended, and an anxious laugh escapes me.

"Noah, you've worked your entire life toward a goal, and you're on your way to achieving it. You're about to have the world at your fingertips, and it's a tribute to what you've dedicated your life to. Here I am, dreaming of being a house-wife, and I haven't even figured out how *not* to burn a loaf of French bread yet."

I go to laugh it off, but Noah frowns, shaking his head.

"Don't sell yourself short. What you want is to give yourself over to the happiness of others. That's selfless."

"Some would call it selfish to want to stay home and raise a family while my partner busts his ass outside of it."

"A good man would disagree."

I blink up at him, and his chest inflates.

"Yeah, maybe you're right." A sigh pushes past my nostrils, and I shake my head. "My dad would like you," I tell him. "Someone who loves his mom, plays football like a boss, *and* cooks like a badass."

Noah glances away, far too humble to face me while I boast about him, but his smile is evident in the creases framing his features.

After a moment of silence, he says, "I went on a picnic once."

My jaw drops. "Once?!"

He laughs, looking down. "Yep. Once. My mom worked a lot, but on my birthday one year, she picked me up early from school, had lunch packed up in a mini–laundry basket, and off we went."

"Where did she take you?"

He meets my eyes. "She took me here."

And my heart melts. "Here?"

He nods. "She gave me my present, a football." He laughs, remembering, and I trace every line of his face. "It was the same every year. She'd ask what I wanted, and I'd say a football. She'd tell me to pick something else, but I'd hold strong."

"You can never have too many."

"That's exactly what I'd say." He peeks at me. "Mason?"

"Yep. My grams didn't have a lot of money, so he always asked for a ball. He knew she'd get him something regardless, so he wanted to be sure it wouldn't cost her much."

"Exactly." He stares, and it hits me.

That's why he did it. He knew his mom couldn't do much more but would die trying, so he made it easy on her.

There's no doubt in my mind she knew. It must have been so hard to have only one parent. One person, period.

212

If she worked a lot, was he alone often?

Does he feel alone now?

I clear my throat. "What did she pack for lunch?"

"Ice cream."

A laugh bubbles out of me, and Noah's follows.

Together, we turn to the ocean, listening to the sound of crashing waves until the chill gets too strong, and then we head back to campus.

Once we're pulling up in front of my dorm, I'm not ready to climb out, so I turn to him and pull my knees up to my chest. "Tell me something."

"What do you want to know?" he rasps, a hidden grin on his lips.

I drop my head against the seat and whisper, "Everything."

Chapter 22
Arianna

It's a little after eleven when Mason, Brady, and Chase are walking through the door.

Brady swings me around in a hug, and Mason plants a grumpy kiss to my hair as he slips by, falling to his ass on the couch, his eyes instantly closing.

"Someone had a long night." I laugh, turning to Chase, who hesitates near the door, last night's encounter likely playing in his head, so I ease his mind, offering a smile. "Hey."

It works, his shoulders pepping up a bit, and he grins, his eyes falling to my outfit. "Hey, you look good."

"Thanks." I smooth my top down on instinct, glancing at my matching burgundy booties. "Cameron said you guys ordered pizza?"

"Yeah, none of us thought we could stand long enough to grill burgers like we planned to."

I laugh, and he follows me into the kitchen, posting himself on the opposite side of the countertop. "The loss hit that bad, huh?"

"Fuckin' sucked. We beat ourselves."

I blow out a long breath. "True, but hey, maybe you'll get your shot at starting this week now. There were three errors from the starting receivers this game alone."

"Hate to admit it, but . . ."

"But that's the first thing you thought?"

He nods.

"Hey, that's the name of the game." I shrug. "Our dads have told you guys time and time again, one man's mistake—"

"Is another man's gain." He frowns suddenly, his eyes lifting to mine.

They hold there, only dropping when the door is thrown open, and Cameron comes inside, some guy I've seen in the halls behind her, pizza boxes in hand. "The food has arrived." They set the items down, and she pats the boy's shoulder, shoving him back into the hall. "Thanks, G-dawg. I owe you one."

"I'll cash in on that!"

"K, bye!" she shouts, turning to us with a grin. "Let's eat so we can tell our parents we're good kids and be on our separate ways. I've got shit to do today."

I get right to passing around plates, thankful for the quick and easy option since Noah asked me to go with him somewhere today.

We carry the boxes into the living room, and this time, the TV stays off.

We sit back, listening to the boys' play-by-plays as if we didn't watch the game on TV, but we don't care. Growing up, this was one of our favorite times of the week when our families would get together at the end of the week and talk shop.

We chat about school and midterms, and the guys let us in on their idea to go camping over the upcoming school holiday instead of going to our beach house as we had thought we would. They scored a Thursday game, so once they get back into town, they're free until Monday. The second we agree to go, the plan is official.

I'm leaning against the coffee table beside Cameron when my phone rings on the ground beside me. Noah's name, or more *Romeo*, flashes along the screen.

"Someone got a new phone." Cameron, being the asshole she is, grabs it, answering on speaker. "Oh, Romeo, Romeo, where for—"

"Shut up!" I laugh, snagging it from her, only to have Brady snag it from me.

"Hello?" He does his best to mimic a woman's voice, failing miserably, making us laugh.

"I'm going to take a wild guess and say this is . . . Lancaster?" Noah's grin is evident.

I smile, and Brady nods.

"I'm impressed, fuckhead. Now, why you callin' our girl?"

"Okay!" I jump up, yanking it from Brady's big ass hands, and hop over my brother's extended legs. I bring it to my ear. "Hey."

"Their girl, huh?" he teases, and my face heats as I realize I forgot about the speaker part.

I quickly whip around so I'm not facing them, turning the speaker off. "Yeah, Mason has tried to retrain the boy for years. It's useless," I joke.

"Noted." Noah chuckles in my ear, and then he's quiet for a moment. "You still mine today?"

Heat washes over me, and I nod, even though he can't see me. "I am."

"Good, because I'm already on my way."

"Perfect." I head toward my room for my purse. "Cameron is about to leave, so I'll walk out with her. Meet you by the doors?"

"Wait inside until you see my truck."

I bite back a grin. "Yes, Noah. Mason happened to train me well."

His airy laugh fills my ear. "Five minutes, Juliet."

"K."

I turn to tell Cameron, let's roll, but the words die on my lips when I find all eyes on me. "What?"

After a second of silence, it's Mason who jumps to his feet and with more energy than I've seen from him all day.

"Nothing, baby sister." He pauses, staring at me a minute before kissing my temple again and heading for the door. "Love you."

"Love you. You don't have to leave."

"I'm not. I'm locking it behind you guys so none of your flirty hallmates try to slip in when you're gone."

I laugh, stuffing my phone inside my bag. "Good idea."

Cameron steps up, pulling a sweater over her head. "Ready?"

"Yep."

We look to the others.

"Bye, guys."

"Later," Brady shouts.

Chase says nothing, facing the TV once more, and we walk out the door.

Noah is pulling up the second I get to the exit, so I slip out with Cameron.

He leans over, pushing the passenger side open for me, and I slide inside, waving at Cameron over my shoulder when Trey pulls up right behind him.

I turn to him. "Hey."

"Hey." He smiles, turns the radio up, and then we're on the road.

He pulls onto the highway, headed the opposite direction of where we went last night, but I don't ask where we're going, and it's not until we're in the parking lot of Tri-City Medical that the sudden need to know sweeps in.

Noah stares straight ahead as he pulls the keys from the ignition, his hand dropping into his lap as if the weight of the lanyard in his palm is too much.

With a deep breath, he begins to climb from the cab, so I do the same, meeting him near the hood.

It takes several seconds, but then he points to a small building near the back, not quite a part of the hospital, but on the same grounds. "That's a rehabilitation center."

I glance to the building with confusion, but his next words clear it right up.

"My mom lives there." He nods to himself. "For about two years now."

My chest caves, the urge to reach out and hold him strong.

"She had a stroke my senior year of high school, lost movement in her left arm." His laugh is sad. "She said she didn't need it anymore since she had a *stud for a son*." He grins, but it falls flat.

217

"Her throwing arm," I guess. "She played catch with you."

"Every day since I could hold a ball." He looks away. "She didn't let it stop her from a damn thing, still cooked dinner, went on like nothing, where she could anyway. She was an accountant for a small firm, so it slowed her down. She lost some work from it, but she was ok, so it didn't matter."

I reach up, gripping the collar of my sweater, the sadness in his tone painful.

"That's why you chose Avix," I realize. He didn't want to leave her to begin with, but after that, he couldn't. He wanted to be there for her.

Noah nods. "She was good for a long time after that, and then the final game of my freshman season at Avix came. We won. I didn't miss a single target that night. Man, I had never been on fire like I was that game." His lips twitch as he remembers it, and I make a mental note to find the highlights later. "All I could think was I couldn't wait to call my mom after, and I did. I was still on the field, still in gear, with reporters flanking me from every angle, but I had to talk to her first. It rang a bunch of times, and when the call was finally picked up, it wasn't her voice. I knew without being told it happened again. I just didn't expect it to be worse than before."

The ache in his voice is too much, so I shift closer, and his eyes come up to mine.

"Let's go inside." I nod, needing him to understand he doesn't need to explain or prepare me. I'm going in regardless. I want to. I need to.

I think he needs me to . . .

"I'd like to meet her."

He stares at me a long moment, and then he nods back. "Yeah, let's go, 'cause she's dying to meet you."

"She knows I'm coming?"

"Yeah, Juliet, she knows," he whispers, turning his body, so it's facing me fully and only a foot away.

My throat runs dry, and when he reaches for my hand, I give it to him.

Together, we head inside the rehab center to meet the woman responsible for the man at my side.

A laugh slips out of me, and I fold my feet in the seat. "To be fair, my mom and dad tried to show me, but it never ended well."

Ms. Riley, who has insisted several times I call her Lori, smiles. "But you're learning okay now, from what I hear."

You hear things?

"Maybe you weren't quite ready for something new before," she says gently, and I nod. "And maybe now you are . . ." She speaks with the wisdom of a mother, warm and kind.

My pulse kicks against my chest and her features soften before me.

"Yeah, maybe. I've got a pretty good teacher." I look to her son, who winks as if he was waiting for me to glance his way. With a smile, I look back to Lori. "My mom would literally pull every recipe out of the book and lock me in a chair until I made magic if she heard me whine how her instructions were lackluster, and then my dad would feel bad and force Mason to help too. And that would inspire my mom to invite all our friends." I sigh. "It was downhill from there."

Lori and Noah both laugh, and warmth spreads through me as, simultaneously, they reach for each other's hands. Noah's leaning against the side of her hospital bed, half sitting on it, half standing.

He just wants to be as close to his mom as he can. He wants her to know he loves and misses her. Appreciates her every word spoken and the inner strength it takes to laugh and smile when her world is a little less than it used to be.

Noah catches my eye, a calm in his I've yet to witness blindingly present.

"You have a large family, then?" Lori asks quietly, pulling my attention from Noah.

"I do, yeah. Aunts and uncles, cousins. Friends who are more like family."

"And they're good to you?"

I can't help but smile. "Amazing. My parents, well"—a low chuckle escapes me, and I roll my eyes—"my brother calls them disgusting, but always with a smile. They're just . . . all the things a person could wish for, you know?" I lift my shoulders. "We've been blessed."

"Brilliant." Her voice is low as if a hopeful whisper.

I look to Noah, who stares at his mother's limp left hand gently placed over her lap.

"Honey," she rasps, facing him. "Will you grab me an orange juice before you go?"

"Yeah, Mom." He kisses her cheek, lifting his bright eyes to mine. "Be right back."

I chew on the inside of my lip, nodding as I watch him slip out of the door.

"Thank you," Lori whispers the moment he's gone, calling my attention to her. She smiles, and though only the right side of her lips lift, I still would have known had they not moved at all. It's in her tone, in the blue of her eyes, nearly the same color as her only son's.

"Thank *you* for letting me come."

"No, sweet girl." She blinks away tears. "Thank you for breathing life back into my boy. It's been a long time since I've witnessed all his shades of blue, but every visit lately, I've been gifted with a little more."

"Lately?" I breathe.

"Yes, honey." She nods, reaching across her body with her working hand, so I push to my feet, slipping mine into hers. "Lately. For weeks now, maybe longer."

My skin flushes, but like her son, she doesn't draw attention to it, allowing me a moment to look away. Clearing my throat, I face her once more.

"Meh, could be because he's basically a football god this season," I tease with a playful shrug.

A loud laugh spurts from Lori, and she grins. "Yeah. Could be, couldn't it?"

We're sharing a smile when Noah slips back into the room, eyeing us with suspicion as he slowly sets a small juice beside her.

"What did I miss?" He glances between us.

"Me getting a taste of that sweet sense of humor you spoke of," his mom says, and my head jerks his way.

His brows lift. "Thanks, Mom." He chuckles. "We should go."

As if on cue, her words begin to slur a little more, but she smiles regardless. "Yeah, honey, you should." Mischief blooms in her eyes. "Take the girl home, tuck her in."

"Mom."

Lori laughs, rolling her head my way. A softness falls over her, her blinks growing slower by the second. "I can't wait to see you again, sweetheart."

A somberness takes over the room, thickening the air in my throat.

I nod, waving as I step out ahead of Noah, giving the two a moment alone.

By the time I've made it to the exit, he's at my side, stepping out into the cooled air with me.

We don't get much of winter here in Southern California, and when you've lived here for so long, you get used to the kind of cold we do have, so while there's a bite in the air, it's nothing our sweaters don't ease us from.

"Your mom is sweet."

"She's impossible," he teases.

Laughing, I slip in front of him, walking backward. "No more than mine."

He grins, but it doesn't reach his eyes.

I realize then how wrong I was before when he said his Sundays were booked, as did his beautiful blonde friend. It had nothing to do with her and everything to do with his mom, but he says his Sundays are fully booked, and his mom was exhausted after a two-hour visit. That means he leaves here every week and does the only thing he thinks he can. He goes home, alone, because after a few hours with the woman who gave him the world but can't quite function on her own anymore, a feeling of helplessness he can't escape weighs him down.

Not today, not when I think I can help take it away.

Inside the cab, I face him. "So, I know it's Sunday and all, and you have practice tomorrow, but it's early enough, and we're young . . ."

Noah chuckles, his head dropped back on his seat, but he points his eyes to mine. "What did you have in mind?"

"Pasco Bella Farms."

He squints, but there's a pinch of amusement in there.

"You know, the pumpkin patch? Where you eat turkey legs bigger than my biceps, drink warm beer, get lost in the corn maze . . ." I gape at him. "Have you never been?"

He grins, shaking his head.

"Well, that is just *wrong*. It's a must, so what do you say, Romeo?" I smirk. "You in?"

Noah stares at me for a long moment, the grin on his lips softening but never slipping. In the calmest, quietest of whispers, he says, "If you're in, I'm in."

My mouth opens, but nothing comes out, and Noah reaches over, guiding my hair behind my ear.

His hand lingers there a moment, his eyes still on mine. "You'll lead us?"

The pit of my stomach lets itself be known, his words weighing as I believe he intended, the double innuendo loud and clear.

He needs me to lead the way.

To the farm . . . and more.

"Lies." Noah dashes forward, tickling my stomach as I spin, evading his hands.

"I saw the terror in your eyes!" We duck under the chain aisle, dashing for the gate before the ride attendant closes it. "You, Noah Riley, got scared by a ten-year-old."

"A ten-year-old in a dress from a hundred years ago, blood on her face and a gash across her eye . . . who jumped out of nowhere."

"Yes, let's not forget all that," I tease, hopping up into the last cart for the corn maze ride.

Noah slips beside me, throwing his arm over the back of the cool metal. "How about we talk about how you *saw my eyes*, Juliet."

We jolt as the tractor driving the carts takes off, quickly facing each other once more.

"Go on."

He raises a dark brow. "Someone was too afraid to look around every corner of the haunted house she was so excited about."

"And someone else was more than willing to do it for me."

"Damn straight."

My toes bend in my shoes, and I lift my chin in triumph. "See, you wanted to be the tough guy who went first."

Noah's tongue rolls over his bottom lip, and he nods. "Yeah, I did."

"There's just . . . one problem with that."

He watches me closely. "And what's that?"

My pulse hammers against my neck, and then I whip around, jumping off the side and disappearing into the stalks of corn.

"What—Ari!" Noah shouts, and then his feet pound behind me.

I dash left, and then right, and then his large hands are wrapping around my biceps, and I'm twisted around.

I gasp, looking up into his blue eyes with a smile.

They narrow, smooth, and then his grip tightens.

I swallow, my chest heaving as I reach up, gliding my hands along his pecs.

"You asked me to lead."

His frown is instant, and he pushes closer, giving the subtlest shake of his head.

My skin flushes instantly, but I refuse to look away.

His blue eyes pierce mine, reaching way past the surface and into my mind. It's as if he's seeing every part of me. It's unnerving yet thrilling.

223

It's Noah.

I roam his every feature, from his liquid eyes to the growing stubble around his jaw and chin, a perfect five o'clock shadow. So manly, yet so soft. I reach out, the sharpness of the short hairs creating knots within my stomach. I peek up at him, but I didn't have to, to know his would be on me. They are.

They always are.

I trace his jaw, gliding my thumb along his chin, and then with shaky fingers, I trace his lips. I start with the bottom, following the curve with precision, and as I meet the corner, his heated breath breaks across my skin, my body shivering before him. For him.

Because of him.

I slide closer.

Noah doesn't move.

My hand moves lower, and I swallow as he does when my touch glides along his throat, to his neck, and down until I'm gripping the soft fabric of his cotton shirt. I pull him closer.

He moves willingly, but he doesn't push.

He waits.

As I lift to my toes, bringing my lips an inch away from his, a storm rages within his eyes, and they become the midnight blue I've come to love.

He doesn't crush his mouth into mine like I thought he might, doesn't press his mouth to mine at all. Noah stares.

He notes the flush of my cheeks, the rapid rise and fall of my chest, and the part of my eager lips, right here waiting for his.

Slowly, with the patience of a saint, he leans in, allowing his to float across my own. The sensation causes me to jump, and the corner of Noah's mouth lifts into a gorgeous, almost cocky, flawless grin.

My core tightens.

In the next second, he kisses me without kissing me, his lips pushing into mine with a pressurized softness I can't quite explain. It's heavy, weighted, while still managing a careful restraint, as if he's allowing me to be sure.

To change my mind.

To pull away.

I won't.

"You remember what I said to you?" he murmurs, the heat of his breath doing far more than it should. "One-time thing, Juliet."

He won't deny me again . . .

I don't want him to.

So, I lead.

I press against him, and that was all he needed.

His hands fly to my face, gripping me, hauling me closer, taking over with a thorough, drugging kiss.

My arms fly around his neck, fingers diving into his hair as his disappear into mine. One drops to my lower back, slipping beneath the hem of my shirt. His fingertips bite into my skin, and I moan into his mouth. His tongue dives inside, swooping and learning the taste of me, coaxing my own to dance with his. I give him what he wants and when he bites at my lip, I whimper.

"Goddamn," he groans, moans, and then his lips are on my neck, teasing. Testing.

I press on the back of his head, and he applies more pressure.

My eyes open on a gasp, pointed at the sky.

The sun has set, the moon is high above us, and the man sucking the sensitive spots on my skin is . . . *perfection.*

And then a light blinds me, and I yelp.

Noah jerks free, simultaneously pushing me behind him as his hand flies up to block the glow.

"Okay, you two, let's go." The security guard flicks his flashlight.

My skin flushes, not that it wasn't already, and I duck my head, allowing Noah to drag me behind him out of the cornfield.

As we cross the dirt path, loud cheers sound, and my head darts up to see the people in line cheering us on.

I look up at Noah, horrified, but when I get nothing but a bright smile back, we're soon laughing with them.

As we're walking away, I realize today was one of the best days I've had in a really long time, and I have Noah to thank for that.

I hung out with my friends and family, enjoying every second of it. It didn't hurt to see Chase, and there was no awkwardness to speak of. It felt normal. Good, and I have a feeling the man at my side is the reason for it.

After that, being with Noah's mom and the soft, loving way in which she spoke eased the homesickness I hadn't realized I was feeling. She is an honest, kind woman and sort of reminds me of my own mom.

And there's right now.

The high.

The kiss.

Noah.

I don't know what it means, but I know I want more.

Noah must feel the same because the moment the security leaves us, having waited until we reached Noah's truck, he grips me by the wrist and tugs me to him.

Noah swoops down, taking my lips with his own once more. "That's the second time security has chased us out of somewhere," he teases, speaking in the gentlest of tones. "What am I going to do with you?"

I press my mouth to his, whispering with a smile, "Whatever you want."

Chapter 23
Arianna

The entire common room is off their seat as Noah drops back, firing a perfect spiral from the opposing team's fifteen-yard line for an epic seventy-yard pass straight into Chase's arms.

Cameron and I scream, jumping up and down, tangling our hands together.

"Come on, come on!"

Our eyes fly across the screen, snapping from right to left as he jukes defender after defender, and then he's jumping up, throwing his arms out just enough to pass the goal line. It's touchdown Avix U.

We freak the fuck out, hugging and shouting and clapping.

"Holy shit, Ari! His first college touchdown!"

We grab our phones to take pictures as they go for a two-point conversion, officially taking the lead in the game with twenty seconds left on the clock.

We record a short video message, yelling and laughing as we spin, capturing the responses of the room around us, then quickly drop it into the group chat we have so they don't miss our reactions.

Cameron pours us a shot, and we throw it back, cheering as they get set to kick it off.

Cameron dances around, slipping close to whisper, "Let's get out of here before we get stuck helping them clean up."

"Good idea," I whisper back. "But first . . ." I slide over to the table, snagging a half-empty bottle, and together, we run down the hall.

227

"Yes, bitch!" Cameron calls, and as we're stepping into our room, the TV left on, the boys are taking the field in celebration of a win.

"Woo! Thank god. Noah needed this."

"Ah, Noah did, huh?" She wiggles her brows.

I flip her off, skipping into my bedroom and pulling my suitcase out from under my bed. I drag it into the living room, dropping it beside hers on the couch.

"Yes, asshole. He needed a raise in spirit."

"Honey, you rose his *spirit,* trust that," she teases, fully aware our Sunday was more than the physical activities she lives to attribute everything to.

I bump my shoulder with hers. "Okay, what are you packing for the trip?"

"Ugh!" She falls onto the armchair. "Do we have to? Can't we get drunk together and talk shit like the good ol' days?"

Rolling my eyes, I spin, grab the bottle and take a swig, passing it to her next.

"Fuck yes!" She pushes our suitcases off the couch and jumps up on the cushion. Cameron swaps over to Spotify on the TV, and we dance around, drinking and making up for all the time we've missed lately.

A half hour later, we're sitting on the floor, taking selfies and scrolling through social media, when my phone rings, my brother's name flashing across the screen.

"There he is!" We fumble with the screen, answering the FaceTime call to find the boys' sweaty faces, eye black smeared all down their cheeks.

"Fuck yes!" we scream, smiling wide enough to match theirs, and Mason and Brady wrap their arms around Chase's neck.

"You saw our fuckin' boy?!" Brady howls. "He caught that son of a bitch with one hand!"

"Hell yeah, he did. That's the strong hand, isn't it, Chase?" Cameron jokes.

Chase dips his head with a laugh, and Mason playfully punches him in the chest.

"You know it," Chase tells her, his eyes on me. "I got your message."

"Oh my god, you Mossed that guy!" I grin. "Wait until you watch the replay! You pretty much jumped over that guy's head!"

"How about I wait and watch it with you?"

My response freezes on my tongue, my abdomen sucking in. Chase chuckles then, pointing his eyes past the camera.

"We've been celebrating!" Cameron smiles, pulling the bottle in her hand in the camera's view.

"Damn!" Mason laughs at our near-empty bottle, moving closer to the phone, so we can hear him better through the growing noise in the background. "Don't get too fucked up. Road-trippin' into the mountains tomorrow night won't be fun if you do."

"To be fair, it was already half gone when we confiscated it from the game party."

"Booze thieves!" Brady accuses.

"Hey, we pitched in for the party favors. We just can't use our fake IDs at that mini-mart to buy the actual shit." Cameron giggles, taking another drink. "Why you think we're drinking watermelon vodka? Like we'd ever pick this out!"

"Is that their locker room?" I ask, leaning to the side as if I can peek around him.

"Dude, yeah, and I feel like a hillbilly in the Hamptons," Brady jokes.

"Here." Chase snags the phone from Mason. "Check it out!"

He turns the phone to face away from them, slowly dragging it along the room. As his team realizes we're on the screen, they whistle and play stripper with their gear, making Cam and me laugh.

"Meet this guy!" Chase quickly flips the phone back around until he and a shirtless, sweaty blond guy are in the shot. "If it weren't for his block, I'd have never hit the end zone."

"That and Noah's bomb of a pass!"

"Fucking right?!" The blond guy laughs, smacking Chase in the chest.

Chase licks his lips and looks away, Mason coming into view in the next second.

"Love you, baby sisters!" He grins. "See you tomorrow! We're getting fucked up!"

"Fuck yeah!" Cam throws her arms up.

"Bye!"

We smile, letting him be the one to end the call.

"Woo-hoo!" Cameron jumps up, dashing into the kitchen and pulling open the freezer. "Our boys are beasts, and I'm starved! Are these fettuccini bowls any good?"

"Stupid good. I'm talking Bella Italia good."

Cameron gasps. "No!"

"Yes."

"All hail the cooking quarterback," she teases. "Come help me."

Pulling up my message thread, I send Noah a quick text.

Me: hey MVP! CONGRATS on a killer game! That pass was highlight gold!

Me: PS Cam is about to get a taste of your alfredo! Be prepared for the aftermath. My girl is not above begging.

I toss my phone, skipping into the kitchen with Cameron.

A half hour or so later, we're stuffed, our drunken haze begins its transition into exhaustion, and we're dropping onto our beds, but two more hours go by, and I'm still awake, so I pick up my phone.

Noah messaged me back while we were eating, saying thanks and that he'd call me tomorrow; they were just getting loaded onto the bus for the long night's drive home.

I text him now anyway.

Me: Are you awake?

He responds almost instantly.

Romeo: I am.

Me: I thought for sure you would have crashed from adrenaline.

Romeo: Nah, I don't sleep well after games. Takes me a long time to knock out. Pretty sure the rest of the bus is out cold. The lights have been off since we hit the highway.

Me: Do you have headphones?

I grin, knowing he's smirking on the other side.

Romeo: I do. Do you have a turtleneck on?

A laugh spurts out of me, and I don't hesitate.

I hit call on FaceTime.

It takes him a few rings to answer, and when he does, he lifts his finger to his lips. Noah slips his earbuds in, shifting, so his body is wedged half against the window, half against the seat.

He pulls his hood up to get more comfortable, the thick gray cotton now pressed against his cheekbones, accentuating the sharpness of his features and casting a low shadow off of his lips. But every few seconds, the window provides a low flicker of light, allowing me to see all of him. It's like watching a thriller, nothing more than a quick flicker of clear sight to get your blood pumping.

Finally, he grins.

"I wish you weren't so far." The words slip from me before I even realize how true they are.

His eyes flick to mine and hold. "Oh yeah?"

Heat spreads through me, and I nod. "Yeah."

Noah rolls his tongue across his bottom lip, drawing my attention to his mouth. "And why's that?"

"Because you can't sleep, and I can't sleep." I smile. "We could *not* sleep together."

Noah's chuckle is low, and he lifts the neck of his hoodie up, slowly gliding the material between his teeth. "I'll be home in eight hours."

"Sorry, invitation expires in seven."

His lips curve to the side, his eyes low and tired. "Of course it does." He pauses, then quietly asks, "You all packed for your trip?"

"We finished a bottle of cheap liquor instead."

He laughs, shaking his head.

"I'm not worried about it. We're not fancy campers. Sweats, shorts, and sweatshirts are basically it. And ponytails. As long as we have some shit in our bags when the boys are ready, we're good."

"You leave right after we get back?"

"We do." I fight a smile. "We want to have as much time there as we can, and it's a few hours away."

He nods, glancing out the side window. "I should let you get to sleep then. You don't want to be hungover on the drive," he repeats what Mason said earlier.

"Yeah, been there, done that." A yawn works its way up my throat, and I scoot down on my pillow, re-angling my phone and propping it up with some smashed blankets.

Noah's eyes leave my face then, and while I'm not quite sure what parts of me he can see, he twists his entire torso, positioning himself fully against the bus wall, drawing his phone even closer. "Okay, I really need to go."

To be playful, I stretch out even more, so my top rides up my hip a little higher.

"Juliet." He warns with a frown. "I'm stuck on this bus with thirty-three other men for the next seven hours, won't see you for another seventy-two after that. Hang up."

A light chuckle leaves me, and I smile. "Good night, quarterback."

Noah's eyes grow soft, the corner of his mouth lifting. "Night, beautiful."

My entire body breaks out in a cool chill, an airy sensation working its way through me. I wave, but I don't hit end, somehow knowing he won't either, and he doesn't.

I pull my covers up to my chin, tucking my hands under my pillow, and his head falls against the glass.

I close my eyes and fall asleep.

As he said he would, Mason texted me his location when their bus was almost at their exit, also reminding us we better start packing now if we hadn't already—he knows us so well, we literally finished packing less than five minutes before his message came through.

The plan is for them to rush home for showers and their bags and to be loading ours up in Mason's Tahoe no more than an hour later, which works, but I'm hoping it goes a little differently.

I lean against the tree, pulling up Mason's location to find they're coming down the road just in front of campus, and a few seconds later, the large blue and gold bus is turning into the parking lot. It's only stopped for a few seconds before the doors open, and the team begins pouring out.

Pushing off, I move closer.

I spot my brother first, and a hint of anxiousness slips in, tightening my ribs.

He moves right for the hatch the driver just opened and starts moving bags around in search of his.

It's Brady who spots me first.

"Ari baby!" he shouts, and several heads glance my way, but they quickly go back to whatever it is they were doing. He jogs over, unable to wait for me to reach him on my own, and pulls me into a hug. "You ready for some fuck-off time?"

"I am." I smile, turning to hug my brother when he makes his way over, a slight frown on his face.

"What are you doing here?" He looks behind me. "Where's Cameron and your bags?"

"She's in the shower, but we're ready."

He nods, his frown deepening, and that's when he looks at my hoodie. His eyes come up to mine, but Chase steps between him and Brady before he can say anything.

His smile is wide, and he comes forward for a hug, as the other two had.

"You came," he says, stepping back. "Tell me you've got the clip? I waited for you."

I scowl but quickly realize what he meant. His touchdown. *Wait, he was serious?*

"I . . . don't. Only the reaction video we sent."

He licks his lips with a grin. "It's cool, should be on Huddle by tomorrow. We can watch it in the mountains."

"Yeah, sure." I nod, leaning slightly to see behind him. The people exiting are coming slower now.

"So what's up?" He glances from Mason to me. "You coming to the house with us?"

"Oh, no, I was—"

I cut off when Noah comes into view.

He's stepping down the bus stairs in a gray Avix U sweatsuit, nearly identical to the one I'm wearing. His hand lifts, and he pushes his hood from his head, running his palm over the back of his hair.

His left foot hits the blacktop, and the second his right comes down to meet it, his eyes are pulled left. Right to me.

He pauses in place, and a low laugh leaves me.

I face the boys, a hint of pink washing over my neck.

"You invited some others, right?" I ask Mason.

His eyes tighten at first, but then he nods.

He steps forward, sighing against my hair as he presses a kiss there. "Yeah, baby sister. I did."

Chase scowls at my sweater, noting the large number nineteen on the sleeve. His eyes come up to mine, narrowing, but as the boys begin to turn, heading for their bags, he follows. Finally, I break away, making my way to Noah.

At first, Noah doesn't move, his head following my brother and the boys, but then slowly returning to me. It takes him a moment, but his attention finally falls to the hoodie I'm wearing, and his eyes snap up to mine. He gets it, that I didn't come for them.

I came for him.

His backpack falls to the ground where he stands, and he erases the last two steps between us.

Before he reaches me, I spin, showing him the back, where his number is boldly printed, but he knows that. After all, he's the one who gave me the hoodie.

I throw my arms out, peeking at him over my shoulder. "Does this count as me wearing it to a game?"

His lips curve up, and he gives a slow shake of his head. "Not a chance."

I spin again, now facing him fully, and step closer. "Does it count for something?"

Noah reaches out, gripping the front of the hoodie, and tugs me to him. He whirls me around until we're half hidden by the open door, his hand gliding into my hair. "You already know the answer to that," he says, and then he's kissing me.

His lips move masterfully, seeking entrance he knows I won't deny, the heated strength of his tongue sending the pit of my stomach into a wild whirl.

As fast as he takes control, he pulls away, and then his pants are in my ear. I only grow hotter, knowing I'm the one who stole the air from his lungs.

"You kill me, you know that?" His chest heaves against mine, and I flatten my palm against it. "Fucking kill me." His lips glide along my cheek until he finds my mouth again.

This time it's a single, soft, slow kiss.

When my eyes finally open, he's already pulled back, bright eyed and excited, but there's a hint of something else in there, too. I'm not sure what it is, but it disappears the moment I say, "Come with us."

His frown is instant. "What?"

"Camping," I tell him nervously. "I knew you'd be exhausted from the game and the drive, and I sort of convinced myself you'd say yes if I asked, so I didn't want to ask you *before* you left, in case you did say yes, and then were too tired to go, but still came just to keep your word, which is a very Noah thing to do, by the way." I pause for a breath, and his lips twitch. "So yeah, I wanted to wait until today, be here to welcome you back, and ask you to leave with me. I kind of figured it was best to ask *after* you'd been gone . . . hoping you didn't want me to be."

"I don't want you to be." His response is instant, and I let out the heavy breath I was apparently holding.

My smile is wide, and I let my head rest against the bus behind me. "So, you'll come?"

"I told you once, Juliet, I won't deny you again." He pushes closer, whispering, "You want me there, I'm there."

"Looks like you're going camping then. You can share my tent."

His gaze rapidly rakes over my face, and he grabs my hands, pulling me back around the bus. "Then we better go get me packed."

I nod, locking our fingers tighter as he walks us backward.

"For the record . . ." Noah pauses, and then he says something I had no idea I needed to hear until the words are wrapping around me. "I would have kissed you in front of everyone if I knew for sure you'd be okay with it, and that is the *only* reason I pulled you aside."

My heartbeat hammers in my chest, and I open my mouth to speak, but nothing comes out.

Noah wants me, and he isn't afraid to show it.

He doesn't care who knows it . . . so long as I do.

I do, Noah.

Noah reads me like an open book and winks as he releases me, grabbing his backpack from where he dropped it. He then jogs over to snag his football bag from the pile set out along the side of the bus.

Mason walks up, a little uneasy. "I take it you're riding with Noah, then?"

"Yeah."

While his jaw is set firm, he nods, spins, and calls his name.

When Noah turns our way, Mason salutes him.

"Crash on the way up the hill with my sister, and I'll have to fuck you up."

I roll my eyes, but Noah only grins.

236

"I crash with your sister, and I'll let you."

I chuckle, and Mason scoffs beside me.

We face each other.

"I could take him." He glares, but his grin slips. "See you at the house?"

"Yep."

He jogs over to Brady's truck, where Chase stands, arms folded over his chest, his hip pressed against the cab.

His eyes brush past mine, and he kicks off, climbing into the bed.

Off they go. Noah and me not far behind.

Chapter 24

Noah

We arrived at Mount San Jacinto a couple hours ago, and the second our feet hit the dirt, we started setting up for the weekend.

I helped Brady unload the barbecue and ice chests from the back of his truck while Mason and Chase got to work on the tents. Cameron and Ari grabbed the rakes they brought and started clearing out the brush, piling it up at the edge of the campsite. The girls popped up a couple tables, and just as Brady and I got the propane tanks hooked up and headed to help with the rest of the tents, Ari intercepted me.

"Noah will start on the food." She looks to me with a proud grin, tugging me toward the bins stacked near the road.

"The things inside this bad boy are all you've got to work with, Chef Riley." She lifts the top one, pushing it into my arms. "Think you can make some magic?"

My hands lock around it, but she doesn't let go. "I haven't seen what's in it yet . . ."

"The magic is in the man, not his tools."

"I hardcore disagree." Cam skips by, snagging the smaller container to the side.

Ari laughs, looking to me as she steps back, and together, we walk the bins down into the campsite. We drop them at the edge of the tables, pushing the one we don't need yet beneath it, and she leaves me to dig through them while she shuffles left to turn on the grill.

Cameron slips over, tying down plastic tablecloths, and then pauses to watch while I do what I can with the seasoning available.

"Okay, Noah." She grins at the foil pan, setting some napkins beside me before she walks away.

It's not too much later when I'm pulling the first few of the chicken legs from the flame, right as several sets of headlights reach the camp from the road above. And just like that, it's a party.

Beers are passed around, more tents are popped up, and by the time everyone has arrived and eaten, there's still a tin full of meat for people to come back to later.

The sun went down an hour ago, and the fire's burning high.

I sit back, watching the others chat and laugh for several minutes, realizing this is the first time in a long-ass time I've stepped away from life.

Damn, if I didn't need it, and I don't believe for a second Ari didn't know it.

She knew, and I didn't.

When she told me she was going camping this weekend, I tried not to think about it when, in reality, it was all I could think about.

Her leaving.

Him being there . . .

A frown pulls at my brows, but I shake it off.

I didn't expect her to ask me to come, not even a little bit, so when she did, I didn't care to think past the fact that she wanted me here.

Because what matters outside of that?

Not a damn thing.

Ari laughs at something someone says, smiling as she swipes the hair from her face, and I can't help but grin.

Sneaking away a moment, I head to my truck, using an old water bottle to rinse my hands and grab the hoodie from the front seat, pulling it on. Despite Ari's offer to share her tent, which I'm almost positive Cameron is also sleeping in, I brought the one I won in a raffle at last year's Award Gala. It had never been opened but was nice and easy to set up. It's a pop-up style, designed for the bed of my truck. It took two minutes to open and tie down, and I brought my mattress pad from home for a bed.

Locking the cab once more, I head back to the campgrounds, and as I step back into the campsite, my eyes immediately find her.

She's in the back of Brady's truck now, singing and dancing around with Cameron and a couple others I don't know. The crazy girl's in shorts and a T-shirt, her shoes kicked off somewhere. Her hair is up in a ponytail, the tips brushing over her back where her top's lifted a bit. She's relaxed in her element, laughing and swaying to the beat, a half-empty Corona in her hand.

Sensing me near, she finds me over her shoulder.

She spins instantly, her body facing me now, a big, beautiful smile on her soft lips, but she doesn't stop dancing. Her hips continue to sway as she beckons me with the crook of her finger, a gleam in her October eyes.

I make my way to her, slow and deliberate.

I want her to feel me coming.

I want her body to heat all over in anticipation.

I know it will.

Once I'm in reach, her soft little hand stretches out, asking for mine.

When I make her wait an extra second, her chin dips all shy-like, and if the glow of the fire wasn't lighting her up, I'd get to witness the way she flushes pink for me.

I hop up into the bed of Brady's truck, a smirk pulling at my lips as I take her hand in mine, but I don't have to haul her to me. She steps in on her own and without a moment's hesitation.

A little hazy from the beer and a half she's treated herself to, she looks up at me, and I lift my thumb, freeing her bottom lip from her teeth. A closed-mouth giggle works its way up her throat, and she pushes up on her toes, her hands loosely locking behind my neck.

"For the record," she repeats my earlier words with a smile. "You can kiss me anywhere you want."

I lift a brow at her playful words, but we both know what she means.

I can kiss her when I feel like it, no matter where we are, no matter who is around, and this girl . . . she'll kiss me right back.

Unable to wait any longer, I push my hood off my head and dip down, covering her lips with my own.

She smiles against my mouth, her grip tightening. Her heavy inhale has me pulling back, but not before I press my teeth into her lower lip. She chuckles, opening her eyes to meet mine.

"Any more, and this would turn into something nobody else gets to see." I press my thumb to her throat, my pulse jumping at the wild beat of hers.

Ari grins and starts rolling her hips again, so I follow her lead, bringing my hands down until they're tucked into the back pockets of her shorts.

We're dancing to the upbeat music, perfect for the bonfire, but I'm not even hearing it.

She mustn't either, because her chin falls to my chest then, her soft whispers reaching my ear as she sings to herself, but the lyrics coming from her don't match the ones from the speakers.

She's listening to that internal jukebox of hers, singing along to the song looping in her mind, Luke Bryan's "Play It Again," and I couldn't agree more.

I want to relive the night with her ten times over and then do it again. And again. It's simple and small, but it's perfect.

She is perfect.

Ari pulls back, so she can look up at me, the golden flecks in her eyes catching against the moonlight and reflecting against my own. It may as well be only her and me up here.

She's all I see.

My Juliet.

Chapter 25
Arianna

Morning comes quickly and early, as it always does out here. Late fall or not, the sun beams against the mesh of tents, demanding your eyes open to appreciate the space around you.

Thankfully, last night wasn't too late of one, and that's because pretty much every single person here plays on the team—minus the girls—so they were barely hanging on when they first arrived. The mountains, though, always offer a second wind, which they ate up, only to crash twice as hard once their buzzes wore down.

"Thank god Brady is smart and only put out half the beer last night." Cameron yawns, flicking on the generator.

"You mean, thankfully, he learned from experience to hide alcohol or be ready for a sober night two?" I laugh, arranging a few logs into the dead firepit.

"That is exactly what I mean."

Cameron gets the coffee going while I take an empty Corona box over to the pile of brush, scooping some up and tossing it over the logs to help kick-start it.

"Smart."

I look up and over my shoulder, smiling at Noah. "Hey."

"Hey." He grins, looking around and coming back with the long-wicked lighter.

He crouches beside me but hands it over, and I glide it beneath the brush, between the logs.

"Camp a lot, huh?" He watches.

"Four or five times a year, yeah. More if you count all the times we put up a tent on the sand at the beach house," I share. "It was always funny when we'd head to the mountains because my dad would have me help him collect wood or climb the ladder to hang the towel line while Mason would be cracking eggs for my mom or helping her peel potatoes." I pause, chuckling as I look at Noah. "Now that I think about it, they were probably afraid I'd somehow burn the forest down if I helped with the cooking."

Pushing to his feet, he tugs me with him. "Good thing you're learning your way around a stove then, huh?"

"Fantastic thing." I go for the dramatics, fluttering my lashes.

Noah shakes his head with a grin and heads for Cam. "Can I help?"

"You can." She pushes him a few feet left, dropping a couple of Ziploc bags of already cut potatoes in front of him. "Toss them in some oil and—"

"Season them?" he cuts her off.

Cameron smiles, digging the creamer out of the ice chest. "I forgot. Bobby Flay is boning my bestie."

"Cameron!" I laugh, and while Noah's doesn't reach my ears, his shoulders shake slightly, giving him away.

"Sorry, I meant *dreaming* of boning my bestie. Better?"

"Oh my god." I cover my face.

"I bet that's *exactly* what you'll say."

This time, Noah's head falls back with his laugh, and all I can do is flip her off when she turns my way. The only reason I don't cuss her out is because she's bringing me a Styrofoam cup of steaming coffee.

"Asshole," I whisper.

"Love you, too." She does *not* whisper.

A tent's zipper opening sounds around us, and a few stragglers tumble out with wild hair and sleepy eyes, the smell of hot coffee likely the only reason they didn't roll back over.

"Noah, my man," a big, burly guy steps up, snagging a water from one of the ice chests. "You a jack-of-all-trades, or what?"

"He is, Georgie," Cameron calls him by what must be his name. "The C isn't only for captain. It's for capable cook and considerable—"

"Cameron!" I warn, and then large arms are around me.

I look up to find Brady.

He kisses my hair and finishes Cameron's sentence like the shithead he is. "Cock."

"Don't encourage her."

"I'm just speaking truths, Ari baby. I've seen it in the showers," he teases, laughing when Noah's head snaps our way.

"That's it, Lancaster, you're last to hit the locker room," Noah jokes.

"I'm good with that, brother. I love to be the last thing the reporter girls see. Makes it easier to remind them who I am when they show up ready to party later that night."

I roll my eyes, saying hello to the guys who start to pile around the morning fire.

A few others fire up grills of their own, some passing off breakfast items to Cameron and Noah to contribute to the meal they've got going.

Chase and Mason emerge from their tents then, and neither climb out alone.

A small frown builds along my brow before I can help it, and I look away, confused by the numbness the sight offers.

Facing the fire, I'm taking small sips of my coffee, and Mason squeezes his chair between a guy named Hector and me. My brother drops his head back, giving me a pouty lip.

My sigh is playful as I climb to my feet.

Noah's eyes flick my way, watching as I grab two cups, filling them with coffee, one with a splash of creamer, the other with a spoonful of sugar. I toss a grape at him, and he grins, going back to mixing pancake batter.

I move toward Mason, passing his off first before walking over to where Chase sits on Brady's tailgate. He runs his fingers through his brown hair, nodding at something the guy to his right says.

As I approach, he looks up, and a grin pulls at his lips. "A spoonful of sugar . . ."

"Helps the nasty shit go down," I finish his sentence, and he chuckles, slowly taking it from my hands. "Thanks, gorgeous."

I freeze a moment but quickly force a tight smile as I turn away. "Yep."

With slow-paced steps, I find my cup and retake my seat, not looking up from the fire again after that, so as soon as Cameron announces the food is ready, I pop up, eager to help get paper products set up for everyone. Standing at the backside of the table, I adjust the trays as people shuffle down the length of it, loading their plates. I figure I'll wait until everyone else is settled before I snag my own, but then Noah's arms are coming around me from behind, and a plate is held out in front of me, the stack of mini pancakes steaming and fresh off the grill.

I peer up at him, and he nods toward the plate, pressing into me slightly to grab a fork from beside me. He stabs it into the top one and leaves the fork there for me to grab.

"Taste."

I do as he says, not taking my eyes off his as I bring it to my lips for a bite. The buttermilk flavor hits my tastebuds, and they come alive when a hint of something sweet follows.

My expression must give away my mouthgasm, because he grins.

"If you add a little shake of brown sugar into the batter, you don't have to drown it with syrup."

"Maybe I like to drown it with syrup."

"Says the girl who likes her potpies nice and flaky, her chicken breaded, and her cornbread with a crisp."

I laugh, my hand coming up to cover the large bite I've yet to swallow. "Okay, fine. You're right. I hate soggy food."

"I know."

"Just like you know you've hit the spot yet again. So good."

"Good. Maybe we'll have to add a breakfast into our menu somewhere."

I spin, whispering, "Would this be a breakfast for dinner kind of thing or . . ."

His smirk is slow. "Or . . ."

I swat him in the chest. "Don't make me say it."

He chuckles and turns to help Cam when she calls him over to the stove.

After eating, everyone hangs around and chats until some people head back in their tents for a nap while the rest of us play a couple games of cards, as another handful of guys begin tossing the football around.

We spend a few hours out on a hike, showing everyone the rock pathways and the small bridge that leads to the opposite side of the mountain.

The rest of the day plays out the same, and only when the sun begins to set, Mason now on the grill, do I bend down behind Noah, who sits sipping on a beer and chatting to a group of guys.

I bring my lips to his ear so only he can hear. "There's a path I purposely avoided today."

Noah tips his head a little, so he can see me, and I drape one arm over him, my fingers tapping along his chest.

"Oh, yeah?" he drawls quietly, his hand coming up to grab mine.

"Mm-hm." I nod, pressing my forehead to his temple. "What do you say, you up for a little walk in the dark?"

Noah answers by setting his water bottle down and pushing to his feet. He slips his hand in mine, and I smile, leading our way.

We curl around the campsite, dropping lower into the trees, and weave around a small trail of rocks. Large bushes block the view, but as we get a little farther, pushing past the thin branches, there it is.

The waterfall leading into a small pool of water, rock walls curling from left to right, closing it off from everything around it.

"Man," Noah says, and I nod, moving closer.

This being the only area around not overlaid with treetops, the stars are visible, creating a glow around us, allowing us to trust our eyes among the darkness.

I slip my shoes and socks off, dipping my toes in the water. It's cold, but not nearly as cold as the ocean, since we've only just come off of summer. A moment later, Noah's at my side.

He steps in a little farther. "I was expecting it to be freezing."

"Not so bad, huh?" I grin, and when he faces away, I shove him a bit, but he's a quarterback and quick on his feet.

No more than his ankle dips in before he's circled me completely, now positioned at my back with his arms locked tightly around my abdomen.

"What was that, Ms. Johnson?" He smiles against my ear. "Your way of telling me you want to go for a swim?"

I tense, squirming in his hold as he inches me forward. "No, no, no!" I laugh. "Hell no."

"But I thought you loved the water?" he teases.

I squeal, my calves now wet. "Oh my god, Noah, I can't!"

"Why not?"

I push into him, trying to find some ground to use as leverage. "I don't do water where I can't see the bottom!"

He buries his face in my neck, and my muscles settle the slightest bit. "What if your feet don't touch the ground?"

"What—"

Noah spins me, bends, and lifts me up. In the next second, we're waist-deep in the chilled water, clothes and all.

I scream with a laugh, hiding my eyes in his chest, my arms and legs clenching around him. Something brushes my thigh, and I scream again, holding on impossibly tight.

"You are so dead. Wait until I get you in the ocean. I'm sticking crabs down your trunks!"

His soft chuckle wafts over my skin, his arms gliding along my back and keeping me close. "I've got you."

"You better."

His lips curve against my neck, and then they press there. Lightly at first but growing firmer by the second.

My legs tighten around him, my toes curling behind his back as he sucks the sensitive skin there, and just like that, the dark waters are forgotten.

My head lifts, and it's only a moment before his follows.

His eyes, a deep midnight blue tonight, are teeming with desire, and behind that, a hopeful tenderness that reaches deep within me.

I feel it, too, the invisible pull from my body to his.

My mind to his.

My heart to his?

I lean forward, taking his lips with my own.

He kisses me back with the same vigor. Our tongues tying, our deep, full breaths turning to quick, short pants, and my body begins to roll.

Noah groans, lifting us a few inches out of the water as he fights to bring us closer, his eagerness in line with my own.

"Careful, Juliet," he warns, steeling my hips with his large, firm hands. "I'm about to lose my gentleman's card here."

"Could you hurry up with that?"

He chuckles into my mouth, and I push my tongue inside his, swallowing the rumble that follows. He whips us around, splashing through the water until we're at the edge of a rock. He presses my ass against it, his hands leaving my body so he can grab hold of my cheeks, making me dizzy with his kiss.

I lean back, taking him with me, and then something glides along the bottom of my foot, and I squeal, jumping backward.

Noah tears back, eyes wide and flying across my face

"Oh my god, a fish is trying to eat me!" I yelp, scurrying farther up the rock, and as I plant my hand down once more, something tickles the tips of my knuckles. I yelp again, jumping down, only to sink up to my neck.

Noah starts busting up laughing, turns, and hauls me up on his back as he takes us to the edge.

It's only seconds before I'm laughing uncontrollably, and as we hit the cold, dry ground, I drop back onto a tree log, my face falling into my hands.

"Ugh!" I can't simmer myself down, and Noah's as enter- tained as I am. "I swear a fish sucked my toe!"

He rubs his mouth to quiet his laughter. "And your hand?"

"Okay, that might have been a leaf or something." His head falls back with laughter. "In the moment, I was positive it was the Loch Ness Monster!" I grin, shaking my head.

"She swims in shark waters with ease, but a tiny tadpole? Forget about it."

I scowl at him playfully, and a small chill runs over me, the mountain breeze having rolled up over the rocks.

"We should head back, get changed." Noah slips his shoes on, stuffing his socks into his pockets, and picks up mine.

He spins again, reaching over his shoulder for my hand, so I stand, giving it to him. Once again, he hauls me onto his back and carries me all the way back to camp.

As we step into the clearing, a few people glance our way.

"What in the actual hell?" Brady shouts, his beer frozen at his lips.

"We fell in a pond," I joke.

"Uh-huh, vagina first or what?" He pops a brow.

Mason slaps the back of his head. "What the fuck, bro?" He glares from him to us, but Brady simply laughs and goes back to his conversation.

Mason's glare deepens, but I, too, look away, and Noah keeps moving toward the row of tents.

"Cameron is going to kill me if I get our beds wet." I grin, tightening my hold around his neck.

"Wanna change in my truck? It's blocked by Brady's." He stops walking, glancing over his shoulder. "We can walk back. Ask her to get you some clothes really fast?"

My teeth clatter. "Okay."

Despite my response, Noah keeps moving straight, his pace picked up a little more. Thirty seconds later, I'm sitting on his tailgate, and he's tearing into the cab of his truck, coming back with a pile of clothes in his hands.

"These are compression pants. I wear them under my gear when it's cold. They might be a little loose, but they'll fit you better than my sweats." He sets a T-shirt and hoodie beside me, a pile of dry clothes for himself bunched under his arm.

He pushes his shoes to the side, doing a double take when I lift my arms and wait.

His brows draw together slightly, the items in his arms quickly forgotten. He lets them fall to the ground and steps toward me.

He starts at the cuff of my sleeves, gently tugging them over my wrists, and moves to the hem next. The wet material has molded to my T-shirt beneath it, so as he slowly lifts it up and over my head, it takes it with it.

My wet hair falls to my bare back then, sending a shiver down my spine, or maybe it's the beaming approval in Noah's gaze that does it. He doesn't look away as he hangs my wet items over the side of his truck, nor when I lean back, my palms pressing into the tailgate, my torso stretching.

He understands, his jaw flexing with his heavy inhale as his hands find the button of my jeans.

My pulse pounds as it's popped open, the soft hum of my zipper creating goose bumps along my legs. He waits, eyes on me, so I lift my hips in request, and he answers, cautiously freeing me of them altogether.

His arms fall to his sides, his body going still as he peers at me, his expression a pensive mix of uncertainty and conviction.

I push up into a sitting position, scooting closer to the edge once more, and grab a handful of his soiled sweatshirt. My legs part and he steps in until his thighs meet the cool metal. He doesn't say a word, doesn't move, other than the way my freeing him of his clothes requires.

My lungs swell as his body comes into view, his chest on full display for me for the very first time. Even on the beach, he wore a shirt that hid it.

"You should take your shirt off more often." My breath is a throaty, desire-filled mess, and I'm pleased when his chuckle sounds just the same.

My eyes fly straight for the tattoo I've admittedly fantasized about.

I wondered how it would curve, what it would hold and how far it reached, but seeing it along his skin is like nothing I could have cooked up.

It's fascinating, dark, and defined.

It spans from his upper arm and stretches along his left peck. There's a goal line and a football that looks as if it's tearing through from inside his skin, but it's the script curved along the threading of the ball that calls to me. It's foreign, Latin, maybe, and beautifully scrolled.

"What does this mean?" I wonder, hesitantly lowering the pads of my fingers to his skin, tracing over the words in slow motion.

"Can't tell you." He shivers, and my lips twitch, my palms flattening over him as I lean closer.

"Can't or won't?" I peek up at him as I press my lips to his chest, scooting more to the edge so I can skate them higher.

I glide along his collarbone to his neck, pausing when I reach his ear. I take a deep breath, and Noah's forehead falls to my shoulder, his hands finding the space at my sides.

I don't say anything, just breathe against him as my touch dares to go lower. I trace the ridges of his abs, getting acquainted with every cut of his masterfully constructed muscles.

He's hard in all the right places, and I'd bet if I went lower, I'd find him hard there too.

I can sense it in the way his abdomen clenches, in the short puffs breaking along my bare chest.

My nipples harden in my bra, and now I'm the one shivering.

That gains Noah's attention, and his head lifts, the heat in his eyes almost unbearable. "It's getting colder."

"I don't feel cold."

His nostrils flare, and he dips down, gripping my hair in his hands and twisting it over his fist, water dripping down his forearm and splattering onto my spine. I jolt forward, and Noah twists to catch my lips with his own. He kisses me hard this time. It's almost in punishment and completely fucking addicting.

"It'll be my fault if you get sick." He speaks between swipes of his tongue. "I can't have that." He reaches for the hoodie beside us, the one he brought out for me, but I dart my hand over his to pause his movements and snag the one he intends to wear first.

He gives a small warning glare, but when my husky chuckle follows, his need to know what comes next has him relenting. With a tight frown, he allows me to pull his over him.

He quickly shoves his arms inside, swiping mine up and preparing to do the same, but I drop my palms onto the tailgate once more and begin scooting backward. I don't stop until my fingers scratch against the nylon of his tent.

His brows dip low as I blindly find the zipper, my hand gliding along until it's over my head, the opening falling against my back.

Noah's jaw tics as he kicks out of his wet bottoms, quickly stepping into his dry pair. He fists the clothes he has for me, and then he's crawling over me, with me, as I guide us into his tent completely.

Still slightly uncertain, he's slow to close us inside, and I want to erase his hesitation that I know only stems from his concern for me because I somehow feel none.

I'm not embarrassed, unsure, or anxious.

I don't have that twist in my gut that's warning me away as if afraid he'll *push* me away.

He would never.

Looking at him, into his blue eyes, my mind isn't muddled. It's calling his name.

There's something about Noah that frees me. With a single look or unspoken notion, he settles parts of me I don't know need settling, and while I don't fully understand it yet, I know I want to.

And right now, I want to get to know him a little better. A little . . . differently.

I fall back onto his pillow, and he follows. While his body hovers over mine, no part of our skin is touching, but the heat of him is present, and a ripple of anticipation works its way through me.

"What are you doing, Juliet?" he murmurs, his eyes falling to my breasts, half spilling over, free from my wet bra.

Tension knots inside me, creating an ache in my chest, and instead of answering with words, I slip a hand behind my back and unclasp it, but I don't take it off. I pull my hand out, letting him decide what to do next.

Noah shifts his weight to one side, his knuckles coming up to glide along my shoulder as his finger hooks under my strap.

"You want me to touch you?" He slides lower.

A small moan works its way up my throat, and Noah pulls the garment from my body, my hands coming back down to grip the sleeping bag beneath me.

My breasts are bared to him, and he takes his time raking his gaze over every inch of me, his attention serving as a heated caress, as do the slow, deliberate exhales fanning along my skin.

His mouth meets my breastbone then, and I pull in a harsh breath.

"Tell me where." His command is gentle, and my nipples turn to sharp points.

My body heats, skin flushing, and Noah peeks at me through his full, dark lashes.

My lips part, and his pull to one side.

"There it is," he rasps. "That's what I was waiting for. The blush." His touch creates a fiery path up my stomach and doesn't stop there. It trails higher until his hand is gently stretched along my throat. I swallow against him, and his fingers twitch in response.

His eyes snap to mine, and he repeats himself. "Tell me where."

I play our game. "You already know the answer to that."

"But . . ." He bites at my stomach, and I squirm.

But he wants me to say it.

Empowered by his mischievous way, I do him one better.

I guide his hand down my torso in an unhurried fashion, and I don't stop the tips of his fingers dipping beneath the hem of my underwear.

That's where I leave him, because while I might not know Noah in this way . . . I *know* Noah.

His eyes snap to mine, narrowing, and I can't suppress the giggle working its way up my throat.

"There."

His features flash with praise, and with that one look, the spark in my core grows to a full-fledged flame. He knows it and fuels the fire, his mouth coming down on my right nipple, clamping over me in retaliation. His lips begin to vibrate, and I squirm.

My legs come up, rubbing together in an attempt to ease the ache, and the move has his hand slipping farther south. That does it.

Noah drives his touch lower, his fingers coming together, so he doesn't miss a single sliver of skin on his way down. He cups me first, applying a teasing amount of pressure with his palm.

My eyes close, his tongue now swirling around my hard peaks as he pushes up onto his knees. He drags his wet lips across my skin, giving equal attention to my left nipple.

His hand skates lower, his chest rumbling as the tip of his pointer finger meets my slit.

"Fuck," he croaks. "Open."

My legs fall instantly.

His touch is hot and strong. I need—

His mouth crashes against mine, cutting off my thoughts yet answering them as he rasps, "I'm about to feel you. I'm gonna find out how warm you are, how soft . . ."

No sooner than he says it, he's there, pushing into me with slow precision.

My moan is instant.

"So fucking soft." He bites my lip. "So wet." My jaw.

When his hand retracts, my eyes fly open, my core straining from the loss, but then his finger disappears between his lips.

His eyes flare, and I nearly choke on air. "So fucking sweet."

I need to come.

His mouth moves back to mine, and he whispers, "You're about to."

His fingers drive back inside, dipping in and out as his thumb presses my clit, his lips playing like a rake against my body. He's on my chest, my ribs.

He's everywhere.

I need more.

I whimper, lifting my hips, willing him deeper, and my god does Noah give me what I want.

He pushes in until the pressure of his hand is hard against my entrance.

"Kiss me," I murmur, my eyes pinching shut. I moan again, blindly seeking out the warmth of his skin. My hands glide up his pecs, and I start to shake. "Now, Noah."

He groans, giving me what I want, working my clit over and over, squeezing, pressing, and then holding as my body writhes beneath him, swallowing the sounds coming up from my throat. Sounds I've never heard myself make.

Sounds that drive him mad, creating fireworks between my legs.

Noah's hand leaves me, but his kiss doesn't.

It deepens, hardens until I cry into his mouth, and then it slows as if in tune with my orgasm. As if he knew the high my body would reach and the slow, sated comedown it would bring me to.

That *he* would bring me to.

Noah lies down beside me, but I don't open my eyes, not yet, and it's only moments later that he begins playing with the wet strands of my hair.

The need to see him becomes too strong, and as if he senses the second I look at him, his eyes slowly lift to mine.

I blush like crazy, and the man smirks, a low chuckle slipping from his swollen lips.

He sits up then, grabbing the long-forgotten clothes he brought me, and he tugs me into a sitting position, pulling the hoodie over my head. His fingers skim along my neck until he's gathered all of my hair, and he frees it from the thick cotton.

"Should I help with these too?" he jokes, and I snag the bottoms he holds out for me.

"I mean, I don't know. I still can't feel my legs, so . . ." I play along, not missing the grin he points at his feet as he slips on dry socks.

Noah climbs out of the tent to put his shoes on, and when I work my way out, zipping up the tent door, he's coming back from the cab of his truck.

"Here." He hands me a pair of long socks, and I pull them on over the 'compression pants,' which is nothing more than a fancy word for man leggings.

I slip my shoes on next and turn to face him.

His eyes flick over my body, cloaked in his clothes, and his teeth sink into his bottom lip. He yanks me to him, presses his lips to mine, but then tears them away before my hands have a chance to wrap around him.

"Come on, if I don't get people around you—"

"If this ends with, *we'll end up back in the tent* . . . it's crap for motivating me to move."

Noah drops his head back, cursing into the air, and I laugh, squealing when he grabs my hand, tugging me toward camp.

When we reach the clearing, he grins at me, squeezing my hand before letting it go.

He cuts left for the ice chests, and I head right for the fire, snagging a chair along the way. Cam sits at the edge of the group circling the bonfire, so I take the empty space beside her.

She's listening to whatever the boys around are saying, but when she glances my way, she does a double take and spins her entire body to face me. Her head cocks to one side, a single blonde brow lifting as she readies to speak, but her words freeze on her lips when a beer is lowered in front of me.

I drop my head back, looking up at Noah. "Why, thank you."

"You're welcome."

I forget to look away, and his water bottle comes up to hide the grin sneaking over his lips. He begins to walk off, and my gaze travels with him.

Cameron claws at my thighs, so I turn to her. Only then does she realize I'm swallowed by clothes that aren't mine, and my hair is a wet, soppy mess. "Bitch." She grips the back of her chair, leaning closer. "Did you hump the humble hottie?" she hisses.

I smile, folding my legs up beneath me, and shake my head.

Her eyes narrow. "He played puppet with your puss, didn't he?"

My head falls back, and I laugh into the air.

Her gasp has my head snapping in her direction again, and I nearly fall over when she yanks at the collar of my hoodie.

"You got a hickey from Kenickie," she jokes, quoting *Grease*.

My hand flies to my neck, my fingertips pressing over the spot it must be, the memory of his lips replaying in my mind.

Peeking at Cam, I bring my beer to my lips, and my girl lifts her hands in a praising motion, holding hers out.

"Way to *go*, sister."

A calming sense of happiness washes over me, and I turn to my friend.

"Tell me all about the kids from your child development class."

Cam beams, shifts as I had, and starts talking. We stay in our chairs for well over an hour, laughing and joking about everything and nothing.

A little while after that, Mason drops a chair beside us, joining in on our conversation, and of course, Brady and Chase follow as soon as they spot the three of us together.

We share some of the stories our parents have told us about their group trip overseas—since we've all gotten different ones—and make plans to spend Thanksgiving at the beach house with our cousins and friends.

Mason busts out the marshmallows, so Brady and I sharpen some sticks into clean points for roasting.

After eating my first one, I put on another, finding my favorite shade of blue across the bonfire.

Noah stares, his friends all around him, mine all around me.

Never taking my eyes off his, I let the treat hit the flame before bringing it to my mouth, but I don't blow.

I let the blaze grow bolder, brighter.

I let the heat take over until it's nothing but a ball of fire.

And in one quick breath, blow it out.

He's too far for me to hear his chuckle, but I know it's there.

He winks, and this time, I feel it in my soul.

Chapter 26
Arianna

I was hoping for an invite to sleep in Noah's tent last night, but not an hour after our marshmallow fun, Cameron was down for the count, which put me on best friend duty.

I did, however, set my alarm for when he mentioned he was getting up, so I could help him pack and say bye before he took off. Knowing the boys, we'll be here as long as possible, cutting it to the very last minute before we have to head back to campus. They're every bit outdoor, hands-on, adventure men.

By six a.m., on the dot, Noah's pulling out of the campsite, headed home for his visit with his mom.

As quietly as I can manage, I snag the last of the logs near Brady's truck and carefully arrange them into a tall point around the mess of ashes. There's enough kindling still burning below that I don't have to use the brush to get it going today—clearly, some campers had a way later night than I did for this baby to still have some life—so I stay crouched, watching to make sure it burns evenly or the fire will weaken sooner than we want.

"You need another log?"

I glance over my shoulder to find Chase stepping up, his hands buried in his hoodie pockets, beanie hanging half off his head as if he forgot to tug it down when he crawled out of bed.

"These are the last of them."

He nods, coming forward. "You're up early. Cam okay?"

I chuckle, pushing to my feet. "Drooling all over my pillow when I last checked. Her ride home won't be fun."

He grins, following my steps.

"Want to help?" I gesture to last night's beer pong mess, pulling two garbage bags from the plastic bin under the food table.

Wordlessly, he grabs the bag, and we start on opposite sides, picking up the empty cans on the ground first, moving to the tabletop second.

"I miss partying like this." Chase looks across the trees. "Well, I guess this is only our third parent-free camping trip, but still. I could go for more of these."

"Good thing we've got all that practice from sneaking onto the back of Brady's grandparents' property, or we'd be coming out here with nothing but tents and an ice chest."

He grins. "Yeah, we discovered the hard way you have to *bring* wood camping, didn't we? That was a failure of a trip."

"We had to leave in the middle of the night, and we slept in the truck outside my house because Mason didn't want to see the grin on my dad's face when he got to say 'I told you so' when they said we weren't ready to go on our own."

Chase laughs, nodding his head.

I gasp, looking to him. "Do you remember summer of sophomore year, when your parents let us have that pool party at your place?"

"Our first adult-free swim session."

"That took *two weeks* to get them to agree to, and in the end, they only hit us with *one* condition . . . " I raise a brow at him.

Chase drops his attention to the table. "No fighting."

"Yes, no fighting, and what do you know, they come home to find their very own son with a black eye because you just *had* to go and hit on Jake Henry's girlfriend."

I laugh, thinking about it, but when I look over, I find Chase frowning at the stream of beer he's pouring into the dirt, so I close my mouth and continue cleaning.

After a moment, he sighs. "You bought a new swimsuit for that party. Pink with white stripes."

My head snaps in his direction.

I did?

"I put you on my shoulders for a chicken fight against Cam and Brady, and we won," he continues, licking his lips as his eyes rise to mine. "I dropped us back into the water to let you down, and I did . . . but then I spun around and reached for you." He holds my gaze. "I pulled you to me, and without a word, you wrapped your legs around my waist. You smiled and then let go. I didn't realize until someone splashed that I didn't. I was still holding on to you."

I shake my head, confused, and his eyes move between mine.

"It was a total of ten seconds, if that," he tells me then. "But that was all it took for Mason to see."

"We were playing a game, celebrating a win." I swallow. "It was nothing."

"It was something, Ari, and he knew it." Chase's lips twitch. "He's got a solid right hook."

Pressure builds along my chest. "It was Mason? Mason gave you the black eye."

My mind spins, anxiously searching for the purpose. For the meaning.

Of what Mason did and why.

Of Chase's words and the reason he's sharing them.

"Why did you lie?" My voice comes out lower than intended.

A shadow falls over him, and while his chin lowers the slightest bit, he doesn't look away. "Come on now."

Because I would have gotten angry.

Because I would have punched Mason back.

Because I would have assumed I meant more to Chase when I was so sure I didn't . . .

Did I mean more to you then?

When did you let me go?

I hastily bend at the knees, my movements jerky as I pick up a few discarded can tabs from the ground.

"Arianna—"

"Why did you tell me that?"

"You said I hit on Jake's girlfriend. I wanted you to know that wasn't true."

But why, I want to ask. That was two years ago, so what does it matter now? I don't ask because what purpose would that serve?

He said he wanted me to know, fine. Now I do. So that's that.

I pop a shoulder with overfed dramatics and do my best to wash away the entire conversation with some lighthearted teasing.

"Well, that's a relief. She was a biatch and matched quite well with her douchey boyfriend, so consider your character redeemed."

"One goal fulfilled," he jokes back. "A dozen more to go."

Looking up, I meet his green eyes, and we share a small smile before going back to the task at hand.

Chase and I tie off the bags, and when he faces me, his beanie slips even higher, now barely hanging on. With a low laugh, I step forward, tugging it back into place. My eyes move to his, and the corner of his mouth lifts into a broken smile.

"Thanks," he mumbles as I step away.

We turn toward the metal dumpsters, located several yards away, but the slight squeal of brakes sounds behind us.

We both look over our shoulders, finding Noah rolling to a stop at the top of the hill.

"I wonder why he came back," I think out loud, taking a step in his direction but quickly pausing, turning back to Chase.

"Must be something he didn't want to leave behind." He stares a moment, slowly facing me, and in the next, his hand is stretched out as a frown builds across his face.

Hesitantly, I pass over my bag.

He's already walking away before "Thanks" leaves me, and so I spin around, jogging up the short hillside.

Noah's eyes are pointed past me but lower to mine as I reach him, a small smile finding his lips.

I'm about to ask him what happened when I notice two hot coffees in the cup holders and two breakfast sandwiches sitting on the dash.

"Couldn't have you burning the forest down trying to make your own," he drawls lazily, his head sinking to the seat behind him.

A chuckle bubbles out of me, and I grip the doorframe, bringing myself closer to him. "Thank you."

Noah stares into my eyes, slowly sliding his hand into my hair and pulling my lips to his. He kisses me slowly, almost achingly so, and I want to fall into him.

After a moment, he sighs and says, "I don't want to leave you here."

I love the way he says what he means. He never leaves me to wonder, and if I ever do, he sees it and answers my concerns without a question asked.

I lower my chin to my forearm and whisper, "So don't."

Noah's eyes grow curious, and I smile.

"I don't have to crash your visit. You could take me home first, or I can nap in the truck. Get reacquainted with cafeteria food," I joke.

Noah licks his lips. "You'd leave with me now?"

I sigh loudly, shrugging my shoulders. "I'd have left with you thirty minutes ago if you had asked."

Noah grips my chin, and my lips press together in a grin. "Go pack your bag, Juliet."

I step back and pull open his door.

He looks at me like I'm crazy, dropping against his seat when I grip the steering wheel and haul myself into the cab, my side squishing against it.

"I'm a good camper, Mr. Riley. Everything stays packed and zipped up tight, so no bugs get in. Cam will grab it for me."

He eyes me, halting me with a palm to my ribs when I try squeezing past him. "Just like that?"

I tip my head. "Unless you have a problem with me looking like a homeless person, whatever you decide to do with me, yes. Just like that."

His nod is slow, his fingers spanning out over my stomach. He holds me there a moment, and then he lets go. I crawl into the space beside him.

Noah waits for me to buckle up, and once I am, he passes me my coffee. "Extra hot."

"Just the way I like it."

Noah smirks to himself, his hand falling to my thigh, and it only leaves the spot when absolutely necessary.

The drive is peaceful, full of laughs and stories, and once we do finally make it back to town, he doesn't drop me off at home. He hops on the opposite highway, headed for his mom's.

As we arrive, he jumps out and reaches for me.

"Not embarrassed to enter with a hot mess like me?"

"Psh." He hauls me out, stepping back to get a better look, his smirk far too cocky. "You look better in my clothes than you do yours."

A laugh pushes past my lips, and I shove him away, taking off ahead of him, but he catches up quickly, his lips at my ear.

"And the mark on your neck you thought I wasn't aware of, we should talk about making it a little more permanent, hmm?"

My steps falter, and he leaves me with his airy chuckle, only turning back once he's at the entrance and holding the door open for me to step inside.

He and I walk into the building side by side, hand in hand, and when we curve the corner, stepping into his mom's room, she smiles wide.

"I prayed you'd be with him today, and here you are," she admits. "Come sit. There's so much I need you to know."

She reaches for me with her right hand, her working hand, so I let go of Noah's and take the opposite chair this time. I glide my palm under her left one, my other coming down on top of it.

Tears brim in her eyes, but she blinks them away, her free hand covering my own.

I don't look to Noah, I couldn't possibly, but there isn't a doubt in my mind that his eyes are on me. I can feel the weight of his gaze. It pierces through me, searing into my soul, where I suspect a piece of him now lives.

"I like your sweatshirt. I think I recognize that one," Lori teases, mischief in her eyes when my cheeks burn a bright red.

"Me too, but it's kind of warm in here. You sure you don't want to take it off?" Noah takes the place on her right, grinning wide when I pin him with an *I'm going to kill you* expression while subconsciously pulling my collar a little closer to my neck.

I give all my attention to Lori.

"Tell me the most embarrassing thing that has ever happened to him."

Noah laughs loudly, and his mom's chuckle follows.

"You know, I hate to disappoint, but he's never quite been the embarrassed type. A little quiet at times, but nervous or embarrassed . . ." She shakes her head.

I narrow my eyes on Noah, his grin still in full effect as he props back in his seat, leaning all lazy and gorgeous-like. "No, I don't suppose he was. He never does leave you guessing."

"Growing up, his friends were his teammates, so each year, as kids got older or moved programs, the new incoming kids would become his friends. He never did much with them outside of that though. He liked to be home."

He liked to make sure you were never alone.

He understood her sacrifices as a young boy and grew up with an open heart and a strong mind, both of which came from the unyielding love and support of his mother. He didn't have an army around him like me, but he had her, and he made sure she felt she was enough.

A tender heaviness falls over my chest, but I try not to show it, propping my chin in my open palm. "Tell me about his first-ever football practice."

"He cried like a baby," she says instantly, making me laugh. "Begged me not to make him go, but I said, son, listen to me," Lori continues telling her story, and slowly, I look to Noah.

He winks my way, but it's soft and different, and when he looks to his mom, I realize something.

Noah isn't all the things the boys are for me.

He's somehow . . . more.

Chapter 27
Arianna

"Brady said this week's game is a big one for them."

I nod, flipping over my flashcard. My shoulders fall.

Wrong again. *Damn it.*

"Yeah." I drop back in the plastic seat. "Noah said they lost to this team in overtime last season, and right now, they're tied for first place." Checking the time on my phone, I begin stuffing my materials into my backpack. "Come on, if I don't get an energy drink or a coffee or something, I might die, and they still have forty-five minutes of practice left."

Cameron jumps up, ready to roll. "I wish we could drive out with them. This is the third away game in a row."

"I know, and they'll be gone for three days this time. It's a fourteen-hour drive to New Mexico. How miserable is that?"

"Ooh, I almost forgot. Someone might go through quarter-back-cock withdrawal."

"Shut up before I push you down the walkway."

Laughing, she leads us down the stadium stairs.

As we get near the final platform, Chase goes out for a route. It's a quick pass, and Noah bullets it his way, but it slips through his fingers, bouncing off his knee pad and right into a defender's hands.

The whistle blows the play dead, and Chase tears his gloves off. Rather than jogging back to the line like the others, he walks.

Noah holds a hand out for each guy as they come in, and each one slaps their palm against his in passing. Each guy except Chase.

Instead, Chase bumps him in the shoulder and gets back into position.

Cameron crosses her arms. "What was that?"

I shake my head, watching as, this time, the receivers run downfield, each guarded by a defender. Chase breaks left, but he's double-teamed, two defenders on his ass and Noah finds his open teammate on the right, so he fires it off, the ball falling right into his intended target's hands.

The whistle is blown, and they begin their walk back, so Noah turns to speak to the linemen while waiting for the others to jog back for the next drive, and I pull in a breath when Chase bumps him again, but this time, Noah's not even looking.

Noah has to jump up to avoid tripping over one of the guys bent down, tying his cleat.

Noah whips around, and Chase pushes his chest into his captain's. Into his quarterback's chest.

People shout, and Noah puts his hand on Chase's chest to keep him back, but Chase slaps it away.

Noah tears his helmet off then, jerking forward and pointing his hand down the field, but Chase screams back.

Not even a minute later, Chase shoves him, and then the entire team is on their feet, screaming at Chase as Noah tries to calm them down, but Chase won't shut up.

Rule number one on the field is never touch the quarterback.

What the hell is he thinking?

"Let's go." I frown, turning into the tunnel that leads to the parking lot.

"Ari, really!" Cameron calls behind me, falling in line beside me a moment later. "You don't want to wait and see what happens?"

"No."

Without another word, Cameron and I leave the stadium, and it's not until we're stepping into the campus coffee shop that she turns to me.

"In case you're refusing to acknowledge what just happened, I'll do it for you." She slips her thumbs through the loops of her backpack. "After last weekend, it would be pretty hard to pretend it wasn't obvious you and Noah are hooking up."

"So."

"So . . . maybe you and Chase need to have a conversation."

Shocked, I gape at her, snapping, "What?"

"Don't what me. You guys never talked about what happened."

"We did. He said it was a mistake, and I absorbed his words like charcoal does gas. There is nothing more to be said. Things almost feel like they're back to normal again between us, so don't stand here and try to tell me that the little fit he just threw over a pass that wasn't sent his way had anything to do with me. Trust me, it didn't."

She tries but is unable to hold her thoughts in. "I just think this is, or that it might be, a little hard for him, is all."

"What exactly is hard for him, Cameron?" I step up to the counter, quickly ordering a drink, and she does the same. We pay and step into the little corner to get away from the others waiting.

"The fact that I cried over him *for months* or the fact that I'm not anymore?"

Her shoulders fall. "Ari, that's not fair."

"Not fair is being the one who skipped out on first college experiences with her twin because she knew his best friend would be there sharing those times with him, and she couldn't stomach the thought of being so close to him. Or how about leaving her own best friend to do those same things, things they talked about doing together for *years* for the same damn reason?"

Tears brim in her eyes, and I shake my head, gripping her hand. "I'm not upset, Cameron. I made the choice. It was all on me, and I didn't want to drag you through it with me. I was fucked up for a good minute, and I didn't know when I'd feel better, but—"

"But now you do."

My lips curve to one side, and I nod. "Yeah. I do. My brother isn't mad at me anymore, or at least he's not acting like it, and Chase and I can be in the same room without a giant ball of tension circling us. Everything feels good. I just want to focus on that."

268

Cameron blinks rapidly to hold back her tears, but this time, they're not sad ones.

She laughs lightly, looking up at the sky as she sticks her tongue out. "Uh, I hate when you're smart and logical and shit." She smiles, throwing her arms around me.

The barista calls our order. We grab it and head out the door.

"Let's blow off the trip to the pub with the boys, eat ice cream for dinner, and watch some trashy TV. What do you say?"

I throw my arm around her, and hers falls over my shoulder. "I say it sounds like a solid plan."

"Fuck yeah, it does."

So, that's exactly what we do.

"So these little FaceTime calls"—Noah grins into the screen, whispering—"you might not want to tease me like before."

"Oh yeah, and why is that?"

Noah holds in a laugh, and his eyes lift over his screen. In the next second, a very familiar voice shouts from somewhere, "That better be my sister you're smiling at, dick."

I drop back on my bed with a laugh and a dramatic eye roll. "Of course, he's your roommate."

"He's playing most of the first quarter tomorrow, so I wanted to try and run over some more things with him without everyone else around."

I fly up, my mouth agape. "He's starting?"

Noah grins. "Yeah. We've got a game plan we think will trip them up, so we're running with it."

"My brother is starting in a college game tomorrow?!" I jump to my feet, running for Cameron's room and stubbing my toe on the way.

"Owe, shit!" I laugh, pounding on her door, barging in a second later.

She tears her headphones off her head, her eyes wide in panic.

"Mason's starting tomorrow!"

"What!" She jumps up, fumbling and falling to the floor, but pops up instantly.

269

"I know!"

We squeal, hugging.

"Ah shit, you told her, didn't you?" Mason's voice fills the line, and I quickly look back to my screen in time to see his head pop up beside Noah's.

"Holy shit!" I smile, stomping my feet.

"I know." A proud chuckle slips from him.

Tears find my eyes, and a playful glare blankets his face. "Knock it off."

We laugh, and I inhale deeply.

"Oh my god, Mase. You're going to rock it."

"Love you, girls." He beams.

"Love you."

Mase disappears, and I squeal at Noah, whose soft eyes are glued on mine.

"I'll let you go to sleep now," he says quietly.

"After this news? Yeah, right! I'm going to try and reach my parents. I think it's daytime in Germany, but I failed history twice, so I could be wrong."

Noah chuckles, letting me know, "I might not be reachable tomorrow."

"Game face, I know the drill by now." I bite my lips. "Kill it out there, Romeo."

"For you, I will."

My smile is slow. "Nineties R and B, I like."

Noah's grin is downright lethal, and I want to jump through the screen. "Bye, beautiful."

With a quick wave to the screen, I hang up.

Tomorrow, my brother will reach yet another goal he set out to accomplish, and I couldn't be prouder.

I know he's earned it; I know he's more than good enough, but I can't help but think Noah helped present him with the opportunity to get to start, and Mason made it his bitch.

*

"Okay, wings are out of the oven. Chips are poured in the bowl and the door"—Cameron skips from the kitchen, turning the dead bolt—"is locked."

"Beers are popped open and volume"—I grab the remote—"is up."

I move to help carry everything to the coffee table, and then it's kickoff time.

On the sideline, we see Mason slip his helmet on, pulling at his collar as he jumps up and down on both feet to keep his blood flowing strong.

Our guy goes down at the twenty, and the offense jogs onto the field, led by my brother.

We clap and cheer, standing too close to the screen as he fills his men in on the play. They break, take their positions, and not five seconds later, Mason calls hike.

The ball is snapped, grasped tightly in his palms, and he spins, fake tossing it to the running back, before stepping back and firing it for a quick first down.

"Woo-hoo!" We clap.

They get set again, and this time, Mason breaks through a gap, running for eleven more yards before sliding onto his hip to avoid the tackle.

"Yes! Two snaps, two first downs!"

"Oh my god, this shit is looking so good to these coaches right now!" Cameron smiles, downing half her beer.

I pick mine up, watching as Mason glances at the sideline. He gives a curt nod and turns back, pointing to his right before lifting and setting his left foot down. The ball is snapped, and he drops back, looking downfield, but the other team blitzes, breaking through his line.

Mason is sacked from his right rear and front left. His torso twists opposite of his hips, his back bending. His helmet flies off on impact, and Mason hits the turf.

Cam and I stand frozen for several seconds before we snap out of it.

"Holy shit."

"Son of a bitch."

Panic sets in, and we jerk closer to the TV.

"No, no, no."

"Ari, he's not getting up."

I fold my hands in front of me, twisting from side to side. "Get up, Mase."

"Ari . . . he's not getting up!"

"Fuck."

Outside of the few who were near Mason, the rest of the team is just now realizing their quarterback has yet to rise.

Brady is shoving his way through their bunched-up teammates on the field as Chase is rushing from the sideline in the same second.

I clench my teeth, tears brimming in my eyes as the fear shooting through the boys blows through me. They get a few feet from Mason, but both are quickly pushed back by several people on the Avix coaching staff. They shout, trying to see beyond the group of people rushing to my brother's side, but are forced to stay put.

Brady tears his helmet off, lifting it as he shouts in rebuttal, but all it does is draw two more linemen his way. They act like a shield, blocking and driving him backward. He tosses the helmet, gripping his head as he turns away, and my hands come up to cover my mouth.

I jolt when my phone vibrates on the coffee table, my chest squeezing as I answer.

"Dad!" I panic.

"Arianna, it's okay," he assures me in a low, calming tone. "Take a deep breath for me, okay?"

I try, but it's choppy and causes a strain along my ribs. "Dad, he's not moving."

"I know, baby. We're watching. Am I on speaker?"

I press the speaker button. "You are now."

"Cameron, honey, you doin' okay?" he asks gently, knowing without asking she's right beside me.

She nods even though he can't see her, biting at her nails. "Mm-hm." She sniffles

"Good, that's good. Your moms are both right here, your dad too, Cam, and the Lancasters," he tells us, and Cameron reaches out to squeeze my hand.

I drop my ass onto the table, and she stays standing beside me.

We stare at the screen as the medics stabilize Mason's neck, three others crouched around him, his teammates not far away.

"Is Mom okay?" My legs bounce.

"She's scared," he tells me honestly. "But we all are. We're all together, though, and that's what matters. Mason knows we're with him, even if we're all in different places."

I sniffle. Jumping to my feet when Noah steps onto the field.

A ref tries to get him to move back, but he argues, and I hold my breath as his coach, standing a few feet from Mason, spots him.

The coach rushes over, saying something, and Noah pats his shoulder, jogging toward the end zone.

"What is he doing?" Cameron whispers, and I shake my head.

"What's who doing?" my dad wonders.

Noah reaches out, grabbing hold of the giant camera just to the right of the goal post, and I gasp when the network splits the screen, Noah's face displayed across the second one.

The commentators stop talking about the trajectory of Mason's hit and begin taking guesses as to what the quarterback is doing, but they don't have the slightest clue.

I do.

Because as soon as he knows for sure he's alive, Noah stares straight into the camera, straight into my eyes . . . and he nods.

Everything inside me cracks, breaks, and then fuses back together. I collapse onto the sofa, tears pouring down my cheeks.

"He's okay," I rasp.

"What do you mean, honey?" my dad urges.

Cameron's head snaps from the screen to me. "How do you know?"

"Noah," I tell them both. "That's what he's saying. He's letting me know Mason's okay."

Cameron's tears fall, and she drops onto the couch. "I fucking love that guy."

A croaky chuckle leaves me, and I smile. "Dad, he's okay."

"Honey . . . he's still not moving."

I nod, but only moments later, Mason bends his knee, and my mother's gasp chokes me up.

The medic staff stands, repositioning themselves near Mason's shoulders, and as they do, Mason lifts his left arm into the air, letting all those watching know he's okay. The cart comes out onto the field, but Mason isn't put on a stretcher. The crowd goes insane as he's helped to his feet and then slowly set on the back. He's carted away, and my parents celebrate on the other end of the line.

We talk for a little longer, and my dad assures me he'll call if they get any news. Mason being eighteen, there's a chance none of us will hear a word until he's able to call us himself.

Hours go by before my phone rings, and when it does, it's from Brady.

Cam and I scrunch into the screen.

"Brady."

"Hey, girls," he says softly, a sad grin on his lips, Chase right beside him. "You heard anything?"

"Not yet. What do you know?" Cameron asks.

"They took him to a hospital a couple miles away to follow concussion protocol, run tests, and shit." He sighs. "That's all we got from Coach."

"Can you go see him?"

Saddened, they shake their heads. "We're getting on the bus from here, but a trainer went with him. Coach says he'll update us when he can, but without Mason's permission, they can't tell him shit. Coach thinks they might have doped him up, so he's probably coming in and out."

"They wanted to take him on the stretcher, but he wanted to walk off." Chase runs his hands down his sweat-covered face. "I think that was for your and the fam's benefit."

I nod. "Yeah, I'm sure. They called. They were watching."

"Damn." Brady glances behind, to the side and back. "One of the guys said he heard him wheezing, saying something about his ribs, so I don't know."

I nod again, gnawing on my inner lip. "I'm going to call my dad. If I hear more, I'll call."

"Same."

"Ari, he's going to be okay." Chase catches my eyes. "He'll be okay. Call Brady or me if you, you know, just want to talk."

"We will." I look to Cam, grabbing her hand.

"You guys try to rest on the bus." Cam drops her head on my shoulder. "There's nothing you can do. Don't worry too much."

Grim smiles cover the boys' lips, and Brady sighs. "We gotta hit the showers. We don't have a lot of time left before we have to be on the bus."

"Go. I'll text you."

With that, they hang up, and we drop against the cushions.

I call my dad to fill him in on the little I found out, and he says he just spoke with the hospital, but to no avail. Cameron and I spend the next several hours pacing, heating, and reheating food after allowing it to get cold all over again.

We were still awake when the sun started to rise, but we must have fallen asleep at some point because suddenly, I'm waking to a pounding at my door. Cam jumps up, rushing to open it, and Brady and Chase hurry in. Brady hugs Cameron first, pulling me in next.

"Anything?" he hopes.

I shake my head, turning to Chase, who wraps me up next. "Why hasn't he called anyone? Why hasn't the hospital called your parents?"

My eyes squeeze shut. "I don't know. We stayed up all night waiting, and nothing. I'm scared."

"I know," he whispers, his hold tightening, and I bury my face in his chest. "I know you are."

A soft tap has my head snapping up, and we all look to the door Cameron left wide open.

Noah stands in the entryway.

"Noah," I exhale, and my muscles go lax.

I rush toward him, and a small smile pulls at his lips as he steps inside, his arms slowly molding around me as I throw myself into him.

I begin to cry, but his lips find my ear.

"Shh, Juliet," he murmurs. "You don't want him to hear you cry."

My head snaps up, and I frown as Noah's eyes soften.

He nods, letting me go as he brings his phone up beside us.

"I'm with her now," he tells the man standing awkwardly on the other side of the video call.

The man nods and shuffles around. There's a click, and then the camera flips, and Mason, laid up in a hospital bed, fills the screen.

A sob breaks from me, and I tear the phone from Noah's hands. "Mase . . ."

"Hey, baby sister." His voice is raspy, and a weak smile pulls at his mouth.

"You're okay," I cry. "Are you okay?"

He chuckles, but as fast as it leaves him, he groans, his hands clenching the blanket lying over him. "Yeah, I'm okay."

Cameron squeezes herself in beside me, and then the boys are right here too, crowding in.

Mason's eyes move along the three of us, and they grow glossy, so he flicks his away.

"You pansies miss me?" Mase jokes, gratitude in his brown gaze.

"Course we came straight here, brother." Brady nods, knowing that's exactly what he would need from his best friends. "Right off the bus."

Mason nods, looking to his lap. He licks his lips before returning his attention to the screen. "Two fractured ribs and uh"—he clears his throat—"a sprained shoulder. I'm out no less than four weeks, maybe longer." His jaw tics.

No one says anything because we know Mason. He doesn't want to hear a word about it. He's accepted it, and that's that.

276

"Way to get out of practice, asshole," Brady jokes, even though he doesn't feel it.

But Mason grins, and that's the point.

"Ari, don't say anything to Mom and Dad. I'm going to call them right now, but I'm telling her I'm bruised up and need rest. That's it."

"Are you sure?"

He nods. "I don't need them worrying or abandoning the trip they spent the last four years saving for."

"Chances are she already booked flights."

He smiles. "Yeah, I better hang up and call her right quick."

"When will you be home?"

"I'm being released right now, just waiting for paperwork. This guy"—he nods at the man holding the camera—"grabbed me some sweats and shit to put on, and Coach hooked me up with a flight home. It's a short jet, some alumni guy was watching, saw the hit, and hit him up, so I don't have to wait around at the airport like this."

"Good. What time should we pick you up?"

He shakes his head, and then a tense expression builds along his brow. "I'm gonna call Nate. Have him come get me and take me back to the beach house."

"What, why?"

"I have to take it easy for two weeks, Ari, pretty much lie in bed, and I can't do that in the football house."

"Stay here. I can help."

"You have class, and we have an entire house unoccupied. I'm going to sleep and lie on my ass. Lolli and Nate are around, Parker and Kenra too. Payton. If I need something, they'll be there."

I glare but nod. I say okay when, really, I want to argue, and he knows it, which is why a small grin covers his lips.

"Ari."

"It's fine." I shrug, sniffling. "But if you don't answer my calls, *one call, Mase*, I'm driving there, I swear."

"Deal." His expression grows tender, and he sighs, dropping his head back when his eyes begin to cloud over.

My heart breaks for him.

"Mase—"

"Love you guys," he cuts me off.

"Love you."

"Call you later." He looks to the man again. "Hang up."

My entire body sags as the call ends, and I toss the phone on the counter, burying my face in my hands. "Jesus fucking Christ."

Someone's hand falls to my back, rubbing soft circles.

"Are we sure he's okay?" Cameron worries.

"He's Mason," Brady says. "This is exactly what I'd expect from him in this situation."

I look over, and Chase is right beside me. He nods, agreeing.

"You want us to stay?" he asks, his tone wistful.

But I shake my head with a sigh. "You guys go home. You look like you slept as much as we did."

"Are you sure?" His voice lowers, but I only nod, and the hand on my back, his hand, falls to his side.

The boys bend, grabbing their bags off the ground, and face us again.

Cameron looks to me. "Trey just texted . . . do you want me to stay or . . ." She glances toward Noah.

"Go. I'm good now." I nod, wiping at my left eye in exhaustion. I look behind me to Noah, who has moved several feet away, now leaning against the wall. I turn to him, and he pushes off, slowly coming closer. I meet him halfway, and he reaches up, brushing my hair behind my ear.

He stares, his blue eyes sick with worry, and so I nod, my hand coming up to squeeze his wrist briefly.

I'm okay now, swear.

He gives a curt jerk of his chin.

"Thank you." My voice cracks.

Noah shakes his head, unwilling to accept because, in his mind, he didn't do this to be thanked. He did it because he knew I needed it, and he was able to give that to me.

"We're gonna head home, girls."

I glance at them, nodding.

Chase stares straight ahead as he walks out the door, and Brady salutes Noah in thanks.

"Call me later, Ari baby." He pins me with a stern expression.

"I will." I hug Cameron quickly, and she closes the door with her exit.

The moment they're gone, I face Noah, and my emotions win again.

Tears fall, so I spin away, pressing my fingers against my eyes.

"I'm sorry," I whisper, trying to swallow back the cry working its way up my throat.

"Don't apologize, and don't hide from me." He steps around, pulling me into his chest. "What am I good for if not to hold you when you need to be held?"

"I can think of a few things," I cry, chuckling through my tears when he does. Sighing, I look up at him. "I'm just worried. Mason isn't Mason without football and his trying not to make us worry only means there's something to worry about."

The pads of his thumbs come up, and he gently swipes them under my eyes. "Maybe he needs a couple days to be angry and come to terms with it?"

I nod, tipping my chin to kiss his hand.

The corner of Noah's mouth lifts, and I blow out a deep breath.

He presses his forehead to mine. "You texted me all through the night. Did you sleep at all?"

I shrug. "I remember the sun coming up and then the boys were knocking at my door."

His strong, warm palms cup my cheeks. "You should try to get some sleep." He releases me, stepping back to grab his phone, and pushes it into his pocket.

I follow him to the door, and he faces me as he grips the handle. "Call me when you wake up? I can come make you something, bring coffee . . ."

He twists the knob, pulling it open, but I catch it by the lock before it's fully free of the frame, and Noah's eyes snap to mine.

My chest constricts as I slide my hand lower until I'm covering his, and I free it from the cool metal.

A slight frown forms along Noah's brows, but he doesn't argue when I push the door closed, the click of the lock the only sound to be heard.

His chest rises with a full breath, and I rise to my toes, stealing it from his lips.

His hands come up, tangling in my hair, and he kisses me back. His mouth heavy and hungry. Healing.

I need this.

I need . . . him.

Our eyes open at the same time, and he must see something within mine because his body quakes with realization.

My heart beats out of control as I glide my palms down his arms until I've reached his hands. I hook my fingers with his and whisper, "Stay."

Chapter 28
Arianna

Noah doesn't say a word, but he doesn't back away either, not that I thought he would.

His eyes stay locked on mine, so I blindly lead us toward my room, and with each step, his frown deepens.

At my door, he pauses his steps, his blinding blues searching, so I release him, move one foot farther, and grab the hem of my T-shirt. Slowly, I pull it over my head, letting it fall between us. Noah looks from me to it, and when I reach behind me to undo my bra, his gaze snaps up.

"If I step inside this room—"

"Step inside, Noah." My voice is a husky whisper.

His jaw clenches, and he moves forward, and when he does, he's full force.

His left palm wraps around the back of my neck, his right cupping my cheek, his body hot against mine. His mouth descends on mine, but at the last second, he evades it, latching onto my jaw.

He sucks gently, teasing my skin with his pillowy lips until he reaches the sensitive spot on my neck. He nips me then, and I gasp into the air, my left hand driving up into his hair.

I don't realize he's ushered me backward until my knees hit the edge of my bed, but when I go to lower us both, Noah bites harder, and my body shivers.

His hands come around me, pushing my bra down my arms. He steps from his shoes then, and when I grab his T-shirt, he lowers, allowing me to pull it off his body, but his lips fall to my stomach, causing his shirt to get tangled around his head.

He chuckles against me, and my toes curl into the carpet. "Someone's ticklish." He squeezes my hips.

I try again, and this time, I get it off him, grinning when he peeks up at me.

He rises, and as he does, he takes me with him, his hands under my thighs. I lock my legs around his body, and Noah smirks, bringing his mouth to mine.

He kisses me hard, groaning into my mouth when I tug on his hair. One knee hits the mattress, and then the other, and his eyes flash to mine.

"I'm not sure you understand what this is about to do to me," he says, his words weighty and strong. His gaze dark and deliberate. Promising.

Mesmerizing.

I tighten my hold on him, and his knees adjust on the mattress.

"I want to tell you something," I say suddenly.

"Tell me."

My chin falls. "I'm embarrassed."

One of his hands comes up, his knuckles teasing along the hollow of my throat, stretching my neck until my eyes are forced to meet his. "Tell me anyway."

The desperation in his tone is almost painful.

My thumbs trace along his bottom lip, and I bring my mouth to his ear.

"I thought of you," I whisper. "When you were gone . . . I thought of you. In the morning, the afternoon, and at night." I kiss the edge of his jaw. "Especially at night . . ."

Noah's chest rumbles, his large fingers tangling in my hair and gently tugging until my chin is in the air.

He pulls until we're looking at each other, the creases along his temples deepening.

I swallow, and his gaze flicks to my neck but comes right back.

"I wondered what it would be like to have you in my bed," I admit, the fire brewing in his eyes intoxicating. Emboldening. "I dreamed about it . . . fantasized about it."

He trembles with need.

"So much so my body ached," I purr. "So I had to—"

"Touch yourself." His forehead falls to mine, his tongue flicking along my lips. "You had to touch yourself?"

I nod.

Slowly, Noah lowers me to the bed, unlocking my legs and hands from around his body.

He glides his hands up my thighs, grips my shorts, and eases them off, taking my thong with them. On all fours again, he presses his palms into the comforter beside my ribs and says, "Show me."

Noah

Her golden eyes widen, her perfect body tensing the slightest bit, so I ease her mind.

I tell her what's been going on in my head, my mouth aligning with hers.

"I did the same, Juliet," I admit. "In the shower. In bed." I drive my tongue beyond her lips, and she eagerly, wordlessly, begs for more. "In *my* bed."

Her eyes fly open, searching for deceit she won't find.

Slowly but free of hesitation, her fingers dance along her chest bone, a blush working its way up her body as her hand lowers, disappearing between her legs.

My body vibrates, my dick hard and straining against my jeans.

"Tell me what I was doing to you," I whisper.

Her face flushes, but she closes her eyes and says, "First, you kissed my neck."

I lower my lips to her favorite spot, dead center on the left side.

"And then you used your teeth and dragged them down to my shoulder."

I follow the path, sucking where I pause, and she pulls in a deep breath.

Her knuckles brush against my pants, her fingers working her clit, and I clench my muscles, desperate to feel her against me.

"You went down from there, but not all the way."

I pull her nipple into my mouth, slowly swirling my tongue around the hardened peak. I suck a little harder than before.

She whimpers, twitching below me. "Your zipper . . . you."

Her hand moves faster now, her eyes flying open when the soft purr of my jeans coming undone finds her. Her gaze drops, her lips parting when she lands on the rod in my briefs.

I free myself of the rest of my clothes, and her head presses into the pillow behind her.

Her thighs clench, and she begins pulling her legs closed, chasing the pressure locking them tight will provide, but when I lower a little, my hard-on rests along her outer thigh, and her muscles ease.

Her eyes find mine. "You didn't use your hand this time." Her cheeks flame, and she pinches her clit between her fingers, her thighs shaking as she grows closer to her orgasm.

I shift again, this time bringing one knee between her legs. I lower my lips to hers, whispering, "What did I do, baby?"

She moans, and I reach between us, removing her hand and pinning it above her head as I bring my other knee between her legs.

"Tell me what I did."

"You pressed against me."

I lower all the way, both of us groaning when our heated bodies meet for the first time.

My jaw clenches, and I bury my face in her neck. She's soaked, and I'm instantly slick with excitement. I can't help myself; I rock against her.

"Yes," she croaks. "Just like that."

I dig my fingers into the comforter on the opposite side. "I slide my cock along you?" I pull back the slightest bit, moving forward with more pressure, and my thighs clench.

"You did," she rasps, her head shifting until her lips are locked onto my neck. She sucks, bites, and whispers, "And then you slid inside me."

I bite her back, and her knees come up, pressing into my hips.

"Slide inside me, Noah."

My chest rumbles, my muscles strained with need. "I don't want to hurt you."

A softness falls over her, and she cups my cheeks, her head shaking the slightest bit. "You would never," she breathes, pulling my mouth to hers. Her kiss is soft and sweet, but her voice when she repeats herself is straight fucking vixen. "Slide inside me."

Pulling back, I do.

I press into her in one long, slow, steady stroke.

She gasps, her neck stretching until her eyes are on the wall behind her, and I lift, looking down at the goddess before me.

She peeks down the bridge of her nose, staring into my eyes as I fill her fully. Completely.

The tenderness that encompasses her has my pulse pumping, and when the silkiest of smiles curves her lips with her next breath, that's it.

It's done.

I'm gone.

I've been gone.

I rock into her, in and out, slow and steady. My strokes are long and deep, a tantalizing torture. A much fucking needed, sweet kind of agony.

Ari brings her legs up around me, her heels pressing into my lower back and driving me forward.

Our pace quickens, and she gets louder.

Her moans, her gasps.

Her heartbeat.

I place my lips over the madly beating organ, and she presses on the back of my head, so I give her what she wants. My teeth.

I bite, and she cries out.

I lick, and she shakes.

I suck . . . and she shatters.

Her muscles tense, her arms locking around me as she begins to come.

But she fights it, yanking my lips to hers. Her kiss is hard and hungry, chasing, and I give her back just as much.

My hips drive in and out, rolling, circling, and pressing, making sure her clit is worked with my body, just as much as her pussy is. I work her over, dragging her orgasm out as long as possible as she pants wildly.

She tears away, finding my ear again, her voice a breathless croak, her body a ball of tension, untethering with jerky quakes. She wants it to go on, fighting the finale she's desperate for, but she breaks. Her back flies off the bed, her moans harsh and maddening as she lifts her hips into me, willing me deeper. Her lips part and she stutters, "And then I c-came."

"On my cock?" I rasp, bringing my knees up, so I'm sitting back on them, and her hips are in the air.

"Y-yes. On your cock."

Her skin flushes, and my body clenches, heat building, and building.

Ari jerks forward, taking my bottom lip in her mouth, her dazed eyes locked on mine as she whispers, "And then you came too."

And I'm fucking done for, she pushes me over the edge.

Locked in a trance by the girl my wildest dreams wouldn't dare imagine, I come. Long and hard.

Her walls clench around me, vibrating from the inside, and I groan, my limbs shaking.

I hold her there, our bodies slick with sweat until we can breathe easier.

Only then do I slide out of her, lowering us both to the mattress.

Her eyes never leave mine, and after a few minutes of quiet, she begins to gnaw on the inside of her lip, her hands folding under her head as she turns her body so it's facing mine.

I reach out, freeing her lip from her cruelty. "What?"

"You really thought of me?"

My chuckle is low, but I nod against the pillow.

"You really . . . touched yourself . . . imagining me?"

I nod again, gliding my hand down her neck and along her shoulder.

My smirk slowly pulls when her hidden smile plays at her lips, and she whispers *exactly* what I knew she would.

"Show me . . . "

I give her what she wants.

I'm pretty sure I always will.

Chapter 29
Arianna

My hand slips under the covers, but Noah catches it with a popped brow.

"You were supposed to get some sleep." His glare is playful.

"I'll sleep when I'm old."

Chuckling, he climbs out of bed, his gloriously naked body on full display. He slips his boxers and jeans on, turning back to me with his shirt.

He slaps the edge of the bed, so I crawl over, and he pulls it over my head, pecking at my lips before tossing me over his shoulder.

I squeal, attempting to cover my bare ass, but he reaches up, palming my left cheek as he carries me into the living room, so I stop trying, enjoying the heat of his touch.

"If you're not going to sleep, you need to let me feed you. Your stomach started growling an hour ago."

He lowers me onto the couch, smirking as he gets a little flashing show when his shirt gets tied up around my waist. He tosses a blanket over my head, his footsteps carrying him into the kitchen.

Unable to contain my smile, I cozy up on the cushions, pulling the blanket up to my chin as I put last night's game on. I pick up where we left off . . . right after Mason was carted from the field, the worry too much at the time to sit through another second.

As soon as I press play and the commentators begin to speak, Noah does too, the gentleness of his tone warming me in places I can't deny.

"You don't have to watch this," he says.

I lick my lips, keeping my eyes on the screen.

"My man's the quarterback." I grin against the blanket. "So yeah, I do."

Noah doesn't say a word, but I know he's smiling, and mine grows because of it.

Whatever Noah makes, I haven't a clue because the next thing I know, I'm waking up to a dark house, and he's gone.

I down a glass of water, and I drag myself into the shower, standing under the warm spray until the water runs cold, replaying the morning over and over again.

When I get out, I head into the kitchen, picking my phone up from the countertop.

I find a text from Noah.

Romeo: I tried to wake you to tell you I had to go, but you didn't budge. Yes. I checked your pulse. Food is in the microwave.

A chuckle leaves me.

Romeo: I'm headed to my mom's. The team's going to a pizza pub a few blocks from campus at seven. Let me know if you want to go.

My chest pinches, knowing my brother won't be there, but he'll be pissed if I don't go just because he can't, all the while hating the thought of me there with a bunch of dudes.

But I'll be with Noah. That, and Brady and Chase will be there too.

So I say yes.

In the microwave are two egg-and-cheese burritos, pretty much the only option there was in the fridge. It's already five in the evening, so I only reheat one, saving room for pizza later.

I FaceTime Mason, relieved when I see he's home, and settled into his bed with a giant plate of French toast beside him that Lolli brought over.

He's smiling and has more color than this morning, even if he still looks exhausted, but it's only day one, so I hang up feeling good, which makes me want to look good.

So I take my time getting ready.

My hair is down in large, loose curls, my eyes lined with shimmery shadow and accentuated with dark liner. My lipstick is as red as my shirt, and my jeans are high and tight.

I've only just finished tying my black boots when Noah shows to pick me up, his gorgeous blue eyes giving him away. The last thing he wants to do . . . is leave this room.

He cocks his head, his lips parting, but all that comes out is a gravelly chuckle.

I bite back a grin and lead our way out the door.

The pizza pub is an adorable mom-and-pop establishment. The silver-haired woman behind the counter is kind and inviting, with a bold mouth that reminds me of my grandmother.

The food is delicious and plentiful, which is the key to success with two dozen athletes running around. Several of which make their way over to me, asking about my brother, and I tell each of them the same thing. That he's good, resting, and can't wait to get back out on the field. I would bet Brady and Chase went home and gave an update similar to mine, but buzzed boys like talking to girls. I'm pretty sure their questions were used as an excuse to come up to Cameron and me and the few other girls who have migrated our way. It's not long before the jukebox is playing something slow and seductive, and the beer-filled boys push a few tables aside. Pretty soon, it's just me left sitting, the girls having all jumped up to join them.

Noah tries to return to me, but Trey is quick to swoop him up as a pool table becomes free.

He looks to me, but I push him away.

"Go." I smile. "He's been hounding you to be his partner since we got here."

Noah lets out a playful groan, following his friend.

Brady comes over then, setting a fresh glass of beer in front of me. "Drink this. I know last night must have kicked your ass 'cause I know mine's bloody and bruised.

"You're not wrong." I lift it in cheers, taking a small drink. "You talk to him again?"

"Nah, he don't want to talk to us yet. Imma give him two days and not a minute longer."

"He'd expect nothing less." I grin, swallowing another sip. My eyes slip over Brady's shoulder, and I lean forward. "Don't look now, but there's a very familiar face that's just walked through the door, and it looks like she's spotted you."

Brady spins his entire body around, and I chuckle. The girl snaps her head away, tucking her hair behind her ear. Smirking, he brings his eyes back to me. "That's the shy little lady from the library, isn't it?"

"It is."

"Woo," he whispers, finishing his drink and lowering it to the tabletop with a hard knock. He stands, leaning closer. "And you said I didn't almost have her."

Chuckling, I salute him on his way, and not a second later, Chase drops into the seat beside me.

He leans back and almost slips off the seat but quickly rights himself, a drunken grin on his lips.

Entertained, I pinch my lips together. "Feeling good?"

He nods, takes another sip, and faces me. "Hi."

"Hi." I chuckle.

"Are you with him?"

My amusement clogs in my throat, my mouth opening, but no words come out. His question, so sudden and unexpected, has me frozen.

His eyes pierce mine, and my muscles seem to coil.

"Are you serious right now?"

"Will you just—" His brows cave. "Just say it for me. Please."

A startling hollowness creeps over me, but I nod. "Yeah, I am." My voice is strong, sure, and I know he hears it.

Chase's chin lowers, and he brings his knuckles down on the tabletop in soft, quiet raps.

"Okay." He looks to the side, and then he walks away.

I watch him go, a hint of sadness washing over me, but it's far outweighed by the relief that follows now that the air is clear.

Cameron falls in the space beside me, eyeing me expectantly.

"He wanted to know about Noah and me."

"And?"

"And I told him the truth, that we're together."

Cameron sighs in relief. "Good. That's good. Maybe he just needed to be sure you were okay now."

I nod, but a frown still forms. "Yeah."

Maybe.

A few hours and several pitchers later, the place is as rowdy as you'd expect, but the bit of energy I gained after going back to sleep this morning is slowly fading away.

I drop my head on Noah's shoulder, and he rubs my back. "You ready to go?"

I peek up at him. "Yeah, but you can stay." I glance Cameron's way. She and Trey are saying bye to a few others at their table. "I think Cameron's going now. I can ride with her."

Noah's knuckles come up to run along my jaw, and I grin. "I want to take you, kiss you good night."

Warmth spreads through me, and I nod. "K."

"Hey, hooker, we out." Cameron slips in front of me.

I push to my feet, and Noah follows. "Us too."

"Cool." Cameron slips her arm through mine, dragging me along.

"I'm going to say bye to a couple of the guys, meet you by the door," Noah tells me, and we move in opposite directions.

"So," Cameron whispers, Trey on his phone a few feet ahead. "I'm kind of staying the night with Trey."

"Oh yeah?"

"Yeah." She wiggles her brows, and the two of us laugh. "You'll be fine?" she worries.

292

"Perfectly." I hug her, and then Trey, and as soon as they're gone, Noah is there.

We're pulling up at my dorm in minutes.

"That was fun," I tell him, sliding my key card in the front door and hitting the button on the elevator.

"After I asked you, I felt like a dickhead."

My head snaps his way. "What, why?"

"Mason." He shrugs. "Shitty timing on my part."

I shake my head, wrapping my arms around his middle. "How are you so . . . you? You're a twenty-one-year-old senior in college who plays football like a badass. You should be such a cocky, selfish prick."

Noah's head falls back, and he laughs, bringing a smile to my face.

"But you're sweet and humble and way too selfless."

A smug grin covers his lips, and he squeezes my hips. "I get it from my mama," he sings, and then it's me who's laughing.

After a moment, I sigh, saying, "I don't doubt that for a second . . . and just so you know. Mason would cuss me out if I didn't go because of him."

"Good."

My mouth gapes, and Noah laughs, grabbing my hands and leading me down the hall.

"Ass." I smack his stomach with my free hand, and he grips my wrist, kissing my knuckles.

Digging my keys out, I unlock the door and look to Noah. "So about kissing me good night . . ."

He smirks, shifting closer, and brings his lips to mine, but I quickly dart my fingers between our lips, and his eyes narrow playfully. "Juliet."

"Noah."

He tugs me closer by the belt loops, making me laugh.

"Let me have those lips," he softly demands.

"Cameron is staying at Trey's tonight."

His eyes flick to mine.

293

I almost chicken out, and he knows it because his thumbs begin drawing circles along my hip bones.

He steps into me, hiding us against my door, his warm, forest fresh scent invading my senses, and my body melts against his.

"You still going to be shy for me?" he teases, his smirk downright sinful. "Even after today?" His hands slide in my back pockets, and he squeezes, grinding me into him. "Even after I've been inside you?"

Heat pulls between my legs, and Noah's lips curve even higher.

Because he knows what he's doing to me . . . just like he now knows what he's *about* to do to me.

I grab the strings of his hoodie and tug him forward.

His chuckle is deep and promising and creates a stir low in my stomach.

Then Noah locks us inside.

Chapter 30
Arianna

Lori presses the nurse call button on the remote at her side, and Noah jumps to his feet, concerned.

"Relax, honey." She rolls her head his way. "I just need a small favor, is all."

"I can help you." He frowns, turning it off, but she presses it again.

"Noah. Stop." She smiles, looking over at the woman who slips into the room. "Cathy, you finally get to meet my son's . . . Ari."

I chuckle, and he looks at me, the annoyance slipping from his face. I wave at the woman. "Nice to meet you."

"And you." She grins, walking toward the end of Lori's bed. "What can I get ya, sweets?"

"You know that new printer you told me about in the lobby?" Lori asks. "Could you take a photo of these two for me? Maybe by the pumpkins you said are on the back patio, if they're still there?"

The woman's smile is kind as she nods. "Of course I can." She looks to us. "Follow me?"

Noah hesitates but slowly pushes to his feet. "Meet me in the hall in just a minute?"

My brows pull together, but I nod. "Yeah, of course."

As soon as they're gone, Lori turns to me. "You don't mind a photo, do you?"

"Not at all."

"I just . . . I want to remember this, my son happy." Her eyes cloud, but she blinks it away. "Most of the smiles I get are glossed with sadness. I worry every time he walks out the door. Not for me, for him. You know he was almost born on New Year's Eve?"

"Really?"

"Mm-hm. I was at the hospital and everything, but he was being ornery. I thought he'd come a few days after that, but nope, he made me wait."

"Until January twenty-ninth."

"Yeah," she coos, as if proud that I know.

I look to the door, quickly leaning in. "I'd like to do something for him, but I'll need your help."

I explain it to her briefly, and her eyes gloss over, her hand shaking as she reaches over to place it on my cheek.

"My, my, sweet girl." Her voice is raspy. "I don't even know what I can say to you to make you understand what you've done for me. What you continue to do for me."

A slight blush washes over me. "So I can call you later?"

"Of course you can." She nods, gently nudging me along, so I rush out to meet Noah in the hallway.

His expression is torn, but he slips his hand in mine, and we follow Cathy out to the patio.

It's a gorgeous stone courtyard lined with large soft bulbs that glow a soft yellow. There are hay bales stacked in the farthest corner, pumpkins of all shapes and sizes strategically piled around them. Cathy ushers us over and pulls her phone out.

"Stand anywhere you like." She smiles.

Noah looks to the holiday decor, and something flickers along his face, the reality of time maybe. So rather than link the moment or thought to a time of year that may weigh heavy later in life, I grab him by the hand and lead us toward the fountain in the center, large stone pots full of Peonies arranged like stairs on both the left and right side.

Noah's gaze finds mine, and with that one look, the unspoken sorrow that swept over him disappears. He lowers onto the edge and pulls me onto his lap, twisting the slightest bit, so my right shoulder is resting against his right pec. He kisses my cheek before facing forward, and I allow my head to rest on his. His arms come around me, and the woman lifts her phone.

"Ready?"

"Ready."

We smile, and she snaps the photo, waving her phone in the air as she walks away.

Before I can stand, Noah glides his hand in my hair, drawing my lips to his. His kiss is so soft, so slow, that my throat threatens to close.

"Thank you," he whispers.

"For what?"

"Everything."

Warmth spreads through me, and we sit there a moment longer, simply staring at one another.

Together, we head back to his mom's room and chat for a little longer, but the visit is cut short when she begins to jumble her words.

We say our goodbyes, and this time, the walk to the car is a bit of a somber one.

He's quiet, too quiet, so once we're on the road, a few minutes having passed, I roll the window down, shocking him with cool air, and his eyes snap my way briefly.

As I knew it would, a small smile finds his lips.

"Take me somewhere."

He reaches over, tugging me into the middle seat, his hand burying itself between my jean-covered thighs. "Where do you want to go?"

"Somewhere you love. Somewhere you could go anytime, and just being there makes you smile."

Noah's teasing eyes move my way, and I laugh.

"Come on, you have to have a place. Everyone does, right?"

"Will you show me yours?" he counters.

"I will."

"I bet I already know where it is."

"I bet you do too."

He chuckles, and then he's making a U-turn.

I swear I could have guessed where we'd end up had we played a guessing game, so I'm not even a little surprised when Noah parks, and we climb out, headed toward the hundred-yard stretch of green turf and white lines.

"Your high school?" I look over the large building to the left, a giant Eagle painted on the side.

"My high school." He nods, and he couldn't wipe the smile off his face if he tried. He sighs, allowing himself to look over every inch. From the field to the track around it, from the stairs to the announcers' box at the top of the bleachers.

He steps out on the football field, tapping his toe along the four-yard line. "This is where Thomas Frolly caught the final pass I made on this field, and he ran it in for the winning touchdown."

I clap, and he gives a teasing bow.

He runs as if running a route, stepping left but juking right and leaping as if jumping over a defender. Where his feet land, he looks back to me, not quite at the fifty. "This is where I stood when they announced homecoming king. I lost."

I laugh, and Noah winks.

He jogs toward the gate, and I spin, slowly following.

He slaps a black-and-white metal sign, warning against smoking on campus.

"Here," he calls me over, "is where I kissed the prom queen."

"Lucky her." I push up on my toes, meeting his mouth with mine. He grins but pulls back, a hint of caution blanketing his features.

He licks his lips. "Paige was the prom queen."

"I knew it." My words escape before I can stop them, and my eyes widen. "Sorry. I don't mean, or I just meant, I assumed you two had history."

"It wasn't like that." He shakes his head but thinks better of it. "Or it was, but it wasn't . . . it wasn't about her and me. Her dad had gotten sick around the time my mom did, and we sort of needed to find comfort somewhere, but that's all it ever was. And never again after high school."

Relief I didn't know I needed hits me as he shares that last piece, and I think of Noah when he got that first call about his mom. How, after that, he went home to an empty house while his mom slept in a hospital bed. I know he had friends, but from what Lori had said, not friends like I had growing up. Not the kind you can run to anytime, for any reason.

Paige was there for him in a way that made him feel less alone because she understood his pain. A sense of thankfulness falls over me, just knowing he had one person he could call.

"You were lonely, and you had each other," I whisper. "If I didn't have my family and friends? I can't even imagine, to be honest. I'm glad she was there for you."

His shoulders seem to ease then. "She's a good friend."

"Yeah," I agree. "She is."

A moment later, Noah smirks, his arms locking around my waist.

"What?" I eye him as a flirty cockiness takes over.

"I had a feeling you were into me more than you realized way back then."

"Oh yeah?" I narrow my gaze, fighting the pull of my lips.

"Mm-hm. You and Cam thought you were slick with that *Prince Charming* bit." He chuckles, pecking my nose, but then his face softens, a tenderness falling over him.

"She thought she was genius."

His pinkie comes up, and he brushes the hair from my face. "She could have said nothing, and I'd have still thought so."

"Do tell, Mr. Riley."

He's quiet a moment before speaking. "I could sense it, sense you, and your thoughts. I've had this gut-deep awareness of you since the day I met you, but every time I saw you or was with you, I tried not to read too much into it."

My throat grows thick, my question a low rasp. "Why?"

"Because I wasn't sure you'd allow yourself time to figure it out."

His words strike a chord deep within me, too many emotions to name trying to break through my chest all at once, and I seek out his lips, kissing him with more than my mouth.

With more than my mind.

With a part of me, I think might be his . . .

The kiss lasts minutes, maybe even longer, and when he pulls back, he hits me with a grin. "That worked."

"What did?"

"You one-upped the prom queen."

My head falls back on a laugh, and Noah bends, swooping me into his arms, so I lock my arms around his neck.

"I better have one *hundred* upped the prom queen."

Noah's chuckle is low and soothing, as is the promise his eyes offer in that moment. "Baby, you beat out every woman everywhere, even in your sleep."

My chest clenches and I bury my face in his neck.

His arms tighten their hold, and he carries me back to the truck.

Noah

Watching her dance around in the seat beside me, smiling wide as she picks pieces of the bun off her burger, eating it like a bird as always, it's as if everything clicks. Right here and now.

I love her.

I love everything about her.

I love the way her facial expressions transform with the words she sings, feeling all the emotions to every song. The way she dips her head and pinches her lips tight when she gets shy on me. I love that she *is* shy, even now, and I love how that, in a twist, she isn't. She's brazen and bold when it's just the two of us behind closed doors. She's open and authentic, loves to share pieces of her life, and asks about mine, not to keep a conversation going, but because she truly wants to know.

I love the smile that curves her lips when she sees me. It's the same one every time, big and bright, as if I show up to surprise her when she knew I was coming all along. I love how she is with my mom, patient and kind, but not in the way of pity, but pride. Like she knows what a good woman she is, like she understands all my mom means to me, and in turn, she means something to her too.

Ari draws thoughts out of me I never had before, about things I didn't really know I wanted but now feel desperate for. Deeper roots and a family.

The love of a lifetime.

I know she's only starting out her journey here, and I graduate this year. I'm expected to go to the draft, first round, my coach says, being I'm ranked as both a receiver, my original position, and a quarterback, where I shined all through college.

My life will be on the road, my schedule nearly full for the better part of the year, every year.

But what if it wasn't?

What if I devoted my life to loving the girl beside me instead? *What if I found a way to do both?*

Right then, buttery-brown eyes shift to mine, catching mine on her, and her head falls against the headrest.

"Hey, Noah?" She grins, licking the hint of salt on her lips. My eyes follow the path of her tongue. "Yeah?"

Humor lines her voice as she says, "You might want to drive."

My eyes jerk up, my head snapping forward, and sure enough, I miss the light, the green turning back to red before I can even take my foot off the brake.

I look her way again, and that smile appears, the soft, warm one she's known to award me with, her laughter light and airy, a glint of something else scripted in her eyes.

I squeeze her knee, needing to touch her, watching and loving the light pink that spreads across her silky skin. My heart beats faster, knowing something as simple as my hand on her skin earns this reaction from her.

"Come with me to the football gala."

She smiles. "A gala? Sounds fancy."

"It is. Black tie and ball gown. The whole bit."

"When is it?"

"January."

"January . . ." She trails off. "That's two months from now."

Slowly, I nod. "Yeah. It is. Tell me you'll come, write it on that calendar of yours?"

Ari bites her lip, her voice low. "You already know the answer." *I hope to God I do.*

When the light turns green, again, I press the pedal, smiling to myself when a soft sigh slips from her.

I'm in love with her, and if I'm right, which I hope to hell I am, she's on her way to loving me right back.

If she could, I'd need nothing else.

Just her.

Chapter 31
Arianna

"I have training in ten. Coach has some meetings, so my day's all messed up. I have film after this and practice at four."

"Sounds like a fun one for you." I grin at the screen. "I'm on my way to a mandatory lecture about *Endless possibilities here at Avix U.*" I mimic the campaign speech my professor showed us today.

"Hey, you might just come out with a major," Noah teases.

"That would be devastating. I already told you my life plan." I laugh. "But bright side, this'll be the easiest *A* I'll ever get."

"There you go." He nods at someone as they walk into the locker room, facing the screen once more. "I should go before people start stripping."

"Or you could leave me on the line."

He shoots a little warning glare my way, and I smile.

"Call me later?"

"You know I will."

We hang up, and I push to my feet.

Heading into the lecture hall, I put my phone on silent, jumping when a hand reaches out, gripping onto my shoulders from behind.

I look up to find Chase.

"Hey." I smile, but a frown quickly replaces it. "Don't you have training right now?"

He shakes his head, falling in line beside me. "Nope. I have a check-in after this, to go over grades and shit, but nothing

303

else until film." He bumps his shoulder with mine. "Trust me, I tried to get out of this thing."

"I bet." I chuckle, then we're quiet as we fall into the long line of students.

We take seats beside each other in the middle of the room, and for the next forty-five minutes, we listen to people talk about how the choices we make now will help shape our futures.

It's kind of boring, borderline common sense, but they do introduce a ton of career options that aren't necessarily spelled out in the course listings.

On our way out, I turn to Chase. "I'm meeting Cameron for a few minutes at the café. Did you want to come?"

He nods but then shakes his head and stops in his tracks. "Can we talk?"

"Yeah, what's up?" I turn to face him.

"No, I mean, can we talk, talk?" He stares pointedly. "About everything. About . . ."

He can't even say the word 'us,' and I'm sure as hell not going to be the one to say it.

"I want to explain. Apologize," he pushes on.

"It's okay. You don't have to." I shake my head. "I don't need to hear it anymore. I get it. I do."

It's the truth. The fact of the matter is I forgave Chase, for all of it. I don't really know when it happened, but it did, and it's not that he felt he needed forgiveness. I don't know if he did or didn't. It's also not because he did something that should require my forgiveness, because that's not necessarily the truth either.

We were consenting adults, both aware of what we were doing, both free of expectations and repercussions.

I knew, in the back of my mind, he could never truly be mine. I'd known it all along. I just allowed myself not to care that night. He offered me something I had wanted for so long, and so with greedy hands, I accepted, consequences be damned.

That didn't mean it didn't hurt when the high wore off, and reality swept in with the morning tide, washing away the memory we made in the sand only hours before.

I was hurt, but that wasn't on him; it was on me.

So I forgave him *for me* because I needed to. Because he's my friend and having him in my life is important for my brother and for me.

Rehashing everything now would be like opening a healed wound, and for what? I've moved on; he's doing just fine, and our group is no longer suffering from our decisions.

"Let me try to make you understand where my head was at and why I was an ass." He reaches for my hand, but I only squeeze his, then pull it free.

"I already know why, Chase. I've known for years. I'm being honest when I say it's okay. *We* are okay. Let's just . . . let it go. Forget about it."

I nod, holding his eyes with mine, and slowly, he nods back.

"I have to go. Cameron's waiting on me."

"Yeah, uh . . ." He clears his throat. "Tell her to call me. I have the notes she wanted for psych."

Agreeing, I rush off, finding Cameron already nestled into the counter booth, drinks and bagels waiting.

It's late that night when my phone dings with a text, but it's not from Noah as I suspected.

It's from Chase.

Chase: what if I don't want to forget it?

The air swooshes from my lungs, and my eyes slice to the ceiling.

Memories crash over me, creating a strain deep in my chest. I press against it to ease the ache and sweat beads along my neck.

This is ridiculous.

I don't know why he's saying this to me. I said my piece. I forgave him for me. He knows this. There's no longer anger and sadness between us.

We're fine.

I'm fine, better than, in fact. I'm fucking happy.

It's not my business what runs through his mind when he's alone. If he doesn't want to forget, he doesn't have to. It's not like either of us really can.

Memories don't die when the possibilities do. They morph into pain.

Pain you have to decide to feed or fight.

I chose fight.

And I won.

I have no idea what to say to him, so I say nothing at all.

Chapter 32
Arianna

Thanksgiving at my house has always been a big event. My aunt and uncle would come down from Alrick with our cousins, and Brady, Chase, and Cameron's families would be there too, plus or minus a few additions they'd bring, depending on the year.

My dad would set up the garage, which served as nothing more than his man cave for him and the boys on a normal day. The wives took care of the indoor food while the men had contests on who could cook the best turkey. We weren't allowed to know who made which one once it was plated but voted on our favorites at the end—Uncle Ian, Nate's dad, won every year.

Pretty sure he'd wink at his wife to swing her vote when she served her plate.

It might be my favorite holiday, tradition-wise, so there's a little sadness this year knowing our parents won't be here . . . but we would never tell them that.

Their once-in-a-lifetime adventure ends just after the first of the year when Brady's dad has to report back to base, so there is always next time.

This year, though, we're trying to ignore the difference by hosting our own at the beach house, and when we leave, we're bringing my brother back with us.

"You didn't get to come inside the place last time, huh?"

"Nope." Noah reaches over the side of his truck for our bags. "You left me out on the sand."

Spinning to face him, I lift a brow. "You shouldn't have hit me in the head with that football."

Noah drops our stuff, rushes over, and wraps me up. He spins me around, planting a hard, quick kiss to my lips. "Best thing I ever did was miss that pass."

"Mmm." I peck at his lips. "And here I was thinking the best thing you ever did was toss me on the bed and—"

"Don't finish that sentence."

I whip around, my smile stretching at the sight of my brother. I kick my legs, and Noah sets me on my feet. I rush Mason, throwing my arms around him, and he groans, his jaw clamping shut.

My hands fly away, my eyes wide. "Shit. Sorry."

"It's fine. Come here." His arms pull me in, a long exhale slipping from him. "I'm okay, baby sister. Promise."

"Yeah?" I blink back my emotions.

"I was fucked off for a couple weeks," he admits. "But I'm good now."

"Thank God for that."

I turn to find Payton leaning against the doorframe, her belly swollen and looking ready to pop.

"Oh my god," I coo, rushing over. "Look at you." I hug her, and when I look to her stomach, she giggles.

"Go ahead, feel me up."

Grinning, I place my palms on her belly, feeling the firmness of the left side and gliding my palm right, where it smooths out again. I then move it back right. "Is this him?"

Payton nods. "He likes to squash my lungs."

"Pretty cool, huh?" Mason steps up.

I cut him a curious glance. "Yeah, it is."

"When are you due? I feel like you've been pregnant forever."

"Next week. Your cousin and I just finished getting the nursery together. You'll have to come see it."

"Kenra?"

"No," she sighs playfully. "Nate."

A laugh flies from me, and she grins.

"Trust me, I was just as surprised while it was happening."

"I bet." I nod, turning to Noah as he steps up, taking Mason's outstretched hand.

"Riley." He raises a brow. "Looks like my sister's still in one piece. This shit serious now, or what?" He frowns.

"It's whatever she wants it to be."

Mason's lips curl up. "Good fucking answer, my man." He chuckles, turning to Payton. "Payton, Noah, Noah, Payton."

"Hi, Payton."

Her cheeks grow a little pink, and I hide my laugh.

"Hey." She eyes him.

"Okay, intros are over. Inside. It's getting cold as fuck out here." He turns, slipping in front of me, and we follow behind.

"Ari, did you know your brother is the bossiest person on the planet?" she calls out.

"Yeah, you get used to it." I grin.

Mason groans, flipping me off over his head, and I can't help but smile. He's feeling better.

Cameron runs around the corner, jump tackling me onto the couch, and Mason takes Noah into the kitchen, reintroducing him to the gang in case his small stopover during the summer is out of their minds.

"Sara and Ian didn't make it," Cam tells me of my aunt and uncle. "Nate said his mom hurt her back when they took the quads out a couple days ago, so he lied and said they'd be out of town for Thanksgiving so that she wouldn't feel bad and still travel while in pain."

"Sounds like Nate. Why didn't he tell me?"

"In case you blabbed about coming this way, I'd bet."

My head jerks her way, and we laugh because yeah. I might have done that on accident.

Payton pushes to her feet, only moments after sitting, and puts one hand on her lower back, the other lowering onto the table. Mason beelines her way, passing her a water and pulling over the chair with cushions stacked on it.

"I'm fine," she tells him, but Mason, being Mason, doesn't move.

Payton lowers into the seat.

"He looks good." Cam nods.

"Yeah. I think so too."

"Think it has anything to do with the pregnant mama he's hovering over?"

"Cameron. Stop."

"I'm just saying," she whispers. "He hasn't left her side."

"She's about to pop. Her brother and Kenra probably asked for help."

"True. I didn't think about that."

Piling into the kitchen, I hug everyone hello as Cameron goes over the tasks for tomorrow.

Everyone is assigned a job, and I flip the others off when I'm stuck with peeling potatoes.

"One day, I'm going to knock all your socks off with a Riley family recipe."

Several eyes widen, teasing glints flicking along the others, and I stutter.

"I meant . . . I was only saying I can cook something he—" Grins pull along their faces, so I laugh. "Oh, fuck you, guys."

Noah squeezes my thigh under the table, but I don't look at him. I'll blush like a madman if I do, and he knows it.

"Well, we'll see just how good the man's family recipes are cause he's on turkey."

"What?!" Brady whips around, half a breadstick hanging from his mouth. "I wanted the turkey."

"You got the ham," Cam argues.

Brady nods and turns back to the open fridge.

We chat a little more, enjoying the fact that we have nowhere to be and no need to rush around.

A little while later, Mase takes the others home since it's dark out now, and they don't want to walk the half mile in the cold with Payton.

Once Mase gets back, Brady looks around, realizing the third piece of their puzzle is missing. "Where's Chase?"

"He went to bed an hour ago," Mason tells them, pushing to his feet. "Speaking of bed. I'm beat."

Everyone nods in agreement, and we make our way to our rooms, but not before Mason pins Noah with a glare. "You're in the guest room, fucker."

"That's what he's trying to do." Brady rocks in his chair, eyeing us.

Noah simply laughs. "My bags are already in the extra room. Thanks for letting me stay."

"Um, it's my house too, and so not up to them."

With a smirk, Noah says, "Yeah, it is."

I give him the evil eye, and Mason pushes on my head, clamping a hand on Noah's shoulder as he repeats his earlier comment. "Good fucking answer."

"Go to bed already," I tease, relaxing into the space beside Noah.

Several of us settle into the living room for a movie, and not an hour after we've split for bed does Mason's shouts wake up the entire house.

"Payton's in labor, and she's scared!"

Just like that, to the hospital we go.

"Does it always take this long to have a baby?" Cameron stands, stretching her neck.

"I don't know." I shrug, lifting my head off of Brady's shoulder. "When's the last time Parker came out with an update?"

"About an hour ago?"

"Here he comes now." Nate nods his chin toward the double doors as they begin to open, Payton's brother on the other side.

He shakes his head. "Nothing yet. They gave her something to speed things along, and she's crying a bit now." A pained expression blankets his face. "They wanted to check her, so she kicked me out, but she wouldn't let go of Kenra's hand."

I nod, rubbing my eyes.

"This baby is already stubborn, and he ain't even born." Lolli grins.

Parker scoffs a laugh. "Right?"

Cam sits back down, knocking her knee into mine. "You heard from Noah?"

"Not since I sent him to the house. Is Trey there yet?"

She nods, showing me a picture he sent her of them sitting by our firepit on the back patio.

I chuckle, shaking my head.

After the first eight hours, I sent Noah to the house. He tried to refuse, but I insisted. Especially since Trey was driving in alone. He needed someone there to welcome him, and who better than his friend?

"Where's Mason?" I look around.

"He was just here . . ."

"He snuck in the door when that doc walked out." Chase looks up from his phone, his attention going right back. That's about the most he's said today.

Parker sighs, frowning. "Course he did. I'm gonna use the restroom and go back in."

Five minutes later, when Parker's headed back through the double doors, Mason comes bounding out from the other side.

"Baby's coming!" he shouts, clapping his hands.

"What?!" Parker's eyes widen, and he starts jogging down the hall as we all jump from our seats.

We crowd the doors, waiting for them to come back out with some news, and it's not long before my cousin Kenra steps out with a smile. "It's a boy!"

"Aww!" I fuss. "She was right."

"Can we go in?" Cam darts forward.

"Yeah, but only two at a time."

Cam and I don't bother looking to the others but dash through the door and around the corner, jerking to a stop in front of her room.

Payton looks up.

"Hi." We quietly enter, coming to her bedside, Mason, and Parker standing just behind her.

The little cocoon in her arms is so tiny, and as I reach Payton's side, his little face comes into view, a little beanie already on his head.

A little baby boy, so precious.

Payton is pale and tired, a mix of emotions written on her face, love being the most obvious.

"Does he have a name?" I whisper.

She nods, tears pooling in her eyes. "His name is Deaton."

After his daddy. Who he'll never get the chance to meet.

"That's a beautiful name for a beautiful boy." I smile, running the tips of my fingers over his soft little hand. He stirs, the sweetest little sounds slipping from him that melts my heart. "Happy Thanksgiving, Deaton."

Exhausted, we pull ourselves out of Mason's Tahoe and head up the deck to the front door.

"Guess it's Door Dash for dinner?" Cam huffs.

"Are they even open on turkey day?" Brady yawns.

"I don't know. I'm fine with cereal at this point. I'm freaking starv—"

Stepping through the door, we're hit with the most comforting of smells, a fresh fire burning, and my grandma's stuffing.

I rush into the kitchen, my stomach swirling as I hit the corner and come to a jerky stop.

The island is covered in Thanksgiving tradition, and my smile broadens.

Cameron comes around as fast as I did, her chest bumping into my back, and she gasps. "Holy shit!"

The others file in around me, slipping forward and examining the dishes alongside me.

There's mashed potatoes and gravy, yams, and green bean casserole. A glistening ham covered in pineapple rings and a bowl of stuffing.

Noah pushes through the patio door then, and in his hands, there's a turkey.

He freezes when he sees us, but a smile curves his lips a moment later, and he continues to the counter, setting the large platter down. "Hey."

"Dude, Noah. Are you fucking serious?" Brady grins, sticking his finger in the side of the mashed potatoes, and getting swatted away by Cameron.

"Bro." Mason steps toward him, clamping his hands. "Thank you, man. This looks fucking good."

I curve around the island, the others still checking out the food, and step into Noah. "You made us Thanksgiving dinner?"

"Did you really think I'd leave you at the hospital just to come back here and rest?"

I pause. "Well, now that you mention it, that was a very unlike you thing to do."

"You were excited for today, and I didn't want you to miss it." He turns me, hugging me to him from behind and toward the food, the others already pulling plates and drinks out. "Some of this I've never made before. I hope it's decent."

"Google?"

Noah chuckles, pushing me forward. "Eat."

We don't argue.

We eat.

Noah had nothing to worry about. Everything was amazing, and while I couldn't possibly tell my mom, Noah's mom's yams recipe was to die for, the crusted marshmallows on top a dessert all their own.

Almost everyone goes back for seconds of something, and it's not long after that we're stuffed and enjoying some mixed drinks by the fire.

I slip away for a moment alone, stepping down the patio and out into the sand.

Leaving my shoes behind, I smile at the sea, moving closer and closer until my feet are at the water's edge. I dig my toes into the wet sand, tugging my sleeves over my hands as the wind picks up, whipping me in the face as if to welcome me back.

I walk a little farther down, until the dock comes into view, and standing right beside it, in the spot we once stood . . .

"Chase."

I didn't mean to speak his name aloud, but it slips from me anyway, and his attention snaps in my direction.

He doesn't move, so I shift a little closer.

"Hey."

He frowns at the ocean.

"Are you okay?" I wonder.

At first, he's quiet, but then his head falls back on his shoulders a bit.

"No, actually," he says into the air, a heavy sense of frustration in his tone. "I'm not."

I wait, folding my arms into my chest.

"I thought you understood." He takes a step toward me.

My head pulls back. "Understood what?"

"Me." He jabs his finger into his chest, and I realize he's buzzed. Maybe even drunk. "I thought you understood me. I thought you got it."

"I don't know what you mean."

"That's the problem." He bends, stressing every word, nearly right in front of me now. "How did this happen? How can you not see?"

"See *what*, Chase? You're not making any sense. What am I supposed to see—"

"That I want you!" He cuts me off with a shout.

Every part of me stiffens, but slowly, I shake my head.

"Yes, Arianna." His brows jump. "I want you."

Oh my god.

My chest caves in, and I turn away, but he grips my arms, twisting me back. "Chase—"

"I want you," he hisses, his entire being softening in the next breath. He whispers, "I want you . . ."

My teeth clench, my mind spinning. "Please don't say that."

"Tell me you want me too. Tell me you didn't give up on me."

"Chase." My voice is a broken murmur, attempting to tug free. "Let go."

But he only shakes his head, pushing closer. "Ari, look at me. Listen to me."

"I'm going to need you to take your hands off her." Noah's voice breaks through the night.

Chase instantly flushes red, anger slipping over him as his eyes point past my shoulder.

Calm as ever, and with his hands pressed into his jean pockets, Noah slowly steps up, his eyes on Chase. "You should go."

"You should fucking go," Chase spits back.

My pulse pounds out of control as I look between the two.

"You're drunk," Noah tells him.

"So?!" Chase throws a hand out. "She's safe with me regardless. She knows that."

"You should sober up. Try again tomorrow." Noah's voice is void of emotion.

My brows crash, and I whip around to face Noah, but Chase is still holding on to my arm.

Chase scoffs. "I'd never hurt her."

Noah stares him in the eye. "You already did."

My spine stiffens, and Chase blanches, releasing me as he stumbles back a step, shock drawing up his features.

"You told him." He gapes at me. "You told this fucking stranger?"

My chin lowers with guilt, but I force my eyes not to fall.

"That was for us! That was *ours*!" He shakes his head in disgust, then jerks around and staggers off.

"Chase!" My body aches. "Wait, I—" I jerk forward but freeze midstep, whipping around to Noah. "Noah, I just . . ."

"It's okay." His face is blank as he nods. "Go after him." His tone lowers. "I know you want to."

"It's not like that," I swear, my throat clogging.

He steps to me, cupping my face as he presses his lips to my cheek. Pulling back, he looks me in the eye. "Isn't it?"

I shake my head. "Noah—"

"Last time I'm going to say it . . . *go*."

"I don't want you to misunderstand. I—"

"Juliet," he warns.

Clenching my teeth until they hurt, I bite back tears, then turn and chase after Chase.

It takes a few minutes, but I spot him about fifty yards in the opposite direction, head dropped in his hands, sitting on a boulder.

"What the hell was that?!"

His head jerks upright, glaring past me, and once he realizes I'm alone, his eyes come back to mine. Something flickers across his face, but he only stares at me.

"Chase," I snap, darting forward. "You wanted to talk, fine, here I am. Talk."

"I'm sick of this shit." He gets right to it.

"Sick of what?"

"Of him. You. All of it!"

"Wha—" I throw my hands out, confused. "What do you want me to do, Chase? Hide away?"

"No—"

"Let you enjoy the life that I belong in just as much as you do so that you feel better—"

"Ari, that's not—"

"Because I did that already, and you know what? It sucked! I missed out on so much, and I'm not going to do that anymore, so you can stop trying to make me feel guilty for choosing to be happy."

"I want you to choose me!" he screams.

My words evaporate, my body turning to stone on the spot.

His eyes soften, and he comes closer. "I want you to be happy, but I want you to be happy with me."

My insides swirl, tighten and pull. "Don't do this."

"I want you to want me again."

"Chase." Everything aches.

"I want you to look at me like you used to."

"Stop."

"I want you to pick me," he whispers, reaching toward my face, but I tip my head, avoiding his touch. "Arianna . . ."

I shake my head, a nauseating feeling fighting its way through me, but he's right there.

And then his lips are on mine, pressing, stealing.

Begging.

Pick me . . .

Stunned, I stand frozen, but my mind shakes me free, screaming no.

Hell no.

That this is wrong.

My hands come up, and I shove him away.

"You . . . are an asshole." My voice shakes, tears instantly pouring down my cheeks. "Why would you do that?"

His features pull, a deep frown creasing his forehead.

"I told you I'm with someone, that I'm *with* Noah, and now you do this?" My words crack.

Chase's spine straightens. "What am I supposed to do when I feel you slipping away from me?"

"Oh my god." I swallow beyond the knot in my throat, but all it does is rise again. "I can't believe you right now. How can you be so selfish?"

Anxious, he reaches for me. "Ari."

"Don't." I jerk back. "For months I sat around wishing you'd show up at my door, knowing in the back of my mind you never would, so don't stand here and say you felt me slipping away when I was right in front of you *for months, years even* if you really think about it. You just didn't see it."

"I saw you." He shakes his head, brows furrowed. "Ari, I *see* you."

I clench my jaw, anger slipping over the sadness and burying it.

"Yeah, well, it's too late."

"I don't believe that."

"Yeah, you do." I swallow, taking backward steps. "You wouldn't have kissed me if you didn't."

The torment of standing before him is too much, so I walk away.

"I see you, Arianna." His repeated words are defeated, broken.

While my feet pause in the sand, I don't look at him but stare straight ahead at nothing.

"I don't want to be seen anymore, Chase." Emotion fights its way up my throat, but I push it down. "I want to be loved."

Slowly, I begin walking again, tension winding around my muscles with each step, but thankfully, Chase says not a word, and he doesn't try to follow.

I want to fall to the sand and cry, to scream into the night around me and beg for understanding I'll never find and that I'm unsure I even want. I don't do any of those things, though.

I head back to the house, my lungs shriveling when I find Noah sitting on the last step.

He looks up then, and as slow as ever, pushes to his feet, the lanyard his keys are clipped to hanging from his right pocket.

Panic whirls through me, but my feet don't move.

I shake my head, tears pricking at the back of my eyes, and he tips his head in encouragement.

"He kissed me." Guilt burns through my veins, and my hand presses against my stomach.

His jaw flexes, but his tone is soft. "And?"

"I didn't kiss him back. I pushed him away."

He nods again, dropping his eyes to the sand where he stands, and when they come back up, the uncertainty within them is almost debilitating.

He comes to me, the pads of his thumbs brushing under my eyes, wiping the tears I didn't realize were falling.

"I pushed him away," I repeat desperately.

"I know." He presses his mouth to my forehead, speaking against it. "I know you did."

"Tell me what you're thinking."

"Isn't it obvious?"

I pull back, forcing him to look at me. "No. It's not. Tell me."

"Come on, Juliet," he murmurs, the ache in his tone crushing my soul. "I can't compete here, not when everything you ever wanted is in reach now, just waiting for you to take it."

"I don't want it."

"Are you sure?"

My lips clamp shut, but I nod, and all that comes out is his name.

"It's okay," he promises.

"No, it's not." I take Noah's hands, pulling them into my chest. "It's not. He doesn't get to do this to us." I shake my head, breathing him in. "*I* shouldn't have done this. I shouldn't have gone after him. I should have come back inside with you. I should have left it alone."

A shadow falls over us, and he strokes my cheek. "Some conversations have to be had. Even if they're tough."

"I know." I lower my forehead to his. "But I don't want any part of anything that could hurt this." My nose begins to tingle. "Noah, I want this. I want us."

"Baby." His hands frame my face, his palms shaking.

"I want you. Only you."

His lips throb against mine, his eyes closing, only to open, satin blue piercing mine as he whispers, "Say you swear."

My chuckle is more of a cry, and I smash my lips to his, my emotions whirling.

He kisses me back, the sweep of his tongue against mine serving as a promise.

An unspoken whisper, from his heart to mine.

A whisper I'm ready to answer with one of my own.

"I swear."

Chapter 33
Arianna

After the fiasco on Thanksgiving, Noah and I have found ways to spend even more time together, be it a quick walk to class or an early morning coffee run, even a few sleepovers a week at my place.

One of the nights he was here was rather embarrassing because my parents called pretty late, so I had to let it go to voice mail, then make myself presentable and drag Noah into the living room with me, so I could call them back. The minute I told them he was here, my mom insisted on a FaceTime call instead, as I knew she would.

She was smitten in an instant, and my dad was won over when Noah deflected every compliment he was given regarding his game, finding a way to roll it over into something that didn't place him in the spotlight but highlighted the team as a whole.

It couldn't have gone any better, and by the end of it, they invited him over for the holidays, which I had to promptly remind them they wouldn't even be home for.

Of course, that only led to Mom casually slipping in how she meant next year's Christmas—her way of claiming him a keeper.

I had to agree.

Mason is back in full force and better than ever. According to Noah's play-by-play of recent practices I had decided to skip. The game plan they went with when Mason was hurt is being rolled out again this week, but with several adjustments on the line.

Brady is an official starter now. He only steps off the field when the ball is turned over, and it's the defense's turn.

Chase is doing well too, I guess, but I can't even look at him, let alone speak to him.

I'm angry and with good reason.

But I wish I weren't because rage always leads to ruin.

And it seems mine was no exception . . .

Noah had to skip his workout this morning because he had an exam he had already rescheduled from their last game, so when he messaged me saying he was going to go to the stadium to use the gym he has a key for, he asked if I wanted to tag along.

He's been beasting it up for about forty minutes now, but I'm shot.

Completely winded, I step off the treadmill, snatching my towel off the railing to wipe my face, and as I turn around, I gasp, my hand freezing midair.

A shirtless Noah stands not ten feet away. His body is angled just right, allowing me the perfect view of his abs, clenching and unclenching, as he works out his delectable arms.

I bite my lip, trailing the beads of sweat running down the center of his chest, over and between the lickable ridges of his ribs and stomach, before disappearing into his waistband.

My breathing grows heavy, my core constricting as his muscles do with each movement he makes, sending a burning desire straight through me. Rhianna's "Skin" plays through my iPod speaker, and all I can think of is the feeling of his body against mine.

My hand lifts, my fingertips skimming across my jaw and slowly dragging down from there, past my throat, until they're sprawled across my collarbone.

Noah lifts the hand weights over his head with fluid motions, his arms bending backward, his elbow bent in the air, giving me a full view of his core working. His sexy scripture tattoo teasing me, begging me to touch it, to kiss it.

To run my hands along it as I have so many times, waiting for the color within his eyes to change.

To darken.

Waiting for my man to lose his patience and take it out on me.

When he brings his arms back to his front, he glances over and does a double take. His stormy eyes lock on mine, sending a bolt of electricity from my head to my toes. Goose bumps rise over every inch of me.

There's my favorite smirk.

Every nerve in my body is on high alert, and I squeeze my legs together, a pathetic attempt to relieve some pressure.

He knows it and holds my gaze hostage and motions for me to come to him.

Hell, at this point, I'm ready to come, but not in the way he's asking.

I don't move.

I feel like a starved animal, crazed and dazed. I should be embarrassed, but I'm not.

This is Noah.

I don't have to hide a thing from him.

Without breaking eye contact, he turns his glorious body toward me, his front now on full, magnificent display as he continues his workout, a small curve holding on his juicy lips.

He knows he's turning me on, and he loves it.

With hooded eyes, he watches me, aware I'm totally transfixed.

My heart rate spikes higher, and I lick my lips, unaware I'm moving until my back hits the mirrored wall behind me.

He begins a new move, bringing both weights in just above his belly button, and throws his arms out wide with the next breath. This requires him to stand wide, steel his hips, and puff his chiseled chest out ever so slightly with each extension of his arms, and I can't take it anymore. I'm burning up everywhere, all over.

It's a raw, desperate need I can't and don't have to fight.

So I won't.

As my palms glide along my silhouette, I imagine they're his, slowly sliding from the sides of my breasts down my stomach. My head falls back against the mirror, and my eyes decide to close.

Just as I reach the band of my gym shorts, a warm hand wraps gently around my neck, and I freeze, a smile curling my lips.

Got him.

I'm too far gone to open my eyes, especially when his heated breath fans over my face in the most erotic of ways, soft and warm and ragged.

I turn my head, unable to handle the sensation growing within me.

Craving release, my fingertips slip into the waistband of my spandex, but he stops me from going any farther by pressing his tight body up against mine.

I whimper, his overheated body pressed into mine too much of a tease when I know the feeling of his skin on mine. Noah groans in response to the sound.

His hand slips down my neck and across my collarbone, and my breath gets lodged in my throat.

He dips his head into the crook of my exposed neck, his favorite place, *my* favorite place, and his tongue darts out, tasting my sweat-covered flesh.

"Mm." He moans. "I love the taste of your sweat." His tongue runs from the bottom of my throat to my ear. "I want to taste all of you."

"You have."

"Not here." He cups me over my bottoms. "Not with my tongue."

My thighs clench, and he takes my ear lobe between his teeth, biting down lightly. He assaults my neck next, earning another gasp from me. His hand presses more firmly against me, gliding up until the tips of his fingers are diving beyond the waistband.

"I like these." He peppers wet, hot kisses to my chest.

"Yeah?" I croak, tilting my head more.

"Mm-hmm," he mumbles. The vibration of his lips against my skin sends a shiver down my spine.

"Then they're all yours," I pant. "Go ahead, take 'em now."

His body bounces with silent laughter.

"I'm so glad I amuse—" I cut off in a moan when his coarse fingers flick over my clit, before settling over the sweet spot.

I push into his touch, my plea desperate and needy. "Please."

He groans, his free hand cupping my ass. Squeezing.

"Tell me, baby," he rasps in the sexiest fucking voice I have *ever* heard. "Tell me what you want."

I squeeze my eyes shut tighter. "Make me come."

My man doesn't make me wait a second longer.

He swiftly pushes a leg between mine, nudging mine open more, and slides a finger inside. And then another.

He moans, crashing his lips with mine, my arousal coating his fingers as he drives in and out. His thumb working magic on my clit.

"You're soaking my hand, Juliet."

"F-fuck." I shake.

Sensing his eyes on me, mine open, and he grins, nipping at my lips.

"You're twitching, just like you do on my cock," he rasps, his eyes darkening.

"So give it to me." I moan. "Let me squeeze you."

"In a minute." His attention falls to my body, and he licks his lips, his eyes coming up to mine as he lowers to his knees on the mat below. His fingers slip out of me, cupping up to tug the hem of my bottoms down, pausing when his knuckles are even with my clit, without fully revealing me. I reach up, gripping the back of his head, and tug him toward me.

"You'll be the first," I admit, knowing what it will do to him.

His eyes flash. "Say yes."

"Yes."

I shake in anticipation, and then his lips close over me and my hips buck, my hands flying to his hair, pressing him into me.

His tongue sweeps, rolls, and sucks, and my gaze flicks past him, watching the muscles of his back move in the mirror across the room as he brings me to the hilt.

I look at myself, taking in my flushed cheeks and wild eyes. It's insanely stimulating, seeing myself, watching my reactions in the mirror as he watches me. As he goes down on me for the first time.

It's too much. I'm about to explode.

"Open your eyes, Juliet. Open those pretty honey eyes and look at me."

I do as he says. His dark blues are even darker, his lids are low, fully hooded, and my pussy is in his mouth.

My breathing picks up, my hands tugging on his hair.

"That's it," he croons. "Come for me, baby."

"Kiss me while I come."

He groans, sucking hard, and when my hips buck again, he darts up, slamming his mouth into mine. The man eats me alive, his tongue demanding entrance, curling around mine and coaxing me through my orgasm.

I rip away, gasping for air Noah can't seem to find either. He's breathing just as hard as I am now.

His eyes take on a naughty glint as his hand dips between my legs, and he slowly pushes inside, smirking as I twitch around him. I whimper even more when he pulls out, lapping every bit of me off of him.

I'm on fire all over again, my body humming in places I didn't know were capable of arousal.

I want a repeat of what just happened. Stat.

My hands shoot up, going for a fistful of his hair as he wraps his arms around me tightly. Possessively.

Something crashes to the floor around us, and we jump.

Noah doesn't pull back or release me as to not expose my body, but he does look up into the mirror my back is pressed against, and his muscles lock.

"Shit," he mumbles, his eyes slicing to mine.

The stiffness within them has my stomach turning, but I shift, peeking past his shoulder.

326

Chase stands in the doorway, staring right at us. The noise was his gym bag falling from his fingertips, crashing to the floor.

A coldness washes over me, and I don't look away, but he does. His face hardens, his glare pinned on the back of Noah's head.

And how fucking dare he.

I run my hand up Noah's arm, gaining Chase's attention once more, and Noah's eyes tighten.

"Let's go somewhere private and finish this."

Something flashes over Noah, but he blinks it away just as quickly as it came. He doesn't say a word but peeks down, adjusting my shorts so that all that needs to be hidden is, before moving over to the weights to get his shirt.

Chase still hasn't spoken a word, but he's looking directly at me, following my every step toward him as I lead Noah and me to the only door that leads in and out of this place, the one behind Chase.

Right as I'm about to pass, I stop, and Noah's body nearly bumps into mine.

"You can have the place all to yourself now," I say, and then I'm out the door, Noah right behind me. I slow my pace to walk in line with him, but he passes me and continues walking.

Suddenly, he stops, his chin lifting into the air before he whips around to face me. His expression is hard to read. It's a mixture of anger and disappointment, of sorrow.

Just like that, I feel two inches tall.

Humiliation burns over me, and I can hardly meet his eye. I dart forward, my hand coming up to cover my mouth. "Oh my god, Noah. I—"

He goes to speak but slams his mouth shut, shaking his head instead.

"I don't know why I did that." I run my hands over my hair. "I'm so sorry. I didn't . . . I don't . . ."

What the hell is wrong with me?

I'm not vindictive, and I don't want to hurt anyone, especially him.

But that, that was downright nasty.

Spiteful.

I'm disgusted.

Vomit threatens to rise in my throat, my shoulders slumping in defeat, and I look away, too ashamed to face him.

After a moment, Noah sighs. "Come here," he says gently, trying to hide the hurt in his tone, but I hear it.

Sense it.

Feel it in my fucking bones.

Like a dog with its tail tucked between its legs, I make my way to him, and he tucks my loose hairs behind my ear, his hand holding there a moment.

"Let's get out of here, okay?" He pulls his keys from his bag. "It's getting cold."

Nodding, I follow him to his truck.

I feel like, no, I *am* such a super bitch that I don't even know what to say to him. There are no words to excuse what I just did.

The uncertainties he voiced less than two weeks ago are likely in the forefront of his mind, and I'm the one who put them there.

I used him to make Chase angry, and we both know it.

Time ticks slowly, the tension in the air tightening by the second and making the car ride home an uncomfortable one.

As we arrive at my dorm, he pulls up in front of the entrance instead of parking like he always does.

A few seconds go by without a word, so with shaky palms, I climb out, forcing myself to close the door. I turn to face him, realizing his hands haven't even left the steering wheel.

"Noah, I really am so sorry."

"I know." His voice is wounded, but the fresh cut bleeds only understanding. "I know."

It's more devastating than anger because it means he thinks there's something to understand in the first place. There isn't.

"But I need you to do something for me," he whispers, his voice hoarse.

"Anything," I swear, preparing my gut for what he has to say and noting how his jaw clenches as if it pains him to do so.

"I need you to really stop and think. About everything. All of it." He drops his frown to the seat, slowly bringing his eyes to mine. "I need you to think about him."

Shock has ice spreading through my stomach, tightening my muscles to the point of pain.

"If you still love him at all," he rasps. "If there's even the smallest of chances for you and him, I need you to let me go."

The air whooshes from my lungs in a quick hiss, my heart beating out of control. "Noah."

"I need you to have mercy on me, Juliet . . . and let me go."

Anguish peaks, my muscles convulsing as a sob threatens to tear through me.

Frantic, I fumble with the door handle, but Noah shakes his head, and I freeze, gripping the frame once more.

"Go inside, Juliet." He faces forward, swallowing. "Please."

It takes a moment, but I manage to let go. I stumble backward, breathless, breaking.

My vision begins to haze, and I press along my temples, doing as he asks as he drives away.

I'm not sure how I managed to get up to my dorm because I don't remember getting the door open or stepping onto the elevator. I don't remember going inside or Cameron coming out of her room.

I don't remember falling to the floor, yet here I am, my best friend right beside me, stroking my hair. Her lips are moving, but I hear nothing, and then I *see* nothing, but goddamn it, I feel every.

Single.

Thing.

Chapter 34

Arianna

The sun brings with it the gloom of the night before, so I pull the blankets up over my head and bask in it. And that's where I stay all day, as well as the one that follows, but by the time the third day rolls around, Cameron is climbing on top of my desk, yanking my curtains down. Literally.

She tosses them on the floor, kicking them under the bed, her hands falling to her hips. "Get up. Shower. I'm making you food."

"I'm not hungry." I flip onto my opposite side, staring at the wall.

She rips my blankets off, and I squeeze my eyes shut, rolling over onto my back.

"Girlfriend, I know everything sucks right now, but you can't do this."

My eyes move to hers, and she offers a small smile. Stepping forward, she pats the mattress. "Get up, get fresh. Plug in your phone."

I wince, and her shoulders fall.

"You know he didn't call," she whispers. "He told you he needed a few days."

Moisture pricks my eyes, and I nod. "I know."

She snags my phone off my desk and walks over to set it on the charging station beside my bed. "Then you have nothing to be afraid of, sister. Now, up. Or I'll pull out the big guns . . . and call Mason."

Squeezing my arm, she smiles and walks out, so before I

can talk myself out of it, I drag myself into the bathroom, locking myself inside.

Even though I spent the last two days in bed, I had no false hope of sleeping, and I didn't. I had lain awake most of the time, searching for words to say to Noah, but no matter how many versions of I'm sorry, please forgive me, I run through, none are enough. Not by a long shot.

Noah came into my life at a time when I needed a friend, and that's exactly what he became. He was the one who inadvertently helped me through the bullshit I allowed myself to fall into after everything with Chase, so he saw how deep my feelings ran. How hard it was to let go and every other embarrassing moment I eagerly shared. Hell, Noah's the one who helped me heal, and I didn't even know it happened until one day something changed. Suddenly, the man I lost sleep thinking about wasn't the one it used to be.

I fell for Noah, and I fell hard.

If you asked me a few days ago if there was a pain point in our relationship, I'd have sworn no such thing existed. Now I realize how blind I've been. He and I, we do have a sore spot.

Chase.

The thing is, only one of us felt it.

The never-ending unease.

The fear that at any moment, the person you want might decide they want someone else.

I knew Chase would be in my life forever, in one way or another. I knew this before and after we crossed the line, and Noah chose to accept that. He got to know me, grew to like me, and showed how much he wanted me while well aware the one man from my past would be a constant in my future.

So, for me to do what I did and carelessly use a moment with Noah to show my anger for the man he feared losing me to was just . . . fucked up.

I fucked up, and I can't take it back.

I hurt a man I'd do anything for.

I've never been so foolish.

All I want to do is call him, rush to his house, and spill my regrets at his feet. I want to beg him for forgiveness.

But I won't. Not yet.

He asked for time, so I'm trying to give it to him.

It's the least I can do.

Unfortunately for me, when I make it back to my room, picking up my phone for the first time in days, the other person involved wants the opposite of space.

A string of messages waits for me, every one of them from Chase.

With a deep breath, I open them up, the first being from the night he walked in on us.

12:05 a.m., Chase: What the hell was that?

12:15 a.m., Chase: Why aren't you answering?

12:25 a.m., Chase: Whatever, Ari. Hope you're having fun.

1:47 a.m., Chase: Can we talk?

Angry tears prick my eyes, and I growl.

I hate this.

Everything is wrong, and I don't know how to fix it, so I do the only thing I can and engross myself in my studies, determined to, at the very least, end the semester with the best grades I'm capable of, all the while wishing that each hour passing will be the hour Noah calls.

But he doesn't, and it's killing me.

Noah

This is fucking killing me.

In the three days since I watched Ari disappear inside her dorm, it's as if I forgot how to function in a world where she isn't with me, because even when she wasn't physically, she was always still there, in the back of my mind, in the *front* of my mind. She was all fucking over.

But with each day passing, it feels like she's slipping away a little more.

A little further.

Before, if I wasn't with her, I was counting down the minutes until I could be.

Now, I sit around watching the clock tick around with no end. The hand turns and turns, tightening my chest like a wrench, stripping me of my threads and leaving me a gutted mess that can't be repaired.

Everyone knows that the only way to fix a fucked-up bolt is to rip it from the stud, and I'm feeling that. It's as if my heart is being torn out, straight through my bruised ribs.

I don't know what the fuck I was thinking, asking her to think of him.

What if she did?

What if that's it for us?

What if she becomes my greatest loss as I turn into her deepest regret?

What if my worst fears are the furthest thing from the fucking truth?

What if my baby is hurting, dying inside like me?

Slowly, and a little more each day?

Twice as hard each night?

What if she misses me, and all she wants is for my arms to wrap around her, for me to pull her in and tell her it's okay? That we're okay, and that I love her with all I am and want her for all she is?

That right there is about enough to kill me.

The mere thought of being the reason behind her pain is too much for me.

I'm sick to my stomach. My muscles ache.

My head and my heart are at war, and I'm not sure either can win.

Because I did this.

I asked my girl to consider that maybe I'm not the one for her, knowing all the while she is the *only* one for me.

I need my baby, and I can only fucking hope she needs me just as much.

Chapter 35

Arianna

How five single days weigh like five years, I don't know, but they do. Every minute is slow passing, every footstep in the hall of my dorm triggering, my mind tricking myself that maybe, just maybe, it's him on the other side. That his knuckles will come down with his knock, and when I open the door, he'll be standing there with a smile, but that never happens.

The anxiety alone made it too hard to stay home, so I've been hiding in the library when not in class, and I forced myself to skip their game two nights ago, but as painful as it was, I did watch it on TV.

Mason's pissed I won't tell him what's going on.

Brady checks on me every night.

And Chase, he's been calling and texting me twice a day, all of which have gone unanswered.

I don't know why, but this morning, it all became too much. I woke with a heavy sense of desperation, of need, and I couldn't help myself.

I called Noah when I knew he should have been free, but he didn't pick up, so I sent him a message, hoping that would work.

He never responded.

Cameron said she's seen him a time or two when visiting Trey, but he doesn't stop to talk with anyone, simply going straight to his room. She *has* talked to Chase.

According to her, he's resorted to coming over now that there's no denying I'm ignoring him. Supposedly, he stopped by twice this week already, both times when I was out, thank God.

With how determined he seems to be to try and reach me, I'm not sure how much longer I can avoid him, a fact that rings true when I round the corner of the library, where I've been hiding myself most days, and there Chase sits not fifteen yards away.

I freeze in place, a million thoughts running through my mind, the loudest of which telling me to make a run for it, but my feet don't move.

Maybe it's time to let him say what's on his mind. To have a real conversation, like we should have done so long ago. The problem is, I wasn't ready for it then, and to be honest, I don't think he was either.

Over the last few days, I've thought a lot about Chase, more than I care to admit, but it was what Noah asked of me, and I realized quickly how necessary it was.

I had blocked out everything, the pain that came with the mention of his name alone was too much at the time, and it caused everything to become muddled. I put him in a box and pushed it away.

I needed to remember, to revisit every moment with Chase, to realize where we went wrong . . . and where we felt right. My memories reminded me of why I fell in love with him in the first place. Alone with my thoughts, I cried and laughed, and then I realized . . .

I missed him.

I miss the guy who would take it easy on me when the others would get on my case about a skirt they thought was a little too short. The guy who slipped Cameron and me a couple beers in secret when Mason said we weren't allowed to get drunk.

The guy who stayed out in the water with me long after the others complained of the cold because he knew I hated when it was time to leave the ocean.

But it wasn't only about him.

I missed our group nights, where no one else was invited, just the five of us.

Me, Cameron, Mason, Brady, and Chase.

Ever since junior high, the only time we were apart was a few weeks each summer when the boys went off to football camp, but even then, we would video chat at least once a day.

Of course, Cam and I would have a blast without our bodyguards, but we quickly missed the other pieces to our puzzle. Even when we were having the time of our lives in St. Petersburg this past summer, where Cam met Trey, we missed our boys.

After the blowout with Chase at the beginning of the school year, things changed, and it wasn't fair to the others, especially since they were pretty much clueless as to why the air in the room was different.

It's time to make it right for all of us, for real this time. I know that, but even so, I can't express how guilty I feel for missing Chase.

How could I miss the man I was so angry with that I so callously hurt mine?

I ache for Noah, deeply, desperately.

The loss eating me away day by day is like nothing I've ever felt. So many times, I wanted to say to hell with it and run all the way to his house, but I held myself back. Barely.

I did head there once when I was feeling extra alone, but as soon as his truck came into view, tears fell, and I turned around.

What kills me most is how I know he's living right now. Alone and in silence.

He doesn't party much, if at all, and he doesn't run in a large crowd. All the free time he had he spent with me, and I know he hasn't filled those slots with anything else.

I know he's as lonely as I am, more so even.

What's worse is what must be running through his mind, doubt I planted.

It's my job to take it away.

It's with that thought in mind that I don't turn around and walk in the opposite direction.

I walk over to Chase.

337

Dressed in a hoodie and sweats with his football bag dropped in front of him, his head hangs. His leg is bouncing like he's nervous, and he stares at his palms as he rubs them together.

"Hey," I call once I'm a few steps away.

His head pops up, unease written all over him. "Hey."

Chase jumps up, his mouth opening, but nothing comes out, so I offer a small smile, and that seems to ease him some.

"You got a sec?" he wonders.

Nerves swirl in my stomach, but I motion toward the table anyway.

He reaches for me, and I let him pull me onto the seat of the picnic table.

My eyes fall to our joined hands, and slowly, I pull away, looking up at him.

He nods, swallowing.

"I miss you, Ari. I miss everything." Apprehension pulls at his features. "I'm so fucking sorry for everything I did and for everything I should have done but didn't."

"I know, and I'm sorry I acted the way I did after. I shouldn't have gotten upset with you when we didn't go anywhere after that night. I knew what I was doing, and I didn't care then what happened after. That was on me."

"Don't," he says sternly, shifting to face me better. "Don't do that. I was, no, I *am* a stupid man. I should have . . . I shouldn't have . . . fuck." A frustrated sigh leaves him, and he meets my eyes.

We stare at each other in silence for several seconds.

Pain and regret gaze back at me, confusion slowly following.

With a small smile, Chase reaches up, tucking my hair behind my ear. His touch lingers a moment, and when his thumb caresses my cheek the slightest bit, I can't help but lean in.

He had so much of my past, and it's not that it's hard to let it go. I'd already done that once. It's seeing the pain he's in that stings. He's never shown it before, not like this.

But the feeling of his skin on mine is all wrong, so I cover his hand with my own, and his eyes gloss over as I remove his from my face.

"I wish we could start over," he says then.

A light laugh leaves me, and I shake my head. "I don't. Yeah, things got shitty, but just because things went wrong doesn't mean that night wasn't special."

"It was," he whispers. "It was special."

My lips twitch, and I lower my eyes to my lap. "I've been thinking a lot."

"So have I," he rushes, gripping my hands, and I look to him. "There's a lot more I want to say, but I'm kind of out of time now. I've been out here for a couple hours already, hoping I would catch you a little earlier," he admits sheepishly. "Think we can talk after practice tomorrow?"

My stomach turns, but I manage a smile, nodding. "Playoffs. That's pretty epic."

Chase chuckles, but his eyes fall to the grass. "Yeah. Pretty epic."

After a moment, he sighs, pushing to his feet, and I stand with him.

Hesitantly, he steps in, his arms coming around me, and while I tense a second, I hug him back in the next.

There's tension between us, it's obvious, so in an attempt to lighten the mood, I joke, "I'm glad you stalked me before practice, or I'd be gagging right now."

Chase chuckles, and I pull back, smiling up at him, but the moment my eyes meet his, my throat runs dry.

A familiar tingle runs down my spine, and I shiver, instantly going stiff.

His brows furrow in confusion, and slowly, I glance over my shoulder.

My stomach hits the ground, an instant wave of nausea rolling through me.

No . . .

Frozen in place with his keys dangling from his fingers, blue eyes sear me.

My hands fly to my sides, and he cuts a quick glance to Chase. He nods, and I shake my head.

"Noah," I breathe his name, desperation oozing from my tone. I step toward him.

He turns away.

"Noah, wait!" I rush forward, but he's already slipping into his truck, and then he's gone.

Tears flood my eyes, and I clutch my abdomen with one hand, trying to get a hold of myself.

"Ari—" Chase begins from behind me.

"I need a minute," I say, without turning around, following Noah's truck from the parking lot.

"Arianna—"

"I said I need a minute. Please." I swallow.

In my peripheral, he nods, grabs his bag, and walks away.

For several minutes, I choke for air, fight back tears, and scream internally.

And then I steel my spine, take a deep breath, and push forward.

I walk straight to the practice field, going the opposite direction Chase disappeared, and I hang back near the parking lot.

Noah's truck isn't in sight.

I go inside the stadium, searching the field as the team takes it.

Noah isn't there.

I wait, and before I know it, the sun's gone down, and the coach is calling it quits.

Noah never shows.

Chapter 36
Arianna

Pushing past the entrance, I curve right and pound on the small door for a solid five minutes before Brady appears beside me. Slowly, he reaches up, grabbing and lowering my hands to my sides.

"Ari baby, I don't think he's in there," he says softly, and I crumble.

He hugs me, attempting to keep me upright, and Cameron slides in front of me, worry carved across her features.

"It's been two days." Tears fall from my eyes, and I look away as a few football players walk by, staring. "He wasn't at practice yesterday, and he isn't here today, so where is he?"

"Maybe he went out for food or something?" Brady's tone is dejected, his attempt futile, and he knows it.

"Come on." Cameron wraps her arm through mine. "We should go home. You need to—"

"Don't say sleep, Cameron." I rub my eyes.

"Honey, he's not here, and we don't know if he has been in the last two days. What are you going to do, camp out in the entryway?"

"If I have to."

"Ari, don't do this to yourself."

"You didn't see his face." I look to them. "He was . . . God, he was . . ." Devastated. "I can't even imagine what he's thinking."

The front door opens, another group of guys arriving home, and I hold my breath, but it's Chase who is the last to step through.

He looks from me to Noah's door and back.

He walks over. "Ari."

"Please, just—" I rush out, my hands flying up as I slip past. "Not now."

"Arianna!" Cameron shouts, chasing me out onto the porch, but I'm already down the driveway and stepping onto the road.

Spinning in place, I scan the area, my hands folding over my head.

My eyes squeeze shut, and I clench my jaw, bending at the knees until I'm squatting in place.

"Fuck!" I finally scream, my body shaking.

Several heads turn my way, but I ignore them.

I jerk upright and start walking.

I walk every inch of campus, circling each building and covering all corners from the center to the outer edge. I don't think I expected to find him, but once there's nowhere left to go, I realize I must have hoped I would.

Defeat washes over me, and I want to drop to the grass and curl into a ball, but my feet don't stop moving.

I walk until the sun comes up, and then I go home. Locking myself in my room, I cry myself to sleep.

Later that day, when Cameron pounds on my door, I tell her to go away, and by the time I wake again, it's after nine thirty, tonight's game likely almost over.

Showering last night's sweat from my body, I quickly throw on some clothes and rush out the door, wet hair and all, but by the time the stadium is in sight, still a good hundred yards away, the campus is already flooded with fans on their way to finish off their Saturday night somewhere. Dropping onto the nearest bench, I go to the school website, where the score is already posted.

The Sharks lost the first round of playoffs, their season coming to an end as of tonight.

That means tonight was Noah's final game as a college quarterback, and I wasn't there to see it.

Hopelessness aches inside me, and I close my eyes.

Noah hasn't accepted any of my attempts to contact him, so it's with a shaky soul and pure desperation that I pull up our message thread, sending him a text I'm hoping he can't ignore.

I turn off my phone, sitting in the same spot until the parking lot is near empty, and then I head for the football house, praying when I get there, Noah will be waiting.

Unfortunately for me, he isn't, but a keg full of cheap beer is. So I fill a cup.

And then I fill another.

Fresh drink in hand, I spin, coming face-to-face with Chase.

I jerk to a stop, smiling, and he frowns.

"Hey." He looks past me toward the guy manning the drinks and then peeks into my cup.

My eyes follow, and I chuckle. "Yeah, he's not the best pourer. It's mostly foam, but it's doing its job." I push past him, move through the backyard and step into the house.

He keeps pace with me, and I can feel his inquisition. "And what job is that?"

"Think about all the reasons people turn to alcohol and check mark every single one."

I glance his way, and his frown deepens.

"This might not be the best time, but we were supposed to talk, and we never got the chance."

"Yeah, we never had the chance for a lot of things, did we?" I stop walking, bringing my cup to my lips. "We feel like a lifetime ago."

"No, we don't."

I scoff, nodding my head. "Yeah, we do."

Sighing, he reaches out, but I bend, evading him.

"Don't touch me." I laugh, finish off my cup, and tip my head at him. "Last time you touched me, you ruined everything all over again, but I mean, hey, I ruined it first, so what's it really matter."

"Things don't have to be this way, you know?"

"How else could it be, Chase?"

"Better." He steps closer. "It could be better for us."

"Please." I roll my eyes. "Until Mason sees, right? Been there, thought that. Got fucked over."

He jerks forward suddenly, and it takes a moment for my vision to adjust to his nearness.

Suddenly, he's in my face. "Tell me I can kiss you, and I will. Right here, right now, where everyone will see." He grips my chin. "Tell me I can kiss you."

"What the fuck?!" Mason's voice booms from somewhere.

And just like that, the chatter around the room dies down, and my brother is gently nudging me aside, stepping between Chase and me.

Chase's eyes widen for a split second, but then he stands up straight, facing off with his best friend.

"What'd you just say to my sister?" Mason pushes on Chase's chest, shoving him back a few steps.

Brady rushes over, Cam beside him.

Chase shakes his head, lifting his hands. "I'm sorry, but . . . you're going to have to get used to this."

"What?!" Mason and I snap at the same time, both our heads jerking toward one another.

He frowns, confused, his glare quickly moving back to his friend.

Cam tries to step up. "Guys, maybe we should head outside?"

"Fuck that!" Mason throws his hands around. "What the fuck do you mean I'm going to have to get used to it? Used to what? Are you fucking my sister?" Mason demands before turning to me. "Are you fucking him?"

"Mason," Brady clips. "Stop."

"No, you know what, it's fine, Brady. Let's have a fucking therapy session right here in the middle of a party." If my words are slurred, it's unbeknownst to me. I pin my eyes on my brother. "No, Mase. I'm not 'fucking' him."

"You better fuckin' not be!" he rears.

And you know what, fuck this shit.

344

"Oh?" I pull back, crossing my arms defiantly. "Why is that? Can't stand the thought of your best friend on top of your 'little' sister?"

"Oh shit," Brady murmurs from beside me.

Cameron tries to interject, but I push her away, and her mouth clamps shut.

"Watch your mouth, Arianna," Mason says sternly.

"Well, guess what, asshole?" I hear Chase's 'no' from beside me but fuck him too. "It already happened!" I watch my brother turn his murderous glare on Chase and start to rush forward before Brady steps in the middle of them, holding Mason back.

"Oh, but don't worry, Mase, I was telling the truth. I'm not *fucking him*. Your friendship was more important than I was, just as you hoped, so congratulations, Mason." I throw my arms out. "He's all yours."

I storm out the front door, ignoring the commotion that ensues with my exit.

"Ari, wait!" Chase yells, hot on my heels, but I don't stop until he's gripping my arm, whipping me around. "Ari, damn it, hold on!"

He jumps in front of me.

"What?! What do you want, Chase?" Emotionally drained, I drop my shoulders. "What do you want from me?"

"Everything!" he yells. "I want everything, Arianna." I go to shout, but he holds his hands up. "Wait. Just let me speak, okay?"

I stare at him for a few moments before nodding.

"Look, I know you said it was too late, but it doesn't have to be. Ari, this summer . . ." He swallows. "I was an ass. Everything that happened between us, it shouldn't have gone down like that. I see that now. I need you to believe me when I tell you that it won't happen again. I won't push you away again, and I won't allow anything to get between us if you just give us the chance we deserve."

I'm shaking my head before he even finishes. "Chase, no. I'm not in the same place I was this summer."

"I get that," he says insistently, reaching out and snagging my hands. "Honestly, I do. I just want you to know I'm ready. I'm here. I know you're scared. I know I'm the one who gave you a reason to be but—"

"Chase—"

My head continues to shake.

He's not getting it.

He doesn't get it.

My fingertips rub at my temples. "Please, stop talking."

I keep walking, but he slips into my space again.

"No. You need to hear me. You need to understand what I'm saying." He gestures toward the door. "I pretty much told my best friend to fuck off just now because I need you to know how serious I am. Just give me a chance to show you I can love you like you deserve, because Arianna, I do love—"

"I don't love you anymore!" I scream, my muscles freezing.

Chase goes stiff, and over his shoulder, I spot my family, all rushing this way, all jolting to a stop at the same second. Slowly, they inch closer, each wearing their version of shock and confusion.

They heard what I said, maybe more.

Tears prick the backs of my eyes, and my nose tingles.

Chase's hands come up to run down his face, and his mouth forms a hard line.

I swallow past the knot in my throat. I never told Chase I was in love with him. This is the first he's heard it. The first my brother's heard.

The irony of this moment is lost on me, how my omission is also my rejection.

How the secret is out, but the need for it is over.

They shouldn't have heard this before Noah.

No one should have.

Not until I've looked him in the eye and spoken it out loud.

Not until he knew, without a doubt, I was his.

I back away, but Chase grabs me.

"Don't do this," he pleads.

"Let me go."

"Arianna, please."

"She said"—my brother slips between us—"to let her fucking go," he growls, shoving Chase hard in the chest.

My body jerks forward as Chase staggers back, but he quickly releases me, and I catch myself on the grass.

Cameron rushes over, but I manage to wobble to my feet, right as Mason advances on Chase, throwing a right hook before Chase can say a word, blood spilling from his lips.

"Come on, motherfucker, don't puss out now." Mase spits to the side, diving for him.

He tackles him to the ground, and Chase gets him into a headlock, but Mason rolls out, bringing his elbow down on his nose.

"Fuck," Brady mumbles, moving in. "All right, that's it."

Brady grips Mason by the arms, yanking him backward, and Chase hops to his feet.

"I can't fucking believe you!" Mason seethes. "You fucked my sister?!" Mason kicks, but Brady holds him at bay.

"It wasn't like that!"

"Yeah, it fucking was. This is why she was depressed when we got here. Because you fucked her, and you left her."

"You're the one—"

"Don't fucking finish that sentence, asshole. You chose to be with her, and then you turned your back on her."

"I didn't want to hurt you!" Chase confesses, but it only makes Mason angrier.

"That's fucked up, and you know it! If hurting me protects her, then that's what you do. That's what I'd want. You fucking know me, man!" He shakes his head. "You know this."

Chase looks away, ashamed. "I didn't want to ruin anything."

"You ruined everything when you took her virginity and left her brokenhearted."

Chase's face is an instant sheet of white, his eyes snapping to mine. Everyone else's follows.

My mouth is agape, my eyes brimmed with tears.

"No . . ." he whispers, subconsciously moving forward. "Arianna, no."

Mason jerks an arm free, shooting it out in time to grip Chase's shirt before he can pass, and he yanks him into his face.

But as Mason looks into the eyes of his best friend and Chase's shoulders fall, Mason's frown finds me behind him. "You didn't tell him?"

My neck is stiff, but I shake my head frantically in apology, in regret.

I look to Cameron, who bites on her nails, to Brady, who hangs his head.

"I . . . have to go." I take backward steps, my hand darting out when I bump into the car on the curb, and I rush around it, crossing the street.

"Ari, come on," Mason snaps, and together, they all move down the yard toward the sidewalk. "Get back over here."

"Arianna, wait!" Chase calls next, and I grip my temples.

"Back the fuck up!" Mason screams.

"I'm going to grab her!"

"You're not going anywhere near her!" he booms. "Ari! Where are you even going?!"

Shaking my head, my vision blurs.

I don't know.

I can't think.

"Don't make me lay you out, Chase, because I fucking will."

"Fuck you, Mason."

"You guys, stop!" Cameron screams. "Mason, let him go!"

I squeeze my eyes shut, blocking them out.

I can hardly breathe.

I have to find Noah.

I want to talk to him.

I need to tell him I know what I want.

That it's him.

I need to tell him that I love him.

Noah

My feet stop, and I bend, putting my hands on my knees. My chest pounds furiously, and I try for a deep breath, but it's easier said than done.

The second I saw Ari's text come through, I was a six-pack in, but I knew I had to get to her, so I locked my truck up and started running.

I ran for no less than five miles without stopping.

My breathing calms a bit, so I stand, and as I get a few feet farther, shouting reaches my ears. I look up, squinting past the last couple houses before mine, and that's when I see her.

Ari, clutching her stomach as she takes backward steps.

I jog toward her, my eyes widening when I spot Mason and Chase shoving at each other, and Mason throws a punch, screaming in Chase's face, but I stop at the edge of the sidewalk.

"Mason, let him go!" Cameron yells.

I step from the sidewalk, ignoring them.

"Juliet," I call to her.

Her body jolts upright as if she's slammed into an invisible wall, and slowly, she finds me.

Her lips part, a broken cry slipping from her lips. "Noah . . ."

The longing in her tone about wrecks me, and I clutch my chest.

Baby . . .

Her shoulders hunch in apprehension, her arms wrapping around herself as if readying for a blow, in case I serve her with one like I did the other day.

Like I've done the last week.

My Juliet, I hurt you, too.

Regret burns through my every vein, and I glance at Mason and the others.

At Chase, who stands not ten feet from me, both his lip and right brow split open. They stand at the edge of the grass, tension whirling in the air around them, both looking from me to her, to each other. I don't know what I walked up on, but I don't care.

I turn to my girl, lifting my phone into the air, and her body sags.

She faces me fully now, her words a hopeful whisper, "You got my message?"

I nod. "I did."

"And you came."

My lips twitch, and I nod again. "I should have come sooner."

Tears fall from her eyes, and a broken chuckle slips from her. "It's okay. Just don't do it again," she teases, but it's not enough to hide the pain in her voice.

Pain that I fed, fearing I was the only one who felt our loss. I wasn't. She felt it.

She feels it.

She's mine.

"Never, baby." My chest clenches. "Never again."

The back of her hand comes up to cover her mouth, and she sniffles as I step around the old truck at the curb.

Her arms fall to her sides, and she smiles, and then she breaks out into a run.

I chuckle, but then a flash catches my eye.

My head snaps left, panic erupting within me.

I dart forward. "No!"

"Ari!" Mason shouts, Cameron's scream echoing around him.

Arms wrap around my shoulders, and I'm yanked backward.

In the same second, the squeal of brakes pierces the air, followed by a boom so loud it shakes my core. Screams fill the air, and I tear free of the body behind me.

Shattered glass fills the street, cutting up my knees and hands as I crawl through it, my body lurching forward as I reach the crunched-up bumper of the old pickup.

A scream tears through me, and suddenly, others are falling beside me.

Someone clutches my shirt.

Someone cries.

Someone pleads.

I don't move.

I can't breathe.

All I can do is stare at the girl I love lying lifeless in the center of the street.

Chapter 37
Noah

Seven hours of no news is excruciating, but the four that follow, when the nurse finally comes up to tell us there's been a complication, are the worst.

They're full of nothing but fear and regret.

Of pain and what-if.

What if I got to her in time tonight?

What if I didn't walk away from her the other day?

What if I never get to tell her I love her?

That she's more than I knew existed, all that I could ever need, and everything I will always want.

Arianna Johnson makes up my entire being.

Without her, I'm nothing.

Not much is said over the next sixteen hours, and that goes for all of us. We pace the room, and every so often, one of us punches a wall or kicks a chair, charging into the hall, just to come right back and bury our faces in our hands.

Finally, the doctor comes out, exhaustion showing in the dark circles beneath his eyes. He pulls his mask down with a nod.

"For Miss Johnson?" he asks, even though he knows the answer already.

"Is she okay?" Mason rushes forward.

Cameron grips my sleeve, shaking.

"She's stable."

A choppy breath explodes from my chest, and I fall against the wall. Pressing the heels of my palms into my eyes, I drop my head back.

A hand clamps on my shoulder, and I look over to find Chase. He nods, his jaw clenching, and we look back to the doctor.

"When can we see her?" Brady asks.

"Soon, but I have to tell you, we're not in the clear quite yet."

"Keep talking, doc." Mason swallows.

He looks over us a moment, and it's obvious he's picking his words carefully. "Arianna suffered injuries along most of her upper body, and we did find a small fracture in her skull. As a result of that, her body went into shock, and we were forced to put her into a medically induced coma."

"Oh my god," Cameron cries, and Mason quickly spins, taking her in his arms. He pulls her close, waiting for more.

"She's in pain?" I rasp.

"Not anymore." He folds his clipboard in front of him. "She was in a great deal of pain, and with her injuries, that can lead to a coma. Her brain would simply shut down in reaction to the trauma, which is why we felt it safest to take the route we did."

"Why?"

"To keep the brain from reacting or responding. We have to give it time to heal as the next step is monitoring her for swelling."

"If that happens?" Chase pushes forward. "If her brain swells?"

The man nods. "Then we have to go in and relieve it."

"How long will you keep her asleep?"

"As long as she needs. A day, maybe two. Maybe a little longer. It all depends on how tonight goes. If we can get through tonight without complications, we might be able to breathe a little easier come tomorrow."

We nod, looking each other over to make sure no one else has questions the rest of us didn't think about.

The doctor nods, and the nurse who was ordered to deal with us when we got here steps up. "Dr. Brian, this is Mr. Johnson." She steers him toward Mason.

The man's face remains blank as he holds a hand out. "A moment in the hall?" the doctor asks and then takes two steps outside.

I close my eyes, spinning around and pressing my forehead against the wall.

My breaths are uneven, and my lungs burn.

The others' soft chatter muffles around me, and I squeeze my eyes tighter.

A flash of her smile appears, an echo of her laughter following.

She reaches for me, but just when I'm close enough to touch her, she fades to black, and then there's nothing.

I'm empty.

Alone.

My knuckles sting, and then a hand is on mine.

I'm slumped against the wall, Brady, Cameron, and Chase kneeling down in front of me, and Mason comes around the corner.

His eyes widen, and he looks to his friends, but as he realizes the blood running down my arm is my own, I follow his line of sight to a hole in the wall. I must have put it there.

His jaw flexes, and he walks across the room, tearing the framed photo from the wall, taking the nail out with it.

He grabs a book off the table and uses it to bang the thing in, covering the damage completely.

With crestfallen eyes, he reaches out. "Come on, man."

My chin falls to my chest, but I slap my palm into his.

He hauls me up, and then he hugs me, for real hugs me, apologizing as if he owes it to me when he doesn't.

When he pulls back, his eyes are red, and he nods.

He turns to Chase next, who stands unsure, but Mason pulls him in just the same.

I stumble from the room, ignoring their calls as I navigate this stupid fucking hospital like the pro I am. I cut left at the end and exit where the nurses take their breaks. I curve around the water fountain and slip between the building until I reach the one tucked away on the left.

I push inside, skipping the sign-in sheet, and blindly walk down the hall.

She's awake when I get there, and the worry that slips over her has my heart shattering.

Everything shatters.

"Oh, honey." Her hand lifts. "Come here."

I drop onto my mom's hospital bed, and I lose it.

The only two people I love in this world are both here, their lives in the hands of someone else, and there isn't a damn thing I can do about it.

I've never felt so helpless in my life.

Tri-City Medical, once again, becomes my home.

All of our homes, really, as none of us leaves for more than a few hours here and there, be it to catch a shower or maybe a few minutes of sleep in an actual bed.

Mason still hasn't gotten in touch with his parents, the end of their trip being their time off the grid, backpacking through Europe, and cut off from communication for thirty days, so they have no idea their daughter was hit by a car, let alone that she's been in a coma.

It was the day before Christmas Eve when the doctor came in with the news we'd been waiting for. After six long, torturous days, the risk of swelling was finally gone, the pain expected to have subsided, and they were ready to allow her to wake up.

Something in me stirs a second wind, and an anxiousness I've never known wakes me up.

Soon, I'd get to look into her eyes.

I'd get to tell her how sorry I am for walking away, for questioning her feelings for me.

I'd promise to never do it again and trust I was enough for her when I know, deep down, she's more than any man could ever deserve, especially a simple man like me.

I don't have a large family to love and adore her. I don't have a home full of memories to take her to or a path to follow to make our own. I didn't have what she did growing up, so I'm already at a disadvantage, but I do have the love of a mother who showed me what it meant to be a man. To work hard and to appreciate the things I have.

To love with all you are, and I do.

I love her with all I am, all I'm not, and all I'll be.

I should have been able to look into her beautiful eyes to tell her all of this on Christmas Day, but I couldn't because Ari didn't wake.

They said we could expect her to after the first forty-eight hours.

It's been four days, and the only change is the slight fading of her bruises.

The deep purple has faded into a soft yellow, and the swell of her lips has disappeared, the perfect pout now a familiar one, a new, tiny scar just below her bottom one.

I reach out, guiding my thumb along the end of her hair, wishing I could run my fingers through it like I have so many times before.

With the help of a nurse, they allowed Cameron to do what she could to hand wash Ari's hair, and then she braided it to one side, just like Ari had done to it the first day we hung out. And every six hours, like clockwork, Cam covered her lips with ChapStick, one less thing she has to recover from, Cam had said.

Ari couldn't ask for a better friend.

Mason doesn't talk much, just frowns at the TV in the corner, though I'm not convinced he's ever watching what's on. He's losing his mind, and he's bound to snap soon.

We all are.

"Anything?"

Cameron looks up from her pile of beads, offering me a small grin. "No, Noah, nothing happened in the point two seconds it took you to take a piss."

A low chuckle leaves me, but it falls flat as I make my way to Ari's bedside.

Cameron's phone beeps, and then she's pushing to her feet. "The boys said they finally put out fresh coffee downstairs. I'm going to go make Mason buy me one. You want?"

"I'm good. Thanks." Gently pushing Ari's hair behind her ear, I lean in, placing a soft kiss to her forehead before lowering into my seat.

I don't have to look up to know Cameron hesitates in the doorway.

"Noah . . ." she whispers, concern in her tone.

I only shake my head, and in the next breath, she slips out.

And then it's just us, a rarity I selfishly want more of.

I slide my hand beneath her lifeless one, the movement a triggering one for me, considering but necessary. I need to touch her. To hold her.

"Juliet, baby, open your eyes. It's time to wake up," I whisper. "Open those big, beautiful eyes and look at me . . . please look at me." The last word barely makes it out of my mouth, and suddenly, I'm overcome with all the emotions I've tried to push down. I clench my teeth to the point of pain, my jaw flexing as I will the moisture building in my eyes not to fall. Not here. Not where she might sense my agony, the way she always does.

Sitting there alone with her, I plead, beg, and pray for something to happen, for anything.

Turning her hand over, I drop my head to the bed, cradling my cheek against her soft palm, and I stay like that, my mind a mess of memories.

I'm not sure how much time has passed when a hand falls on my shoulder, and I look up to find Cameron standing beside me.

"Why don't you go home for a little bit?" Her smile is soft.

I sit up, clearing my throat as I look around the room, the boys in their usual spots.

Shaking my head and running my hands down my face, I tell her, "I'm good."

"Noah, you haven't left the hospital." Mason sits up, leaning forward to rest his elbows on his knees. He lifts a single brow. "You shower here, sleep here, eat here . . . when you eat at all."

"I eat when I'm hungry."

He nods, glancing toward Chase when he stands, his eyes following his friend as he comes to me with a cup of coffee.

"It's not steaming anymore, and it tastes like shit, but it's warm enough." Chase holds it out. "Looks like you could use it."

This is his peace offering, as was the uneaten pizza last night and the breakfast sandwich the day before. I didn't want any of that, and I don't want this, but it's got nothing to do with who's giving it to me. My stomach won't accept anything. No matter what I try to force down, it comes back up.

I'm in knots from my mind to my fucking feet.

He probably thinks I want to bash his face in, and that's fine. Sometimes that's exactly what I want to do, to punch him square in the jaw.

Him and every other thing in reach.

He just keeps standing there, so I accept the drink in his hand.

"Thanks." I take a small sip, trailing him as he moves back to the seat by the window.

"Where's Lancaster?" I ask Mason, just realizing the tripods missing a leg.

"Should be on his way by now. He had an early training session."

I nod. "Good, that's good. He needs to keep his routine. Coach said there's an offer out for a center they're hoping to snatch up for next year."

"I heard about that." Chase sits up. "Some high school senior from Detroit. He's supposed to be a beast."

"He is. I watched his film."

"Doesn't matter." Mason shrugs. "Brady's stats this year were fucking wild, and he's only getting better. No one can read the line like him."

"Yeah, he's quick with adjustments. With you leading, you guys should go far next season." The moment the words leave my mouth, I wish I could take them back, knowing I left this one wide open, and all we have is time to pass, so they'll keep the conversation going.

The second I look down, Mason speaks up.

"So you ready for the draft, my man?" Mason asks with a hint of excitement, the first I've heard from him in weeks. "That shit must feel surreal, being so fucking close after years of hard work?"

There it is, the exact topic I don't want to discuss, especially with promising hopefuls I spent the last six months leading.

"That's months away still."

I don't look up; Mason's delayed response tells me he's growing curious.

"Yeah, but you've got a lot of work leading to it. Shit, the Senior Bowl is just a few weeks away now. You probably fly out—"

"I'm not going."

From her place on the ground, Cameron spins, facing me, but I don't look up.

I run my fingers over Ari's, brushing along the smooth lilac nail polish Cam painted on for her.

"You mean you're not going too early to get familiar . . . just waiting until game day?"

"I told Coach Rogan to give my spot to someone else. I'm not going." I turn Ari's hand over, gliding my fingertips along her inner palm the way the nurse suggested. "Pulled out of Pro Day, too."

"Oh my god," Cameron mumbles, Mason's voice nearly cutting her off.

"Wait a fucking minute," he snaps.

I look up.

Mason glares, Cameron stares wide eyed, and Chase frowns at the floor.

"You did what now?" Mason tips his head.

"Don't." I speak as sternly as I can manage. "I already got shit from every coach on payroll, and the rest of the staff, for that matter, including the trainers. It's done. End of story."

"Noah, man." Mason furiously shakes his head. "Don't do this. You worked your ass off for Avix and earned this shit. Not to mention all your years of high school and youth ball. Don't let that go. You'll regret it."

"Regret?" I don't mean to laugh, but that's what happens. "Regret?" I deadpan.

"Noah, damn it—"

"You think I give a shit about my football career right now?" My voice raises an octave with every word, and I release Ari's hand to protect her from the anger vibrating through me. "You think I've thought about it since I've been here? Since *she* has been here? Because I haven't, not fucking once."

"I get that this is fucked up, and shit's not normal right now, okay? Don't fucking forget that is *my* sister lying there!" Mason shouts, pointing his finger at Ari. "But don't think for one fucking second that this is what she would want you to do because it's not." He's standing right in front of me now. His glare is sharp, but his entire face falls, as does the pitch of his voice. "It's not, man." His eyes soften just a bit, and his voice lowers. "It's not, man. She wouldn't want this for you."

I just stare at him a minute, slowly nodding.

"I hear you. Honest, I do, and I know you're right, but if there's ever a time for me to be selfish, this is it. Because despite what she or anyone else might think is right for me right now, there is no way in this fucked-up world we're currently living in that I could go out on that field and do a damn thing while my reason for breathing is lying here." I shake my head slightly. "My regret would come from leaving her, not from staying. I could never regret being where I am right now. This is where I belong. This is where I'm staying. Nothing changes that, and *nothing* is more important."

Mason's jaw flexes, his brows caving. He reaches out, clamping my shoulder, and gives me a little shake. "That right there, my man, is why I haven't kicked your ass yet," he says on a chuckle, making the rest of us join in.

The mood settles a moment, and everyone goes back to what they were doing a moment before, so I take a deep breath, swallowing a few mouthfuls of warm coffee.

"You realize it doesn't matter if you pulled out of Pro Day, right?" Chase says, not bothering to take his eyes off the TV.

360

"You already completed your college eligibility, and you were already confirmed as a prospect." He looks my way. "The compliance department already signed off with a big green go. You're in it."

I hold his gaze until he looks away, only then dropping mine to my lap, forced to consider his words.

He's not wrong. I know what I was signed up for, just like I know who's interested.

I also know I'll pass on every single offer that comes in.

Lifting Ari's hand, I lean forward and bring it to my mouth, placing a small kiss along her knuckles. My eyes close, and I press them a little firmer, cupping her hand with both of mine, speaking against her skin without a word whispered.

I imagine her thumb brushing along mine, just as it does.

My body goes stiff, my eyes flying open. I don't dare move.

Don't dare speak.

Her thumb twitches once more, and my head darts up. I jerk closer.

The others fly from their seats.

"What?! What's wrong?!"

"What is it?!"

"Noah!" Mason snaps.

"She—" I shake my head, not taking my eyes off her face. "She moved. Her hand. She moved."

My eyes fly from her face to her hand, back and forth, and her wrist jerks next.

Cameron's hands clamp down on me, squeezing. "Oh my god! She moved! Mason, she moved!"

My head turns to look at the others, but my eyes wait until the last second to flick their way.

Mason's eyes gloss over, and he glances from me to her. "Is she finally . . . think she's . . ." He swallows, unable to say the words out loud.

I open my mouth, but nothing comes out, so I turn back, release her, and reach up to cup her face in my palms. Slowly, I stroke her cheeks.

361

"Open your eyes for me, baby," I breathe as Mason grips my shoulder tight for support. "Juliet, open your eyes."

Her lids begin to flutter, and the room fills with small gasps.

My heart rate spikes, my lungs squeezing, pleading she'll fill them with hope once more, with purpose.

"This is it," Cameron croaks, tears falling from her eyes. "She's waking up. Ari, come on, girly, wake the fuck up."

"Baby . . . come on," I whisper, trying my damnedest to keep my emotions under control but failing.

I watch, waiting for my world to start spinning again, as my girl ever so slowly opens her eyes.

A half laugh, half cry whooshes its way out of my chest, and my forehead falls to her stomach. My body shakes with relief, and I pinch my eyes to try and calm myself, if only for a second.

She blinks a few times, her eyes widening as she slowly flicks them around the room.

They settle on Mason, and she lifts her left arm.

The sight alone has my smile spreading wide.

Movement from both sides.

Thank God.

Mase pushes closer, gripping her hand and giving it a squeeze.

"Hey, brat." His voice cracks. "You scared the shit out of us."

That gets a small smile out of her, and all our sob-muffled chuckles follow.

She tries to sit up a bit but winces, her hands shooting to her ribs.

"Try not to move too much," I tell her softly.

Her eyes flash to mine and hold.

Just like that, my tension-riddled body goes lax. Every part of me settles, the left corner of my mouth lifting more and more until I couldn't possibly smile wider. "Hi, Juliet."

My voice is strained, and her chest rises, her mouth opens, but then her hand shoots up to touch her neck.

She tries to clear her throat, wincing once more.

There's a shuffle in the room, but she doesn't look away until someone is lowering a cup of water in front of her.

She looks, and her lips turn up at the edges.

"Hey, stranger." Chase smiles back, passing the cup into her open hand.

The second she takes a small sip, Cameron is there to snatch it away. Water spills all over the floor as Cam throws her arms around Ari, careful not to squeeze her too hard. "I can't believe you're finally awake! You scared me, you bitch." She laughs through her tears.

Ari's low, raspy laugh runs through me, waking me up even more.

Every nerve in my body is firing to life, I can hardly sit still.

Ari takes a deep breath, dropping her back onto the pillow behind her.

Reaching up, I use the knuckles of my index finger to push her hair from her face, and she peeks through her lashes.

"How are you feeling, baby?" I ask, realizing how fucking stupid the question might be, but I need to know. I need to hear her speak. I need to know she's okay.

She hesitates at first, a curious pull between her brows, but then she nods. "I'm okay. My body aches everywhere, and my head is starting to pound, but I think I'm okay."

I swallow, clenching my teeth, so I don't scare her by breaking down, but her voice . . .

I fucking missed it.

I missed her.

God, I love her.

I couldn't bring myself to admit it before, but for a moment there, I wasn't so sure I'd ever get the chance to tell her.

"Wait." She tenses, looking around again. "Why am I here? What happened?"

My eyes meet Mason's a moment, and then I lean forward, catching her attention. "You walked into the street."

"You ran me over?" She clutches the blanket, and the monitor behind her starts beeping wildly.

363

"What? No." I frantically shake my head, tipping my chin, so she's looking in my eyes. "No, baby. A car was coming, and I couldn't get to you in time. They didn't see you before it was too late."

She visibly relaxes, but her breaths are short and labored, and she winces again.

"It's okay, little sister," Mason rasps, reaching out and placing his hand on her ankle. "You're okay now."

"What the fuckity fuck? My girl's awake, and no one called me?!" Brady tears through the little bubble we've formed around Ari. "That's some bullshit right there!" He grins, leaning down to place a giant kiss on her cheek, and I want to wipe it away, replace it with my own. "Glad you're back, Ari baby. Our boy here turns into more of a vagina with each passing day." He looks her over, humor his way of working through his worries. "I told him you just needed your beauty sleep, ain't that right?" he teases, knocking his fist into my shoulder.

"Funny, Lancaster." I grin, sitting back in my chair.

Ari's brows draw together, and she laughs. "Missed you, too, Brady."

"What's all the noise, gentlemen? I told you hoodlums no more watching football in this room if you guys can't . . . oh! Well, hi, honey!" Nurse Becky beams, spotting Ari awake in bed. "Thank goodness you're up. These men are worse than toddlers. So needy." She teases with a wink.

"Don't let her fool you, girl. She loves us." Brady nods.

Nurse Becky lets out a playful sigh. "Yes, I do."

She smiles and walks over to Ari, gently patting her leg. "I'm Becky. I've had the pleasure of being your daytime nurse since you got here, and I've got to say, it's damn good to see your eyes, sweetheart. I see those golden flecks that boy of yours was whispering about."

I open my mouth but close it, chuckling from being caught.

Mason nudges me with his knee, smirking to himself.

"I know you just woke, but I can bet you're exhausted and have lots of questions. Let me run and grab Dr. Brian."

"Thank you," she responds, the soft hum of her tone coming back more and more with each word spoken.

I squeeze her hand, and she looks toward the contact, her eyes flying to mine as if she only realized now I'm holding on to her.

I allow her the moment she wordlessly asks for, saying nothing as she takes me in from the light scruff building along my jaw, from refusing to spend an extra ten minutes shaving when I knew she was sitting in this bed without me, to the wrinkle of my clothes, pulled from a messy duffel bag I had my buddy drop off.

Slowly, her eyes make their way back to mine and hold.

"Hi, beautiful." I tip my head. "I've missed those chocolate eyes."

I smile wider when a hint of pink colors her cheeks, but then she looks away. Slowly, she eases her hand out of mine and begins adjusting her blanket.

Something stirs in my gut, and I lick my lips, slipping to the edge of my chair.

"Well, hello there." Dr. Brian rushes in with a smile, quickly washing his hands in the sink across the room.

As he comes forward, the group steps back to allow him some space. I don't move.

"I'm Dr. Brian." He tips his chin. "And you are?"

She frowns. "Um, Arianna Johnson."

"Yes, you are." He nods. "Passed the test."

A worried chuckle leaves her.

"Like Nurse Becky, here, I've been tending to you since your arrival. I'm going to ask you a few questions, and then we'll talk about your injuries. Does that sound all right?"

"Yes, sir," she mumbles nervously, wringing her hands in her lap.

"Okay, good. I assume it's okay to speak now?" He lifts his hands as if referring to us, and she nods. "Good. Let's start with an easy one. On a scale from one to ten, ten being the highest, how would you rate your pain?"

365

"About an eight."

"Big baby." Mason speaks only to ease her, clearing his throat as emotions take over.

It works. Her mouth pulls, but she keeps her attention on the doctor.

"Okay." He nods. "Where are you hurting the most?"

"My head is throbbing more so than anything else." Her palm flattens just below her breast. "And my chest. It's hard to breathe."

The room grows stiff with worry as we listen, and I draw my lips in.

"That's normal, considering." He clasps his hands together, letting them hang in front of him. "Before I break down your injuries, let me ask. Arianna, are you aware of what happened? How you ended up here?"

Her face contorts a bit, and she looks to Mason with pleading eyes. He gives her a small nod for encouragement, and she looks back at Dr. Brian.

She shakes her head. "I was hit by a car?"

"Yes, that's right." The man nods. "You took quite a hit. Your legs and arms went mostly unscathed, but your right shoulder had to be popped back into place. Your right lower rib is fractured, but it is very minor and nothing to be concerned about, but your left is where it gets tricky. See, two of your upper right ribs are broken." He refers to his own body, so she can visualize, as he explains, "When that happened, you suffered a traumatic aortic injury. Your aorta, the main artery in your body, was ruptured, causing extensive bleeding. Thankfully, your body did its job, and the surrounding tissues contained it as long as we needed it to. Had your lung been punctured, we might not be here to have this conversation, but we won't go down that road."

Ari nods, letting him know she's following, and my leg starts bouncing uncontrollably as I hear the doctor's explanation of what happened to my girl for the first time.

"You also suffered a basilar skull fracture on the left side of your skull, just around your left eye. Initially, we were worried about cerebrospinal fluid leakage, but after running some tests, we were able to rule that out. Because of that, though, you were placed in a medically induced coma for the first few days for monitoring. After that, we stopped the medication and waited for you to wake on your own, and now, here we are."

"Wait . . ." She pushes up higher, her eyes scanning along her body. "How long have I been here?"

"Eleven days."

Her eyes bulge, and he lifts his hands.

"I know it's a little scary and confusing, but you're here, your family has been here the entire time, and you're going to be just fine."

Her shoulders draw up, but she nods.

"Thankfully, all the hard stuff is done. Conservative treatment is all you need. We'll keep you as comfortable as we can with pain management, and we can also give you something for the nausea you'll likely still experience. Obviously, we will be keeping you for a little while longer to monitor you, but it shouldn't be more than a day or two."

"Okay." Ari's voice is small and scared, and I just want to reach for her. "That doesn't sound too bad."

"Yes, you were extremely lucky." Dr. Brian clears his throat, his expression goes somber, and Nurse Becky looks down, busying herself with Ari's file.

Something's off. I can feel it.

"Ms. Johnson, after the accident, your body went into hypovolemic shock due to the amount of blood you lost."

"Okay . . ." She waits.

He nods. "Your organs began to shut down as a result of your injuries. A blood transfusion was necessary . . ."

I jump to my feet, unable to sit still any longer. "Dr. Brian, with all due respect, can you spit it out already? Because I'm starting to freak the fuck out over here, and I know you're getting at something."

"Noah, come on, man," Mason mumbles.

"Don't. You got a full break down and that"—I jab a finger in Dr. Brian's direction—"is not what you told us. You made it sound like she bumped her fucking head! I had no idea all that other shit was happening."

"Please, Noah," Nurse Becky tries to soothe. "This is a lot for everyone to take in. Maybe now is not the time?"

I look back at Ari, who is frowning at her lap, and I instantly feel like a dick. I nod, lowering into the chair once more.

"You know what, actually . . ." Mason jumps up just then. "I think we should go out while you talk to her." His voice shakes nervously. "You know, give her some privacy."

"Are you fu—" I'm about to lose my shit when my girl speaks up, cutting me off.

"No, don't go," she pleads, holding his gaze for a few seconds.

Finally, his features cave, defeat building across him. His eyes flick to me before he drops them to the floor, his arms coming up to fold around the back of his head.

"Dr. Brian," she prompts.

He nods his head. "Mrs. Johnson?"

"Miss," I correct automatically.

"Miss?" The doc looks from me to his file. "Becky?" He turns to his nurse in confusion.

She flicks her gaze to Mason. "*Mr.* Johnson? Are you or are you not Arianna's husband?" she asks him in a very motherly tone.

The others chuckle at her mistake, but my glare would cut through him, if possible, especially when he refuses to lift his eyes from the ground. "No, ma'am, I'm her twin brother."

"What the *fuck* is going on?" I step around the bed, eyeing him.

"Oh dear," Becky whispers, her eyes sliding my way. "I guess I assumed the situation was a little unconventional."

"Mason," I snap.

"Noah, please." Cameron grabs onto my arm and turns back to the doctor. "It's just a misunderstanding."

I frown, turning, so my body is facing Ari's, the doctor standing to her right.

"It's fine. Please, say what you need to say," Ari urges.

"I'm very sorry to have to tell you this, but by the time we were aware, it was too late—"

"Too late for what?" she cuts him off, tension enveloping her as she clutches the blanket in her hands.

"I'm sorry, Ms. Johnson, I'm afraid you lost the baby."

Chapter 38
Noah

I jolt, my muscles spasming as a sheet of ice falls over me, immobilizing me from the inside out. Gasps fill the room, and my body becomes too heavy to hold, someone beside me now holding mine up. The doctor's lips continue to move, but his words don't reach my ears.

A wave of nausea hits me, and I sway.

A hand falls on my shoulder.

Confusion, hurt, anger, rage, sadness, loss.

I feel everything.

Agony, true and complete.

I can't breathe.

Baby. My baby.

Our little baby . . .

Gone?

"I . . . what?" My beautiful angel's voice cuts through the haze, and my eyes lift. "I was pregnant?" Her shattered whisper cuts through me, and my hands ball into fists.

It takes all my might to push myself up, and even then, someone helps me to my feet.

The doctor says something else, and then he's gone.

I swallow the bile threatening to spill from my throat. "I'm so sorry, Juliet. No one told me. I didn't know."

"Oh my god," she cries, tears spilling down her cheeks before she buries them in her hands.

"Baby," I crack, anger and sadness stinging my eyes in the form of tears, and I snap out of it, making my way to her bedside.

Her head finally lifts, and my heart breaks at the sight.

She opens her eyes, but they don't shift my way.

She reaches out, but not in my direction.

And then she whispers, but it's not my name she cries.

She calls *for him,* and every orifice in my body tightens, twists, and tears.

She calls to him, and my world goes up in flames. Lava, pure, hot, obliterating lava boils within me, bringing beads of sweat to my skin. I force my eyes to his.

Chase stays rooted in place, not daring to move an inch, the entire room now a cell of silence.

"Chase," she cries for him. "We were going to have a baby?"

I choke on air, my pulse flatlining.

"Oh shit," someone rushes out, and then a body is in front of me, arms caging me in, and then there's another.

I don't realize I'm fighting my way to the wide-eyed asshole across the room until there's one arm around my neck from behind and another around my back from the front.

"Noah, don't," Mason hisses in my ear. "Please, not now. Let's . . . fuck, just hold on."

Cameron rushes to Ari's side, wrapping her arms around her.

"Noah, man . . ." Chase shakes his head. "No. Something's wrong." He looks to Mason. "Mason, I swear. I . . . she—" He shakes his head again, peeking at Ari from the corner of his eye.

"Fuck me," Brady croaks under his breath.

And then it hits like a ten-ton truck down a straight slope.

"Hm-mm." My head shakes frantically as I tear myself free of Mason's hold. "No."

I rush to her bedside, falling to my knees beside it.

"No," I repeat on a whisper, unwilling to believe what's happening.

"Look at me." My words are a soft demand.

The room falls quiet, and when her shoulders draw up in hesitation, my blood pressure spikes, my heart beating against my rib cage like an animal trying to escape.

"Ari?" Cameron whispers, but she makes no move.

Gently placing my knuckle beneath her chin, I lift it from Cameron's shoulder.

I bring her gaze to mine, searching, praying I find what I'm looking for.

"Juliet . . ." I whisper, so only she can hear.

She looks deep into my eyes, tears in her own, and her body shudders as that one word from me travels through her entire being, the way it always does. The way it has since the moment we met, even when she didn't realize it.

But I see beyond the response she can't control.

I see the unsure, curious flicker behind her big brown eyes, the one she had all those months ago before she let her first love go.

Before she opened up to us.

Before she became mine.

My hand goes limp, dropping to my thigh with a loud smack. Cameron weeps beside her, having just realized what I've already figured out.

I stagger backward, falling onto my ass, quickly crawling back to my feet. Stumbling over nothing before I reach the door and trip again on my way through it.

I hustle from the room before I lose it completely.

I hear them as they shout my name, but I don't stop. I keep moving.

Away from the hospital.

Away from the place my unborn child died.

Away from the man who hid it from me.

Away from the bastard in love with my girl.

And away from the girl I love . . . who has no idea she loves me back.

Chapter 39

Arianna

The repetitive beep grows longer and louder, piercingly so.

It gets faster and faster, creating a sharp echo in the back of my mind, and then someone is shouting.

My body is burning up, the heat making me nauseous, and when I try to fill my lungs, I'm denied.

There's a scream, and my cheeks are covered with clammy palms, but I don't know whose.

It's so blurry.

The face, my mind . . . my life.

It's all blurry . . . but then I close my eyes, and suddenly everything it's clear.

The haze is gone.

I can see.

My stomach is swollen.

My smile is wide.

A hand slides into my hair, large and strong, yet gentle. And then his eyes open, and a calm settles over me.

His eyes, they're the most gorgeous shade of—

Voices creep in and steal the dream away.

"What did you give her?"

"It's a sedative. We need to get her heart rate down."

The beeping is back, and then everything goes black.

Noah

It's been a couple hours since I left the hospital, and not five minutes after my ass hit the seat of my truck, Mason called. And then he called again and again, but I didn't pick up.

While he was calling, Brady set up a new message thread in GroupMe, the app the football team uses for group chats and sharing information. He created it with a handful of guys he must assume I talk to the most, Trey being one of them, asking if anyone has seen me and, if not, where they think they can find me. A couple guys name the obvious places like the gym, field, and my house, but the people I've been living at the hospital with know better than that, and minutes after that, my phone starts ringing again. Both Mason and Brady try call after call, text after text.

I should appreciate their concern and the fact that they give a damn where I am and what I'm doing, but my mind can't hold any other thoughts right now, so I turn off my notifications, hit the corner store, and drive a few miles outside of town without a destination in mind. The first turn after the city limits sign is the one I take, and I bury my truck in the middle of an orchard. Hiding my keys in the glove box, I drop the tailgate and climb up.

I'm not a drinker, never have been, but tonight, I'll drink like a pro.

Some bottom-shelf vodka is the liquor of choice. It's disgusting, burns like a bitch, but I couldn't bring myself to walk toward the whiskey, not when I would have done nothing but picture drowning in a certain set of eyes, so I drown in clear liquor instead.

I drink until the last drop, the need to get trashed high.

I want to blackout. To shut down fully and completely because if my girl doesn't remember us, I don't want to remember anything.

Not even my own fucking name.

For the first time in my life, I wish I were someone else.

I wish I were him.

Chapter 40

Arianna

A flash of blue jolts me awake, and when I open my eyes, Cameron is there.

"Hey, girlfriend." She yawns, her upper body bent over in her chair, her head lying on my legs. She folds her arms under her cheek and smiles. "How's the head?"

"Heavy, but not excruciating anymore. My ribs are an entirely different story."

"I bet."

Glancing around the room, I spot Mason draped over the corner chair, the rest of the space clear.

"Brady and Chase went home a couple hours ago to shower and get some sleep. Mase wouldn't budge, of course."

The corner of my mouth lifts, but I look away when moisture builds in my eyes, and I don't even know why. "What day is it?"

She's quiet a moment before she whispers, "It's still December twenty-ninth. You were only asleep for a couple hours." Her tone is thick with worry.

I nod, but my lips begin to quiver, and she sits up, Mason quickly coming to my side. "I'm sorry. I don't know why this keeps happening."

"Don't apologize. It's been less than twenty-four hours since you woke up. Of course you're going to be emotional, we understand, and we're just happy you're okay."

"Am I?"

Mase reaches out, but I shake my head, wiping the tears away before they fall. My chest aches with my full inhale, but I suffer through it, trying to force away the millions of emotions dizzying up my mind.

"Ari—"

"I wish Mom and Dad were here." I cry, my shoulders shaking, and Mason shifts, sitting at the edge beside me on the bed now.

"I know you do. Me too." He hugs me to him, his voice cracking. "I've tried everything, but they'll call us as soon as they're back on land. Should only be two more days, tops."

Two more days until I'll get to hear my mom's voice. Until my dad is here, promising everything will be okay, and begs for instructions on what he can do to make it better.

I don't know what can be made better if anything.

I'm too afraid to think past what I know, and apparently, I don't know shit. Nothing recent, anyway.

The doctor said this happens more than people realize that memory loss, while less common than not, isn't abnormal in concussion-related injuries. He said as soon as my brain has had time to heal, things will slowly come back to me, that they're hopeful, and I should be too.

I want to be, but there's this helplessness I can't shake, and I think my twin senses it.

Sniffling, I look up, and he wipes my tears with the pads of his thumbs, attempting a smile, but it never quite breaks free.

"If you do get a hold of them, I don't think we should tell them until they're home." I try to busy his mind with something a little less about me. "They'll just stress the whole way back."

"I was thinking the same thing." He nods, rubbing his eyes like he used to do when we were little.

I reach out, gripping his hand. "Go home, Mase."

His head jerks my way, and he sits up straight. "What? No, I'm good."

"No, *I'm* good, I promise." When it's obvious he doesn't agree, I add, "Plus, I want to try and take a shower. Nurse Becky said I could, with help. I just have to work around my IV."

"I can help," he argues.

"Mase, your sister will be naked in said shower," Cameron teases, knowing he didn't think it through. "Just go, I went home for a few hours last night, and we both know Ari will be bored of hearing us and ready to pass out again in another hour anyway." She pokes fun.

Mason scoffs a laugh, aware of what she's doing, but he's exhausted, and he knows I'm in good hands. The risks are gone, so if there's a perfect time for him to go, it's now.

"Yeah, all right. I've got something to do anyway."

"Yeah, like sleep."

His smirk is small as he presses his lips to my hair. "Be back soon, okay? Have Cam call me if you need me. I'll come right back."

"I know, and I will."

He grabs some things off the chair, and with one last look back, he walks out.

My shoulders fall instantly, and when I turn to Cameron, her eyes begin to water.

"Come on, girlfriend," she whispers as she stands. "Let's get you all fresh."

It takes several minutes for me to get up on my feet, but it's faster than it was the day before when the nurse asked me to walk across the room and back.

Everything still aches, but I've got some of my movements down to know which ways sting a little less.

Cameron pulls my IV bag as close as she can, allowing for the most stretch possible, and I slip under the spray, Cameron not a foot from me the entire time.

Once I've washed my body the best I can manage, I gently apply shampoo in my hair, careful not to touch the scrapes now scabbing over on the left side of my head, in fear of it stinging.

Cameron pokes her head in to help squeeze some conditioner into my palms, and the minute I lather it into the ends of my hair, my eyes decide to close, a strange flicker of something bringing a frown to my face.

I lean against the wall, lift the tips of my hair to my nose and inhale again.

The soap, it has an almost piney eucalyptus scent, but fresh and clean and . . . familiar.

An unexpected warmth washes over me, but it brings tears of confusion with it, and suddenly, I'm gasping for air I didn't know I was denying myself.

"You okay?" Cameron asks from the other side of the curtain.

"Mm-hm." My closed-mouthed response gives me away.

Cam pokes her head in, a shadow falling over her eyes as they meet mine. "Ari . . ."

"Can you, um, help rinse with conditioner really fast?" I ask, letting her know I don't want to talk about it without saying it. "I can't stand here any longer."

She pushes the curtain back with a nod, unfazed by the water splashing all over her sweat suit, and gently spins me, grabbing my hair in her hands. "Let's just wash this out. I brought leave-in for you days ago, just in case, so we can work some of that in once you're sitting."

I nod again, and she gets to work. As she's turning off the water and passing me a towel, I whisper her name.

"Cam?"

"Honey bunny."

"Thank you." I don't mean to cry. "For this. For being here. For all the things I can't remember, but I'm sure you were there for the last few months."

"I'll always be here, Ari, you know that." Cameron sniffles as she ties my gown back into place, gently moving my hair to one side. She slips in front of me, tears wobbling in her eyes. "No matter what."

I nod again, stepping into my best friend, who hugs me to her. No matter what she said.

That's the scary part about all of this, isn't it? The reality behind it all.

That this could be the beginning.

How things could get worse.

If that's the case, where the hell does that leave me?

Stuck in the past . . . or lost in the future?

379

Noah

The crisp California air wakes me, and with the cold comes a hangover I didn't think through. I can't even roll myself over without wincing, but I manage to make it to my feet and stumble to the cab of my truck. It takes all my might to climb inside, but the sloshing around has my stomach turning as beads of sweat form along my hairline. Spinning, I quickly lean my upper body out the door, just in time to keep from throwing up in my lap.

It feels like forever before my stomach is empty of the poison I fed it, and even then, a dozen dry heaves follow. Huffing, I strip my shirt from my body, using it to wipe the sweat from my face and head. I rinse my mouth out with half the water bottle I left on the seat, using the other half to force down some ibuprofen—something I learned to keep on hand after my first week of practice my freshman year at Avix.

Dropping my head against the headrest, my eyes close again, a pain I've never known burning its way along my bones, and it's got nothing to do with the drumming of my temples.

A month ago, my life felt full for the very first time, imploding with a peacefulness I never knew existed. Twelve days ago, that peace was shattered, completely crushed as my girl was taken by ambulance to fight for her life, and unknowing at the time, our child's. And last night, last night, my heart was obliterated, pulverized as I looked into the eyes of the most amazing person I have ever known, eyes that looked at me as if *I* was the prize, as if *I* was the most amazing thing in her world, only to find them rid of us.

Just like that, my world fell apart, and I don't know that it can be put back together.

And that's just too fucking much.

Squeezing my eyes closed, I replay every moment, from the first smile to the last laugh, and then I do it again.

I must pass out again after that, because the next time they open, it's later. I don't know by how much, I never did look at the time, but it must have been at least a couple hours as my vomit is dry in the dirt and the pounding in my head has gone from heavy metal to two-tone punk.

It's beating up my temples, but it's bearable now.

Lifting my phone from the seat, I check the missed calls and messages, but when neither my mom's facility nor my girl's name is among the dozens in red, I toss it.

Instead of heading home, I dip into what's left of my financial aid from this past semester, and check into a hotel room, where I stay the next two days, repeating the one before it.

It doesn't help. The distance or the distraction.

Every time my eyes open, reality rocks me to the core.

That's the thing about alcohol. It's a temporary fix, one that leaves you more fucked up than before. And believe me, I am fucked up.

My mind, my body.

My future.

I clench my jaw, dropping back against the shower wall, holding my breath as the water rolls over my face.

What future?

I slap the wall and then bang my forehead against it.

And then I fall to the fucking floor.

I hear the footsteps coming before his face pokes around the corner, and I'm almost humiliated enough to turn away.

Almost, but not quite.

The last thing I want is for the guy I've worked hand in hand with all season, coaching him to be the next leader of my position, to see me with my head hung in a room that reeks of liquor when the man he knows me to be has never once stood in front of him drunk.

But I'm not even standing.

I'm sitting on the floor of a shitty balcony at an overpriced hotel, my back flat against the wall.

"How did you find me?"

"Only four hotels within a five-minute drive from the hospital. Knew I'd spot your truck at one of them." He's angry, rightfully so. "You need to come back to the hospital."

Sighing, I drag myself to my feet and move toward the edge of the banister. Crossing my arm over the cool metal, I lean forward, looking down at the empty playground. "You think I don't want to be there? That this isn't killing me? That I don't feel like shit for walking out and leaving her there?" I glance at him over my shoulder. "Because I do."

"Doesn't seem like it."

"Did she ask for me?"

"Does she have to for you to know she needs you?"

Fuck.

His words are a sharp insult wrapped in glass, cutting as deep as he intended, because no. She doesn't. That was part of the beauty of us. Her pain was mine as mine was hers. We never needed words to know the other was hurting . . . but she doesn't remember that.

I face forward. "She doesn't remember me, Mason."

He says nothing for so long, I half expect he's walked away, but when I turn around, he's still standing in the same spot.

His lips press into a firm line. "I saw the message she sent you. The one from that night."

My eyes narrow, small pricks drawing my shoulders up tight. "You read our private conversations?"

"No." He stands tall, unapologetic. "I didn't, but I would have if I felt like I needed to. What I did do was take her busted-up phone down to the store, got her a new one, and had them flash everything from the old one over. Had to open it up to make sure it worked before they trashed it. Her message to you was the last thing she touched on that phone."

My chest clenches as I stare at him.

"That's why you came home that night." He moves closer. "To come get her. To tell her you love her, too. Right? You love her too?"

Grinding my teeth, I go to push past him. "I'm not having this conversation with you."

Mason slides in front of me, brows caved. He's angry, but it's more than that. The inability to protect the one person he's spent his life protecting is eating him up.

I know the feeling.

The only two people I have ever had in my life I couldn't protect.

Mason shakes his head, admitting, "I don't know why, but in the back of my mind, I told myself my sister cared for you but being with you was her way of doing what she could to be happy while she secretly held on to something else."

"You mean someone else. There's no reason not to say his name." I throw his hand off of me.

"So you do know everything that happened with her and him?"

"Why do you think I gave her space in the first place? Why do you think I pulled back?" I don't give him time to answer. "It was because he suddenly realized what he was losing and knew he had to at least try. It took him months, years really, to see what I saw the minute I met her, and I can't even fucking blame him because the fifty-fifty chance is worth the risk if it ends with her in your arms."

Mason's expression twists. "But she chose *you*, you know that, so why the hell aren't you at that hospital where you belong?"

"Because fate stepped in and showed his cards, and I'm not even in the deck, let alone at the bottom of it."

His jaw tics angrily, and I glance away.

"Do us both a favor and delete our message thread before you give her the new phone."

"What, no." His body tugs backward. "Fuck no. Why you acting like shit's over? Like it's done, and her memory is gone and not coming back?"

I swallow, the possibility too damn real to stomach. "Maybe it is."

"Don't make me knock you out, man." He glares, his fists clenching at his sides. "What the fuck's the matter with you? My sister is lost right now, and you give up on her? What kind of shit—"

I've got him by the collar, his back slammed against the wall behind us in a split second.

"I will never give up on her." My body shakes. "Ever."

"Then what the fuck are you doing getting trashed while she's barely able to fucking breathe?" he seethes.

"I don't know!" I admit, the muscles in my neck straining. I tear away from him, running my hands on top of my head until I'm gripping my hair. "I don't fucking know what I'm doing, man. I don't know shit. I'm fucking terrified that if I go into that room, I might do or say something that'll only make this harder on her, hurt her more, and I couldn't handle that."

"You think I'm not?" he rasps, and I bring my eyes back to his. "Trust me, I am, we all are, but she needs . . . I don't know what she needs, but it ain't me. Ain't Cam or the others. It's got to be you, man. It has to be."

Shaking my head, I step around him into the room, his shadow following. "She doesn't remember *us*, Mason."

"I know that."

"Yeah?" I drop onto the edge of the bed, looking up at him. "Do you know how to tell a woman who thinks she's only ever been with one man that *you* are the father of the child she lost?"

As if he hadn't paused to consider this side of things, my side, the shitty, helpless fucking side, his muscles go limp, and he falls into the chair across from me. Mason drops his head back, staring up at the ceiling in defeat because he gets it now. He knows what I know.

That you can't.

You. Just. Fucking. Can't.

Chapter 41
Noah

A little over twenty minutes of my sitting beside her bedside passes before her eyes begin to flutter open, and I force as much of a smile as I can muster.

"Hi, Mom."

"Honey, you should have woken me." She places her palm over mine, and as she gets a better look at me, her face falls. "Noah, no. Is Ari . . . did she not make—"

"No, no, she's okay." I shake my head, my voice hoarse and thick with exhaustion.

"Noah?"

I bite the inside of my cheek, looking away as my eyes begin to cloud.

Outside of being a young boy, my mom has only seen me cry once, and that was the day I came here to tell her about Ari's accident.

In the eleven days Ari was out, I wouldn't leave the hospital, but when the doc would make his rounds, asking us to clear the room while he and the nurse ran through her vitals, I'd run over here to see my mom, something I could never do during the football season, and thank fucking God for those few minutes I was forced to step away from my baby's bedside. If I didn't have that little time with my mom, I'm not sure what I would have done.

It might have only been for twenty or so minutes at a time, less on days she herself would get too anxious and tell me to hurry back to my girl, but it was the only thing that kept me sane.

But I don't feel sane anymore.

My mom squeezes my hand, and I drop my chin to my chest, pulling in a full breath.

"She doesn't remember me, Mom." I look to her, her face blurry from the mess my eyes threaten to make. "She woke up, but she woke to a world I wasn't a part of."

My mom's shaky inhale has me swallowing, trying to be a soldier for her sake like she always does for me, but I can't find a drop of inner strength inside me, and the look in my mom's eyes says I don't have to.

"Come here, baby." She tugs on my hand, and I allow my body to fall against hers.

Her hand rubs along my back, and I hate that I've come here like this, that I've pulled her into my nightmare, but she wouldn't have it any other way.

I close my eyes, reminding myself I'm lucky I'm not alone in life, that I need to be grateful for the things I have, but my mind fights back, screaming for me to shut the fuck up.

That I am alone.

That I do have nothing.

Because what will my life be without Arianna Johnson?

Empty, that's what.

Ari

"I think I want to know," I admit, and Mason's anxious gaze finds me.

He steps around the doctor, coming to stand near Cameron on my opposite side. They share a look, both facing me.

"Ari," Mason grasps my hand as he drops onto the bed beside me, a torn expression carved along his face. "You sure that's a good idea? The doc just said—"

"That it could be triggering or traumatic, I know, I was listening, but what do you think waking up and realizing your mind is stuck in July feels like?" Proof of my botched emotions warms my cheeks, and Mason's grip tightens. "I need to know why everyone is looking at me like I'm not even me. Did my life really change that much in one semester?"

Mason looks down, his eyes glossy when they finally rise to mine.

"Why don't we pause on that a moment, okay?" Dr. Brian intervenes. "And get back to understanding where we are. Does that sound all right to you?"

Mason waits until I nod to face forward.

"Okay, as you said, the last thing you remember is leaving the beach, correct?"

An anxiousness pulls at me, but I clear my throat. "Yeah. We spent the end of summer at our beach house, but I left a little earlier than planned. I remember leaving, but I don't remember the drive or getting back to my house."

"You mentioned bright lights?"

I close my eyes, thinking back.

It was nighttime when I stepped out of the door, my dad's

truck waiting for me to climb inside for the trip home. I crossed the roadway, and I saw a truck parked a ways down. I couldn't be sure, but I thought it might have been Chase. Before I could get a better look, the headlights flicked on. I lifted my arm, trying to see past the shine, but it didn't help.

The brightness blinded me.

And then . . . darkness.

"It, um, it was headlights. I was crossing the street, and they flicked on, shined right into my eyes."

The doctor nods, looking to Mason when he speaks.

"Just like that night." He frowns, looking to the doctor. "It's almost the same. She was crossing the street, and then the truck came. She looked, but"—he swallows—"it was too late."

My heartbeat spikes slightly, and I wince as I attempt to drag in a full breath.

Dr. Brian folds his clipboard in front of him, tipping his head slightly. "Arianna, did something happen that night? The night you do remember?"

Panic washes over me, and while I'm not sure if it shows, the monitors I'm hooked up to give me away.

Mason's posture stiffens, and Cameron's palm finds my upper arm, afraid I'm going to have another panic attack.

"Hey, hey, calm down," Mase rushes out, and when I look into my brother's eyes, finding his soft ones on mine, I take a breath. "I already know," he says quietly.

Nodding, I hold his gaze. "You do?"

"Yeah, sister, I know about you and Chase. Maybe not every little thing, probably not every little thing, but I do know the big stuff. I know . . ." He looks to the doctor briefly, swallowing hard as he brings his attention back to me. "I know he hurt you, maybe even . . . broke your heart." His brows pull into a frown.

The urge to cry out creeps over me, so I squash my lips to the side because his tone, it's telling, as is the sorrow in his eyes.

"Mase . . ."

He understands, shaking his head as he hangs it.

Chase hurt me, broke my heart, and this is Mason's way of telling me his best friend didn't put the pieces back together.

Squeezing my eyes closed, I nod again, salty tears falling into the corners of my mouth.

"Arianna," the doctor eases. "Is that the way you remember that night?"

Nodding, I force myself to look at him. "Yeah. It was a rough day." To put it lightly.

He nods, flipping a few pages and reading over something in my file. He closes it and faces me once more.

"Oftentimes, in amnesia cases like this, the brain will link trauma to trauma, and I believe that is what we are dealing with here."

"I don't understand."

"It's sort of as I explained to you about why we had to place you in a coma. Your injuries caused you a great deal of pain, and your brain was at risk of shutting down because of it. What we are facing now is the same idea but related to memory instead. You experienced trauma, and your brain connected it to past trauma, erasing the time in between."

My throat runs dry, my legs prickling. "I don't think I'm following. What trauma? *New* trauma?"

What could have possibly happened to me that ached like that night did?

Was it about the baby?

Had I already lost it?

My sniffles grow choppier, and it doesn't take long before my chest is fluttering, the movement creating an ache through my entire upper body, reminding me of my wounds on the outside, but it's nothing compared to the pain within.

I was going to be a mom, something I've always dreamed of but imagined would happen later in life. It was the only thing I was certain of, the one thing I wanted more than anything else, and I can't even remember if I knew about the little blessing before I lost him.

A good mother would remember that no matter what.

Wouldn't she?

Dr. Brian says something, but I have no idea what, and then he walks out.

My eyes close.

I was told I was only seven weeks pregnant, not far along enough to know the sex . . . and not far along enough to have gotten pregnant over the summer.

That means Chase wasn't the father. That's what my brother shared.

Unless we found each other again and nobody knew it?

He would have come to me when I cried, held me, and cried with me if that were true, wouldn't he have?

My body racks with silent sobs, and when I force my eyes open, my brother's find mine.

He hesitates a moment, and I curl my toes in my socks, anxious. "Ari—"

He's cut off when there's a soft rap against the wall.

All our heads snap toward the door, and my stomach drops at the sight.

Broken blue eyes flash in my mind, and my hand twitches, remembering the feel of the one that held mine the day my eyes opened in this room.

Juliet, open your eyes . . .

My brows cave as I look him over.

Dark hair tousled, eyes a deep, depthless blue.

It's the guy I met this summer. The guy from the beach.

A friend of my brother's.

A friend of mine?

"Noah," I don't mean to say out loud, but it slips from my lips.

My brother jerks beside me, and a choppy exhale pours from Noah's lips.

My stomach tightens, and his forehead follows suit.

"I was hit by your football."

He swallows. "You were."

"You came to the bonfire."

"I didn't stay long."

"I know, I remember."

He licks his lips, giving a stiff nod. "I have that effect."

A small laugh slips from me, but I cut it short the second I realize, and something softens in his gaze. As if it takes effort, he jerkily tears his eyes away. He looks to my brother, but only for a moment before his gaze comes right back to me.

There's something a little different about him, but I can't put my finger on what.

"I, um," he begins, the rasp in his tone rattling my throat. "I can't stay."

Mason flies to his feet so fast his shoes squeak against the floor, and a strange sense of unease builds behind my ribs.

"Okay."

Noah looks up at the ceiling a moment, and when his gaze comes back, it's beaten. "I found some people you'll be really happy to see," he tells me.

I don't take my eyes off his as he glances behind him, and then he moves aside, someone else stepping through.

Relief whooshes through me, and my face falls into my hands, full, heavy weeping instantly tearing from me, completely overcome with the most welcome sight.

I sob, my body shaking, and then strong arms wrap around me, holding me close. "Dad."

"It's okay, baby girl." His voice cracks. "It's okay. I'm here. Your mama's here."

Mason sniffles beside me, and then my mom is there, running her hands over my hair. I fall into her chest, and my dad holds us close, but not before my attention is called across the room.

To Noah.

Who is already staring, and while he seems to ease before my eyes, his tell a different story. Only, before I'm given the chance to look further, he's gone.

Noah

Outside the door, I fall against the wall, my eyes closing as I drag a deep breath through my nostrils, slowly blowing the air from my mouth.

I left again. Walked out.

I looked into my baby's eyes, saw that familiar flicker burn within them, and watched it fade away.

Again.

It took all I had not to go to her, to drop to my knees beside her and kiss her. To kiss the spot that would soon grow with our child if the world had been kinder.

It's not. I know this from experience, but I'd have given anything to have been able to keep her from ever finding out.

Palming my chest, I push off the wall, but I don't get two feet from it before footsteps fall behind me.

"Where you going?" Mason's voice follows me farther into the hall. "Why even come if you're just gonna cut out again?"

"Your mom saw me in the parking lot, asked me to walk her up. I couldn't say no, but maybe I should have."

"Why were you in the parking lot?"

I swallow. "Go back in with your family, Mason."

"You go back in with *your* family!"

At that, I whip around, ready to tear into him, but the smirk on his lips throws me off.

Of course, it's only there long enough for that, falling flat in the next second, and that same helplessness eating away at me washes over him. "You're family, Noah. The minute she decided you were, that's what you became." He steps closer. "Don't leave. She needs you."

"She doesn't even know me."

"You heard her; she remembers everything that happened over summer. It's everything after her last day there that's fuzzy for her, but she remembers you."

I shake my head, a heavy throbbing creeping in.

Goddamn it, why does that almost feel worse?

"She remembers some guy from the beach who she sat and talked to for a minute, just like she remembers being in love with someone else that day. The same someone who she sat in that hospital bed and *reached for* when the *entire* room found out she was growing a child inside of her and lost it. Our child, *my* child that she thinks was *his*. That she sat and mourned with another man in mind, not me." A burning sense of torment spreads through me, and I swallow. "I didn't get to comfort the woman I love after a loss no one should have to face, and I will never forgive myself for that. Ever."

Grief-stricken, his face scrunches. "That wasn't on you, Noah."

"But it will stick with me. Always. Just . . . go back in there. I know your dad wants to talk with you."

"Come with me, man. The doc said she linked two traumatizing events, and that's why her mind jumped backward or some shit, so we need to find a way to help her separate them. I need you there for that. Come back inside."

The elevator doors open beside us, revealing Brady and Chase.

We stare as Brady steps out, Chase right behind him, a bouquet of flowers in his hands.

A cool current travels through my veins, and my muscles draw up.

"Noah, what the fuck, bro?" Brady comes closer, but Mason holds his hand up, and they pause.

"My parents are in there, go say hi," he tells them, not looking their way, and with hesitant steps, they do as he says, slowly moving toward the hospital room.

With their every foot forward, a sharp ache picks at my spine.

They slip inside, and I jerk away, unable to stand there and watch as they do the one thing I wish I could.

Just fucking be with her, near her. Anything.

The elevator doors close again, and I can't wait for it to come back. I head for the stairwell.

"I told her!" Mason shouts before I can disappear.

My body freezes, and the swinging door comes back, almost slapping me in the face. Anger ripples through me, and I glance at him over my shoulder. "What do you mean, you told her?"

Mason looks away, and I push closer to him.

"Mason." I slip into his space, pinning him on the spot.

"She knows the baby wasn't his."

Swear to God, something cracks inside me. "Do not mess with me on this."

"Why would I?" He presses right back but softens after a few seconds. "I made that one point clear, but I didn't spell out anything else."

My hands find my hips, my cheeks filling with air as I look off. Biting my tongue as I fight to keep from breaking down.

"I don't know what to do. I need her to know she's not alone," he stresses.

Knots form in my stomach. "She's not. Ever."

"I know." His tone is low, understanding. "Noah, she's bound to ask questions, and as much as I hate to admit it, I'm not sure I have all the right answers. Please, help her remember."

My pulse flips, tightening my tendons. "If she doesn't?"

"Then fuck remembering."

A scoffed laugh leaves me, and a small grin slips over his lips.

"She fell for you once, right?" He shrugs one shoulder. "Give her the chance to do it again."

Swallowing my fears, I ask the question that's been haunting me. "And what if she doesn't want to?"

Mason tips his head. "Come on now. This is Ari we're talking about. She's still her, and you're still you." When I hesitate too long for him, his features pull. "Noah, please. I need to know she's going to be okay, and the way I see it, she can't be if she's not with you."

394

"You don't know that."

"I'd bet on it."

If I were thinking straight, I would too. I'd bet on her, on us, but the world keeps finding ways to remind me life is rough and for every good comes a handful of bad. Every time I think things are turning around, that I'm finally getting past the heavy, a rockslide comes tumbling down, and I have to fight my way through it. But this time, I can't do that.

I'm at the mercy of a mind I no longer hold a place in.

My sigh comes next, and I look to the door Chase and Brady disappeared into. "She doesn't even like flowers."

A laugh spurts from him, but the sorrow within it isn't missed. "Yeah, man, I know. That would be my dad's fault."

My eyes flick to his, the smallest hint of warmth flickering in my chest. "Yeah?"

He smirks, the man knowing he's got me, his words offering a little more of my girl to me, but the answering "yeah" comes from down the hall.

We turn to find Mr. Johnson closing in.

I stand straight, and he clamps his son's shoulder, facing me.

"Flowers are pretty, but they're prettier in the dirt and don't die after a week." His mouth curves into a wide smile. "My girls are spoiled with food, treats, and shit."

My lips twitch, and Mason lifts a brow in victory. "Why you think she was all about cooking meals with you? You were winning her over when you didn't even know it."

Memories of the first time I cooked for her sweep in, and I look away.

"That's sort of why I'm out here." We both look to Mr. Johnson. "She's starvin', and she doesn't want what they brought in."

"I can go get her a spicy chicken from Popeye's?" Mason's already fishing his keys from his pocket.

"No, she, uh, she was pretty specific with what she's craving." His brown eyes move to mine, a hidden thought within them. "Know where we can find a potpie around here?"

My muscles lock, a spark of something jolting me from within, the smallest hint of darkness morphing into daylight.

Unable to speak, I nod.

"Then lead the way, son." He tips his chin. "Our girl's waiting."

I pray to God, somewhere deep down, she is.

And then I remember the man she thinks she loves is with her right now, and any flicker of hope I might have felt is gone.

Chapter 42

Arianna

Stuffed, I drop my head back, happy to have my parents home. "That was so good."

My dad takes the Tupperware container and tosses it into a bag on the countertop. "Yeah, that Noah sure knows how to cook."

"Noah Riley?" I look to my dad. "He made that?"

"Oh, yeah, and straight from scratch. Pretty impressive, if you ask me. Why do you think it took us three hours to get back here?"

"I didn't think it was because Avix U's quarterback seconded as a chef, that's for sure." I gasp, looking to Mason. "Oh my god! Your season? How was it? Did you play?"

Mason chuckles, opening his mouth, but I cut him off before he can speak.

"Wait, don't tell me! I changed my mind," I tell my family, and all eyes slide my way.

Once my dad and Mason got back, we were able to call Dr. Brian back in, and this time, he was joined by a specialist. They broke everything down once more, so my parents could fully understand, and the way the specialist explained what I'm facing made me think about things a little differently, leading me to my final decision.

"I don't want anyone to tell me about the last few months."

"Ari." Mason shakes his head. "There are things you need to know."

Subconsciously, my hand plants on my stomach, and I nod.

"I know, and I will ask some about some things, but I want the chance to do exactly that when I need to. The doctor said someone else's thoughts could confuse me more than I already am, and I don't want to risk that. I want to remember on my own. They said I can."

"Of course you can, sweetheart." My mom pushes my hair back. "There's no pressure. Whatever you decide, we're here."

"About that, I get released tomorrow, and I don't . . . I don't want to go home."

My mom looks from me to my dad, and Mason guesses, "Beach house?"

I nod, looking between the three of them. "It's the last place I remember, and I want to stay closer. I also want to go back to school when the semester starts."

"That's less than a month away."

"And the doctor said I could remember any day. The accident was fifteen days ago. Everything should come back soon. Tomorrow even."

The room is quiet a moment, and my mom offers a small smile. "And if it takes a little longer?"

A wave of nausea hits me, but I steady myself. "I still want to go back, especially then. Being on campus, hanging around the same areas and the same people could help. I did end up on campus, right?"

"Course you were." Mason clears his throat. "I think that all sounds good. I'll have Cameron pack you some things tonight, have it ready for tomorrow."

Worry pulls at my dad's brows, but he nods, putting his hand on my mom's back as she stands.

"Dad and I can hit the stores, stock the fridge and things." My mom nods, anxious. "But if you think I'm going home, you're crazy. I'll stay in our condo down the beach."

I reach out, squeezing her hand. "I figured you'd say that."

She winks, and then they're all on their feet, visiting hours almost over for the day, and now that I'm no longer critical, the standard rules apply. Honestly, it's a relief and admitting that makes me feel guilty, but they see my heavy eyes and tell me to rest. It comes from a place of love, but if they knew the way my stomach turns at the thought of nightfall, they'd worry themselves to death.

So, as they say their goodbyes, I put on a mask of ease, but the minute they're gone, it slips away, anxiousness crippling me.

Soon, all the lights will be out, and no chatter will come from the halls. The nurses won't shout out from their stations but speak quietly among themselves.

The floor will fall silent, and exhaustion will bleed in.

I hate it.

The mere thought of sleep is terrifying.

What if I close my eyes and lose more?

What if I close my eyes and they never open?

What if they open, and I don't even know who I am?

Right now, I'm still me, just missing a couple pieces.

What if tomorrow I'm a stranger stuck in Arianna Johnson's body?

Dropping my head back, I push away the tears with a growl.

A light tap has me jolting upright, surprised when it's Noah I find in the doorway, a plastic bag in his hand.

"Casper getting on your nerves again?" His tone is tense but warm.

I blink away the moisture. "Yeah, he's being a dick. Keeps pouring water in my eyes. I'm kind of sick of it."

A low chuckle leaves him, and he nods as if understanding what I mean.

I'm sick of crying.

"I brought you something." He hesitates in the doorway a moment, but when I say nothing, he walks in.

He hands me the bag, and slowly, I reach out to take it.

"What is it?"

"A little something to get you through the night." He turns for the door, but something has me calling out.

"You don't have to leave . . . unless you want to."

He doesn't look back at first, and when he does, there's a heaviness that settles over the room.

He doesn't want to leave; I can sense it.

How can I sense it?

I clear my throat. "You could wait until someone comes to kick you out? Shouldn't be too long."

Slowly, he nods, his hands sliding into his hoodie pocket as he comes closer, taking the seat beside me.

He watches me closely as I reach into the bag, pulling out a pair of earbuds and an old iPod.

Warmth washes over me, and I look to him. "You brought me music?"

His eyes hold mine. "Thought you might need to get lost for a little while."

How do you know I can't sleep? That music will help?

How do you know what I need?

"Thank you," I whisper, and when I get the thing turned on, and the earbuds hooked up, I pass him one.

Noah keeps his gaze on mine as he slides it into his ear, and I drop back against the bed. I press play, and three chords in my eyes close, the story playing out behind them.

Something settles within me, and my breaths grow deeper, fuller.

"It's so good to see that man finally getting some sleep."

I look up to find Nurse Becky coming in, unsure of how much time has passed, but it must have been a while because when I look to Noah, I find he's asleep, his hand lying on top of my mattress, at my side.

"Sorry," I whisper. "I know visiting hours are over."

"You've got the whole room to yourself; they won't bother you." She waves a hand, her jacket hanging over her arm. "Besides, I'm off the clock, just wanted to pop in and say goodbye in case I don't see you tomorrow before you go."

"Thank you for all you did for me."

"It was my pleasure. It was nice to see such a loving family. It's sad how rare that is in here." She sighs, smiling

400

as she looks over at Noah. "And that man, he didn't leave your side."

My stomach sucks in. "He didn't?"

She shakes her head, staring at him with a motherly notion. "Poor thing only closed his eyes for an hour or two a day the whole time you were unconscious, and even less the last couple days while he was hiding out in the waiting room down the hall. If he wasn't in that shower, he was right there in that chair, as restless as a kid on Christmas Eve."

A frown builds along my brow.

"Looks like he's sleeping just fine." Her eyes come up to mine, a low gleam within them. "I'll go before I wake him."

Nodding, I wave, but as soon as she's gone, my eyes shift to Noah, to his hand, an inch from meeting my blanket-covered thigh.

I stare at it a moment, at his long fingers and the slight bend of his knuckles. At the softness of his skin and the veins of his lower forearm as his sleeve pushes up the slightest bit.

I look to his face, to the long lashes lying against his cheekbones. His dark hair pokes out from beneath the hood, and there's a light stubble on his jaw.

His chest rises and falls with deep full breaths.

I put the earbud back in my ear, and before I know it, morning comes with the seat beside me empty and a tap on the door.

My eyes open, my smile instant.

"Chase."

Noah

A little over an hour of my sitting on the curbside bench passes before Ari's voice reaches me, snapping me from my thoughts, and the moment I turn my head, she appears, her eyes instantly finding mine as if I spoke her name.

"Noah." The joy in her tone has my pulse jumping, and I can't help the small smile that appears.

I want to grab her, hug her. I want to hold her.

Instead, I stay sitting, locking my hands together because I don't trust myself not to reach out. "Juliet."

Her eyes narrow a little, but then she laughs, and goddamn, it's so fucking good to hear. She remembers the nickname I gave her that first day.

"You know." She tips her head. "They talked to us about the danger of stalkers at orientation."

My nerves spark, my words drawn out. "Did they now?"

"Mm-hm," she teases. "And you sitting out here shows borderline-stalker tendencies."

I swallow. "What if I said I wasn't here for you?"

"I'd call you a big fat liar."

I chuckle, the ease of this conversation settling in a way I can't explain, but a weight comes with it because while I was sitting here waiting to see her walk out, she should know why else I'd be here on a Sunday afternoon. She came with me so many times. I push the thought aside and climb to my feet, her chin lifting, so she can keep her eyes on mine. "You'd be right."

Her lips begin to curve, but she pulls them in, and then she looks behind her, and the warmth brewing in my chest dies on the spot.

Chase steps out with a smile, but the moment he spots me, it falls flat. He looks away a moment but back the next. "Hey, man."

Guilt, it's written all over him, as it should be.

My brain refuses to allow me to respond, but then Cameron and Brady file out, and the roar of an engine revs behind me. Mason pulls up at the curbside.

He quickly jumps out, and the others put the bags into the back as he comes over, Ari still standing on the sidewalk a foot in front of me.

"I called you twice last night." He glares at me.

My eyes slide to Ari's, and she drops her chin, nibbling on her lip, and Mason's eyes narrow, curious.

Everyone climbs into Mason's Tahoe, but the two of them and Ari looks to me, the circles beneath her eyes a little lighter today.

"We're spending the rest of break at the beach house," she tells me, and my chest tightens.

"Oh yeah?"

She nods.

Come on . . .

"Are you . . . do you have plans with your family?"

You are my family.

I shake my head, my pulse quickening, a mixture of emotions flowing through me.

"Oh." She pauses.

Almost.

"It's just the five of us staying, and we have an extra room if you want to come," she says as if I haven't been there. It kills me, but not as much as the hint of uncertainty in her tone.

In her eyes.

In the way she stands.

I want to wash it all away, to tell her she never has to wonder where I want to be because the answer is, and always will be, wherever she is.

Right beside her.

But I can't say that.

So I keep it simple. I keep it us.

"You know the answer to that."

"Do I?" She laughs, but she has no idea why, and for once, it brings a smile to my face because while she doesn't remember, her mind makes the subconscious connection. "Maybe I want to hear it?"

At that, a small smirk builds.

Of course you do, baby.

"Yeah, Juliet," I tell her. "I'd love to go."

Her lips press together in a smile, and she gives a curt nod. "Then it looks like it'll be a full house."

It takes her a second, but she steps around me, slowly slipping into the front seat, where Mason's got a couple pillows waiting for her.

He steps beside me. "What kind of girl would invite 'some guy from the beach she sat and talked to for a minute' to sleep down the hall from her for two weeks?"

My lungs fill, and I turn to him.

"The kind that remembers a topic from her freshman orientation."

His brows snap together. "That . . . that was after she left for the summer. Weeks after."

A small smile pulls at my lips, and I nod. "I know."

With that, I move toward my truck, leaving Mason to explain why I don't have to run home to grab some things before we make the short trip.

I already packed.

Chapter 43
Noah

Two days turn into four, and four turns into a week, and still, Ari's memory hasn't come back. That's twenty-two days in total, and with each passing hour, my days grow a little darker.

The subconscious memory about orientation is the last and only comment I've caught that holds any kind of proof her memories are still in there somewhere. As far as I know, it's the only time she's referenced *before*, not that she realized it. Again, as far as I'm aware.

A cold bottle of beer slips into my view, and I look up to find Mr. Johnson.

Not wanting to be rude, I plan to take it, but I hesitate a moment too long, and a low chuckle leaves him.

"Yeah, I know that face." He lowers into the seat beside me, takes a slow swig, and sets the second bottle between his legs. "That's the face of a man who found himself on a first-name basis with the guy at the liquor store."

My mouth curves slightly, and I look to the wooden deck beneath my feet. "His name was Darrel, and he's got a thing for cherry soda."

Mr. Johnson flashes a small grin, but it doesn't meet his eyes. His features smooth, and he nods. "You think you can be straight with me?" he wonders.

"I have no reason not to be, sir."

He waves me off. "I like that answer, but no sir. No Mr. Johnson. Just Evan." He lowers his chin, and I nod.

"I won't lie to you, Evan." I look him in the eye. "I might choose not to answer based on the question, but only out of good intention. Nothing more."

"What kind of question would you choose not to answer?"

I open my mouth, but he laughs it off.

"I just want to know how you're doin', son, how you're *really* doing."

"I'm not really sure," I answer honestly. "All things considered, I'm fine, but *all things considered* and uh . . ."

"And you're a fucking mess?"

My eyes snap his way, and he grins, drawing a chuckle from me.

"Yes, sir." He lifts a brow, and I raise my palms. "Sorry, curse of an athlete. If you weren't a professor of mine, you were sir or coach. It's not an easy one to break."

"It's a good problem to have." He nods. "About that whole athlete thing."

I look away. "This might lead to one of those 'choose not to answer' questions."

"Because you don't want me to tell you not to walk away from your dreams."

"If that's what you said to me right now, sir, I'd thank you for understanding why I'm here and not anywhere else."

His jaw clenches, and he looks away with a slow nod, attempting to shield the moisture building in his eyes. "Evan, son. Not sir." He takes a long drink from his beer, and when he looks to me, he nods again. "How you doing? Truly, Noah. I know your mama is still healing, you've got your last semester coming up, and football is up in the air. And with everything happening with Ari, it worries me for you. It's a lot for anyone to handle, but where my daughter is concerned, I imagine your position is the worst to be stuck in."

"I don't feel stuck, sir, or Evan. A bit helpless, a little overwhelmed, yeah, but not stuck."

"I know it's hard, and I don't know that I necessarily agree with her choice to keep all our mouths closed like this, but I appreciate you going along with what she's asked." He scoffs, shaking his head. "Pretty sure I'd have locked my wife in a room with me and broke down every detail that first night."

My laugh is low. "Yeah."

I'd love nothing more than to do exactly that. It's on my mind all the time, how I would start and what exactly I would say. I've had the imaginary conversation with her a hundred times now, but at the end of each one, tears brim in her eyes, confusion swimming within them as she stares at the man telling her she loves him while internally swearing she loves another.

I won't hurt her just to help myself.

I look to Mr. Johnson. "Biting my tongue has never been too hard for me. It's just another thing that comes with being an athlete."

"A coachable athlete anyway."

I nod.

As an athlete, a coachable one, as he pointed out, you don't always like what you see, hear, or are asked to do, but you do it anyway for a number of reasons.

"This is a lot different, Noah." He speaks my exact thought out loud.

"Yeah, it is, but it's not the 'holding the words back' part that's hard for me."

Understanding draws his features in, and he sighs. "No, son, I don't imagine it is."

Both of our gazes lift then, pointing toward the ocean, toward the waterline, where Ari stands, her hair blowing around in front of her face, a wide smile spread along her lips as she laughs . . . at something Chase has said.

Tension builds in my sternum, and I force my eyes to my feet.

Sitting back this time means watching firsthand as my future grows blurrier by the day, but what she wants is what I want for her, so really, there's no decision to be made on my part.

I'm here until she's ready for me.

Or until I'm forced to let go.

"You love my little girl." Mr. Johnson speaks low, turning to me.

"I'm not the only one." My lips press into a tight line, my eyes lifting to the sand once more. "I'm beginning to wonder if I'll ever get the chance to tell her."

His hand clamps onto my shoulder then, giving a little squeeze. "If it begins to look like you won't, you might have to go on and do it anyway." His chin lowers, and I manage a nod.

Slowly, he pushes to his feet. "It's an honor to have you here, son."

"Thank you, sir."

He glares, and a low laugh slips from me.

Mason comes out of the house then, looking between the two of us, but his gaze is quickly pulled forward to Chase and Ari. A deep frown pulls at his forehead.

Mr. Johnson chuckles, slaps his shoulder, and heads around the side. "I'm walking down to snag my wife for lunch. See you, boys."

He leaves, and the two on the beach walk back this way, pausing not too far from us now.

Chase says something, and Ari's sweater-covered hand comes up to cover her laugh, but it still echoes in my ears.

My lips twitch, my body confused by the happiness her laughter brings and the devastation bleeding through me that I'm not the one who earned it.

"Fuck." Mason sighs, and we glance toward each other. "What are you doing, man?"

"Wondering how to show a girl who's wanted one man all her life that she doesn't want him anymore."

Mason winces, his glare sharpening more and more as he stares at the two. "Fuck this."

He jolts forward, and I dart to my feet, catching him by the wrist, halting him in place.

His eyes narrow on me. "Noah."

"I need you to promise me something."

His brows furrow. "Don't."

"Mason, come on. Please."

Angry, he plants his feet. "What?"

"When he tells her he had a change of heart, don't interfere."

"What the fuck?" he throws back. "Are you serious right now?"

"Yes, and I know you don't want to hurt her. Going apeshit will do just that."

"This isn't about keeping my sister from my friend. It might have been before, but it's different now. This is about her getting back the life she lost. You've got to get that."

"Trust me, I do, but I'm trying to do what's right here. This is what she wants."

"What she wants is you."

"Mason."

"She loves you, bro! That's what's right, end of fucking story!"

"Keep your voice down," I warn him, but it's too late.

Ari hears her twin's shouts, and sure enough, her eyes are pulled this way.

She stutter steps, tucking her hair behind her ear as she tugs the corner of her lower lip between her teeth. Her chest rises with a full breath, and she doesn't look away.

She doesn't move at all.

But her eyes, they aren't on Mason. They're on me.

"Look at her, Noah." Mason's whisper is desperate. "Just . . . fucking look at her. It's written all over her, and she doesn't even know it. She's yours, man. Don't let her lose what she always wanted and finally found."

A knot forms in my throat, and I swallow past it. It does nothing to hide the turmoil in my tone. "In her mind right now, she loves him. She wants *him*. I need you to let her figure it out on her own."

Frustrated, he runs a hand over his face. "Tell me why."

"Because she's lost, you said it yourself. She only has what she knows, and what she knows is—" I swallow. "What she knows is the way he makes her feel."

We're both quiet a moment before I add, "He's the only thing that makes sense to her right now."

"You know this is fucked up, right? That it could backfire? If he really loves her and she gives them the chance they didn't get 'cause I'm a bastard, this could mean you losing her." He faces me fully. "Are you prepared for that? 'Cause it could fucking happen."

The arteries surrounding my heart squeeze, and it gets a little harder to breathe.

Ari smiles then, waves, and everything fucking aches. Burns.

Clearing my throat, I turn away. I look Mason in the eye.

"I'm not asking you to push her to him. I'm just asking you to allow her the chance you took away if she decides she wants it."

Mason shakes his head. "This isn't some dude off the street. There's history, family ties. Friendship that spans years." He eyes me. "Chase is a good man, Noah."

"If he wasn't, I wouldn't be standing here."

He sighs, long and loud. "Fine. But for the record, this is a bad idea, and you might learn that the hard way." With that, he storms down the steps, cutting right and disappearing down the beach.

Ari and Chase both watch as he disappears, and as her attention moves back toward me, I drop back into my seat.

I press my knuckles into my eye sockets, hoping that I'm doing the right thing and wishing there was a way to find out, but how can I possibly find the answer when I don't even know the damn question?

Life has never been simple for me, but this is on another level, and I'm not handling it well.

I want my girl back.

I want the future I dared to dream about.

I want her.

Chapter 44
Noah

"Thanks for coming over to chat with Kalani," Nate, Ari's cousin, says as he walks me out. "I imagine the last thing on your mind right now is football, so it means a lot that you entertained her."

"I don't want you to think I'm not interested in playing for the Tomahawks." I turn to face him. "I am. I'd be honored to be a part of any team, especially one that wants me to transition back to my original position, but I just . . ."

"Can't think past the hour?"

I nod.

"Hey, I know the feeling, man. Trust me. My world shattered for a minute, too, before we got to where we are now. Not like yours but—"

"Nah, don't say that. Heartache is heartache, right?"

"Shit burns either way," he agrees, offering me a hand, so I slap my palm into his. "You'll come to the barbecue on Sunday?"

"I'll be here." I salute the man and make my way back to Ari's beach house.

On the way, Trey tries calling, making this his fourth attempt to reach me since Ari woke up from her coma, but I can't bring myself to answer, just like I couldn't answer Paige or my coaches' messages either.

I don't know what to say to them, or anyone else for that matter. I imagine they've heard something, but I can't be sure, and I'm not ready to have that conversation with anyone.

Talking about what's happened will only make it more real than it already is, and I'm not okay with that.

It's not long before I reach the deck of the beach house. Brady and Cameron are sitting on the couch, playing on their phones. As I reach the top, Cameron looks up from hers, a smirk on her lips.

"What?" My steps slow.

"Martha Stewart has officially arrived." She draws her legs up, snagging a chip from the bowl in Brady's lap. "Get on in there, Snoop Dogg."

"I'm not following . . ."

She looks back to her screen. "You will."

With a small grin, I shake my head and walk inside.

I get a single foot in the door, and instantly, my senses are assaulted, the aroma one I could recognize anywhere, and my feet freeze, my eyes darting around the room.

Mr. Johnson sits at the table reading a sports magazine, and Mason leans against the kitchen island.

And behind it, facing the stovetop, is . . . Ari.

She's stirring something in a pot, and if my memory isn't playing tricks on me, I know exactly what she's taking extra care tasting.

The recipe I shared with her. Made with her.

My mom's recipe.

My throat clogs, and slowly, I push closer, joining Mason against the counter.

"Mom, did you find them?!" Ari shouts, dipping her finger in the spoon to taste the steaming sauce.

"No, honey, there's none back here." Mrs. Johnson comes around the corner, her face lighting up when she spots me. "Noah, you're back. How'd it go with Lolli?"

"As wild as expected, I'm sure." Mason pumps my elbow, and a low laugh leaves me.

"She's sweet. It was a good conversation."

Ari looks over her shoulder then, and my chest inflates.

"What uh, what were you looking for?" I wonder, peeling my jacket off and setting it over the chair. I push my sleeves up, cautiously making my way around the side of the island.

I pause beside her, and a nervous smile pulls at her lips.

"Ma was looking for some peppers," Mason offers.

I nod, trying to keep my breathing steady because I think I know where this is going. "There're some jalapeños in the fridge."

"You think that would be okay?" Ari wonders, glancing my way briefly.

"It might, but what kind were you looking for?"

"Crushed peppers."

I purposely don't say a word, and she looks to me. "You know, like pizza peppers?"

I fight a grin, my pulse flipping. "Right, right. Pizza peppers."

Ari's hand freezes midstir, her head snapping my way. A small frown builds over her brow, but a small smile slips in the next second. "Wait!" She walks over to the side drawer and digs around, pulling out a few packets of peppers from Benito's pizza. She holds them up in triumph. "I knew these would come in handy."

She comes back, tears them open, and pours them inside.

I lean my elbow on the counter, facing her. "That should give it a nice little kick, huh?"

Her smile is wide. "Exactly."

Her eyes freeze on mine, and a knot forms in my throat. *God, she's so beautiful.*

"Oh, shit!" Brady comes in with a shout, and damn it if it doesn't break the spell. "We got fire extinguishers, right?"

"And homeowner's insurance?" Cameron adds.

"Ha ha." Ari shakes her head. "They swear I'm useless, Noah."

I slip a little closer, her elbow brushing along my chest as she stirs, and her chest rises with a full inhale.

Her eyes lift to mine, her long, dark lashes fanning along her cheekbones.

"Looks like you're doing just fine." My tone's a bit huskier than I'd have liked, but I don't care.

413

She blinks, a flicker of something flashing across her face, and then she tips her chin, that sweet shyness I love coming through.

I miss you.

She frowns but quickly washes it away, jerking her head over her shoulder. "Yeah, I'm doing just fine. Maybe I don't suck so bad after all." She pauses. "*Mother.*"

"Hey." Mrs. Johnson leans against her husband, pulling a coffee mug to her lips to hide a smile. "I didn't say it."

The room laughs, and before I look away, Mr. Johnson catches my eye.

He winks and goes back to his reading.

My eyes don't move off of her after that.

She's working off of memory, one that I gave her, and she doesn't even know it.

Mason and I are tossing the football around in the street when Ari stumbles out of the house, tripping over Mason's shoes.

"Shit, Mason!" She laughs, catching herself on the chair by the door.

"My bad!" he shouts, glancing behind him when the roar of Nate's Hummer grows near.

"Crap, tell them to wait. I forgot my phone!" She hustles back inside, and we turn to face the girls.

The windows are rolled down, the music is loud, and Lolli doesn't press the brake until she's right in front of the house, finally coming to a screeching halt.

Payton and Lolli's cousin Mia smiles from the back, leaning half out the window.

"Sup, boys?"

"Not much, playing some catch." I point to Mason, who walks up with a frown.

"Where's little D?" He tucks the ball beneath his arm.

Payton looks to him, her eyes briefly flicking past mine. "Ari seems to be keeping her distance from him, so I—" Her eyes flick to mine, and her lips press into a tight smile. "Sorry, Noah."

414

A sharp pain stabs at my chest, and it doubles, knowing Ari is avoiding being around Payton's son, but I shake my head, not wanting to make her feel guilty when she shouldn't. "It's okay."

"I didn't want to make her uncomfortable, so I left him with my brother."

"I could have helped," Mason argues.

Payton's cheeks turn red. "I didn't need your help."

Mason turns to me, tosses the ball, and jogs back into the house.

Lolli flips around in the front seat, lifting a brow at Payton.

Payton busies herself with her phone.

"Sorry, ready." Ari rushes over, her hair dripping wet and tied in a knot on her head.

"Girls' day?" I wonder.

"Yes. It should be fun."

I grin, happy to see her getting out for some fresh scenery. She hasn't left the house much since we got here, other than to walk down and be near the water.

"I'm here by force, in case you were wondering." Lolli frowns.

"Shut up, Lolli. We'll feed you Patron. Don't worry," Mia teases.

"We're going into the city to look at some boutiques," Payton says, without looking up. "Kenra heard about the 'gala' and lost her mind."

My muscles lock, and it takes effort to pry my lips open.

I look to Ari. "Gala?"

She smiles. "Yeah, your team event is coming up superfast, so I've got to go find something now, or I'll be screwed."

My stomach stirs, my limbs tingling.

"You—" I swallow.

She remembers?

I must look crazy because she giggles.

"At first, I wasn't sure I was up for it, just in case, you know?" she says, and I eagerly nod, desperate to reach out and brush the loose hair from her face. "But then I decided, screw it, I need some fun."

415

"Yeah. You do." We do, baby.

"So I said I'd go." She shrugs, tugging the door open to the back seat.

"Said you'd go."

Said she'd go?

A knot forms in my throat.

In my gut.

In my fucking chest.

Ari nods, a sudden anxiousness drawing her shoulders in. "Um . . ." Confusion swims in her eyes, and so I clear my throat, trying to offer a smile for her benefit, but I'm not sure I manage.

And then I spin around, heading back toward the house, but I don't go inside.

I storm around the back, my ears ringing when voices reach me from the patio.

My vision pulses, blurring in and out of focus, but I only need one clear view.

One clear fucking shot.

And I take it.

I pull back, my fist connecting with Chase's jaw.

He falls from his chair, tumbling to the ground, and when he jumps to his feet, his head snapping toward me, I grip him by the shirt, driving him backward until his spine hits the railing.

I trap his arms behind his back and lift his legs a bit, so he's half hanging over the deck's edge. I press my forearm against his chest, forcing it to hold all of my upper body weight.

He groans, trying to break free, but I press harder.

He cries out in pain this time, and Brady appears at my side, a door slamming behind us, and then Mason appears.

"Noah, let him go."

I press into Chase's gut with my elbow and dig the heel of my palm into his shoulder blade. I could pop it out with just a little more force.

"You're gonna break his arm." Brady's hand closes over my wrist.

My stomach turns. "Maybe he deserves it."

My body shakes, my teeth clenching, and I push off of him, but I don't step back.

Chase is forced to stand before me, right in fucking front of me.

Blood drips from his lip, and he dabs at it with his thumb.

My shoulders fall, and I shake my head.

A twisted type of torment burns within me; it's a mix of anger and guilt, making it hard to breathe because here I am angry at the guy in front of me when I'm the one who placed him there.

I did this. I tried to do the right thing, laid on the damn sword because that's what she asked for, that's what she needed, and being any and everything she needs is all I've ever wanted. It's all I'll ever want.

So I followed her lead, stepped back, and this motherfucker . . .

He slid right in.

But I don't get it.

I shake my head. "Why you doing this?"

Chase has the audacity to wince, and he looks away.

"Really? You're man enough to make the move, but you're not man enough to say it out loud?"

His head jerks forward at that, and he throws his hands out. "What do you want me to say, Noah?"

"I want you to tell me why I shouldn't knock you the fuck out. Why I shouldn't go to her right now and remind her of exactly what her life became after you because it was better. She was happier. She was—"

Loved. In love.

She was mine.

"I just want to be here for her, Noah, and I want her to know that I . . . that I am here if she decides she—" He cuts himself off.

"How you going to be half the man she needs if you can't even admit what you want out loud?"

"I'm sorry, but I don't have to say anything to you."

"No, just keep pretending to be the guy she begged you to be months ago and see how that works out for you."

"Do you think I don't know that I fucked up?" he shouts. "Because I do, all right. I do, but I can't walk away now. For months, I've watched for some sort of sign that what we did was right, that we are what's right, and I can't ignore the fact that this is it. This is the most straightforward sign if I've ever seen one."

A humorless laugh leaves me, and I try to swallow beyond the knot in my chest. "A sign." I nod. "You've been sitting around for months, years even, waiting for someone or something to come along and convince you she's worth it?"

Again, he looks away, but I push closer, getting into his face, and finally, he brings his eyes back to mine.

"I've known that girl was worth the world since the moment I met her." I blink hard, willing myself not to lose it while staring into the eyes of the asshole trying to steal my world from under me.

Mason's hand falls onto my shoulder, but I jerk myself free, spin, and begin to walk away, but I only make it a single footstep.

"She loved me once, Noah . . . she could again. Maybe you should start considering that."

Ice spreads through my stomach.

I whip around so fast I feel sick, dizzy, but my knuckles crack across his nose, and the pain it creates is welcomed.

"Fuck!" Chase touches his face, blood pouring down it.

Mason hangs his head, and Brady looks away. Neither says a word, because really, what can they say?

This was a long time coming, and they know it.

Needing to get away and quickly, I take the steps two at a time, dragging myself around the property so they can no longer see me.

My body is shaking in cruel punishment. A vicious ache working its way up my throat, and it wins out.

I stumble toward the trash can in the corner, my stomach draining into the black garbage bag, taking the little bit of hope last night brought with it.

Maybe I'm making a mistake.
Maybe this is the wrong way to do this.
Maybe I need to go against what she asked.
Maybe I should hang my hat and walk away.

Chapter 45
Arianna

Rushing down the stairs, I jog out front, quickly slipping into my mom's car.

"Sorry." I wipe the rain from my forehead and buckle up. "Mia had me pinned up on a pedestal longer than expected, trying to get my dress to fit right."

"When is this dance?" She pulls onto the street.

"Mom." I laugh. "It's not high school. It's not like prom. It's basically an end-of-season award ceremony."

"That is set for formal wear and in a rented-out hall, from what I heard."

"True." I smile, looking at her. "Anyway, yeah. It's next Wednesday."

"Hm," my mom muses, her eyes shifting toward me.

"What?"

"Nothing."

"Mom . . ." I turn in my seat, eyeing her.

"Nothing, sweetie." She pats my leg. "It's just soon, is all, and school begins the following week, right?"

"Yep. The twenty-seventh is the first day back. Chase is taking me to see my dorm a couple days before. It's so weird that I have no idea what it looks like, but I lived there for an entire semester."

We pull into the parking lot of the hospital for my follow-up with the behavioral neurologist. Parking in front of the building, she turns to me. "You've been spending a lot of time with Chase."

Heat works its way up my neck, and I shrug.

She tips her head, a tenderness in her gaze. "How's that going?"

"It's going." A low chuckle leaves me. "We're having fun. Making up for what I assume was lost time. He's constantly asking me to go with him places, even if it's just down the beach. At first, it made me anxious, but now it's, I don't know . . ." I trail off, a small swirl stirring in my stomach.

"Exciting?" she whispers.

A smile curves my lips, and I look to her, the creases around her eyes deepening, but she smiles through what troubles her, her hand coming out to touch my cheek.

"It's strange. It's like he's the same Chase, but not. Only, I can't figure out what's changed about him, but I feel it, you know? Something's different." It's frustrating, at times, how the invisible fog won't clear, but constantly stressing over it makes it hard to function, let alone breathe, so I try and keep busy, so I don't have to think past the moment.

I don't tell her that.

"Have you wondered if maybe it's not him who has changed?" My mom smiles softly. "That maybe it's you who's different?"

"I—" I shake my head. "I'm not different. I lost my memories, but I'm still me, and besides, they're coming back any time. Tonight maybe. Maybe after this appointment."

My pulse spikes, and I dig my fingertips into the cheap leather of the armrest.

"I didn't mean your accident changed you." She grabs my hand, unease in her tone. "Ari, sweetie, you came into your own at Avix, and sure, it might have only been a semester, but that first taste of change was good to you."

"And soon, I'll remember all of it." I nod, squeezing her hand. "I should go in before I'm late. I know they said no one is allowed in the room, but are you sure you don't want to come up to the waiting room?"

"That's okay," she rasps. "I'll grab a coffee down the road and come back, read while I wait for you. I'll be right here when you get out."

Nodding, I slip from the car.

As I step out, my eyes are pulled left, toward a small building beside the main one with the name, *Tri-City Rehabilitation Center,* in large, bold letters hanging over the double doors.

Pressure falls over my chest as I stare at the dark windows.

"You okay?" My mom's voice shakes me out of my head, and I force a smile.

"Yeah. See you in a bit."

I walk into the building, and while it feels like hours of waiting, in reality, it's only a handful of minutes, and then I'm sitting on a velvety sofa, the man who joined Dr. Brian in explaining what might have happened to me sitting behind the desk before me.

He smiles, and I sit on my hands, a little anxious all of a sudden.

"It's good to see you again, Arianna. You're looking much healthier."

"Yeah, I can move without feeling like I'm being stabbed now."

He chuckles, crossing one leg, and I do the same. "So, I read over everything again and—"

"I'm sorry, not to be rude, Dr. Stacia, but can we not do any of the basic lead-up stuff?"

The man offers a small smile and sits forward. "Why don't you go ahead and tell me what's on your mind, and we can go from there? Does that sound all right?"

I nod, stretching past the tension in my chest.

"I don't remember anything," I blurt out. "It's been a month now, and nothing. It's like I wake up, and there's this layer of fog over my eyes, but I can see just fine. My mind is constantly running, but only with half thoughts. I look at something and lose my breath, but I don't know why. I hear a sad song, and I cry, but for what? I smell familiar scents that aren't even familiar if that makes sense, and it's like my throat swells, and I can't breathe. Almost like everything is on the tip of my tongue, at the tip of my fingers, but when I move forward to grab it, there's nothing to hold on to.

"There's this . . . this feeling I keep getting." Tears prick my eyes now. "It's like an overwhelming sense of urgency, demanding my attention, almost like need or awareness. It keeps screaming that I'm missing something, something big. Something that's a part of me, but I don't know what it is. It's physically painful, like beneath the bones, painful, where I can't touch it, can't find it, but it's heavy, and the desperation that falls over me when it happens is debilitating.

"It's so often that now I'm avoiding the things I do know, and I'm afraid I won't be able to do that soon, and I'll go crazy. I feel like I was tossed out in the middle of the ocean, and if I lie back and try to float, try to remember, I'll drown, so I keep swimming. I keep busy. But lately, I'm running on empty. My family has been amazing, but that's because I smile all the time, and I don't know how much longer I can do that."

I take a breath, looking up at Dr. Stacia.

The man nods, considering everything I have said, and as he begins to speak, breaking down what I've expressed and relating it to my situation in a way that medically makes sense to him, a weight falls over me.

I want to scream, to cry. I want to run away.

But instead, I do what I've been doing for the last several weeks.

I push it away, bury it with a smile, and when he lifts from his seat, offering me his hand, I shake it, pacing myself as I walk out the door, wishing I never walked through it.

As promised, my mom is waiting just outside the building, and as I slip inside the front seat, saying not a word, my mother reads it on my face.

Her tears are as instant as mine, and when I turn away, she faces forward.

I zone out, and the next thing I know, we're pulling up to the beach house, my dad's truck parked behind Chase's in the driveway.

When I don't get out, my mom asks, "Want to come back to our condo?"

Shaking my head, I bite at the inside of my cheek and jump out.

I head inside, my movements jerky, eyes watery, and cheeks red.

Everyone's sitting in the living room watching TV, but the moment they set eyes on me, it's paused.

My dad's eyes fly to my mom, and Mason frowns, leaning forward.

Chase stands, starting toward me, but I throw my hands up, toss my purse to the floor and keep walking.

I need . . . I need . . .

What the fuck do you need, Ari? Goddamn it!

I'm out the back door and running for the beach in seconds.

The wind whips my face, burning my skin, but I don't care. I keep running.

About a half mile down the beach, my throat swells, my tears choking me, and I growl, swiping them away with angry movements.

I jerk to a stop and something has me spinning around, looking forward, and that's when I see him.

Noah.

My shoulders fall, and as if I spoke his name aloud, he turns, spotting me in an instant.

He frowns, gripping the edge of the dock his legs are dangling over, but he doesn't move when something tells me he wants to.

Before I realize it, I'm four feet from him, and he's looking up at me.

"I don't feel like talking right now." I'm not sure why I say it when I'm the one who walked over, but that's what comes out.

Noah nods, his brows nearly touching in the middle. "Talking's overrated."

A chuckle slips from me, and I sniffle, catching the small twitch of his lips.

Folding my toes in my shoes, I hold a hand out. "We could . . . not talk together?"

424

His tongue comes out, running across his lips, and a heaviness settles over me as I wait for his response, but I'm not sure why because when he nods again, it's as if I knew what his answer would be before he made it.

Something tells me I did.

Noah

Ari stares down at me, a small smile on her lips, her hand outstretched and eyes red rimmed. I knew the second I saw her she was upset, that she'd been crying, but I also knew she wasn't in the mood to share. She needs time to herself to process her thoughts, just like me.

So, I take her extended hand.

The moment my palm touches hers, it's as if a needle pricks our skin, and she jolts from the small shock.

A laugh slips from her, and I can't help but grin as I leap to my feet.

Once standing, I turn, so my body is facing the same direction as hers, and this time, offer her my hand. It's with a coy smile that she grabs hold.

Her head tips back the slightest bit, so she can see me fully, and slowly, very slowly, a softness falls over her. Her eyes roam along my face, her fingers twitching in mine, and before she realizes, before she grows anxious and pulls away in confusion, as she's done every other time she allows herself to be close to me, I nod.

"Let's get to that 'not talking' then, huh?"

Ari smiles and leads us down the long dock, but instead of walking to the end, where the wood meets the sand, she turns us halfway.

We leap over the side, the ground not three feet from us.

The second we touch the sand, she looks to me, and the glimmer in her brown eyes has my muscles flexing.

I quickly let her go, burying my hand in my hoodie pocket, and she does the same.

With nothing but the sound of the ocean around us, she leads us farther down the coastline to a boat ramp about a mile away.

She bends and begins untying a two-person paddleboat.

"Should I be on the lookout?"

Over her shoulder, she throws me a smile, and I want to drop to my knees beside her.

"It's Lolli's. She won't mind."

I nod, jerking closer when she starts to climb in, but she doesn't need my help.

She's done this a million times.

I hop in beside her, and off we go, paddling out into the open ocean but sticking close to the land.

It's not for a good hour, and after our second time passing her beach house, that she stops peddling and lets her butt fall to the floorboard, her legs thrown over the top, head tipped back on the seat.

She stares at the cloudy sky, and I join her.

"You ever wish you could go to a new place and take on a whole other life? Like, tell everyone your name is John, and you're a carpenter with no family and moved on a whim?"

"No."

Her head snaps my way at my quick, flat response to her wishful notion.

"I'd tell everyone my name is McLovin."

She laughs, her body shaking, and when she looks back to the sky, it's with a sigh. "I love that movie."

I know.

A somberness falls over her, and I wait.

It takes a minute, but then she closes her eyes, and when they open back up, they focus on the yellow nail polish she's now chipping from her thumb.

"I had a doctor's appointment today, you know, to check on me after the accident."

I knew this. It's why I came out here in the first place, to the one place I could feel like I was close to her, even when I wasn't.

I should have been there with her, sitting in the waiting room, so I could take her hand and hold her when she came out, celebrating the good or comforting through the bad.

A knot forms in the pit of my stomach.

"They, um, they think I'm blocking the memories. They said sometimes people who are . . . severely depressed do that." Tears build in her eyes, and she shakes her head. "How am I supposed to know if that's the problem when I can't remember if I was depressed in the first place?"

I fight not to let out the shuddered breath lodged in my chest, the pain in her tone too fucking much. Her silent cries shake her body, and she looks away, embarrassed.

She's breaking beside me, and I can't take it. Can't do this.

She wants to learn things on her own, but she needs something to hold on to. She needs to know she is okay. That she'll be okay.

My knuckle finds its place beneath her chin, and when my thumb falls to the space between there and her bottom lip, her lips part with a low gasp, and her eyes fly to mine before I've even turned her face my way.

There's a plea within them, but goddamn it, my baby has no idea what she's asking for.

It's subconscious, her heart and mind knowing I'm right here, dying to take away her pain, to comfort and support her through anything. Always.

Forever.

Her chest inflates, and my lips curve into a small, gentle smile.

"You were hurt, and it felt like the worst thing you could imagine." Her lip quivers, but she doesn't dare look away. "You cried a lot, hid away, and pretended things weren't as bad as they were, but slowly . . ." I swallow. "Very slowly, the light slid back into your eyes."

Her blinks grow slow, her tears slipping and rolling down to meet my skin. "Why do I get the feeling you helped with it?" she whispers.

I force my hand to fall and will my eyes to follow.

"Did you help with that?" She tries again.

I know she wants to remember on her own, but I already messed that up by sharing what I did. Now she's asking for more.

For a tiny piece.

I promised I'd never deny her, so I won't.

I clear my throat and answer the best way I know how.

"I hope so."

Her smile is unhurried, and she faces the open waters, murmuring, "I think you did."

I think I'm losing you . . .

Chapter 46

Arianna

White twinkling lights hang from the wall, sheer blue curtains weave around them to create a dreamy, winter wonderland–type atmosphere. Large pillars span the corners of the walls and at the front, raised on a small stage, is a table full of trophies and plaques.

The guys are dressed in sharp suits and the girls in flowing gowns, all but the coaching staff, who opted for their sideline attire.

The music is soft and the food a sampler-style cultural mix.

After the staff has the tables cleared from dinner, champagne flutes are passed around to those with wristbands. Sparkling cider for the rest of us. The head coach takes the stage, taps on the mic, and begins to welcome everyone to the ninetieth annual winter gala.

"It's not uncommon to have a good team and a decent season. I've been here for twenty-two years, and there hasn't been a single year I couldn't claim the same, but there is a difference in good and gold, and this year, boys, the Avix U Sharks football team was fucking gold."

The room erupts with hoots and hollers, Brady's loud bark heard above each and every one.

The man goes on about his team, giving praise to them as a unit, sharing some of their trials with those of us who were none the wiser, and then he pauses. The man grabs the edge of the small podium he stands in front of and nods his head, a smile forming on his lips.

"You know, as a coach, there's only so much I can do, and I do it as best as I possibly can, but I know many of my boys cuss me out in their heads on a daily basis. A coach is only a coach." He nods. "The true hero of this season's success lies in the heart of the captain."

People whistle, and my stomach swirls. I subconsciously lean forward.

"Now, unfortunately, Noah Riley isn't here tonight, but if he were, I'd take my hat off to the man. He took a team, built on a third of rookies, and led us to the playoffs in a year we were expected to be at the bottom of our division. He pulled many of you under his wing, and you all might not know this, 'cause he surely never said a word, but that young man shifted his entire schedule around to be there to train and mentor every one of you who asked. He made us a family."

The backs of my eyes sting.

"For that reason, he's, without a doubt, and unanimous in votes from all thirty-nine of you on this roster, this year's MVP. I'd like to invite Trey Donavon to the stage to accept this award on Noah's behalf."

The room erupts with cheers, and Cameron, his date for the night, screams from her seat beside me.

Trey pushes his sleeves a little higher, and a few guys give catcalls, making him smirk in response.

"Hey now, I got a girl, and she's the jealous type," he teases, and I playfully swat at Cameron.

He clears his throat, lifts the small trophy, and looks it over. "Noah's been my best friend for three years now, and I know I'll be able to say the same thing thirty years from now."

"Hey," Chase whispers, and I reluctantly glance his way. "Wanna go get a drink? My buddy's manning the bar."

I shake my head, facing the stage once more as Trey continues.

"There ain't a man out there more hardworking and deserving of all the good the world has to offer more than him. I, uh, I know Coach asked me to accept this award, but there's someone else here I'd like to invite up to do it instead." Trey looks to

Cameron behind me, and a frown builds along my face as he tears the mic from its holder and leaps off the stage, headed right for her. But then he says, "Arianna Johnson," into the mic, and my spine straightens. Trey smiles. "My butterfly's bestie, you might be thinking I'm crazy right now, and I sort of am, so that's fine." He's in front of me now, and I look to Cameron when he drops to his knee with a wink. "Accept this award for our boy Noah?"

"Uh . . ." My mouth opens, but all that comes out is a nervous chuckle, knowing all eyes are on me.

"Come on, please?" He gives me big puppy dog eyes.

I lift my hands, shrugging. "Sure." I laugh, taking it from him.

The room cheers and he laughs as he heads back to the stage, tossing the mic up at his coach.

The coach gives out a few other awards, Brady being the only freshman to receive one, and then the lights dim, the music growing a little louder.

Chase turns to me, extends a hand, and nods toward the dance floor.

"No one is dancing yet."

"So." His smile is bright. "I want to dance with you, and I don't want to wait."

Warmth spreads through me, and I push to my feet. Chase's grin widens as he takes my hand, leading me to the center of the floor.

He spins me, making me laugh, and a blush rushes to my cheeks as I peek around to find several sets of eyes on us, some not as friendly as I'd have hoped. My muscles tense a bit, and Chase shakes his head.

He leans in, pressing his cheek to my face as he whispers, "Ignore them." He pulls back, his palm gliding around my body, his right hand clasped with mine but drawn in at our sides. His soft green eyes hold mine as his lips part, and he presses them against my knuckles. "You're beautiful, Arianna. So beautiful." His tone drops even lower, and my chest clenches from the sound.

A few others join us on the dance floor, but I don't pay them any mind.

I stay focused on the man before me.

"I used to dream of things like this," I admit. "Dancing with you, holding on to you . . ."

His forehead falls to mine, and my eyes close.

"It's all I've been thinking about," he confesses. "I wasn't sure I'd ever get the chance. I was a fool before, but no more. I'd choose you over anyone, Ari. No matter what. I'd choose you."

My stomach dips, and I bury my face in his neck, inhaling his scent.

It's sweet and peppery, subtle.

Where's the cedarwood and sage, the minty breeze?

My lids open, a frown building along my brow, but then Chase's hand leaves mine, and his soft palm falls against my cheek.

Where's the rough texture, the heated skin?

I pull back slightly, and his eyes lock with mine.

"Ari," he whispers, slipping closer, and my chest seizes.

But I can't tell if it's in anticipation or apprehension.

It's confusing, and it aches, but maybe it aches for him?

For us.

For more.

So when his eyes fall to my lips, I lift my chin in invitation.

Chase's mouth falls to mine, and my eyes close.

My heartbeat pounds hard against my rib cage, and he presses closer, his hand diving into my hair.

That's when a sob breaks through me, and I tug back, but before I'm forced to look at him before he can say a word, my brother is there.

Mason slips between us, pulls me into his arms and buries my head against his chest. He shields my face from the rest of the dance floor. I clutch his suit jacket, and he sways us slowly.

"It's okay, honey," he rasps, kissing my head. "It's okay."

"I don't know what's wrong with me. I don't know why I'm crying." I shudder, and his arms tighten. "I think it's just overwhelming, you know? I've waited so long."

Mason's sigh rolls over me. "Yeah, I know."

The pained frustration in his tone has me lifting my head. I swipe at my eyes and meet his.

"What?"

"Nothing."

"Mason, what?" I beg. "What is it?"

His chin falls, and he shakes his head. "It's really hard to stand back and let you lead. It scares me, that's all."

"That's not all, and you know it." We stop moving. "Does it bother you to see me with him?"

"Not the way you're used to."

"I don't know what that means."

"I know, but you won't let me tell you what it does mean." He reaches up, swiping at the edge of my eye and showing me the small black streak on the pad of his thumb. "It's okay. Just promise me you'll . . . move slow. Think things through before . . . anything."

Pink darkens my cheeks, and I nod, a low chuckle leaving me. "I should probably go find my date, so he doesn't think I'm crazy."

"He knows better than that." Mason's lips pull to one side, and he releases me. "Go."

With a deep breath, I nod, spinning on my heels.

To my surprise, Chase isn't far, and he isn't fazed. He waits for me, not fifteen feet away, champagne flutes in hand.

Biting at my lip, I step up to him, accepting the glass when he offers it. He quietly takes my hand, leading me to our table.

"Thank you for coming with me tonight." He brushes his palm along my arm. "This shouldn't have been our first dance. I should have taken you to the homecoming dance freshman year and to every other one after that. I should have shown you how important you were to me a long time ago, and I want to make up for that," he rasps, pressing a soft kiss to my shoulder. "Let me take you out this weekend. Just us."

"Are you asking me on a date, Chase Harper?"

A hint of bashfulness washes over him, and he nods. "Yeah, I am. So what do you say? Go out with me?"

My stomach swirls, and I nod, earning a victorious smile from Chase. We face forward after that, sitting comfortably as we listen to the music play.

As I look around at all the smiling faces, our friends only feet away, one spreads across my own.

And for the first time in a long time, a small sense of hope sparks within me.

This feels right.

So why does it take effort to hold my head up?

Later that night, once we get home and settled in, I search for Noah to show him the award he won, but he's nowhere to be found, so I set his trophy on my dresser and slip out of my dress for a quick shower.

My smile is wide as I step into the warm spray, the evening replaying before my eyes, the promise of tomorrow strong, but just as the excitement builds in my gut, it twists. It twists until it's painful, and suddenly, I can't breathe.

The calm from moments ago washes away with the water, swirling down the drain, taking me with it. Before I realize I've moved, I'm tucked into the corner, my legs drawn tight, my head buried against my knees.

I begin to cry.

At first, it's emotionless, confusing tears, but slowly, the ache lets itself be known.

The shame seeps in.

And the guilt is nearly too much.

For weeks now, as I told the doctor, I've been silently screaming to remember what I've forgotten by blocking out what I knew because what I knew was too painful and what I didn't, I was desperate for.

So I pushed it all away, the good, the bad, and the sad.

The precious.

A sob racks through me, and I give in to it.

I let it consume me.

Alone in the corner of the shower, I cry for all the things

I've tried to force from my mind but ache within me every day, nonetheless.

I cry for the child I lost, who I can hardly bring myself to acknowledge because the agony and loss it brings is unbearable. Downright devastating.

Being a mom is what I want most in the world, and here I am, too weak to even think about the little life that's no more.

The door is thrown open, and Cameron's wide eyes appear. "Oh, sister . . ."

Taking the towel off the counter, she quickly turns off the water, drops to her knees beside me, and wraps me in it, hugging me.

"I don't know what's wrong with me. Today was so much fun, but—" I break off in another choked sob.

"But what?"

"I don't know!" I shout. "I don't know what the 'but' is for, but I feel it. Constantly. It follows me. Every step I take, the 'but' is right there."

Something fucking stings, and she doesn't understand.

No one does.

Not even me.

An overwhelming sense of self-hate slips in, and my shoulders coil.

"I haven't allowed myself to think of what I've lost in weeks, Cameron. I pushed away the one thing I knew for certain. Who does that?!" Tears pour down my face. "Who pushes away a memory that should be treasured?"

I haven't spoken of or permitted the smallest hint of remembrance of the child that was growing inside me. My child.

I can't even bring myself to go near Payton's. That's how hard it is.

"It hurts, Cam. My bones literally feel like they're cracking when I think of him." I admit. "I think it would have been a him. A boy. I don't know why." I shake my head. "But every time I touch my stomach or accidentally wonder about him, I feel like I'm having a heart attack."

436

"It's okay, Ari," she murmurs.

A bitter laugh leaves me, and I swipe at my nose. "No, it's not. You just have no idea what else to say."

"It is okay—"

"It's not," I snap when I don't mean to. "I'm just pathetic. Completely fucking pathetic."

Panic flares behind my chest, and it swells, locking off my airway, and I start to sweat. It's as if my brain starts flashing all these moving pictures and words, each blurrier than the last.

I might vomit.

"I don't want to hide from myself anymore, but I can't do this. Sometimes I want to swallow a handful of sleeping pills and hope when I wake, everything is different."

"Don't say that."

"I feel that, Cam. I won't, but I want to. I'm helpless. I feel like a fucking fraud, and I don't know how to fix it."

My muscles win out, and my body hangs like deadweight.

My head falls to the tile, and while my eyes are open, I see nothing.

I think I scream, but I can't be sure.

I hear nothing.

But a loud bang has me blinking, and I find my brother standing there.

His eyes are wide, and his nostrils flared. He bends, scooping me up off the floor. When he speaks, his voice cracks, "Come here, little sister."

He lowers me to my mattress, and Cameron quickly tosses a blanket over me, dragging the towel off me from under it.

Tears roll down my face, soaking the pillow beneath me. "I can't do this, Mason."

My brother's grip on my hand tightens. He holds my gaze a long moment, his chest inflating with his full breath. He licks his lips, but he doesn't speak until my lips pull into a small, encouraging smile.

Nerves have him fidgeting, but then he sets his shoulders straight, his eyes trained on mine.

"I know you're confused and heartbroken in ways I can't even imagine, but I need you to know something, something I'm dead fucking afraid to say, but that needs saying regardless." He shifts on his knees, his free hand clasping over our joined ones. "I need you to know that as much as you're hurting right now, as much as you've been, that there *is* a man out there who is hurting just as fucking much, with every breath he takes." I suck in a choppy breath, and my brother's eyes gloss over. "And not for himself, but for you." His attention falls to my stomach. "For *both* of you."

My lips tremble. "There is?"

"Yeah, baby sister." He blinks, moisture shining along his lash line. "There is."

My eyes squeeze shut, and I nod. Slowly, he leans forward, kissing my temple before he releases me and falls against the wall at his back.

Cameron crawls into bed beside me, facing me on top of the covers.

Slowly, my breathing settles, and a soft smile pulls at her lips.

Tears fall from Cameron's eyes, and when I reach up, wiping them away, she chuckles.

My eyes close, and a little while later, the sound of my door opening and closing has me stirring. My brother is gone, but Cameron is sound asleep in front of me. Whispers from the hall reach my ears.

"Tell me she's okay."

"She's not. She's pushing it all away. She's going to break."

"I'm going in."

"I don't think it's the best time for that."

"She's mine, Mason. I should be the one to hold her. To remind her that she's stronger than she knows."

I drift off again, my dream full of a flashing color.

Of blue.

Of a bottomless, brilliant, ocean-at-night blue.

His.

I'm his.

Whose?

438

Noah

Yesterday was rough. Last night was worse.

That seems to be the downward trend.

I wake wishful, and I go to sleep weak and weighted. I keep waiting for the moment when things will get better, but they don't. Every day brings a new mountain to climb, and it only gets higher, steeper. It's as if I'm at the bottom with a broken harness and no rope.

Except there seems to be an invisible one wrapped around my chest, and it tightens every time I look up to see her smiling face, pointed at a man who's not me.

My mom's going to realize things are getting worse the moment I'm in front of her, so I make a quick stop in the bathroom, splash some water on my face and take a moment to mask the broken man in the mirror.

It takes a little less effort when I reach her, finding her bed raised to the highest sitting position and a smile on her face.

"Hey, Mom." I slip closer, my grin feeling a little foreign. I notice the wheelchair beside the bed, and then Cathy steps around me.

"Hey, Noah." She offers a small smile, meeting my eyes for a moment before focusing on my mom. "This young woman here has been watching the clock for you today."

My mom swats at her playfully, and then she does something I've yet to see her accomplish, maneuvers her hips at a ninety-degree angle on her own.

Her eyes come up to mine, and a low chuckle leaves me. "Whoa, now. What's this?" I rush around, unable to control the smile on my face as she reaches for me.

Taking her right hand in mine, I guide her, ready to support her left side, should she need me to, but she twists, planting right into the seat. Bent at the knee, I look up at her, and I'm almost overcome, but I don't want to spoil this, so I swallow it back. "Someone has been killing it in therapy, huh?"

My mom laughs gently. "I'm feeling great, son."

"That's what I like to hear." I push to my feet, leaning in to hug her. "So, where we going?"

"Cathy says there're little cakes in the cafeteria next door. Thought we could try it out, see if it's anything like mine."

I chuckle, my knee bouncing. "Doubtful."

"Well, we'll just have to see. Besides, the coffee here tastes like used grinds, so I could use one step up."

"You know I would have brought you something if you'd have asked."

She waves me off, patting at the wheel, so I slip behind her, gripping the handles. "I wanted to go with you. I hear the decorations are still up in there."

Smiling, I nod at Cathy, and off we go.

Two slices of chocolate cake and an abandoned cup of coffee later, my mom sighs, her eyes on the giant nutcracker outside the long windows. She trails along the lit-up garland to the snowman holding a Christmas book.

"Do you remember the year we spent Christmas in the mountains?" She looks to me. "You said you didn't want any gifts, but a night in the snow, so we booked that small cabin for one night?"

"And then we got snowed in and got to stay for another night for free."

My mom laughs, a softness falling over her. "Yeah, we got lucky, didn't we?"

She turns back to the table, picking at the frosting left on her plate, her eyes roaming the room with such joy my throat thickens.

I've waited for this for so long, to see her up and around and happy to be in the world again, but her body has been too

440

weak. She would try, but moving into the chair alone would take so much energy she'd be too tired for anything other than a short walk around the rehab facility.

The hardest part for me was not knowing the way she felt when she was alone, but I imagine the undeserved guilt she had, in the beginning, seeps in sometimes, and a wave of helplessness follows, but she still has so much life in her; I see it when I visit her. Every time I step into the room, she's the mother I've always known, kind and loving and selfless.

Today helps prove it.

She's getting stronger, there's light in her eyes, and her movements have yet to grow heavy, even though we've been sitting here for over an hour now.

I needed this.

My world is so fucked up, but right now, seeing my mother turn to the woman a table over, chatting about the poinsettias and how red is the classic color everyone should stick with, everything feels okay. For the first time in forever, I feel like I can breathe.

A little while later, it's time to take my mom back.

Inside her room, she gestures for me to sit, so I drop in the chair across from her.

"I had a dream last night," she whispers softly. "It was Christmas Eve, and you were sitting by a tree with a box in your hand. You opened it and this . . ." She digs inside the small pocket over her chest. "Was inside."

A small frown builds along my brow as my mother lowers a wedding band into my palm.

"Do you remember this ring?" she wonders.

Shaking my head, I lift it, eyeing the little diamonds along the side. "You found it when you were six or seven. You saw the neighbor using his metal detector, and he let you borrow it, so we took it down to the pier. We spent hours walking around and didn't find a thing. Not even a bottle cap. You were about to give up, almost in tears, when suddenly, it beeped."

A vague memory settles over me as I set the ring in my palm and look to her.

"This is the ring you dug up. You wrapped it and gave it to me for Christmas that year."

"I do remember," I rasp, a smile tugging at my lips. "You cried."

She laughs. "I did. And then I had it properly cleaned, and I saved it for you. I almost forgot about it until last night."

"Your dream?"

She nods. "Yeah, it was sitting there in the box, and your hands started shaking when you pulled it out, but they stopped the moment you slid it on her finger."

I swallow, and my mother's eyes grow soft. She takes my hand, squeezing.

"Mom . . ."

She reaches up, cupping my cheek as tears pool in her eyes.

"I am so proud of you, Noah Riley. You have become the man I always hoped you'd be."

Moisture builds in my gaze, and my jaw flexes. "I had one hell of a woman show me the way."

"You did, didn't you?"

My chuckle is laced with emotion, and she smiles. "I love you, honey. With all my heart. Always."

"I love you, too."

With a deep breath, she pats my cheek, and I help her into her bed. "Today was a good day," she whispers, a heaviness growing in her words, and I know it's time to go.

I step out into the cool January air, and I ignore the moment of reprieve I feel.

Pulling my phone from my pocket, I scroll to the long list of missed calls and hit send.

Trey answers on the first ring. "Well, fuck me, he's alive."

I point my smile to the sky. "How about that beer?"

"I'm already headed out the door, my man. See you in twenty?"

"I'll be there."

Climbing behind the wheel of my truck, I roll down the windows and turn the music up.

Feeling lighter than I have in a long time, I head toward campus.

Chapter 47
Arianna

Out front, Chase jumps from his seat and runs around the hood, reaching my door right as I push it open.

He pins me with a victorious grin and reaches for my hand.

"You know." I scoot closer to the edge, slipping my palm in his. "I've jumped to my feet from this very seat several times."

"Oh, I know." His free hand comes up, taking my other one, and I hop to the ground, his fingers tethering to mine as he draws me closer. "But tonight's a little different."

"Yeah, and how's that?" I play along.

"You were here as my friend all those times."

Something sparks in my gut. "And tonight?"

"Tonight, you're here as my date," he whispers, and my calves tighten. "And I'd like to kiss my girl good night before we go in, and I don't get the chance."

I laugh lightly, about to respond, but something over his shoulder catches my attention, and I gently nudge him to the side.

Mason, Brady, and Cameron have stepped from the house, and unease washes over me.

My eyes roam them once more, and I take note of who's missing. The same person I've searched for but haven't set eyes on in the four days since before the gala, though I was told he came back that night but left before morning.

Noah.

Tension wraps around my shoulders.

Cameron wrings her hands before her. Opens her mouth, but her palm lifts to cover it, and she shakes her head. She looks to the ground, shifting to the side, and my eyes flick toward the front door.

Soft eyes meet mine. "Hi, Ari."

"Paige." I frown, my stomach shrinking. "Where's Noah?"

Her eyes widen, and she stutters, "Um, he-he's . . ." She trails off, erasing the distance between us, and grabs my hands. Her eyes begin to water, and my teeth clench.

"Paige . . ." My blood runs cold. "Is he okay?"

Her lips tremble, and she shakes her head, tears falling from her eyes.

Something in me cracks, and my cheeks run warm as a sob breaks from me. Suddenly, it's hard to breathe, and my vision blurs. I don't realize I'm shaking until my brother's palms latch around my forearms from behind, steadying me. I turn into him, and he whispers in my ear, but his words are muffled.

Soft hands find mine, and I look up.

A broken smile curls Paige's lips as she nods. "Can I tell you what happened?"

I quietly climb from the Tahoe, turning to look at the long line of trucks pulling into the parking lot, each one loaded down with three or four Avix Sharks football players. One by one, they file out, somberly joining us at the curbside.

Tears brim in my eyes, and I nod when his coach steps up, gripping my arms briefly as if they understand the pain I'm in when I, myself, am still trying to figure it out.

Once all the cars have parked, Mason, Cameron, Brady, Chase, and I lead the group around the back, where the service is about to begin.

I can't say for certain this is what Noah would have wanted, but I think it is. It feels right.

As we step around the corner, Trey and Paige come into view, both sitting in the only row of seats brought out into the yard, the officiant standing before them with a Bible in his hand. He looks up, spotting our large group and a small smile brims his lips.

It isn't until we're in the clearing, the pond, and flower garden now in full view, that his body comes into view.

With shaky steps, I move down the small path, and with tears pooling in my eyes, I lower into the last free seat.

With trembling limbs, I look to his closed eyes, placing my palm over his folded ones, my words a croaky mess. "I'm so sorry, Noah."

Noah's body tenses, his eyes snapping left to find me at his side.

Shock shakes his features, but only for a moment, and then a shuddered breath blows past his lips.

His hollow gaze grows misted in an instant, and he pulls his left hand free, closing over our still clasped ones. His touch tightens, and with that, every muscle in his body seems to ease.

Mine does the opposite, the weight on my shoulders doubling as I stare at him.

He's so sad, hurt, and maybe a little hard-fought anger making him up. I haven't seen him in days, and in that time, I know he hasn't slept much.

He's exhausted, destroyed.

I would be, too, if I lost my mom.

The team begins to shuffle in behind us, and Noah frowns, reluctantly looking away from me and toward the growing crowd at our backs.

His jaw sets tight as he nods, silently thanking those he can see. Turning back to me, he nearly loses it, gratitude bleeding from his every pore.

"I thought you could use some backup."

He swallows, not trusting his own voice, and then his hand comes up, gliding along my cheek as he pushes my hair behind my ear. It's the most soothing and settling sensation.

I don't realize I've closed my eyes until they're reopening and his hand is, once again, wrapped over my own.

Past Noah's shoulders, Paige nods, a small smile on her lips as she faces forward.

Moments later, the yard is silent as the man before us reads the eulogy of the woman who gave the world Noah Riley.

What an incredible woman she must have been.

A few hours later, we're facing the parking lot, watching as the last truckload of football players loads up, honking on their way out of the parking lot.

Mason turns to Noah then, moving in to give him a bro-like hug, and when he steps back, he looks to me. "Are you riding back with us?"

I look to Noah. "My parents are at our place making a bunch of food, and they've got the firepit going. Trey and Paige were invited."

He frowns.

"Come home?" I don't mean to whisper. "I mean, come back. Please? You shouldn't be alone."

Noah nods. Glances off and back again.

For some reason, I push closer and lift my chin to look at him. "I don't want you to be alone, Noah. Please come with us."

Though loss burns in his gaze and longing screams in the deep blue staring back, Noah's lip twitches. His attention falls to my hand, so I take his. Something stirs in my gut, and he tips his head the slightest bit.

"Ride with me." He squeezes.

I squeeze back.

Everyone chats around me, drinks in hand, and stomachs full of my mom's best comfort food. Mason invited a handful of other guys who he said Noah had mentored closely, as well as a few he had been close to over his four years at Avix.

I can't believe he's a senior. It's his last year of college life, and his mom won't get to see what he becomes after, whatever that might be.

He's all alone now. He must feel so empty.

My joints stiffen, and I drop my eyes to my lap.

He's all alone . . .

Noah has no other family.

My head snaps up, landing on him not twenty feet away, and the pain in my back deepens.

Noah sits, staring off at nothing, Paige at his side in support.

Noah

My mind won't stop, but it's odd because it's as if my mind is blank, like nothing's running through it, yet here I am. I'm dead on my feet, winded from a race I can't recall.

Today is a little too much, and that seems to be the theme.

Monday tests me, and Tuesday's worse, but then Wednesday gets here and gives the other two the bird. Thursday does its damage, and then Friday fucks me sideways, leading me into the weekend like 'hold my beer.' It's a never-ending high rope with no bell to be rung, shredding my limbs with each attempt to scale.

I have no energy, no drive.

You have nothing, Noah.

My chin falls to my chest.

"I can guess the answer, but for the sake of asking, do you want to talk about it?" Paige eases, her voice hesitant but tender.

Shaking my head, I force myself to look to her.

She sits one chair over, her body twisted, so she's facing me, a hot cup of tea in her hand. Paige smiles, dropping her head against the back of the chair as she watches me.

Her nose turns a little red, and she tugs her mouth to one side, trying to fight the tears consuming her.

I want to look away, I don't want sympathy, and I hate that how I'm feeling is affecting the people around me. I don't want anyone sad because of me.

I don't want anyone to feel what I'm feeling.

Completely and totally defenseless.

"Paige." I reach over, placing my palm on her knee, and she sniffles through a nod.

Her eyes glide past me, and her chest inflates as they come back to mine. "Has she remembered anything?"

My brows cave and I face forward again. "Not exactly." I think of how she mentioned orientation and her comfort in the kitchen. "Nothing she's realized, or that's triggered anything else, as far as she's shared anyway."

"She called me by name."

My head jerks toward her, and Paige nods.

"I didn't get the chance to tell her who I was. She saw me and called me by name."

My gut spins. "What did she say?"

"She asked for you."

Hope spears my chest, but it suffocates in the same breath.

It's not so simple now.

Now, if Ari were to remember, there's no guarantee.

Chase's hand is in the pot, and all she has to do is grab hold. *Something tells me she's close.*

It's in her eyes, a glint that was reserved for me when the universe decided to steal it.

It's delicate, but it's there, developing more with each passing day.

I knew when I met her, she wasn't free to be mine, as I knew when I fell harder, the climb back up would be rugged, if possible, but the knowledge of how things might end wasn't enough for me to turn back.

The path to the three-way junction is one I'd take ten times over, no matter where it leads because loving Arianna Johnson is worth the risk.

Being loved by her is priceless.

The time was worth the torment.

Especially when I was forced to face what I tried to deny, a possibility I hadn't thought of before.

Falling in love with me didn't mean she fell out of love with him.

It meant she loved us both.

I want her to love me more.

449

Spinning the ring my mom gave me in my pocket, I close my eyes, picturing the smile on my mom's face the other day. It didn't even click then, like it should have.

That was her last sunny day.

The last time her soul would shine over this cruel world before it took her from it. From me.

People say that day comes once you've accepted the end of your life; it's that last burst of energy and final laughter with the ones you love, shielded as faux hope.

My mother loved only two people when she died, one was me, and the other the girl who doesn't remember her.

How could she accept the end when she didn't know where it led?

Shame falls over me at the thought, and I say a silent prayer, thanking whoever will listen for the dream she was given before it was time for her to let go.

She saw me happy, and that was all she ever wanted from this world.

Her son's happiness.

I'll do what I can to give that to you, Mom. I'll find it.
Somewhere.

Paige's hand falls to my shoulder, and blindly I reach up, accepting the warmth it offers as, on the inside, a frostiness is taking over, and I don't know how to stop it.

A second hand falls to my knee, and I look up to find Mrs. Johnson's kind eyes. "Everyone's outside now," she whispers, reaching up to touch my cheek, just as my mother had, and something soothes within me.

I nod, and she straightens. I watch as she walks over to Ari and perches on the chair behind her. Ari, who is staring right at me, doesn't look away as I rise to my feet.

Clearing my throat, I gather everyone's attention, and the chatter around us stops.

"I um . . ." I clear my throat again, unable to find my bearings, unsure of what I want to say and wishing I didn't ask Mrs. Johnson to let me know when a good time might be to speak, but as I look up, right into the softest, most perfect pair of brown eyes, the words become clear.

"I woke up at dawn today. The sun hadn't risen yet, and you couldn't see past your hand. The fog was so thick. I knew I was about to walk through a nightmare, and I wasn't sure how I was supposed to make it to nightfall, but then you showed up." I speak, staring into Ari's eyes, watching as hers grow glossy before I face everyone. "See, my mom, she was a selfless woman, the most selfless person I've ever known, in fact. All my life, I witnessed her going out of her way to help and please others, taking little to no care for herself. It took me a long time to realize that was how she liked it.

"If she wasn't doing something to make my, or someone else's, life better, then she wasn't doing it at all. She was kind and generous in that way." I square my shoulders, looking around the groups of people. "I thought I'd stand before the pastor today, just my mom and me, and I thought that was all I needed, but I was wrong. She deserved more than that."

"She . . ." I hesitate, looking to Ari once more. "She told me once all she ever wanted was to be a mom a child would be proud of, and she accomplished that." A curious, thoughtful frown builds along Ari's forehead, and I look away. "She deserved to be honored by the people who respected her life's mission, and that mission was raising me, so it means the world to have all of you here because I know you value our friendship. In doing so, you've made my mom's one dream come true. Today was bearable because all of you were with me."

Ari clutches her chest.

Because you were with me.

"If my mother was here, she'd thank you for coming, but not for her, not even on a day that's meant to remember her. She'd thank you for me, so I want to do what she never would, and I want to ask you to think of her a moment. Not me."

A moment of silence falls over the group, and then Mr. Johnson steps up, wrapping me in a hug.

A few others walk to me to pay their respects on their way out, and the moment I can break free, I do.

I don't mean to, but I can't help but wonder if she'll chase me down the sand as she chased him.

When twenty minutes go by, I accept the answer for what it is.

Fucking painful.

Chapter 48
Arianna

The ocean is much like life, ever-changing and unpredictable. I've always found that to be the beauty behind it, but lately, I wonder if that's true.

Where is the beauty in the possibility of a hurricane with the power to destroy everything in its path, both memories of the past and forecasts of the future? Isn't that why we return to places we love? For the peace it offers and the memories it brings?

What happens when that's washed away, and there's nothing to look back on?

How are you supposed to move forward knowing that?

The breeze picks up, and I cross my arms over my chest, but something pulls my eyes left. Thirty feet in the distance is Noah, and he's headed right for me. My feet are moving before I even realize it, and then I'm meeting him in the middle.

A small smile forms along his lips, and he slowly passes me one of the two coffees in his hands.

Eagerly accepting, I use the heat of the paper cup to warm my palms. "How'd you know I'd be out here?" I tease, pretending the reason he's out here is me.

"You always are." He doesn't miss a beat, and for a moment, my muscles clench.

Noah knew where to find me, so much so that he took a little detour to the coffeehouse first, knowing I'd be in the place he expected when he came back.

There's a deep pull low in my stomach, but I breathe through it, and without a word, we walk toward the firepit, sitting down along its edge together.

I lift my cup, inhaling the rich scent.

"Don't worry." Noah adjusts his lid. "It's not caramel."

My head jerks his way, and the softness of his gaze has me whispering, "What kind is it?"

"Peppermint."

My favorite. Noah knows my favorite.

He knew I'd be out here, close to the water.

Confusion whirls within me, and I think Noah sees it. He answers by breaking eye contact and bringing his cup to his lips, making me curious.

"What's yours?"

"Spiked."

A chuckle bubbles out of me, and his lips pull to one side.

"Well . . ." I take the lid from mine and hold it out. "Share."

He studies me a moment, and with a hint of amusement in his gaze, he pulls a small bottle from his hoodie pocket, adding a splash of Bailey's in my cup.

I give it a gentle stir, taking a small sip. "Nothing like a little liquor before lunch."

"It's not even eight yet."

"Yeah, but lunch rhymed."

Noah chuckles. "Surprised you didn't hit me with a little Allan Jackson and say, 'It's five o'clock somewhere'."

My smile is instant, and I admit. "I thought it."

A soft hmm leaves him, and something warms inside me when his eyes meet mine. "I bet you did."

My smile is broken apart with a yawn, and Noah's blue eyes soften.

"Still not sleeping well?" His voice is scratchy with his own restlessness.

I wince. "That obvious, huh?"

Noah shakes his head, slow and steady, whispering, "No. It's not."

He stares into my eyes a long moment, and an equally foreign as familiar warmth blankets me. No, it's not obvious. He simply knows.

Because he knows you, Ari.

I blink.

You know him.

I blink again.

We stare at each other, and it's he who faces the water first, so I follow.

We sit in silence, enjoying the heat our drinks offer and the calm each other's company brings. I've been on edge for so long, but this is the first time in a really long time that I've felt like I can just be, like I can let my pain show where it will, without worrying about others and the concern they try to hide around me.

My family tries to pretend everything is normal, and I know how hard that must be.

Noah doesn't do that. He's simply here with me, and that's it.

I don't feel like I have to smile and that alone is invigorating.

Only once I can see the bottom of my cup do I decide I want to share something with him, even if I'm not sure what it means or why I need him to know.

But I do need him to know, so I shift to face him.

"I looked for you last night." My voice is lower than planned, and Noah's head jerks my way so fast air lodges in my throat. His blue eyes search mine, a mix of shock and settlement, of unspoken pain clouding his own.

"I thought maybe you left with Paige."

His frown is deep and instant. Noah shakes his head, licking his lips as if biting back words he wishes to speak, so I nod, silently asking for them.

"Paige is my friend," he tells me, tension tightening his features as he adds, "From high school and from Avix."

My pulse beats a little harder, and I wait for more.

"I know you didn't realize this, but that's where you met her. At Avix." His eyes move between mine. "Not before. Not in the summer. On campus, weeks into the semester."

My lips part, my shoulders drawing in. "I met her at school?"

He nods.

"Why would I remember her face and name out of everything else?" I wonder. "Was she important to me?"

He shakes his head again. "No, not necessarily."

The deeper implication of his words strikes me, and an unexpected sense of dread follows. "She was important to you."

His face contorts, a million thoughts flashing across it before he speaks, "Not the way you might be thinking."

"I don't even know what I'm thinking," I admit quietly. "It's like I have thoughts and worry, or anger and sadness, but I don't know why or where to direct it. I keep wondering if I made a mistake. That maybe I should have let everyone fill in the holes, but I didn't want what someone else thought I felt to smother how I actually did, because does anyone actually share their every feeling with someone else? I mean, truly, and without selection?"

Noah stares me directly in the eye and says, "We did."

Two words, so tender and candidly spoken, create an ache so deep in my bones, I have no idea where it ends or begins, no idea if it's my pain I'm feeling . . . or his.

Noah tips his head. His smile is tight, but his words are genuine. "I disagree, by the way. I think what you're going through is brave. Anyone could have sat there and listened to someone else tell the story of their life, but you chose to live it instead. Regardless of the confusion I know you feel, and no matter the pain you can't shake. You're strong, Juliet." He swallows. "So much stronger than you know."

She's stronger than she knows . . .

My throat runs thick, and as I stare at Noah, my mind sparks.

Like lightning during the day, the flashes are there, but by the time your eyes follow, there's nothing in sight. No proof of what you witnessed, no sign of what was.

"What are you thinking?" he wonders.

"About how proud your mom was of you." Pain flickers across his face, and his chest flares. "She must have been."

His eyes fall fast, and he nods, facing away from me for a quiet moment. "I saw her the day she died. She was . . . it was a really good day. She gave me something we found years ago, something I'd forgotten about, and right over there by that pier is where we found it." He sighs. "I can't remember exactly where but somewhere near there."

That brings a grin to my face, and I look to the water. "The ocean always offers a surprise. I hope it's a long time from now, but I'd like to be cremated, too."

Noah turns to me, and for the first time, I feel like he just learned something about me he didn't already know. "Yeah?"

I nod. "That way, my ashes can be buried or spread, and it'll be like being in my favorite place forever." I look to him. "Want to know where that is?"

"I know where it is."

"Oh yeah?" I chuckle, his response quick and unexpected. Noah nods. "Here. At the beach."

My mouth gapes. "How did you . . . never mind." I grow a little embarrassed and look away.

"Juliet . . ." he calls. My eyes return to him. He's slowly shaking his head. "You didn't tell me. You asked me to take you to my favorite place once." *I did?* "So I asked if you would do the same."

"I brought you here?" I whisper, my stomach whirling beneath my palm.

"You agreed to show me, but I said I'd bet I already knew, and you said . . . you bet I did too." His grin is small, and then it's gone. "I never confirmed what I thought, but you just did."

"This was the first time you guessed?"

"It was, but it doesn't feel like a guess." He swallows. "Feels like I knew."

A shiver runs over me, and I bite at my cheek. "Because you know me."

"Yeah. I do. Just like you knew what I needed to make yesterday the least bit okay."

Pressure falls on my chest, and I brace for the dizziness, for the fog and suffocation, but the panic never comes.

Curiosity does.

So, I turn to Noah, asking, "Where was your favorite place?"

At that, his eyes go soft, his voice nothing but a whisper when he says, "I could show you . . ."

Eyeing the length of the football field, I pull my legs up to my chin. "I wonder if this would be Mason's favorite place, too, if I asked him." I turn to Noah, my neck stretching to follow as he jumps to his feet.

He holds a hand out, so with a critical squint, I allow him to pull me to my feet.

Noah chuckles, and then, without hesitation, he tugs me into him. One hand plants on my hip, the other keeping hold of my right. Slowly, Noah begins to rock us, and only when silence falls over him, and it does, the soft melody reaches my ears.

Peeking behind me, I spot his phone on the turf and look back to him.

"You owed me a dance," he whispers, the heat of his breath sending an electric current down my spine.

My pulse plays leapfrog, and I try for an easy grin. "Do I now?"

Noah only nods, and we continue to move.

It's a strange kind of torture, the soft purity being in his arms offers, and the devastating story the words the song playing around us gently tells.

It's bone-cracking torture, but Rascal Flatts will do that to you.

The song is about love and good graces. Of wishing nothing but the best for someone. But most of all, they sing of selflessness, of acceptance that only comes with loss or the possibility of goodbye, and Noah's lips move to the words of the song as if silently singing them.

It's as if Noah knows what music does to me and is speaking to me through the lyrics.

He wants me to be happy above all else, and I wish I understood exactly why.

You must know why, Ari. Remember.

I blink, swallow, and then the song changes, and it only gets worse.

Because this time, Noah's grip isn't simply him holding me. It's him needing me.

I can feel it deep in my soul. I feel him.

The defeat, the loss the song tells a tale of, it bleeds from him, and I ache to take it away.

It tells of missed chances and future dreams. This is a song about the agony that comes from the 'what-if' life leaves us with. That so-close moment, when everything seems possible, your happiness dangling within reach, all to be torn to bits and burned.

When there's nothing you can do but sit back and watch the ashes disappear into the wind.

A sense of helplessness washes over me, and it's as if a weight dropped along my shoulder when Noah's forehead falls to mine.

My ribs ache, growing worse as I try for a deep breath, and I realize why when his shuddering one fans across me.

Noah is breaking before me. It's obvious in the creases deepening along his brow. In the way his eyes squeeze tight, and his movements begin to slow. He's barely keeping it together.

My intuition is proven true when his next breath is an apology as he excuses himself.

I stand there, all alone in the middle of the end zone, wondering why with each step away he takes, my body grows heavier.

Chapter 49
Arianna

My knee bounces restlessly as we pull into the parking lot in front of my dorm room.

It's odd to recognize everything so fully, but not know if it's from the visit we took here last year or the semester I called this place my home.

Since all five of us needed to come and go through our things, we decided to ride up together in Mason's Tahoe. The boys carry Cam's and my suitcases, chatting about the mess they left their rooms in as we make our way inside and onto the elevator.

Cameron presses the number three, and I log that into my memory. The boys speak, and I smile in response, but I have no idea what they say. My heart is pounding in my ears, leaving no room for anything else.

Maybe I shouldn't be, but I'm nervous.

What if I hate it?

Does that mean I'm different? That I changed, and I don't even know it?

What if I walk in and all my memories come flooding back, overwhelming me?

What if I walk in and they don't?

Before I realize it, I'm standing in front of a cheap wooden door, the number 311 hanging beside it. Pulling the key from my pocket, I slide it in the lock and turn.

The door swings open, and I hold my breath.

It's with shaky steps that I ease inside, and the moment I cross the threshold, the weight on my shoulders lessens.

A smile breaks over my face as I look to the candles on the countertops, a translucent bowl half full of wine corks and bottle caps between them.

I glance at Cam.

She picks it up, shaking it a little. "This is everything we consumed as besties since move-in day. Group caps are unworthy."

"That sounds solid." I run my fingertips over the counter, slipping into the living room.

The pillows are purple and white, fluffy, and there're two matching blankets folded neatly—definitely not by me—and hidden under the glass of the coffee table.

The remotes are in a giant cup that reads 'size does matter', and the rug beneath my feet is a fuzzy black. "I see I won on the rug."

"Yes, you did, and thank God, cause Brady totally spilled root beer float all over it."

"Guilty as charged," he shouts from the entryway.

I turn to them, all three pretending they're not waiting for me to have a mental breakdown, understandably so.

I haven't talked much since everything with Noah. Granted, it was only two days ago, but still. It's noticeable, maybe even more so, when I learned he left for the campus, without a word, only hours after we got back from his favorite place.

"I'm going to go check out my room," I tell them. "You guys can go to your place. Just come back when you're done."

No one moves, so I do, and only then does Cameron turn to them and begin to whisper.

She promises we're fine and that she'll call if there's a need, but I don't stick around to hear the rest.

I step into the room that has my name stenciled across the door, quietly closing it behind me and quickly spinning to face the plywood a long moment before I convince myself to turn around.

My stomach churns, but as I allow myself to glance along the small space, my mind eases.

461

I smile at the wall of string lights and walk over to find the power button located on the outlet cube. Turning them on, the bright white lights begin to twinkle, earning a low laugh from me, and I plop onto the fluffy white comforter my parents bought me before move-in.

There're Post-it Notes scattered along my mirror and pink pens in an Avix mug, sitting on my dresser, a few other knick-knacks sprinkled around. Above my headboard hangs a giant splatter paint picture with a pair of puckered, pink bleeding lips in the center. Textbooks are in a pile by the closet, so I move that way and lower to the ground to check them out.

I open to the first sticky note hanging out the side and read over a passage about the pains in American History. Beside it are some scribbly thoughts in my handwriting, a proposal on how we, as the next generation, can do better.

I don't remember writing it.

I don't remember this room.

But I don't hate it either.

I love it.

Does that mean I'm still me?

Pulling myself to my feet, I peek out the window, and when I do, I gasp.

Noah is here, sitting in the parking lot with his truck idling.

I can't see his face from here, but he's looking forward, in the same direction Mason's truck is still parked.

I pull my phone from my pocket, preparing to text him, but then his truck begins to roll, so I lower my phone onto the nightstand beside me.

There's a soft rap on the door, and when I glance that way, Chase pokes his head inside.

His eyes flick around, a small smile pulling at his lips, and I realize then this is the first time he's seen it.

He's never been in my room.

My skin prickles with unease, and he walks closer.

"We're going to head to the house, but I wanted to check on you first." He pushes my hair behind my ear, and a small frown flickers across my face from the action. "How you feeling?"

"I'm good." I nod. "Honest, I just want to look around and get reacquainted with the place."

"K," he breathes, and when he leans closer, a knot forms in my chest.

I try to smother it, to press it down, but it doesn't work.

His lips fall to my forehead, and that knot tightens, my breastbone caving in, but when my eyes open, meeting his soft green ones, it becomes a little more bearable.

He grins and walks out, closing the door behind him.

Blowing out a deep breath, I lower to my bed, burying myself in the mountain of pillows, and close my eyes.

I inhale deeply, and my muscles clench.

I inhale again.

And again, and then I'm sightless in a thick, cloudy haze.

My senses go haywire, searching.

I'm hit with mornings in the mountains and evenings on the ocean.

With spice and pine and mint.

My eyes open as a flash from the hospital comes to mind.

The scent was there, it lingered, and under the heated steam of the shower, the aroma was brought back to life, invading and overtaking my senses.

It calls to me, soothes me, and then it pulls me under.

I'm not sure how much time passes before Cameron's soft voice wakes me.

"Hey, sleepyhead," she whispers, curling up in front of me. "Nice to see you actually knocked out for once."

"I feel like I slept for a day."

"It's only been an hour."

"Well, the comfort of home for the win."

We chuckle, and Cameron begins biting at her nails.

"What's wrong?"

She frowns. "I'm nervous for you."

"Don't be. I feel fine."

"You're still having panic attacks, Ari. How are we supposed to go to class, not knowing if you're okay on the way to your own?"

"You can't babysit me all the time, Cameron."

"I know, but . . . what are we going to say to people in our building? Should we make like a photo diagram like they did in *The Parent Trap*, so you can pretend you know them? I mean, is that even allowed? Would the school be okay with you as a second-semester student when you don't remember the first? What if you fail? Get kicked out?"

"Whoa." I laugh lightly, sitting up, and she follows. "Chill, okay. Seriously. It's going to be fine. I'm—" Over her shoulder, I spot a calendar tacked to the wall.

"Ari?" She shifts on the bed, looking where I am. "Oh my god," she gasps, jumping up and tearing it from the wall. She tugs it into her chest, and then I'm standing on the bed.

"Cameron."

"Ari . . ." She shakes her head.

I jump off, my blood pressure rising. "Give it to me."

Tears pool in her eyes, and she closes them before handing it over.

Spinning away, I hold it out in front of me, and my limbs begin to shake.

My eyes are pulled to the bold blue letters, cased in with pink, purple, and yellow hearts over the date of January 19th, but it's the words written in the small square box that sends a pulsing pain through my entire body.

Gala with Noah.

My breaths come in short, deep pants. Every ounce of air expelling with each puff and not nearly enough circulating back.

I grow light headed, fall to the floor and pull the cheetah print calendar closer.

My stomach lurches, and I groan. I look to Cameron.

"What the fuck is this?"

"Ari," she cries.

"Cameron," I snap, shaking the thing. "What the hell is this?"

Her shoulders fall, and with hesitant steps, she walks toward my closet.

She peeks at me and then pushes the doors open, her chin falling to her chest.

Hanging there in the middle, and facing forward, as if I wanted to see it clear as day every time I stepped into this room, is a gown.

A sleek, side-shoulder mermaid-style gown.

It's shiny and silky and a brilliantly beautiful . . . blue.

My hand comes up to cover my mouth, and I cry, burying my face.

Cameron falls before me, wrapping me in a hug. "I'm so sorry, but you asked us to promise not to say a word. We were just trying to follow your lead."

"How could he . . . why didn't . . . " I growl, rip the sheet from the rest of the calendar, and jump to my feet. I'm out the door as fast as my feet will carry me.

"Ari, wait!" Cameron quickly follows.

I break out in a run, opting for the stairs, and soon, her shouts echo above me.

"Ari!"

But I'm already flying out of the exit.

The January air has a chill, but the sun is out and bright and warming by the minute.

I keep running.

Through the parking lot, around the coffee shop, and across campus, I run until I'm standing three feet from Noah's truck, Mason's not far from it.

I charge forward just as Mason's flying from the front door, his phone locked to his ear.

He spots me instantly and lowers his cell, tension written all over him. "Ari . . ."

I push him in the chest, and his hands lift.

"How could you let me become this girl?!"

"That's not fair."

"I told him I was going with Chase to that stupid dance, and he stared at me with this . . ." My ribs tighten. "Oh, god, this just brokenness, and I didn't get it, and I thought he was just . . . sad, and now I know it's because of me. It was him, wasn't it? He's . . . he was . . ."

"Ari, you have to calm down."

"I don't want to calm down! I want to remember!" I cry. "I want my life back!"

My brother's eyes water, and he tugs me to him, holding me against his chest as our dad would do if he were here.

"I know you do, sister. I know." He hesitates a moment, and then he looks down at me.

"I'm going in there, Mason. I need to talk to him."

"Are you sure that's a good idea?"

"I'm not sure of anything, so what could it hurt?"

"Him."

I turn to find Cameron, her hands on her hips, breathing shallow.

She walks to us, a somberness on her face. "It could hurt him, and he's been nothing but hurt since the day you were hit by that truck, which was on this street, by the way. Right here, in front of this house."

"Cameron," Mason snaps, but she pushes on.

"It was right after their last game of the season, a loss in the playoffs. You came here to find him, but Chase found you first."

I frown, shaking my head.

"You had something to say that night, to Chase and to Noah. But you only got the chance to talk to one. Face to face anyway."

"Cameron!" my brother screams.

"You texted the other."

My skin prickles and I draw into myself.

She tosses me my phone, and I catch it.

"If you're really ready for all this, resync your cloud, Ari."

Mason jerks from me, getting in her face. "What the fuck are you doing?"

"What you should have done a long time ago." She glares. "You were the one who got her a new phone, flashed her account over."

My eyes fly to Mason, his glare still pointed at Cameron.

She shrugs. "I'm her best friend. I know her passwords too, and after she decided she didn't want to know, I went to her phone planning to do the same, but it was already gone. The entire thread. You deleted it, didn't you?"

"I did what was asked of me." After a moment, his eyes meet mine, shame weighing them down. "He didn't want to make things harder on you."

He . . .

Noah.

My chest rises and falls with several breaths, and then I whip around, rushing into the house. I lock the door once I'm through, and Mason's hard bang beats down instantly.

Someone comes around the corner, frowning at me as he heads to unlock it, but I'm already tearing open the door that leads to Noah's room.

As I reach the last step, Noah pokes his head around the corner, and we both freeze.

"I . . . um." I blink, glancing behind me and back. "No one told me where your room was . . ."

Noah's brows pull, and then slowly, he nods.

"Yeah," he answers the question I didn't have to ask. "You've been here."

"A lot?"

"That's up to interpretation."

"Noah."

"Yes, a lot."

I nod, looking down, and that's when I remember why I came in the first place.

I step around him, into the space, and I'm nearly knocked off my feet.

It's the scent. The mint and pine. It's Noah.

"Ari . . ."

I lift the calendar and turn to face him, slapping it into his chest.

He has a choice to watch it fall or grab hold of it and read it, and he chooses to let it drop to our feet.

A tenderness falls over him, and his head tips the slightest bit. He already knows what's on there.

"I'm sorry you had to see that," he rasps.

A humorless chuckle leaves me, and I shake my head.

"What?" I stare. "That's what you have to say about this?" I shake my head again, spinning away from him and moving farther into his place.

"I don't want to hurt you," he says quietly, the warmth of his presence growing closer. "But more and more, I have no idea how to accomplish that." He's right behind me now. My body senses his. "Lies hurt people, and I feel like all I do is lie when I look at you."

I gulp. "So don't."

"Don't what?"

The hairs on the nape of my neck stand as the heat of his breath reaches me.

"Lie." Slowly I face him, and my lungs expand. "Don't lie to me, Noah."

His blue eyes pierce mine, and he gives a curt nod. "Okay."

"Say You Swear."

A broken breath pushes past his lips, and he nods again.

With anxious waves rolling over me, I point to the calendar on the floor. "The gala. I was supposed to go with you."

He nods, and an ache forms in my chest.

"I had a dress."

His lips tip the slightest bit. "You did?"

"You didn't know?"

He shakes his head. "I bet you wanted to surprise me. What color?"

"Guess."

He points his smile to the floor as if he knows but doesn't say a word.

"The gala. That's what you meant when you said I owed you a dance. Because I should have danced with you then."

Another nod.

Tears prick the backs of my eyes, but I hold them in. "Why did I draw hearts all around the date?"

"You didn't."

Frustration blooms and I bend, snatching it off the ground and slap it into his hand. "You swore."

"You wrote it on the calendar. I drew the hearts."

"Y-you drew the hearts?" I stutter. "In three colors? On the calendar in—"

"In your bedroom." He stares, hesitating, but only for a moment. "And in your school planner. And on the one in mine."

"In your . . . what?"

"Bedroom," he whispers.

My throat swells. "Show me."

Nodding, Noah holds a hand out, so I slip away, slowly moving through the small living room area and through the open door that leads to a fresh-made bed.

A pair of shoes sit at the foot of it, and papers litter the small desk in the corner.

I freeze when I spot an old T-shirt tossed in the corner, one that looks a lot like Mason's old high school shirt, the one I stole as sleepwear.

My head snaps over my shoulder, my cheeks heating when Noah nods.

He slips ahead of me, pulling the standing calendar from his desktop, and hands it to me.

It's still on December, which is completely blank, and so I flip it over, and sure enough, it's there, hearts and all.

My hands tremble, and I brush my thumb over the writing. "Noah . . ."

"We were excited," he rasps. "That's all."

"How could you allow me to go with Chase?" I look up.

"I didn't allow anything." His shoulders fall. "It was your choice."

"But I had already made one. If I would have known, I wouldn't have said yes."

"But you didn't know."

"That's your fault too!" I don't mean to shout, and guilt wraps around my ribs.

"You can blame me. Anything you want to blame me for, do it. Please." His tone is shattered, helpless, and the ache bleeds into my own veins. "I'll carry that weight. Gladly. Happily, if it takes any off you. I don't want to hurt you." He steps closer, nearly begging to take the pain from within me as his own. "If I went against what you asked, if I looked you in the eye and told you anything from before, I would have risked scaring you away. I couldn't take that chance."

"You wouldn't have scared me."

"You don't know that." Torment burns in his eyes, and my lips begin to quiver.

"Did you ask Mason to delete something from my phone?"

He visibly winces, silently pleading for a pass.

I don't give him one.

You swore . . .

Noah nods.

"What was it?"

He swallows. "A message . . . all of our messages."

There was a lot?

"Did you delete them from yours?"

Noah hangs his head. "No."

"Why?"

He closes his eyes, and when they open, they're clear, and I'm captivated by the sorrow within them. "Because I needed to hold on to what you gave me with the last message you sent."

"What did I give you?" I whisper.

"Purpose, Juliet," he whispers back. "You gave me purpose when I wasn't so sure I had one."

My eyes close, and I'm made aware tears have fallen when the heat of Noah's thumbs meets my skin, shocking me, warming me.

Soothing me?

My lids fly open, locking with his.

His touch halts, but it doesn't leave.

The calendar falls, and my hands press against his chest.

I jolt, but then I flatten them there. His heart beats against my palm, and my pulse follows his lead. It starts stuttering, slow, and with each passing second, the rhythm picks up and up, and my eyes rise with it.

Noah's fingers twitch against my hair, and he swallows.

I rise onto my toes, and his features pull.

"Juliet . . ." he rasps. "What are you doing?"

"I don't know," I admit, his lips so close now.

"I don't know how I feel about that."

"How do you feel about me?"

He says nothing, so I look up, and when I do, suddenly, his silence makes sense.

Noah doesn't have to say a word. The truth is written all over him.

He couldn't hide it if he tried, and I think he might be trying . . .

Noah

Goddamn it, she's gorgeous, perfect.

Here.

She came to me in anger, found me on memory, and now stares at me with need.

But my baby has no idea what she needs when the answer, while hard to find, is so simple.

It's one word, one thing.

It's me.

The ache in her voice, it cuts me. It's fucking killing me.

How do I feel about her?

My knuckles run up her cheek, my palm flattening against it a moment later, and she blinks slowly.

I love you, baby. Every part of you.

I love the way you link life to lyrics, how you smile at the moon and love like the ocean, far and wide, and without apology. I love how selfless you are, how honest and kind, even though life hasn't been so kind to you lately. I love how you try to be brave for your family because you don't want them to hurt, even when doing so hurts you a little.

I love you so much I want to come home to you, wake beside you, and spend a lifetime worshiping you. I want the house you spoke of and the family in your dreams. I don't only want to be the man you need, but the one you want. The one you can't live without. I want to love you for a lifetime, and even more after that.

But most of all, I just want the chance to make you mine again.

Because I'm yours. Always.

No matter what.

"Noah," she rasps, and I blink back to now.

To the vulnerable girl standing before me, confused by the way her heart beats when she's close to me, and understanding exactly what it is she's feeling while she is.

She feels safe and calm. She's at peace and taken aback by the fact that she senses no need to run, how she knows she has no reason to.

Because with me, she's home.

I am home for you, baby. Please remember . . .

Ari takes a deep breath. "Do something for me?"

"Anything."

"Show me how you feel about me," she pleads.

My gut curls, but my mind beams with light.

She nibbles on her lip. "I know I'm messed up and—"

"You're not messed up."

"Nothing has felt real since I woke up, but being here . . ." Hesitantly, her hand glides up, and it doesn't stop. "I can't explain it."

My blood pumps wildly, every muscle in my body contracting. "I made you a promise once."

"What promise?"

"Never to deny you, so I need you to think really hard about your next move because I'm not strong enough to be a better man here. A promise to you is something I will never break, even if you don't remember me making it, but I'm not sure if this is me being noble or if it's being selfish." My hand lowers, my thumb gliding along her lower lip. She shivers, and heat spreads through me. "You should walk away, Juliet."

"I don't want to." Tears fill her eyes, and her head lowers, so I meet her forehead with mine. As slowly as possible, she presses her lips to the corner of mine and holds there for a long moment.

I can hardly fucking breathe, hardly keep my hands from driving into her hair, but I somehow manage to keep myself still.

When she finally pulls back, it's with the softest of smiles. "Do you think we can maybe talk for a little while?"

Possibility sends a spark through my chest, and the muscles in my neck stretch. "Always. As long as you want."

I thought maybe she'd lead us to the living room, but she simply lowers to the floor, leaning her back against my bed, so I do the same, mine against the wall across from her, and wait.

Ari

Noah stares as I pull my legs up and drop my chin against my knees.

"Tell me something," I ask.

A tenderness blankets him, and he looks down, biting back a smile as if he has a secret, and suddenly, I want to know all of his.

With humor in his gaze, he meets mine. "What do you want to know?"

"Everything."

His eyes pierce mine, and I swear they grow glossy, but in the next moment, they're clear and enthralled by me.

Noah smiles, and something in my chest stirs.

He starts speaking, and I hang on his every word.

Chapter 50
Arianna

It was well after midnight when my brother finally decided he could no longer hold back and called Noah. I met him at the bottom of the stairs, and we piled into his Tahoe, Chase and the others already tucked inside.

We didn't speak much on the ride back to the beach house, and by the time we arrived, everyone was ready for bed.

Once again, I didn't get much sleep, the events of the day looping through my mind, thoughts of what might have happened whirling around. It's hard not knowing if what I see is a memory or a twisted fantasy that stems from the desperate need to know I find myself burning in.

By the time the sun rises, I'm already getting out of the shower and heading straight for the first place I felt the need to be.

As I suspected, she's up and spots me through the bay window.

With a small smile, Payton pushes open the door, her hair a messy pile on her head, her eyes tired.

"Ari, hi." She ushers me in, retaking her place at the counter, where she's mixing a bottle for her son. "What are you doing up so early?"

"I . . . Payton."

Her eyes lift to mine.

"I'm sorry."

"For what?" She frowns.

When I pin her with a knowing look, she sighs, walks over, and wraps her arms around me.

"Trust me, Ari. I understand."

I nod, squeezing her back and blowing out a long breath when she lets go.

"Any chance you could use a little more sleep?"

Nerves swim through me as her steps pause, and she glances over her shoulder. But then she walks to me. "I could use an uninterrupted shower . . ."

Chewing at my lip, I nod, take the bottle from Payton's hands and curve around the corner.

I step up to the bassinet, quickly turning to Payton before she's gone.

"Payton."

She halts.

"Thank you."

With a small smile, she nods, and then she disappears down the hall.

I run my hands along the edge of the plush blue blanket, and as my face comes into view, Deaton's eyes find me.

"Hey, buddy," I whisper, chuckling when he kicks his feet.

With a deep breath, I gently lift him into my arms, his little cooing sounds warming parts of me I was afraid to feel.

As I lower into the rocking chair with him in my arms, moisture builds in my eyes, but it's not from sadness. I'm not really sure what it's from. All I know is that the baby in my arms is precious. He latches onto the bottle with ease, his hands coming up to cover mine as if he's determined to hold the thing himself, and a low laugh leaves me.

"Already trying to be a man."

I look over to find my brother stepping through the kitchen.

"Hey." I squint, looking him over. "I didn't know you were up."

He nods, comes to sit beside me, and as soon as Deaton spots him, he smiles around the nipple of the bottle. Mason chuckles. "What's up, my man?"

"Or maybe you didn't know *I* was up. Mase?"

He shrugs, falling into the chair on the couch beside me. "I walk over in the mornings sometimes. Parker's gone for work a lot, and Kenra stays busy too."

My eyes narrow, but he says nothing else.

Mason looks from the baby to me, his features softening. "I was wondering when you'd make it down here."

"Yeah," I whisper, running my fingers over Deaton's soft hair. "Me too."

Holding an infant brings a sense of peace like nothing else can. It's as if time slows, and your lungs open beyond their ability. It's like holding your breath and breathing deeply at the same time, an unmatchable warmth that fills you from head to toe.

"You okay?" my brother whispers.

"I am," I answer honestly, my hand tingling as I run the pad of my thumb over the baby's soft cheeks. "I wish I would have spent more time with him over the last few weeks."

I look to my brother, and he nods, but a small frown builds as he stares at the little boy in my arms. "If you did, it, uh, might make it a little harder for you to leave tomorrow."

"Is it?" I wonder.

He looks to me.

"Is it going to be harder for you to leave tomorrow?"

Mason's chest rises, but again, he speaks not a word, and worry washes over me.

"Mase . . ." I shake my head. "She's not ready."

"I know." His eyes fall to Deaton.

Several minutes go by, and it's not until I'm lowering the baby into his bassinet, sound asleep, that Mason speaks again.

"What are you going to do, Ari?" he asks. "About Noah and Chase?"

Shaking my head, I turn to him. "I don't know."

"What's your heart telling you?"

Shame falls over me as I whisper, "That I want what I always have and that maybe it's finally mine."

"That *he* is finally yours, you mean?" I look down, and he

continues, "I know you, and I know learning a little bit about you and Noah has made things harder for you."

"I just . . . I don't want to hurt anyone."

Mason sighs, a gentleness falling over him. "I know you don't, but no matter what happens, someone gets hurt, sister. It's inevitable."

"Yeah, I know."

My parents have always said you should follow your heart, that it will never lead you astray, but mine's malfunctioning.

Because if your heart is the leader, your body and mind should fall in line.

Mine have not, and I have no idea what to do about it.

Cam and I spend the day unpacking while my mom works her magic in our little kitchen, restocking and organizing all the crap we simply tossed into the cupboards in a hurry. She cooks steaks and mashed potatoes, and the boys come over for our first dinner back.

A few hours later, once everyone has gone home, I lock myself in my room.

I open my window to better hear the pitter-patter of the rain and pull the calendar from under my bed before settling on top of it.

You can do this.

I give myself a little pep talk, and then I flip it back to September.

Outside of a few test reminders and game day reminders, as if I needed them, there isn't much, so I flip to the next page.

My mouth falls open, and I draw it closer to my face.

After the first week, there're at least two days colored in, little hints to plans I had made written in. Plans I have no idea if I followed through with or not, but the little doodles on the notes section at the bottom make me think I did. But then I turn the page again, and I nearly lose my breath. October was nothing compared to November.

Cooking with Noah.

Movie night with Noah.

Road trip with Noah.

Noah's game.

About halfway through the month, I stopped writing in his name, but the plans look very much the same. The entire month is filled, the doodles on the bottom of unrecognizable foods and familiar movie lines, a mountain, and splashes of water.

Of hearts with smiley faces.

I turn to December, and there's a pull in my chest.

I shake my head, reading over everything, and unease coils around my shoulders when a few days in, it begins to look very different.

The words 'I'm sorry' are scribbled a few times, broken hearts and small flames littering the edges.

"Something happened," I whisper to myself.

But what?

Did he leave me?

Hurt me?

Were we even dating, or was it . . . what were we?

And then I get to the last entry on the page.

December twenty-third, so after the accident, the words pick up the CB, with an address attached.

I Google it, finding it's a printing company not far from campus. I try calling, but they're closed.

The rest of the night, I'm stuck wondering what I could have possibly ordered, and by the time morning rolls around, I'm more than ready to find out, but classes begin today, so whatever it is will have to wait.

Noah

I woke up this morning with a little less weight on my shoulders.

Nothing is good, not by a long shot, but she came to me without direction. She looked at me like she used to.

She felt me like I feel her.

All over, in every part of her, she just didn't understand it. I should have kept my mouth shut and kissed her but kissing her would be the cruelest form of torture, and I'm not so sure how much more I can take. My mom's not here to talk me through this, and I won't bother my friends with problems they can't find a way to fix.

It's been the longest six weeks of my life, but I'm hoping it gets better.

We're back on campus now. Back to the hustle of college life, and I'm hoping everywhere she goes, everywhere she looks, she sees me as I do her.

I see her in the fountain we sat on the night I found her at the bar.

I see her at the coffee shop and on the picnic tables.

In the library and on the track.

The gym, field, and every other inch of this place, because I've held her hand across every part of it. I've kissed her in every corner.

I've loved her in secret, but I'm not so sure how much of a secret it was.

I think she knew.

I hope I showed her what she meant to me.

What she'll forever mean to me.

If she isn't mine in the end, I'll still be hers.

It's torture.

But it's true.

There's no coming back from a girl like her.

The hope is I won't have to, but as I step out of the coffee shop, I'm reminded of why I left hope behind long ago, after my mom's second stroke.

Ari stands off to the side of the building, a peppermint latte in hand, no doubt, extra hot like the one burning my left palm this very instant. Chase a foot before her.

My baby smiles up at a man that isn't me, and when he wraps his arm around her shoulder, mine fall.

I slip into the shadow of the tree as they start walking this way, my eyes closing as her laughter threatens to tear my heart from my chest.

Only once they're gone do I step out, throwing the coffee I bought her in the can untouched.

I have class in an hour, but I don't care.

My feet carry me to my truck, and my truck leads me to the highway.

The same highway I drove her down more times than I can count.

It's like I said, she's everywhere.

My Juliet.

A bitter laugh leaves me, and I shake my head.

Maybe the answer to our ending was given from the start.

If I'm Romeo and she's Juliet, maybe this is the fate I put on us that very first day. Love forbidden, but in our story, we're forbidden by fate.

Maybe I was the placeholder, as Mason wondered.

Maybe I'm not the man of her dreams but the understudy who did the noble work. Who befriended a broken girl. Who showed her what it meant to matter to a man, how it felt to be loved. She knows now that she's worth the world and deserves even more.

Ari is strong enough to demand what she's always wanted now, and the person she still believes she wants it from is ready to give it to her.

Chapter 51

Arianna

By the time I'm done for the day and manage to track Mason down about borrowing his Tahoe, the printing shop is once again closed. They couldn't say much over the phone, other than confirming I had an order that was getting dusty on the pickup shelf.

Chase has called a few times, but after his unexpected arrival this morning, when I was really hoping for a little time to explore campus alone, something I think he should have realized, I've let his attempts go unanswered.

Thankfully, Mason agrees to drop his keys and car off to me tomorrow morning before class, so I make the executive decision to skip the first day of my second set of classes.

I make sure to email the teachers before bed so that I don't get dropped from the courses, and I'm on the road the next morning, minutes before the place opens.

It takes about fifteen minutes to get to the place, and I smile at the large neon sign above the door that reads, Paper Dreams and Things.

The woman behind the counter smiles as I enter and turns to the giant wall made of little cubes.

"You are going to love the way this thing turned out!" She shakes her head, placing a shoebox-sized package in front of me. "Let's pull it out so you can make sure it's all correct." She begins tugging on the gold tie holding it closed, and I dart a hand out.

"No, wait," I rush out.

She freezes.

"I, uh, it looks so pretty with the ribbon. I don't want to mess it up. I'm sure it's perfect." I nod anxiously.

"Oh, no problem at all." The woman folds a few pieces of paper, places them on top of the box, and pushes it toward me. "Oh, I almost forgot! This . . ." She removes a sticky note from the side of the box I can't see, pressing it down on top as well. "A woman came in and left this address. Asked that we tell you to come back after you picked this up. I guess she's been tryin' to reach ya, too."

"Yeah, sorry about that. My emails are buried right now."

"Well, hun, you have a happy holiday."

And just like that, she moves on to another customer, and with tense muscles, I carry the box, no heavier than a pair of shoes, to the car.

Rather than pull it open, I put the address on the sticky note into Mason's GPS, and fifteen minutes later, I'm pulling into a parking lot I'd be happy to never see again.

Killing the engine, I climb out and hope I'm headed into the right area, a little unsure when I get closer and see the name of the place.

Tri-City Rehabilitation Center.

I remember this place. I saw it when I came back for my follow-up.

With a deep breath, I head inside, and a wave of nausea hits me.

The woman behind the counter smiles, waving me forward, so with slow steps, I do, and as she hangs up the phone, she beams.

"Sign on in, honey. Who you here to see?"

"Oh, um—"

"Ari?"

My head snaps left to find a woman around my mom's age walking up, a clipboard in her hand. "Hi."

"I'm so glad you made it by! I've been trying to reach you for days. I was going to call Noah, but she made me promise not to."

My heart beats wildly, and I nod.

Who made her promise?

She frowns, slowly moving behind the counter. "Give me a minute, okay, hun?"

"Yeah, sure." I swallow, consider turning and running away, but I don't know why. There's a heaviness creeping over me, threatening to knock me over.

A little less than ten minutes go by, and the woman comes back, a sealed envelope inside, something hard within it. "Sorry about that. Here." She passes it over, speaking gently. "So sorry for your loss. She was very loved here."

My smile is tight, and I nod.

"Take care of yourself, Ari."

"Thanks, Cathy." With that, I leave the building but freeze right outside.

Cathy.

How . . .

I shake it off, more confused now than I was before.

I drive back to campus, my knee bouncing the entire time, and rush up to my room. Thankfully, Cameron isn't home, so I lock my door and set both the box and letter before me.

Minutes, maybe even hours, pass, and I don't move. I pace my room, combing my hair a dozen times, never once taking my eyes off the top of my comforter.

My phone rings, but I ignore it.

My stomach growls, but I ignore that too.

"Fuck it."

I jump onto the bed, tear the envelope open, and pour the contents out.

My mouth gapes when *another* sealed envelope falls out, a folded piece of paper falling on top of it addressed to me.

A letter.

It's a letter.

It takes a moment, but I find the courage to open it, setting it down before me.

Grabbing a pillow for support, I bury my mouth against it as I hug it to myself, and I hold my breath.

485

And then I look down and read.

Dear Arianna,

I'm not quite sure how to start this letter, so I'm just going to dive right in and tell you that you, sweet girl, are a gift I never thought I would receive. You are the gift. The one that has allowed me to breathe for the first time in a very long time. Because of you, my daily struggle has lessened, and I'm finally able to put my white flag to rest.

What does that mean? Well, it means that my mind and heart are finally on speaking terms with my body. And if I'm understanding the secrets my body has shared with me, I've left him.

I've left my son.

If you haven't guessed, this letter is from me, Lori Riley, Noah's mother.

I gasp, my hold on the pillow tightening.

I know you don't remember me, but we're good friends, you and I, but we can come back to that. Back to Noah.

As you once knew, I was all he had in this world. For all of his life, it was simply him and I, and while I wouldn't change a thing about the lives we lived, I came to regret a lot of it. With that regret came resentment, and it pointed straight back at me.

See, I failed to realize that by loving him, by pouring every ounce of energy I had into our lives and his future, I didn't leave room for more, something I didn't realize until after I had my first stroke Noah's senior year in high school.

From that day on, in the back of my mind has been fear.

Fear that something would happen to me and my son would be left all alone in this world.

And then I had my second stroke, the one that landed me here.

The fear became crippling, but I tried to hide it, and I held on with every bit of power I had left. Some days I could barely speak at all because my body was trying to tell me it was time. That I needed to make peace and let go, but I couldn't. Not yet. Not when in doing so, Noah would be left with nothing but heartache. I never felt like such a failure.

I was a woman who, not so long ago, was proud of the job she did raising such an amazing man on her own, and all of a sudden, I hated myself. I was drowning in helplessness I saw no way out of. I was going to wither away slowly before my son's eyes, trying to hold on.

Defeat consumed me.

And then I met you.

Tears pool in my eyes as I grip the paper, pulling it closer.

I felt I knew you before I met you, and I loved you the moment I did.

As I said to you the day you asked me to help you make my son a gift, you put life back into my boy. It had been so long since his eyes shined. Since his smile was real and not placed there for me to see. That's not to say he wasn't happy. He was. He did what he set out to do and earned his place at Avix U, something I know deep down he did for me. So yes, he was happy, but his happy came in moments that didn't last past nightfall. My son walked with the weight of a man on his shoulders, and because of that weight, he closed himself off from the things a person needs to keep going.

Until you came along.

He fell in love with you, Arianna, maybe even the day he met you.

You were hurting, and he yearned to be the reason you healed. And he was.

Sweet, Arianna, my Noah became your Noah, and honey, he was your everything, just as you are his.
You fell for him right back, and you never got up.

Love, Lori, the mother forever in debt to the woman who loves her son.

Tears fall from my eyes as I read the last line, and then I move to the text beneath it, written in a different language.

Non temere la caduta, ma la vita che nasce dal non aver mai saltato affatto.

My fingers are drawn to the script, and I slowly glide the pads of my fingertips across it.

A flash flicks before my eyes, and I freeze.

Holding my breath, I do it again.

Another flash.

Again.

And then the page morphs.

Suddenly, my fingers aren't tracing the words on college-ruled paper but on the tan, smooth chest of a man. A man who lies in the center of my bed.

My hand tingles as his comes down to cover mine, and a shaky breath escapes as he glides my touch along the warmth of his body, and I follow the path to his lips.

He kisses my knuckles, then his body lifts off the pillows until his breath brushes along my skin. He leans in, and my eyes close, a flash of blue revealing itself on the other side.

But not just any blue.

It's deep and depthless.

Bold and brilliant, like the center of the ocean or a mountain's night sky.

They're tender and limitless and locked on mine.

"Juliet . . ."

I gasp, choking on nothing. The paper falls from my hands, and I stumble from my bed, hitting and sliding down the wall.

I can't see before me, but I see.

I see him.

I see the night of the bonfire and the night at the club.

I see the morning coffee and the daytime cooking.

I see the bumper boats and his mouth an inch from mine.

I feel his hands on me as I sit on top of the kitchen counter and the heat of his eyes.

The warmth of his body.

The beat of his heart . . . pressed against mine.

I feel him. All over.

Everywhere.

A rush of yearning hits me, forcing the air from my lungs, and my body racks with sobs. "Oh my god . . . Noah."

Chapter 52
Arianna

If I could go back in time, I would do so many things differently.

It's sad how it takes a solid blow to learn a hard lesson.

How loss shakes your core in a way love can't.

Love aches, but love is a blessing, something you'd be lucky to experience.

Loss hurts, but loss is necessary, something you *have* to experience.

Loss makes people realize what they want. It lights a fire on a blind path and guides you through the flame, burning the uncertainties standing in your way as you go. It drives you to discover what you want because life is short. Too short.

And unpredictable.

Loss forces you to recognize who you can't live without, who you refuse to lose. Loss makes you reckless because loss? It sets you free.

At least, this is what it's done to me.

It's strange how a person trapped in their own mind walks without fear.

Fear is the one thing I'm not sure I've felt this entire time.

I've been nervous and anxious and unsure, on edge, but never afraid.

But right now, I am.

I'm fucking terrified.

Because I'm about to break someone.

People say to love someone with all you are is the most selfless thing you can do, but I find the opposite to be true.

Love has made me selfish because I can't live without the man my heart belongs to. The man it *truly* belongs to.

I did a lot of thinking during the night. Reflecting on the last four years of my life, and when I woke this morning, it's as if my eyes were clear for the first time.

That means I have to break the heart of a man whose only fault is my need for someone else.

It's going to be hard.

Maybe even devastating.

But as I said . . .

Love made me selfish.

Loss made me see.

And longing I can't live with.

Which is why I'm already out the door.

It's time he knows where he stands.

That this is real.

And we're forever.

I take the steps two at a time, and as I reach the front door, the man I came to see appears.

His eyes find mine instantly, and a soft smile appears.

Mine follows.

"I called."

"I know."

Chase holds out his hand, and I take it.

Chapter 53
Arianna

Nothing forces a man to admit his feelings for a woman more than witnessing the interest of another man.

That's what Noah said to me the day we met.

Chase was across the fire, watching with worry as a man I'd only met held my attention, and held it he did.

That was when 'we' began.

The massage in the living room.

The ice cream in the kitchen.

Our night on the beach.

Once we crossed that line, the one there's said to be no going back from, back we went.

Chase made a choice, and while it hurt, I understood.

I respected his decision, and then I fell apart.

That's when Noah came along.

Little by little, I was put back together. I fell in love, and then my world was turned upside down, and I realized I was already in love. Before.

Long before.

Sitting here today, I see what I didn't then. The beauty in the subtle touch, the longing in the stolen glance. Those things came back to me in wild waves, as did their timing.

After the note with Noah's number on it.

After the hoodie with his number on it.

After I took back what I'd given away and offered it to another.

And this time, the man I begged to accept it didn't only love me back.

He loved me first.

Once Chase realized this, fear shook him, drew him out of the corner he placed himself into, but by then, it was too late.

I was already gone.

But when I think about our time, there's no sadness anymore. I don't feel shorted or cheated. I realize now that it had to happen as it did. Chase had to be the one, or things would have ended a lot differently.

I think he knows it too, which is why his green eyes fall to his clasped hands when he asks, "So, uh, if I would have never pushed you away? If I would have fought for you from the beginning?"

It takes him a moment, but he looks to me again.

"Then I would have been the one who hurt you." My tone is gentle but honest.

Chase nods. He knows what I'm saying. Guilt washes over him, and he sighs. "I'm really sorry, Ari. Truly. I wish like hell I didn't hurt you and that things were different for us, but I understand. I've understood, to be honest. I could see the way you loved him, and when you suddenly didn't remember him, I thought maybe that meant you were supposed to be mine all along. I shouldn't have stepped in. I should have waited to see what you decided and been there for you when you needed me to be . . . if you needed me to be. I was afraid, and I have no other excuse, but I am ashamed, and I do care about you. I hope you know that."

"I do." I nod, and when I stand, he stands with me, pulling me in for a hug.

"I have to go," I whisper.

"I know you do." He releases me, the smile on his lips sad but encouraging. "I'm happy for you, Arianna. You deserve a man like Noah."

With a small smile, I turn and walk out.

What I said to Chase was true.

Had he not been the one to hurt me from the start, I would have hurt him in a much different way because I still would have found Noah. There is no doubt in my mind.

Just as there's none in my mind as to where to find him now.

The sun is minutes away from setting as I'm pulling off the road, so I say a silent plea he's still here, and I'm not disappointed. The moment I turn the corner, his truck comes into view, so I throw the Tahoe into park, grab my things off the seat and rush up the small hillside.

As I reach its peak, my entire body warms. He's sitting exactly where I expected, the glow of the sun creating the perfect Noah-sized silhouette.

My steps are near silent, yet he still knows I'm coming, and he whips around so fast I jump.

His eyes widen, and then narrow, and then he's hastily shoving something into his pocket, but not before I catch a glimpse of what it is.

My heart seizes, and I lower to my knees beside him, my body facing his as he sits facing forward.

I set my backpack aside and offer a small smile, fighting off the prickling feeling threatening tears.

"Can I see that?"

Moisture clouds Noah's eyes, and without taking his off me, he digs into his pocket and pulls out what he tried to hide. A football, but not just any football.

A tiny white, fluffy one, no bigger than the palm of his hand.

Taking it between my fingers, I spin it around, and my throat grows thick.

Stitched along the front, where the seam of the football should be, is soft yellow threading that reads *Little Riley*.

"This . . . this is for—" I swallow, meeting his gaze.

Noah's jaw is locked tight, but he manages a nod.

"We didn't even get to love him. Her." My voice cracks, the tears dropping. "Not even for one day."

Noah grows rigid, his gaze sweeping over my face with urgency.

Holding the tiny football close, I reach for the backpack at my side, blindly digging inside.

It's with shaky hands I place the small bag between us. I try but fail to keep the cracking out of my voice as I meet his stare once more. "Happy birthday, Noah."

His nostrils flare, his nose turning red. "Juliet——"

"Open it," I murmur.

His body shakes as he pulls the tissue paper free, and as he sees what's inside, nothing but a single twenty-dollar football, the same gift his mom would give him every year for his birthday, but isn't here to do so today, the moisture in his eyes doubles.

Noah's chin falls to his chest, and he buries his face in his hands, his shoulders shaking with silent sobs, and my own grows choppier.

I jolt forward, and the second my hand touches his, he looks up into my eyes, and he sees it.

He sees me.

His palms lift, cupping my cheeks gently, and I lean into his touch, reaching up to hold him there as he stares longingly. "Baby . . ." he mutters desperately. "Did you come back to me?"

"My god, Noah." I choke on my own tears, pressing my forehead to his. "I'm so sorry. I'm so, so sorry. I'm sorry I wasn't there when she died, and I'm sorry you've been alone, and I'm just . . . I'm so sorry," I cry, gripping his hands with my own. "I abandoned you."

"Shh, baby, no." He swallows hard, shaking his head. "Don't be sorry. Never be sorry. You just had to find your way back." His eyes close. "I thought I lost you. Are you mine?" he worries, his voice lower than a trembling whisper. "Please . . . say you're mine."

I nod rapidly, my hands gliding along his face. "Always. Forever."

A harsh breath pushes past his lips, and he shakes. "Say it."

My eyes pop open, locking with his as I grip and hold him still, whispering, "I swear."

Noah doesn't hesitate. His mouth crushes mine.

His kiss is hard and deep. It's devastating and awakening. It's claiming.

His kiss is a promise from his soul to mine that no matter what happens, this is home.

He is home.

Epilogue
Arianna

Valentine's Day

In the weeks that have passed, Noah and I have grown so much, both as a couple and as individuals. Together, we decided to take a semester off from school so we could process and come to terms with all that happened to us. My parents were more than understanding, and while I didn't want that for Noah, for his final semester as well as graduation, to be delayed, he was the one who suggested it.

With everything that was going on, he had no time to heal. He was torn in half in December, only to be shredded into a million pieces come January. He thought he lost me, he lost our child, and then he lost his mother. Not only did he want time to heal, but he also needed it. We needed it.

So we took the time we deserved. Packed up my dorm as well as his captain's quarters since neither of us would be returning to campus until the fall when a new captain would be moved into Noah's old space. And then we left for my parents' house. My dad surprised us when we arrived, his man cave having been turned into a cozy little studio that he insisted Noah and I stay in.

Everyone wondered why we didn't simply stay at the beach house, but I wanted a fresh start somewhere where he and I shared no pain, so that's what we have.

But it's Valentine's Day today, and Noah wanted to bring me to my favorite place, so who was I to deny him?

With a long, settling sigh, I look out the window as we roll to a stop in the driveway; my excitement peaks, and I'm in a rush to jump out.

So, as soon as Noah puts the truck in park, I reach for the handle, but he quickly presses the lock button, and my head snaps his way.

With a smirk, he climbs out, then reaches back in and tugs me to him. He steps between my legs and kisses me, his hands sinking into my hair. I breathe him in, my chest swelling, my arms wrapping around his neck. He lifts me from the seat, his hands cupping my ass as he presses my back against the side of the truck.

"We should go inside," he says between kisses.

My pulse spikes and I nod, pressing on his chest, so he lowers me to my feet.

As I round the hood and skip to the front door of the beach house, I can't contain my smile at the fact that Noah and I have it all to ourselves for the entire weekend.

Once I unlock the door, I quickly spin, my shoulders falling against it as I watch my man walk up to me.

The prolonged anticipation is killing me, making my heart beat out of my chest, and Noah senses it. A single dark brow lifts as he grows suspicious.

"Juliet . . ."

"We missed so much time, Noah. I want it back."

"Baby." Anguish fills his voice, deep creases forming along his eyes as he reaches for me.

I grip his wrist, freeing his hand from my cheek and folding his fingers closed. I kiss his knuckles, and a frown builds across his face.

Twisting the knob, I push the door open behind me, blindly taking backward steps inside because I don't want to miss his reaction.

It takes him several moments to force his eyes from mine, but reluctantly, his are pulled to the living room.

His eyes widen, flicking across the space, and then they land on me.

"Ari . . ." he barely whispers.

I snag the red and white hats off of the back of the couch and walk to him. He bends the slightest bit, his gaze never leaving mine as I tug the Santa hat onto his head, and when I go to pull mine on, he takes it, placing it on me himself.

His arms come around me, his thumb teasing beneath my bottom lip, and the smile that curves my lips is soft. His eyes leave me then, and he looks to the white flocked tree, standing tall in the corner of the room. It's decorated in red and green lights, shiny silver bulbs covering it from top to bottom, a single present wrapped beneath it. Each wall is lined in colorful bright lights, and two stockings hang from the fireplace.

"Merry Christmas, Noah," I whisper.

His jaw flexes as he stares at the Christmas tree and then the mantel, where a tiny, porcelain set of angel wings sits, a red ribbon tied along its base.

And then he's kissing me again. It's slow and tender, and the ache in my chest deepens, but this time, it's with longing and love.

Grabbing his hand, I lead him into the kitchen, freeing us both of our Santa hats and tossing them on the floor as we curve around the corner.

Silver and gold tinsel hang from the ceiling, matching confetti glittering the floor.

I let go of his hand and step toward the corner and click on a switch, and the mini disco ball sitting on the kitchen island flicks on, spinning and sparkling across the walls.

Hopping up on the counter, I look to Noah.

His chest heaves as he glances around the room, and he reaches up, gliding his fingers along one of the streamers hanging above him.

His eyes snap to mine, a war of raging emotions behind them. "Come here."

He does, and I open my legs for him. Noah slides right in, his hands coming down to grip my thighs, squeezing.

I grab the plastic tiara behind me and slip it on my head, and then I place his top hat on his.

Handing him a blow horn, I hold mine in my hand.

"Hey, Google," I speak to the Google Home system, "Press play."

Noah's eyes narrow, and then a ten-second countdown begins.

Noah's lips twitch, and a light laugh leaves me.

I count down the last four seconds, and he follows my lead, lifting the horn to his lips, and together, we blow.

But Noah quickly tears it away, slamming his lips to mine, and this time, it's not soft or slow.

It's deep and dirty, and my core clenches.

I moan into his mouth, and when he finally tears away, he bites at my lips, a raspy groan leaving him.

"Happy New Year." My words are choppy, needy and his eyes darken even more.

His eyes clench closed, and his forehead falls to mine.

Sliding from the countertop, I push up on my toes, kissing the corner of his mouth, and whisper, "Wait right here. I'll be right back."

"Baby—" He grips my hips, halting me, seeking out my lips, but I evade with a smile, chuckling when his warning glare meets mine.

"One minute, Noah." I smile and quickly walk away, pinning him with one last look. "Stay."

I run into the downstairs bathroom, where I hid what I need, knowing he is likely to hunt me down if I take any longer than the one minute I promised.

Tearing off my leggings and T-shirt, I quickly change, carefully pulling the strategically placed bobby pins from my hair. Up, it looked like a mess, but down, as I shake it out, it's as if I just pulled hot curlers from it.

I dash out, grabbing the stereo system remote on my way, and when I step into the kitchen, I don't know why, but nerves swirl through my stomach.

He senses my approach and glances back.

His entire body stiffens, and as if it's set to slow motion, his body slowly faces me.

His eyes fall to my feet, inching their way up, and my god, does he take his time, being sure to cover every inch of my body before he finally meets my gaze. His lips part, his shoulders fall, and he swallows hard.

My heart beats out of control, and I slip closer, hooking my finger with his and slowly dragging him beside me.

He doesn't watch where we're going, doesn't resist. He stares at my face, and I could cry at the struck expression on his.

Pushing the sliding door open, I lead us to the back patio, clicking the switch just before I exit.

The lights flick on, twinkling above and around us. The patio furniture has been pushed against the deck walls, and I laid a blue carpet across the cherrywood.

Noah's lips press into a tight line as we step into the center of it, and he knows what to do.

He takes my hand in one of his, the other planting across my lower back.

He yanks me flush against him, the satin of my gown now flat against his chest.

"Look behind you," I whisper.

Noah's gaze narrows, his eyes staying on mine until the last possible second, and then he flicks them toward the wall, where a small banner hangs, reading Avix Football Annual Gala.

His hands twitch against me, clenching. He presses me closer, his eyes coming back to mine.

I smile, and then I press play, tossing the remote to the side.

His head darts up when his coach's voice comes over the speakers, and he stops moving, listening to the kind words the man who mentored him for the past four years spoke of him that night, the words he missed.

His chest rises and falls, a shattered breath slipping past his lips, and when Trey comes on, asking me to accept the award on his behalf, Noah chuckles, and my god, it's a settling sound.

In the next moment, Noah is hugging me to him, squeezing me tightly.

"Baby." A heavy breath pushes from his lips, and he pulls back, his palms flattening on my cheeks. "What did you do?"

"I told you . . ." Tears brim in my eyes. "We missed so much, and I'm not okay with that. I wanted it back. So I gave it to us. I was gone for what should have been our first Christmas, New Year's, and the football gala." I shake my head. "I refuse to miss a single thing that was meant to be ours."

A shuddered breath leaves him, and he brings his mouth closer, gliding his lips across mine.

"I love you, Noah. With all that I am and more."

"I love you, baby. Always." His eyes gloss over, his hands shaking against me. "I need to feel you."

With a sly smile, I slip my arms around his neck and whisper, "Then take me to my room."

I yelp, when in the same second, I'm tossed over Noah's shoulder, and just like that . . . we're headed to my room.

Noah

I take the steps two at a time, and when I push into her room, my feet jerk to a stop. Holy shit.

Fuck me.

Slowly, I lower her to her feet, my eyes flicking to hers.

"Happy Valentine's Day," she whispers, a hint of bashfulness washing over her cheeks.

I squeeze her palms but quickly release her, moving to the calendar lying open on her bed, red rose petals all around it.

The room itself is lined with red dimmed lights, and flameless candles are lit all around the room, something I should be doing for her. Something I planned to do for her, the items in my bag in the truck, proof of that, but this . . .

The calendar.

The item that led her back to me.

But it's not the same one. It's open to February—this month—and the image on the top half is of her, wearing my letterman's jacket. Wearing *nothing but* my letterman's jacket.

She's angled to the side slightly, sitting back on her knees, her legs bent just right to hide what's mine, the jacket pulled in close, but only enough so that the buttons of the jacket hide her nipples, the swell of her breasts, her breastbone, and stomach on full display.

Her brown hair is down and silky straight, her eyes covered in golden glitter, her lashes thick and painted black. Her arms are bent as well, gripping onto the collar as she stares straight into the camera, the tips of her blue-painted nails the only thing showing through the sleeves. It's so large on her tiny frame.

I pick it up and look to her.

She smiles from the doorway, her gown glowing against the shine of the candles in the room.

"Wait until you see the ones in your jersey."

Heat pulls at my groin, and I stalk toward her, but her hands dart up, halting me, and I glare.

Ari chuckles softly, her palms gliding up my chest. "Turn to July."

"You covered in red and blue paint?" I picture it, her body dripping with color and nothing else.

Laughter leaves her again, and she shakes her head, a softness falling over her.

Eager for more, I quickly turn to August, and my muscles grow weak. I don't remember moving backward, but suddenly, I'm sitting on the edge of the bed, staring down at a photo of her and me, the one my mom's nurse took of us back in November.

But the photo, it's not the one I saw. It's not the one where we're smiling for the camera, the one my mother had up in her room for her to see, for us to see. It's the moments before.

When I was overcome with Ari's understanding as she led us to the fountain rather than time-stamping sorrow to the memory of fall pumpkins and hay bales.

I'd sat down, lowered her into my lap, angled her, so she was sideways, her shoulder pressed into my chest, and called her eyes to mine. The shot was taken right then, when she looked to me, and I see it there, what I had hoped for then, but couldn't dare claim, just in case.

Her love for me.

It's so obvious.

My Juliet.

"Where . . . where did you get this?" My voice is a raspy whisper.

She comes to me, steps between my legs, and lifts my head, her hands gliding into my hair.

"Your mom . . . she left it for me."

My lungs squeeze, and I grip her, gently dropping the calendar to the floor on the other side of the bed.

"There's more——" she begins, but I've pulled her down, taking her lips as my own.

Because they are.

Every fucking part of her is mine.

I kiss her savagely, my tongue tangling with hers, and then I'm sucking hers, biting at her lips, chin, neck. "More will have to wait. I need inside you. Now, now. Right now."

"Then why are your sweats still on?"

I groan, tossing her on the bed, kicking my joggers off in one motion, and then I'm settled over her, between her thighs and that hint of wild clashes in her brown eyes.

My hand slips under the dress, my palms clamping around her lower thigh, and I drag the material with me. "Is this the dress? The one you were going to wear for me that night?"

She nods, licking her lips as she watches my hand grow closer and closer to her sweet spot. "My favorite color."

I groan, and then my muscles lock because as I reach the apex of her thighs, there's no soft cotton, no silky string. No panties to be found.

Ari bites her lip, presses her head into the pillow, and smirks. "Exactly what you'd have found that night. Me, bare for you."

I groan, sliding my knees back on the mattress, my eyes holding hers as I lower, hovering an inch over her clit.

My tongue slips out, swiping across her so fast she doesn't have a single second to enjoy the heated feeling. A hint of a glare forms at the edges of her eyes, and then I blow warm air over the wet spot, and her chest rises.

"Don't be a tease."

"What song you got for that?" I pinch her clit between my knuckles, and she squirms.

Her mouth opens, and when nothing comes out, it opens wider, but this time in shock.

"Did you just stump me?" she pants with a frown.

"I told you I would, one day."

"This is trickery, Mr. Riley."

505

Chuckling, I lower, wink, and then I've got a mouthful of pussy.

I suck her slow, rolling my tongue along her clit, and when she begins to yank on my hair, I glide two fingers inside her, offering the pressure of a cock and the heated magic of a tongue.

Her knees come up, clamping over my ears, and I wrap my free arm around her, squeezing her thighs as I sit up on my knees. Ari's lower half is off the mattress completely, nothing but her shoulder blades and head lying flat.

She wriggles around. "Oh my god, Noah, please. More."

She dances against my face, searching for her orgasm, and I'm about to give it to her.

But then she yanks free, my hand sliding from her, and she shoves me backward, my head meeting the edge of the bed.

My baby climbs right up, right over me, and with her royal-blue dress clung around her waist, the tail of it pulled around us, her pussy sucks my cock inside her.

"You want to drive?" I push her hair over her shoulder, and her eyes flash. "Hm?" She clenches around me, and my eyes close.

"Hold on to me, Noah."

My chest rumbles, and I do as she says. I squeeze her ass, giving it a sweet little slap, and her palms fall to my chest.

Her hips begin to circle, and I draw my legs up, allowing her ass to fall a little lower, my cock to slide in a little farther, and she moans.

"Faster, Juliet."

She picks up her pace, her hips lifting, then coming back down with hard, full slaps. I reach up, hooking my finger around the strap of her gown, and tug her to me.

Her lips clash with mine, her tongue diving inside my mouth instantly, and I lift my hips, pressing back into her. She tears at my hair, and when she rips away, burying her face in my neck, her whimpers send chills down my spine.

She starts to shake, her pace slowing, so I scoot down the mattress until my feet hit the floor, and then I stand, taking her with me.

She yelps, a low laugh escaping her, but she claims my mouth once more, her body rolling over me, searching for more.

"One second, baby. This is going to be so good, I promise, but the dress, the dress has got to go. I need to see these." I bite her through the fabric as I spin her around, setting her on the edge of the dresser. Her hands leave me, and she hardly reaches behind her, unzipping her gown, but my hands come around to finish the job. I tug it up and over her head, letting it fall to the floor.

Ari's shoulders hit the wall with a thump, and she uses it as leverage to rock her hips into me. I tug her ass to the edge, bringing her knees up, so the arches of her feet are pressed along the edge.

Driving my hips forward, I sink into her at an angle we've yet to try, and it's a fucking keeper. "So deep," I rasp.

She answers with a thrilling little mew, her tongue sneaking out to wet her lips.

Bending forward, I capture her right nipple in my mouth, and her back arches into me. I roll my lips around the hard peak, fucking her deep and hard.

And she cries for more.

"Noah." My name is a soft demand.

"You want more?" I bite her a bit, pressing in hard and grinding against her clit. "You want me to go faster?"

"You know I do."

I withdraw, and she whimpers, her eyes flying open.

My cock aches, but she loves this. The anticipation, the burn low in her core.

"But?"

She shakes, not finishing the game we play, but goes straight for it, saying what she wants. "Give me what's mine, Romeo. Faster. Harder . . . *now*."

A growl shakes in my chest, and I curl my palms beneath her ass for a better grasp. "Lock 'em tight, baby, and quick."

Her legs cross behind my back, her arms wrapping around my neck, and stretching until her chin is pointed at the ceiling when I tug on her hair, now tethered tightly around my wrist.

And then I give her exactly what she asked for.

I fuck her hard, fast, and raw.

The loud clap of slick and sweaty bodies meeting fills the room, and she whimpers into the air, her muscles locking around me.

"Suck on my cock, Juliet. Squeeze me."

She does, her pussy walls clenching around me, flexing over and over, and then she starts to shake.

Blood surges through my veins, and my toes curl, my fingertips biting into her skin. I release her hair, and instantly, her mouth comes down on mine, but she can only begin to kiss me because in the next second, she's coming.

Her lips part, her eyes clench closed, and a long, heady moan fills her throat.

She grips my face, pulling my lips an inch from hers, and whispers, "Your turn. Come for me, Noah. Now."

"Always, baby."

I drop my mouth to her neck, sucking her skin as her pussy sucks the cum from my body. It's fucking powerful.

All-consuming.

Moments later, her body collapses into mine, and I gladly accept her weight, pulling out and scooping her into my arms. But as I move to the bed, she shakes her head, lowering it to my shoulder.

Her hand comes up to glide along my jaw, her smile so soft my damn chest grows tight.

"Take me to the living room. I want to show you something."

Without a word, I push her hair behind her ear, snag the blanket hanging off the bed, and lay it over her. She drags it up to her chin, her eyes glued to my face as I do what she asked.

I carry my baby out the door, down the stairs, and into the living room, where our missed Christmas awaits.

Arianna

The moment Noah lowers me to the fluffy rug in front of the tree, he moves over to the fireplace and lights the logs set inside. He slips behind me, pulling my back to his chest as we watch the flames take over, adding a little more light to the twinkling Christmas surrounding us.

I glance under the tree, and my stomach swims with anxiousness.

This is months in the making, long before my accident, and I've never been prouder of something in my life. I'm about to give Noah a gift that I have no doubt will mean more than even I can fathom.

Stretching my toes from beneath the blanket, I tap on the red wrapping, and Noah's head shifts, his cheek pressed to mine.

"Is that for me?"

I nod against him. "It is."

"That's not fair, Juliet." He kisses my temple.

"I can think of several ways you can even the score . . ."

He groans playfully, his hands coming down to tickle my ribs.

I chuckle, dropping my head back on his shoulder so I can meet his eyes, and he lowers his lips to mine. I smile against him, whispering, "Open it, Noah."

He holds my gaze a long moment and then gently sets me aside and leans over, snagging it from beneath the tree. He eyes the packaging, the label reading from Santa to Noah, and a small grin forms across his face.

He looks up again, and I nod, my hands tethering together, my nerves at an all-time high.

As if in slow motion, he tugs the ribbons, and they fall from the side. The packaging is torn, and he gets to the white box beneath it.

My lips press together in a tight line, and then Noah is lifting the lid, the contents of what's inside coming into view, freezing his hands in midair.

His entire body is frozen, but ever so slowly, he allows the top to fall, and it's with shaky hands that he reaches inside, freeing the soft, black leather book.

Reluctantly, his eyes come to mine, but only for a second, before they go right back.

Noah falls onto his ass, and he swallows hard. "Juliet . . ." he hardly breathes. "What is this?"

Tears prick my eyes, and I fight to keep my breaths from growing choppy.

I scoot closer, slowly tracing the cursive on the cover.

The title no more than two words.

Riley Recipes.

Noah's hand comes up, clenching over his mouth and jaw, and he shakes his head. "Baby . . . I can't," he croaks, his eyes clouded as he looks at me.

"Look inside."

A shuddered exhale leaves him, and he squares his shoulders, doing exactly that.

The moment his eyes land on the crisp, cream page, the recipe book falls to the floor, and he buries his face in his palms.

When he looks up, it's to grab me, to drag me to him and drape me across his lap, to bring my lips to his, so he can kiss me with every bit of himself.

It takes several moments for him to pull back, and when he does, I smile softly.

"Can I read it to you?"

He nods, locks his arms around me, and closes his eyes, hiding his face in my chest as I pick up the cookbook.

This book is for my favorite boy. The boy who gave my life meaning and purpose. It's for the boy who made me a mother, the one thing I aspired to be since before I could remember. It's for the boy who surpassed my every expectation and grew to be a man I couldn't be prouder of. Truly, my soul can hold no more pride as you've taken up every inch already, and I know you'll only come to be even more astonishing.

This recipe book is for you, my sweet Noah, and inside, you will find me in memory. My heart is so full, as I hope that one day your wife and children's bellies will be as you turn the page and create for them all the meals I created for you. And just like that, you'll find I'm forever with you, alive in aromas that shall one day fill your home as they filled ours.

My hope is that you'll add to this someday, create more Riley family recipes with the woman who holds your heart in the palm of her hand, just as you hold hers.

With every bit of my love,

Mom.

Tears fall from my eyes, and Noah's thumbs come up to catch them, his own cloudy with emotion.

"On one of our visits with her, I asked her if she would be willing to help me make this for you, and of course, she said yes. I started calling her when the timing worked out, and I'd record while she spoke. Some days we'd only get through a half of a recipe, and others, she'd fly through two. I typed them all up, and the people at the print company helped me get them all together."

Noah's throat bobs as he swallows, and he shakes his head. "This is . . ."

He's speechless, but he doesn't need to use words for me to understand what he's feeling.

I just do.

His eyes cling to mine, and I'm overcome by the pure adoration within them.

This man loves me with all that he is . . . and more.

I'm not sure what I did in my life to deserve him, but he's everything that I have ever hoped for, beyond so.

I spin in his lap, my legs coming around behind him, my hands gliding up his neck until my thumbs are sliding along his jaw, the tips of my other fingers grazing the edge of his fade. "I love you, Noah Riley."

A broken breath escapes him, his eyes clenching closed. "Santa did so good."

A laugh escapes me, and a small smile curves his mouth.

Noah kisses me then, his hands sinking into my hair, as he has always done, but it's now his new routine each time we leave, arrive, meet, or part. His touch is never far. Ever. It's as soothing as it is painful, but only because of how deep the reasons for it run.

Noah's afraid. Afraid that, at any moment, something could come along and take me from him, but we won't let that happen. Not again. *Never* again.

Beginning the night my memories came back, I had lain in Noah's arms and written down the night he and I met, the conversation we had, as well as the bonfire that followed. Every night after that, I did the same thing, telling our story in a journal with doodles and scribbles, and yes, colorful hearts. I've already filled two, having cracked open my third just yesterday.

"I can't wait to add today to my journal."

"You just started on our camping trip last night. You've got a long ways to go."

"I know, but still."

Noah's lips graze mine, his eyes closing, his tone oh so soft, as he says, "What if . . . you're never caught up?" A small frown pulls at my brows, and Noah blindly curls a piece of my hair around his finger. "What if I keep giving you more to write about?"

The hand now tracing his tattoos pauses, and my eyes fly to his. He takes his time, watching as he releases the dark lock, and then pushes it from my shoulder when it falls. Only then do his eyes come to mine.

"What if every day that follows this one, I give you something else to write?"

"Noah." My heart pounds wildly.

His lips curve into a small smirk, and he hooks his finger beneath my necklace, the gift he gave me the moment I woke up this morning, a silver heart dangling from it.

He said it will tarnish in time, the sterling unable to hold its shine, but said maybe when that time comes, he'll be able to afford a real one to replace it.

"I told you my mom gave me something the day she died, something she and I found at the pier, but I never told you what it was." He spins the heart until its clasp is in the front, and he undoes it, holding it in his open palm. His eyes never leave mine. "I want you, Arianna Johnson, like no man has ever wanted a woman before. I'm sure of it. I want to give you the life you dreamed of, the one you shared with me. I want to give you a home on the ocean, one that will be ours, where the back deck faces the ocean, so we can sit outside at night while the sun sets, but only so we can watch the way the moon bounces off the water the way you love. I want to come home and cook for you while you sit back and watch our little one in your arms."

My tears fall in heavy streaks down my cheeks, but I don't even want to blink. I don't want to miss a single expression on his face.

"I want to give you everything you could ever want, and then I want to give you even more. But first." He opens his palm, and then that heart that was around my neck is opened, and a small, silver band falls out, right into my hands.

I gasp, having had no idea it was a locket. "Noah . . ."

"First," he repeats, his knuckles lifting my chin, calling my eyes to his. "First, I want to marry you."

A cry slips past my lips, my hand coming to cover my mouth.

"Marry me, Juliet. We can wait until you're done with school, or we can drive to a chapel right now. I don't care. Marry me."

I'm nodding before he's even done speaking, my lips smashing with his as I pull him as close as I can get him, and it's not close enough.

It will never be close enough.

But forever is a damn good start.

"You will?" he rasps.

"Of course I will."

His palms shake as he grips my cheeks, his eyes piercing mine. "Say you swear?"

Placing my palm over his tattoo, I recite its meaning.

"Fear not the fall, but the life that comes from having never leaped at all." I smile through my tears. "I'll always leap if the jump leads me to you, Noah Riley. Always."

"And forever."

"I swear."

He kisses me, and I get lost in the man before me.

My Romeo.

My fiancé.

My everything.

You made it to the end!!! How are you feeling?! LOL

Man, I have no idea how to express what the completion of this book has done to me. This baby is 5 years in the making. Literally, I started writing it 5 years ago, but the fear was real with this one. I didn't think I could tell the story as the characters intended, but I cannot tell you how proud I am of how it came together.

Say You Swear is a book about a growth and coming into your own, about finding yourself and stepping outside of what you've always known to discover all you were meant for. And holy shizz, our boy Noah???!!! MY GAWD THAT MAN! *DIES*

I think the term book boyfriend has been obliterated, because that man is straight up book husband material! LOL

Deep, happy sigh

From the bottom of my heart, I thank you for reading. This story is the one that inspired me to begin writing, and I am truly beside myself that it is now in your hands.
Xoxo,
Meagan

Stay in touch with Meagan Brandy:
@MeaganBrandyAuthor
@MeaganBrandy
@MeaganBrandyAuthor
@MeaganBrandyBooks
www.meaganbrandy.com

Acknowledgements

This one is easy. I have a few people to thank for helping me get through this, and trust me, it was not easy! This book nearly killed me. As I always try to do, I poured everything I had into this story, but something about this baby weighed differently. It was heavy, and deep, and not a single line from it could be forced or rushed, so HUGE thank you to the man of my house for picking up my slack the last few months while I was engrossed in this story for many, many sleepless nights. And for loving Gordon Ramsay as much as I do! LOL

Rebecca, you have no idea what you did for me in this book! Your honesty and feedback had such a huge impact! So much so that I can say without a doubt Noah and Ari's story wouldn't have become what it did without you here for the process. I will forever be grateful for your hard work and support. You went beyond and I can't thank you enough for that.

Melissa! As always, you talked me off the ledge and pushed me to keep going! Your encouragement and friendship means the world to me and I'm so happy to have you as my main bish. Sorry I tortured you with a couple chapters at a time! LOL

Serena! Thank you for being a part of this journey! Your input means a lot!

Ellie and team at My Brothers Editor, thank you so much for always working with me on such tight deadlines! I'm a mess, but that's why I have you!

Bloggers and early readers!! You guys are so such an important part of the process! Thank you so much for taking time out of your busy schedules to meet my newest couple and help spread the word!

And lastly, to my readers!!!! YOU GUYS ARE THE REASON I AM HERE TODAY!

Thank you so much for following me along this journey! I'm so honored that you choose to read my words and fall in love with the worlds I create. I will forever give my all and never release a book I am not 100% sure of because you guys deserve that from me! THANK YOU for allowing me to write what I feel and being here for it!